The book 'Hindsight' inspired by Glenn Beck and Bill O'Reilly's penchant for truthful and educational reporting, tells of the man-made nuclear disaster, triggered Christmas Eve 2111 in the Middle-East that would have extinguished mankind if it were not for time-travellers from our future who return with hindsight to certain points in our timeline to adjust mankind's attitude, thinking and decisions which over two centuries contributed towards this extinction event.

Based on current and historical events, this educational book exposes how greed and progressivism contaminate the media, political and banking systems, causing systemic corruption undermining the integrity and fabric of society, ultimately threatening humanity's survival.

Hindsight's story line incorporates data about depleted resources, corruption, insidiousness of Progressivism, statements and actions by famous influential people, all interwoven into a rich tapestry of intrigue, exposing greed, corruption, and deceit, which has been overlaid with a gripping love story, using fictional characters from the future.

HINDSIGHT

WHEN HINDSIGHT FROM OUR FUTURE BECOMES TODAY'S FORESIGHT

ARDEN WEDZLER

HINDSIGHT
WHEN HINDSIGHT FROM OUR FUTURE
BECOMES TODAY'S FORESIGHT

iUniverse books may be ordered through booksellers or by contacting:

iUniverse
1663 Liberty Drive
Bloomington, IN 47403
www.iuniverse.com
844-349-9409

ISBN: 978-1-5320-7066-2 (sc)
ISBN: 978-1-5320-7067-9 (hc)
ISBN: 978-1-5320-7068-6 (e)

Library of Congress Control Number: 2019903068

Print information available on the last page.

iUniverse rev. date: 02/15/2021

DEDICATION

This book and characters within, has been dedicated
to those who were truly wonderful people, I was privileged
to know and proud to call my friends in the
Class of 1972
of
Que Que High School
Southern Rhodesia now known as Zimbabwe
and
**My Beautiful Loving
Wife**
who is also my soul mate and life-long best friend.

* * * * * * *

PREFACE

Earth....... the wonderful unique planet we all live on that gives us life. This planet is the only place we have where we can exist, so why are self-serving and corrupt elements of mankind, wantonly decimating our planet because of their greed and selfishness?

Many people believe that Earth has been heading for a collision with a man-made disaster ever since the industrial revolution. For Mother Nature, that collision may have already happened, many have said that mankind has proven to be the most pervasive virulent and destructive "virus" that she has to continually battle against, just to maintain some kind of ecological harmony.

If the above happens to be the truth and intelligent individuals did nothing about it, then God help us all. This is because, we will end up regretting our ignorance and apathy in years to come when it will be too late for mankind to do anything about the devastation, to recover the situation.

This book explores elements of that ".... *it is sadly too–late*" scenario.

The storyline of this "*Factional*" book, set in the future tells us of our world in their past, where systemic greed and endemic corruption within the halls of power, including political houses, governments and banks sets in motion the engine of humanity's downfall. These are the very organisations that have been guilty of inciting wars and conflicts between tribes, religions and countries. Wars manifested by the flawed "interventionist" foreign policies of America, which were funded by the Progressive elitists and the banking industry, many of which grew out of control, causing horrendous deaths, pain and suffering for billions of innocent people.

The storyline reminds us that, because of all its posturing and indecisiveness, the United Nations were unable to change the final outcome. We learn from six teams of time travellers who enlighten us how, by the year 2110, mankind was driven into self-destruction by wealthy elitists, corrupt politicians, corrupt bankers and greedy, self-serving Progressives.

The time travellers inform us that on Christmas Eve, of December 2111, self-destruction and mass extinction would be only moments away. Mankind's greed and corruption had manifested a destiny that was like a runaway train without brakes at the top of a mountain pass: it could only end in catastrophe.

This book, a gift of insights from our future and is dedicated to those remaining elements of sanity, integrity and humanity within each and every one of us. This book says what people would really like to say about doing things right, but because of "Political-Correctness" are too scared to say for the fear of castigation, retribution or being oppressed.

The six time-traveller teams who are sent back in time from the year 2612 AD, had been forced into stasis for an intended 5,000 years because of the man-made nuclear disaster in 2111 AD, which was about to be mankind's extinction. Owing to technical difficulties, however, the time travellers are forced to come back in time to a point prior to the disaster of 2111 AD in order to visit six key historical events and persuade people of influence to make subtle changes to their thinking and actions in the hope that if all six events could nudge mankind onto a slightly different trajectory, so that the man-made destruction of 2111 AD could be averted.

These time travellers have the advantage of hindsight, which in this book becomes the foresight of those people who are visited further back in the timeline. The time travellers are hoping those whom they choose to visit are wise enough to see mankind for what it really is, and can get past their two biggest enemies, ego and self-importance, to prevent the stupid mistakes that accumulatively created a critical mass of human horror that would ultimately, through convergence, cause mankind's extinction.

For any of you extinction doubters or deniers out there who cannot see the wanton destruction and extinction that mankind causes every day, you need to maintain an open mind, open your eyes to help broaden your horizons, look around you and overcome your bias, read reports from the non-mainstream media, such as those listed on zerohedge.com so you can examine both sides of every story objectively, and not be phlegmatic about mankind's plight.

Hopefully, this book will help our Politicians, Government Mandarins, Bureaucrats, Elitists, Corporate Moguls and those architects of Progressivism with their journey towards living with integrity and enlightenment. The Author, who himself has minimal education, lived a simple life working to make an honest living hopes that you too will be enlightened by this story and will see through the spin and the lies that the Politicians, Banks, Governments and their elite wealthy cronies have been feeding you through a corrupt media system.

If you think the world is running "hunky-dory" and many of those problems you might have heard about for a short while, which miraculously disappeared from the media as quickly as the story appeared; it is because they were suppressed by ignorant, wealthy-elitists or self-serving journalists or politicians who purported those incidents to be a conspiracy by some lunatics on the fringes of society. Well, congratulations, you have been deceived and, more poignantly, you are showing your ignorance and deceiving yourself at the cost of your grandchildren and their grandchildren's wellbeing.

By touching on all the excellent work mentioned in the acknowledgements below, the real message that the Author has attempted to deliver is as follows:

- *"No matter how insignificant we may feel as individuals, we cannot continue to put our heads in the sand and hope the problem goes away.*
- *We, the people, need to collectively rally to the call for integrity, transparency and accountability in politics, government and banking and add our contribution with our resources, votes, and intellect so that pragmatic caring movements such as Green-Peace or derivations of similar humane and empathetic organisations that operate on a basis of integrity who are attempting to do what is right, for the right reasons;- only then will we*

be assured of our continued personal liberty, wealth, health and the very survival of our planet and other living creatures.

- *Now is the time for a new-breed of honest enlightened leaders to be put into the halls of power so that they can finally do what is right."*

If you really care about the futures of your children and their grandchildren etc., the Author urges that you read this book with an open mind so that you can see how the citizens of most countries have been indoctrinated and continue to be surreptitiously manipulated and controlled like sheep by the elite and powerful with their insidious Progressivism and Globalisation Game-Plan.

Spread the word, much change is needed.

ACKNOWLEDGEMENTS

While based on historical events that occurred in the time travellers' past, (our past and present), the time traveller storyline is fictional. The author would like to express his great amazement, admiration and deep gratitude to all of those clever dedicated people who have collectively contributed, hundreds of thousands of hours of research into material for projects such as Wikipedia, or their own articles, published or unpublished, that authors for books like this rely on as a source. It is this plethora of valuable information from which the Author lays down a background that resonates with a realistic scenario that the wider mass populace is familiar with and can relate to.

The author attempts to reference these contributors within the book as well as where appropriate in the appendices, together with all material utilised as part of the background that articulates the historical happenings alluded to in the book. Sadly, many articles and links have vanished or have been purged in attempts to rewrite history on the internet over the last 8 years since this book was first being researched and written.

As eloquently quoted by G. Edward Griffin in his best-selling book;

The Creature from Jekyll Island

> *"It should be said that one who blatantly takes the work of another and presents it as one's own would be termed a plagiarist, while one who takes from the work of many is deemed a researcher."*
> *It is a roundabout way of saying that the authors of books like Hindsight are hugely indebted to the efforts of so many before that have wrestled with the broad range of subject matter*

that needed to be covered in a fictional book like this to make the message work and resonate with true life experience of many millions.

Almost all historical research was undertaken using that wonderful Internet search engines, including Wikipedia, hence factual integrity and poetic license speaks for itself and thus events, alleged comments, alleged quotes, alleged statements, alleged actions and alleged scenarios described in the story as being done or said by real people are just that; "alleged" - when they are interacting with the fictional characters in this book. View them as products of imaginations of the fictional characters such as Joe and Karyn from the future to fertilise your imagination allowing you to imagine a world where you had the power of a "What-if" simulator and a time machine.

So, remember, all historical events, comments, quotes, statements and actions made by real people cited in this story are alleged-to-have-happened because they have been or are recorded as alleged activity by various other forms of written medium including but not limited to those such as Wikipedia or news articles. In many cases for the reasons of historical authenticity and staying true to actual events, some text used within this book has not be tweaked if copied from published works and is used in the raw state to help the reader with resonance to our tawdry war torn if colourful, but brutal history.

That said, the actions of some people who form part of the actual history may have been ever so slightly tweaked to create a more gripping and congruent storyline that unfolds over a 600-year period, which should be taken into consideration when reviewing the factual happenings over this period. It has not been the intention of the author to malign or defame any living individual or organisation / corporation, it is a mission of this book only to reflect the unvarnished brutality of life for millions of people at the bottom of the social pyramid.

The author attempts to create a fictional representation for interactions with surrounding actual historical events presented in this book to be used as metaphors illustrating what may have gone wrong, or may have been the cause of subsequent later behaviour or happenings in our history!

Also, some of the science quoted herein should not be taken seriously as it was used as poetic license to be purposely far reaching as it played into the narrative of being futuristic and geeky.

Enjoy the journey.........

CONTENTS

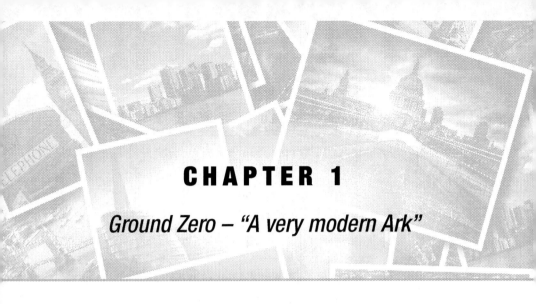

CHAPTER 1

Ground Zero – "A very modern Ark"

The countryside near what had once, when such things mattered, been the border between Scotland and England, shook violently under the onslaught of an earthquake that measured 7.7 on the Richter scale. Suddenly, with a loud crack that reverberated through the bitterly cold air, the entrance to a secret, secure military bunker that had lay undisturbed deep underground became exposed to the atmosphere and open country-side.

Over several centuries of harsh summers and winters with temperatures ranging between -30°C and 28°C, water had found its way into the perimeter walls of the bunker through cracks in the surface, and the continual freezing and thawing had caused the cracks to widen. If intruders had found their way in via this breach, they would have been faced with a large empty hangar, with steel doors that stood 8 metres wide and 4 metres high, leading into the hillside. They would have heard no sound other than the howl of the 30 to 50 mile an hour winds that scoured the surrounding terrain, detected no man or animal noises, and seen no ape-like beasts, no birds scurrying away in fright. Confronted by nothing but an eerie silence, they could not have had any inkling of what it was they had stumbled upon.

The secret underground bunker consisted of over 100 miles of environmentally controlled, reinforced concrete corridors that connected a mixture of over 3,000 storage rooms and cavernous hangars. These hangars contained mankind's legacy, an archive of all things valuable, rare and sacred, kept safe for the future in the event that

1

a disaster happened. During the latter part of the second millennium and early part of the third millennium, there were those pragmatists who could see how mankind's arrogance and ignorance was spiralling into a kind of self-sabotage which could result in the destruction of the human race. They worried that famine such as that predicted in the late twentieth century by scientists like Richard C. Duncan, caused by a combination of overpopulation and depletion of non-renewable resources, aggravated by the probability of related events such as wars, global criminality and pandemics, might not merely reduce the human population, but might extinguish it altogether.

In fact, at the turn of the third millennium, essential resources had become critically short. Between 2080 and 2110, there were over 100 fiercely fought battles or wars between countries over resources such as oil, water and essential minerals.

The earth was quickly running out of the very materials that mankind desperately needed to prosper and survive. Terrified by the mass extinction of animal species which was being caused by mankind every year, the pragmatists knew that the DNA for all animals, insects, birds, fish and plants had to be preserved for the continuation of life on the planet. Programs like the Norwegian Doomsday Seed Vault and Kew's Millennium Seed Bank Partnership were set up to help save the world's plants and habitats from the risk of extinction. Most of the seeds saved at Kew, and now stored in the bunker, would remain viable for hundreds of years, thus providing resources for medicines, new plants and the restoration of destroyed habitats.

It wasn't only seeds that were stored in the bunker. It contained the DNA of almost all known animals, as well as humans that were deemed to be healthy and productive. Any intruders could not have suspected this, but, halfway through the third millennium, there was no one left to intrude.

Now, however, the bunker perimeter had been breached by the extreme elements and the earthquake, triggering a series of safety protocols which were designed to ensure the wellbeing and security of the environment. The first of these would awaken the Guardians, six very special humans currently in a state of suspended animation, a form of deep sleep that dramatically slows down ageing and bodily decay, inside six stasis pods.

The date inside the bunker was 30th March 2612. In the world outside, dates had long since ceased to have any significance.

CHAPTER 2

Day Zero - The Awakening, 2611 AD

There was utter silence, no noise, no light, just peaceful, blissful darkness.

Suddenly, dim lighting came on, and the silence was broken by music which began to play quietly in the background. It was Mozart's Piano Concerto No. 21 in "C" major – it sounded so familiar. Joe felt warm and content. He was in a drifting half-sleep and everything he wanted was there, right now.

His blissful state was abruptly disturbed by a beeping sound and a yellow flashing light, which pulsed against his eyelids as he slept cocooned in a sleeping pod. Joe became conscious of the repeated dot-dash-dot-dash of the light, like the Morse code used in the twentieth century. He had been dreaming of his parents, Joseph Gilroy Senior, his father, Serena his mother, and his younger sister Elizabeth. In his dream he had just turned sixteen and they were somewhere warm; he could feel the warm air brushing over his skin. The yellow light was flashing more intensely, more rapidly, as if it was coming from behind the overhead bedroom fan. Yes, that was it, they were in their Mediterranean villa on the Greek island, it was warm and Elizabeth was playing her favourite Mozart piece on the piano. God had been good to them and Joe felt blessed with a wonderful loving family.

Damn, Joe thought, that bleeping must be the oven; his mother Serena must have left the timer on and gone for a walk outside. They spent splendid holidays at the villa, where the smell of the olive groves, the distant high-pitched sound of the cicadas shrilling their mating call in the heat of the sun, reminding them that they were in the Mediterranean, the place where you could enjoy peaceful afternoon siestas without feeling guilty. Man, it was great to be alive! The afternoon siestas with his parents and Elizabeth in the Mediterranean heat under the bedroom fan made life worth living.

Hell, that bleeping is still going, where is everyone? He decided the noise was too irritating; he had to get up from his siesta and see to the oven so the food would not burn. He tried moving. He couldn't, he was paralysed, his eyes were closed, yet many of his other senses were beginning to kick back in, panic and fear . . . Oh my God, Joe thought, I'm having a stroke! He tried to shout out. All he could hear was Mozart and that damn bleeping. Then, too exhausted to struggle any more, sleep came back to him, the panic subsided, and he fell back into a deep sleep.

Beep . . . beep . . . beep . . .

Two hours later, there was a sudden whooshing sound, and a rush of warm air brushed his face. Joe could hear a gruff hoarse voice calling his name.

"Joe, wake up, Joe, *wake up* . . . Joe, *are you ok?*"

As Joe came to his senses, he was expecting to see the ceiling of the Mediterranean villa with the familiar ceiling fan and his mother Serena or his sister Elizabeth calling him for brunch, so who did this gruff hoarse voice belong to?

Joe opened his eyes; the reality and emotions came streaming back to him, as he became aware of all the tubes and cables hooked up to him and the memories of the horror, the devastation, and the cold reality of mankind's extinction. His heart was beating at 150 beats per minute; he felt nauseous, frail and weak. As he tried to sit up, his head spun and he almost lost consciousness. He knew that this was the effect of his circulation beginning to return to normal functioning, and started to massage his limbs to help the process.

He desperately craved a date with his toothbrush. Two of his fellow Guardians helped him sit up, and as his eyes began to focus, he could see the five of them, all in different stages of undress, looking as if they had just crawled out of bed, as indeed they had.

Joe and the other five were the six Guardians who had been in a long sleep in stasis pods.

As was drilled into them in their training, Joe assumed they had all been sleeping in deep stasis for over 5,000 years. They all thought the awakening had started, and suddenly realised that this was it, this might be the new beginning for mankind they had worked so hard for.

There was no time for niceties. They had a lot of work to do and the clock was ticking.

The first day out of stasis was going to be the first day of mankind's resurrection.

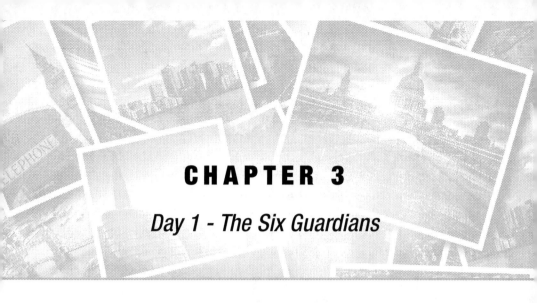

CHAPTER 3

Day 1 - The Six Guardians

The six Guardians had been hand chosen, specially selected from thousands of extraordinarily talented candidates who desperately wanted to work on the "Noah 5000" project. Competition for these positions had been fierce. The Guardians were going to be the most important people on the Noah 5000 project; these were going to be the heroes that kept the lights on, the ones who would keep the special lucky *"chosen ones"* alive and safe. The Noah Guardians were the overseers who would guarantee that the human race survived mankind's self-induced extinction caused from a global nuclear war.

Joe Gilroy was an outstanding, three times decorated officer in the elite British Special Forces 22 B squadron, Special Air Service – known as the SAS. He spent his first eight years of military service on campaigns in the Middle East and South America from 2101 to 2109. In what was his final year, while holding the rank of Captain, Joe was assigned as the special military attaché to the Noah 5000 project. Joe's father, Joseph senior, was also a military man, had retired as a Brigadier the year Joe was assigned to the Noah 5000 project.

Early in his military career, Joseph senior had married his high school sweetheart, Serena. They were married in Pateley Bridge, a picturesque small market town in Nidderdale, North Yorkshire, where Serena had been born and brought up. Joseph and Serena were both extremely proud of their son Joe when he was assigned to the top-secret Noah 5000 project. At the age of 36, Joseph Gilroy held the rank of Captain, which was when Joe junior was sixteen years old and his daughter Elizabeth was thirteen. Joseph Gilroy was eight years older than Joe junior, when Joe junior secured the rank of Captain.

By the time the Noah 5000 project doors finally closed to the outside world Elizabeth was twenty-five years old, was the second love of his life, and she was the very reason why he saw to it that Joe junior secured the military attaché role. It offered him a chance to save Elizabeth from the oncoming cataclysmic events that were then about to unfold. His great sorrow was that he could not save Serena, since only young people were selected for Noah 5000, but in any case, Serena would not have left his side, preferring to die with him than live without him.

As part of the Guardian team, Captain Joe Gilroy was in charge of security of the Noah 5000 bunker; his expertise in surveillance, covert operations, military strategy and tactics were deemed necessary in the event of threats that might occur in their future.

The custodians of the project had chosen well in selecting Joe. He had an Intelligence-Quotient (IQ) of 179, and he was top in all his classes in school, university, and the military academy. In his short military career, his proven ability and achievements in the field as a military leader and tactician were revered by his colleagues while at the same time feared by his enemies.

Joe's first task after recovering from the awakening was to reconnect with the environment, they found themselves in and familiarise himself with the status of the terrain surrounding them and the state of their security. He entered the command and control centre. The lights came on automatically, and he set about his initial tasks with quiet confidence. The copious amount of training before stepping into the stasis pod had obviously worked. He began by bringing the Bunker's command and control centre back to life. There were dozens of large, thin, flat-screen monitors set in ergonomic work stations arranged in banks with comfortable computer chairs positioned so that each one faced a massive visual display screen on the south wall. Joe was looking at what was probably the most up to date technology of its time when it was installed. He was now able to take stock of the command and control centre, which was fitted out to facilitate seventy people, each of whom would have specific tasks to fulfil when fully operational.

He sat in front of the vast array of computers and started looking through gigabytes of data, which included the inventory of what was held in the Noah 5000 bunker and weather telemetry data collected by sensors and satellites while they had been in stasis.

"What the hell does that mean? That's only a tenth of the time we should have been in stasis," Joe muttered. The data he was scrutinising told him that they had been awakened prematurely; they had only been in stasis for 500 years and not the planned 5,000 years that had been thought would be necessary. Still pondering, he moved on, scanning hours and hours of data until he thought his head would explode.

Suddenly, he froze. "Oh shit," he groaned, "Shit, shit, shit!" He had just pulled up the stasis pod status report, which showed there were 200,000 occupied stasis pods. The cold facts that he was reading plunged him into despair. Feverishly, he scanned the records showing which pods were allocated to which people. He sank back in his chair, overcome with grief, then reached across the desk and pressed the internal alarm to summon the other Guardians to the first of what would prove to be many emergency meetings.

CHAPTER 4

Day 2 - The Irony of a Man-made Disaster

The six Guardians had gathered in the briefing room and listened intently to the revelations that Joe needed to share with them. Looking strained and pale, Joe said, "I have some dreadful news. The data on the stasis pods shows that over 2.7% of the pods have suffered catastrophic failure, which means that we have lost more than 5,400 of our people." He did not tell them that one of these people was his beloved sister – Elizabeth, since he was aware that the other Guardians might also have close relatives in the affected pods and did not want to parade his own grief. "As yet," he continued, "I don't know how this happened, but I do know that those pods failed and their occupants died at different times over the past 500 years."

Cassandra Mountain, who was one of the world's brightest botanist and plant life genome specialists, was the first to speak after Joe's revelation.

"How could this have happened? The system was supposed to be fool proof – it had fail-safes to back up the backups, for God's sake! What the hell went wrong?"

Gibbs, a remarkably good-looking man with thick jet-black hair, green eyes and chiselled features, the nuclear scientist and nuclear fusion expert on the team, said that he would investigate the disaster immediately, and left the room. The remaining five Guardians waited silently, deeply immersed in their own thoughts about the loss of such a significant number of their charges.

When Gibbs returned, he explained that from what he could

ascertain, one of the reactors was taken offline because of fuel rods not being accessible to the robotic arms that serviced the reactors. Debris from a damaged roof strut had fallen across the track and prevented the equipment from delivering new fuel to the number four reactor. This event would have triggered a failsafe protocol and the computers would have done a calculation on the energy usage for the full 200,000 stasis pods correlating it with the timeline to the projected neutralising of the radioactive atmosphere above, which was estimated to be about 4,500 years hence. The computer would have calculated that each month a certain number of stasis pods would have to be turned off to allow for the fact that one of the reactors was no longer functioning in order to optimise and maximise the population yield at the projected time of the awakening.

As the Noah 5000 project's nuclear scientist and one of the finest brains in the nuclear industry, Gibbs was not one to sugar coat the truth. He believed in facts, hard empirical evidence and reliable data. "This is the problem," he began. "The debris has also blocked the lead-lined steel doors that separate the fuel storage from the reactors, preventing them from opening. The debris will have to be moved, but both rooms are highly radioactive and any human being exposed to such an environment will die a horrible and painful death from radiation poisoning."

Cassandra asked, "Is there another entrance into the fuel chambers other than through the blocked doors?"

Gibbs shook his head. "No, so the only solution is to reprogram the robots that deal with the fuel rods to clear away the debris." He took a deep breath, and then delivered the worst news. "The life preservation protocols that were inserted into the computers mean that the yield optimisation cannot be overridden. This is a failsafe to avoid tampering and the accidental or deliberate euthanasia of certain genetics. The longer that reactor is offline, the more lives will be lost."

The Guardians had been well trained, and they recognised that this was a major issue that would need immediate attention and all of their wits, intellect, imagination and powers of innovation to overcome. They initiated the crisis evaluation protocol, which meant that if they did not have the necessary skills to overcome this event, they would have to select some other personnel from the stasis pods who had the necessary skills, and awaken them, so that they could build up a contingency task force to deal with the problems.

Gibbs would head this task force. Further analysis of the issue was needed within the next 48 hours, which included selecting the task force personnel that would need to be targeted for awakening.

CHAPTER 5

Day 5 - Nuclear Winter & Snowball Earth Effect

All six of the Guardians had worked twenty-hour days to wade through the relevant data, so as to be in a position to report back the status of their areas of responsibility to the group.

It was only Day 5.

The computer expert in the team, Michel Raider, nicknamed "Orb" because of a glass eye he wore in his left eye socket after an injury caused by a cricket ball hitting him during his junior school years. Orb had been looking at various ways to hack the primary protocol in the main computer to delay the stasis pod termination decrement cycle. While he had some success in finding the area within the programme that was responsible for the "decrement cycle", he was unable to make any changes as it was encrypted with two interchangeable 5,120-bit encryption keys which were unbreakable, even with all the computers working together simultaneously, using Shor's algorithm, named after mathematician Peter Shor, which is a quantum algorithm (an algorithm that runs on a quantum computer) for integer factorization formulated in 1994.

What Orb was able to do was reprogram the nuclear fuel service robots in the fuel depot to act on a new set of instructions which he could transmit using robotic simulation gloves. He had some success in removing some of the debris from the doorway access, but very soon determined that some of the concrete chunks weighed in excess of five tons apiece while the robots were rated to a maximum load of two tons.

The data also confirmed that on Christmas Day, 25th December

2111, the most devastating nuclear war that mankind had ever experienced broke out; the devastation was caused by 1,261 nuclear explosions in Europe, Russia, and Asia; including Egypt, Saudi, Iran, Iraq, Turkey, Israel, Afghanistan, Pakistan, India, China, the Korean peninsula and Vietnam, while at almost the same time there were 1,103 nuclear explosions in the Americas, spread between the USA, Canada and several Latin American countries. By the time the last explosion happened, the Noah 5000 project had already sealed the doors and the stasis pods were being occupied by their 200,000 residents, being prepped for a rather long 5,000-year stasis sleep.

Ever since the Cold War ended at the end of the second millennium, where nuclear disarmament was promised by Russia and USA, it was believed this scenario would never occur because of the theory of "mutually assured destruction" (MAD). This was a key doctrine for military strategy and national security policy in which full-scale use of nuclear weapons by two opposing sides would effectively result in the destruction of both the attacker and the defender. It was thus decreed that a war that had no victory or any armistice, but only total destruction would be futile. It was based on the theory of deterrence, according to which the deployment of strong weapons would be essential to threaten the enemy in order to prevent the use of the very same weapons. The strategy was deemed to be a form of Nash equilibrium in which neither side, once armed, has any incentive to disarm or go to war.

There was also the threat of nuclear terrorism by non-state organisations which was very much an unknown factor in nuclear deterrence thinking; as states possessing nuclear weapons were susceptible to retaliation in kind from those they targeted, whilst non state actors were not. The collapse and breakup of the Soviet Union at the end of the second millennium led to the possibility that former Soviet nuclear weapons might become available on the black market (so-called "loose nukes"). While no warheads were known to have been mislaid, it was alleged that suitcase-size bombs may have been unaccounted for.

At the beginning of the oil and water wars during the 2080 to 2110 period, terrorists used nuclear devices designed to disperse radioactive materials over a large area using conventional explosives, called dirty bombs. These dirty bomb detonations did not cause a nuclear explosion, nor did they release enough radiation to instantly kill or injure a lot of people. However, they did cause severe disruption to food sources and necessitated potentially costly decontamination. These acts contributed comprehensively to the famine which was rife at the time, and thus were indirectly responsible for the death of millions of innocent people.

What the superpowers, Russia, China, USA and European Community did not count on was the total collapse of some of these super-states due to anarchy and existential failures of their political systems, exacerbated by corruption. Evidence emerged that nuclear weapons were sold to the highest bidders in a desperate attempt to raise funds by the bureaucrats in power in those states. Essentially, the terrorists had won the day; they wore down the superpowers by creating systemic failures in their financial and political systems, which finally resulted in Armageddon.

Compared to conventional warfare, nuclear warfare was known to be vastly more destructive in range and extent of damage. It was known for many decades that a major nuclear exchange could have severe long-term effects, primarily from radiation release but also from possible atmospheric pollution leading to nuclear winter that could last for decades, centuries, or even millennia after the initial attack. An all-out nuclear war was considered to be the most dangerous risk for civilisation on Earth, purely because nobody could clean up the mess due to radioactive waste and fallout. The Noah 5000 project was the only form of defence in this scenario, essentially a time capsule filled with people and resources that would begin the resurrection of mankind when the radiation had either dissipated entirely or had reached a level at which it was less dangerous.

Orb, of course, knew all of this, but when he stood before the Guardians to deliver his report, it was with a heavy heart. "More bad news, I'm afraid," he began. "The telemetry data is showing that over 95% of the world's land mass is covered in radioactive ice. It looks like a "Snowball Earth" is in progress out there."

For several moments no one spoke, and then the air was filled with a hubbub of cries of shock and half-formed questions.

Orb held up a hand, and gradually the room grew quiet. "I don't know how or why this happened. The forecasts made in 2111, at the start of our project, were predicting that by around the year 7,000 the nuclear winter would be over, and most of the radioactive dust should have settled, been washed into rivers and eventually the sea, and that much of the earth's surface would be getting enough sunlight to allow life to be sustainable again. Instead, it seems as if the earth is fast becoming covered in deep glacial snow and ice."

Joe asked, "If we hadn't been awakened early, if we'd been in stasis for the full 5,000 years as was intended, would the "snowball" have melted?"

"Probably not," admitted Orb. "Archived records indicate that around seven hundred million years ago, Earth's oceans were completely frozen over. No rivers flowed, no rain or snow fell. But, deep in the centre of the Earth, there was activity that led to surface volcanism. Volcanoes belched carbon dioxide and other gases into the air, which accumulated over millions of years, eventually producing global warming –"

"– which melted the ice," interrupted Cassandra.

"Exactly," agreed Orb.

"The greenhouse effect," muttered Joe.

"That's the one," said Orb. "Now, between 570 million and 750 million years ago, this icehouse to greenhouse cycle occurred several times. Glaciers turned Earth into a "snowball" that stayed frozen for millions of years until volcanic gases finally freed it."

"OK," said Gibbs. "Hence Snowball Earth."

Orb nodded.

"And that's what we've got out there?" asked Gibbs, waving his arm in the general direction of the outside world.

"Not yet. It's not a full snowball effect. The telemetry shows that the temperature out there did not once rise above -20°C in the past 100 years, and the strong freezing winds have created a wind-chill factor that has reduced this even more, to between -40°C and -70°C."

Orb looked around at his stunned and depressed fellow Guardians. "But there still appears to be some open water in the tropics, although the telemetry shows that the ice gap is closing rapidly. Rather than a snowball, it might be a "slush ball" at present."

Orb then explained "the initiation of a Snowball Earth event would involve some initial cooling mechanism, which would result in an increase in the Earth's coverage of snow and ice. That increase would in turn increase the Earth's albedo, which would result in positive feedback for cooling. If enough snow and ice accumulate, runaway cooling would result. This positive feedback is facilitated by an equatorial continental distribution, which would allow ice to accumulate in the regions closer to the equator, where solar radiation would be most direct."

"Yeah, I know about that," said Cassandra. "It was something people were worried about with the diminishing of the Arctic sea ice back around the time towards the end of the second millennium, beginning of the third."

Joe had been sitting with his head in his hands, looking deeply depressed. Now he raised his head. "OK," he said. "Things are pretty bad. Orb, can you feed in new algorithms to get us a new forecast, based on the data you now have, which might tell us when this "snowball effect" could be over?

"In other words, a new Noah 5000 awakening date to coincide with a predicted thaw date?"

"I've already started it, Joe, but it'll take weeks for the computers to process the data. The computer has over 600 years of new weather telemetry to contend with."

Global warming associated with large accumulations of carbon dioxide in the atmosphere over millions of years, emitted primarily by volcanic activity, is the proposed trigger for melting a Snowball Earth. Due to positive feedback for melting, the eventual melting of the snow and ice covering most of the Earth's surface would require as few as 1,000 years.

The satellite data showed that low levels of radiation had pretty much covered the whole planet; however, it was most heavily concentrated in vicinity of the Euro-Asian, Russia, China and American states where the full force of the blasts were experienced.

Fresh water supplies would be affected as the ice melts and eventually the radiation would concentrate in the ocean, rendering all opportunities of fish stocks thriving rather moot as they would become sterile and thus become extinct.

It was previously estimated by scientists in the nuclear industry that the radiation fallout from a nuclear bomb would have spent itself within 10,000 years. Unfortunately, Noah 5000 project was only equipped to survive for 5,000 years, and it barely made 10% of that target before the first critical issue arose that created the first awakening of the Guardians.

It was going to be a very long 5,000 years.

CHAPTER 6

Day 31 - Not Many Days Left to Avoid Extinction

The date was 30th April 2612 AD, one month after they first awakened; the six Guardians sat in their early morning progress meeting, where Joe stated, "So this is what we know so far."

He pulled up a slide, and, reading from it, ticked off the points on his fingers as he spoke.

"One, the Noah 5000 project has lost 25% of its fuel for power, a situation that looks irrecoverable.

"Two, a "Snowball Earth" scenario appears to be getting a foothold outside as a result of the nuclear winter and it seems that there is nothing we can do about this phenomenon.

"Three, the nuclear fallout from the 2111 event is trapped in the snow and ice and will not wash away off the land until the big thaw begins, which, according to the forecasts made by Orb using all the available data, looks likely to be in about 15,000 years' time.

"Four, if a full "Snowball Earth" did indeed develop, similar to the events of 570 million and 750 million years ago when the "snowball" stayed frozen for millions of years until volcanic gases finally freed it, this would be terminal. The volcanic activity of 570 million years ago and the volcanic state now are vastly different. Nothing would change the CO_2 levels sufficiently to trigger a warming effect.

"Five, the Guardian awakening event happened earlier than anticipated, triggered by one of the intruder safety protocols, and the programme had only progressed along 10% of the original intended journey.

"Six, the stasis pod decrement cycle is still running and as yet Orb hasn't figured out how to disarm it. This means that we would lose a minimum of 10 lives per year until the awakening, which would be another 50,000 lives in all, which was circa 25% - that would be a disaster."

Joe finished with a grim statement. "This would be bad enough to cope with during several full lifetimes, but we have only thirty days to sort this out."

There was a long silence; everyone in the room looked at the six points as if they were a death sentence. The first to speak was Svetlana Bowker, the doctor and renowned scientist specialising in human DNA and the human genome on the team. Svetlana, or Lana, as she preferred to be known, was one of two sisters; both of them were beautiful and gifted with incredible intelligence and vision. Svetlana had discovered the DNA sequence and genes that needed to be manipulated to changed the ice-forming properties by combining the fluids in the cells with a sucrose which bound the ethanol and oxygen that enabled stasis to be feasible, allowing living tissue to be put into a state of deep stasis for very long periods without ageing and precluding damage from ice particles or shards.

Lana said, "If we have two issues out there that we are unable to resolve, then surely we have to look at alternative strategies to see what can be done to change these disastrous circumstances. If we cannot alter our present state, which inevitably means that our project is doomed, then we have to alter the steps leading up to this series of events."

There was stunned silence and looks of incredulity. Was Lana, one of the world's most celebrated visionary scientists, actually suggesting time travel?

Unknown to the rest of the Guardian team, Lana's elder sister Venetia was one of the "Chosen Souls" in stasis. Venetia was employed by the American military and had been working on a top-secret time travel project in Area-51 before being ordered to report to Harrogate in England on the 30th October 2110. Venetia was designated the officer in charge of several sealed containers marked "Experimental Equipment

USA.".'" Venetia was to see the containers delivered safely to Noah 5000 project and report for inoculation. That day in Harrogate was the last time Lana saw her sister, and she had no idea that Venetia was one of the "Chosen Souls".

Briefly, she allowed herself to think about her family. Venetia was the tall slim, vivacious and very sexy Head Girl at their high school who had all the senior boys and teachers eating out of her hand, whereas Lana was the shorter, plump child who had an enchantingly beautiful face and charming character and was seen as the swot and a bookworm. Lana was one year behind her elder sister, and always envied Venetia's charisma and amazing ability to wrap the boys around her little finger. Lana's only way to compete was by always beating Venetia's best score in any of the exams they sat. Not surprisingly, both girls achieved straight A's and were top of all the classes they entered; each of their IQs was in excess of 160. When they were at school together, when they worked together as a duo, they were unbeatable at debating, problem solving, and inventing solutions for the most complex problems.

Both of their parents were professors at Harvard. They were both talented and expected their girls to excel and be the best at whatever they put their hands to. Lana thought of them now with sorrow. Neither of her parents were selected as those fortunate enough to be a "Chosen Soul" because they were both over seventy years old when the selection was done. Most of those selected had to be capable of hard work and reproducing; all were tested for their virility and capability to yield viable eggs and sperm. The loss of many wise elders would be a cost to the new brave world, and she was saddened at the clinical but understandable selection process they underwent.

She was jolted out of her reverie by Joe asking the other Guardians if they had any other ideas. Facing again the harsh reality of their situation, she sat and pondered what she had just said to the team. Had she mistakenly let the cat out of the bag about her having knowledge of the time travel project her sister had been working on? If so, they would very quickly ascertain that there was a security breach that must have happened prior to the 2111 event.

"I think that we have to awaken everyone who we think can add particular skills that might help us find a way out of this situation," Joe said. "Otherwise, as our resources have been calculated to last for only 5,000 years, we are all going to die, whether in functioning stasis or not." Joe had asked Orb to run a series of searches on the database to determine which people's skills, best suited the situation they found themselves in. They would be assigned to workshops and think-tanks to try to come up with a workable solution.

Orb presented a shortlist of seventy-five names with brief resumés for the team to review so that they could agree and select fifty-six names, which would be input into the awakening sequence. Eight of those names had been specifically selected for non-workshop or think tank duties and would report directly to Orb. The remaining names would be divided up into four groups once they had become accustomed to their current environment and appraised of their present status.

"Orb, you will work with Lana to manage the awakenings," instructed Joe. "We cannot afford a single casualty."

CHAPTER 7

Day 41 - Disaster Recovery Not an Option

The date was 10th May 2612 AD.

It was the tenth day after the "think-tank" stasis awakenings, and all the new recruits had been thoroughly briefed on the situation. They had been given various tasks to fulfil during their recovery and acclimatisation, which helped them to prepare and deal with the challenges that they were facing, and had been allocated to four working groups.

One was tasked with trying to find a solution to the structural integrity of the project. In particular, to find out whether the loss of the fuel for power could be redressed, whether the debris could be cleared, and what needed to be done to prevent further structural decay within the bunker.

Another group was to concentrate on the climate change issue, to try to establish where they were in the "snowball earth" cycle and to explore whether there was anything that could be done about it.

The third group had to calculate – when and where it would be safe to venture outside the bunker into the world, given that the telemetry data showed that the nuclear fallout from the 2111 events was trapped in snow and ice. They were the "Habitation and Environment" team.

Finally, a team was given the task of helping Orb to work out what options might be available to disarm the stasis pod decrement cycle and prevent the loss of a further 50,000 lives. They were given one month to come up with their first assessment and any ideas for possible solutions.

Orb had chosen his team carefully, for he knew that advanced computer skills would be needed in all of the working groups. The "Geek Squad", as they became known, would prove invaluable to all of the teams, as the data needed to help them find solutions for each problem would have to be supplied by them.

One of the brighter Cambridge Computer Science graduates, Robert Dell-Russell, had done some work with GCHQ and MI5 in the UK prior to being commissioned for the Noah 5000 programme. His work on satellites was proving immensely useful for the Habitation Environment and Climate Change workgroups. Robert had discovered that at least twelve satellites orbiting the earth were still functional, but had not been assigned to feed data into the Noah 5000 programme. Robert and three other computer hackers set about taking control of the satellites so that they could be "persuaded" to put their vast array of military utilities at the Noah 5000 programme's disposal. One of Robert's team, Zhou Zhi-Wei, (pronounced Chee-Way), (whose family name comes from the very old Zhou Chinese dynasty (1122–221 BC) in the Republic of China); he had worked with the Chinese mainland military satellite task force. "Eureka!" he cried, as he unlocked the security on four Chinese high security military spy satellites, giving full access to the Noah 5000 Geek Squad. Robert, who had been looking over his shoulder, said, "I think you mean "Open sesame!"

"Whatever!" Zhi-Wei grinned, enjoying his moment of triumph and examining the data he had gained access to.

One of the utilities, codenamed "Hotspot" was capable of identifying mineral and essential resources anywhere on the planet, up to depths of two miles underground. The map that he pulled up illustrated its power and showed radioactive material; both processed and as yet undiscovered deposits such as uranium. They could see the entire unused ordnance that the military had not fired off during the December 2111 events. What was scary was that they could see the location of the Noah 5000 bunker. They could pick out the four storage locations and the four reactors.

"That is phenomenal technology," breathed Orb in fascination. "Look at the depth of resolution those satellites are returning!" He could hardly believe the power of the ground penetrating "X-ray" technology. Zhi-Wei shrugged. "Well," he said, "it hardly matters now, but for some time the Chinese were using a technique that nobody else on the planet had thought of. They were using neutrinos in a specific way to achieve the ground penetrating capabilities you can see now."

He continued, "Neutrinos are subatomic particles like electrons or quarks, or the Higgs Boson that have almost zero mass, a neutral charge, *thus their name*, and travel at close to the speed of light. Unlike almost every other particle in the universe, neutrinos are unaffected by electromagnetism, *because of their neutral charge*, which means they are only subject to gravity and weak nuclear forces. This means that neutrinos can easily pass through solid objects as large as planets. Every second, 65 billion neutrinos from the Sun pass through each square centimetre of the Earth at almost the speed of light. That said, there are four states of neutrinos, of which only three were known by the rest of the world; electron-neutrino, muon-neutrino and tau-neutrino, all of which could interchanged into each other's state due to oscillating changes in their respective frequencies. The Chinese discovered that a fourth state existed, a unique frequency which was transmitted as each neutrino passed through different materials, which triggered their state changes."

Orb interjected, "Whoa there *boss*, neutrinos were notoriously hard to detect and damned expensive to do at that. Even with the huge MINERvA collector at the Fermi National Accelerator Laboratory (Fermilab) near Chicago, which was a large, multi-ton slab of metal, they could only detect one neutrino in 10 billion!"

"Yep you are correct, so you are not just a computer whiz, you also know about *quantum physics* and the *standard model* that was used to understand the universe and how it was made up." Zhi-Wei retorted.

Zhi-Wei explained, "During the first quarter of 2000, the Antarctic IceCube experiments run by the British and Americans in what was one of the first U.S.-UK Science and Technology Agreements signed where both countries commitment to collaborate on world-class science and innovation.

"The IceCube experiments used high energy neutrinos so that they could be seen by the Antarctic detector. The Chinese leverage the fact that high energy neutrinos were a critical factor since the higher the energy, the more likely the neutrinos were to interact with matter and therefore be absorbed by minerals in the Earth.

"The sensors did not directly observe neutrinos, but instead measure flashes of blue light known as Cherenkov radiation. These flashes were emitted by muons, which are produced when neutrinos interacted with the minerals in the earth. What the Chinese discovered was that whilst the IceCube detector experiments focused on readings in the detector, they were able to setup sensitive Cherenkov radiation muon listening devices along the horizontal plane between the transmitter and detector devices.

"By measuring the multi-TeV Cherenkov radiation muon frequency patterns emitted from these interactions along the pathway of the IceCube detector array experiments, the Chinese scientists were able to calculate something called the neutrino "cross-section Cherenkov radiation" frequencies generated by different material types with a high degree of accuracy."

"Which is why" he continued, "the Chinese scientists exploited that much less expensive route and focused on the energy output that was created as their particle accelerator shot a stream of concentrated neutrino-beam pulses underground along the horizontal plane to interacted with these different materials. In doing so, the different nuclear properties of the respective materials caused the neutrinos to oscillate between their present states, emitting concentrated pulses of these unique multi-TeV Cherenkov radiation radio frequencies, which cumulatively became sufficiently aggregated and thus become detectable."

He added, "By cataloguing these unique radio frequency bursts against known metals, or materials, and using some extremely sophisticated mathematics, including the time-independent Schrodinger equation, they were eventually able to determine four things: the type of material the pulsed neutrino beams passed through, GPS map coordinates relative to the terrain, and because of the known distance between the hearing devices and the speed of the neutrinos, they were also able to calculate the depth from the surface and–most important of all–the magnitude of the geo-strata or material or mineral deposits."

"Clever or what?" he said, grinning.

Orb thought about this. "Does that mean that the Chinese could have known the map co-ordinates of every other country's nuclear devices before the 2111 disaster?"

Zhi-Wei smiled. "Oh, yes, for more than thirty years, actually, though that was not the primary aim."

Orb whistled, half horrified and half admiring. "Of course," he marvelled. "With this kind of technology, they would have been able to pinpoint the location of key resources anywhere in the world. Essentially, the world would have been their oyster and they would have been able to plunder resources with surgical efficiency!"

"Yes," agreed Zhi-Wei. "We know that early in the third millennium many African states saw China as their new benefactors because they made massive investments in infrastructure such as telecommunications and electricity in those states in return for contracts giving them the right to harvest their riches –"

"Whereas in fact," interrupted Orb, "Those African states were just pawns in an international game of mineral and resources chess!"

"Yes, *financial colonisation* by economic stealth, without firing a single shot." Zhi-Wei chortled.

The Chinese satellites gave them a global picture of the spread of the nuclear fallout, which served to confirm their suspicions that a nuclear winter had indeed occurred. The outside world was not going to be habitable for at least another 10,000 years. If the Noah 5000 project was going to be successful, it was going to need to double its nuclear fuel and pray that the infrastructure was going to last the course. All indications showed that both of those requirements were nearly impossible.

The Structural Integrity working group had exhausted all of their options as well. There was no way to move the debris with what was inside the fuel depot, which meant they would have to breach one of the walls with plasma cutters and insert additional equipment that could be utilised as part of the extraction operation.

While this was not entirely ruled out, it meant they would face contamination of all the surrounding facilities and corridors leading up to the depot. That would render a lot of resources inaccessible for a very long period of time. As they reported in their assessment, this was a last resort option.

The Climate Change Working Group (CCWG) concluded that the "Snowball Earth" scenario was still in the process of happening and that a radical influx of CO_2 into the atmosphere would go some way to slow it down or alleviate the threat somewhat. There was far too much land mass that was essentially in a "white-out" state, which reflected too much sunlight back into space, and the telemetry data showed that the gap between the tropics had been gradually closing every few years.

They also came up with a last resort scenario, which would probably cost some of the people in the Noah 5000 project their lives, as they would have to somehow get to one of the nuclear silos and manually reprogram the target co-ordinates, point them at certain volcano structures, and set off several volcanic eruptions around the world in the hope that they would emit sufficient CO_2 to warm the atmosphere and stop the "Snowball Earth" from progressing. A very long shot at best.

The Solution Integrity working group was unable to break the decrement cycle code. However, they did manage to crack the security on a number of ultra-secret secure military projects around the world that were stored in various locations within the bunker. Being the Geek Squad, they were delighted to be able to hack military systems to their hearts' content without the threat of being prosecuted and going to jail.

What was pointed out, which was obvious, was that because they had woken up some of the people, the drain on the power was slightly reduced and thus they probably had about two- or three-years' grace before the decrement cycle activated the next stasis pod switch-offs.

The month had flown by as they all worked eighteen-hour days, searching through data and exploring all the options. However, even with fifty of the brightest brains on the planet they were unable to come up with safe plans to move some rubble, extend their power range, and blow billions of tons of CO_2 into the atmosphere.

The exercise was a bust!

Joe called a crisis meeting for 06h00 the next morning and everyone was asked to come prepared to make some hard decisions. After that meeting, he asked the other five Guardians to remain behind, and after everyone else had left, closed the door and locked it.

Joe had a stern, pensive look on his face. There was a deep furrow between his eyebrows, which none of the Guardians had noticed there before. He said what he was about to show them and what they were about to discuss could have grave consequences. They sat down as Joe motioned to Orb to continue with the presentation he had prepared.

Orb began by saying that there were two issues he needed to cover.

He brought up some specification data on the stasis pods, which showed quite clearly that they were reusable, so that if someone was accidentally brought out of stasis, they could be inserted back into the pod with the original DNA profile and their programme restarted. Naturally, when the supplier demonstrated the systems during the sales phase, this all worked, and they were told that they had to deliver 200,000 units within twenty-four months of the order date. There were specifications that were modified to accommodate the long duration DNA stabilisation requirements, which had been specified and tested by Svetlana and her team prior to signing off the specification and before committing to an official order.

The units that were delivered did not have a key piece of the solution that stored the person's original DNA and their profile to hardware. All the stasis pods were designed to take a real-time sample, and after running real-time tests with the occupant inside, it would create their profile which was held in its operational memory, and store the original profile to a chipset that was interchangeable between different pods in case of faults developing with a pod. In theory, this all made sense and during the trials and tests, all of this worked to the satisfaction of the specification and was signed off.

Unfortunately, the memory storage devices were never inserted and could not be found anywhere in the bunker, which meant either that the supplier short-changed them, or ran out of time and never installed them.

"The crux of problem," summarised Joe, "is that if we were to go back into stasis, we could begin with a DNA sequence that is flawed because of potential radiation exposure, or with a gene sequence that could have been corrupted, which means that during a prolonged stasis process, where faulty genes and DNA are utilised to automatically mend or remove and replace the faulty elements with the correct material based on the original sample, corruption could be introduced and resources could be over utilised and the stasis integrity would fail."

Svetlana was asked to work with Orb to look into whether there was a fix that could be made using whatever technology was available. The ramifications of not solving this problem meant that everyone who had been awakened could not be guaranteed to live through a second attempt, as they might run out of their own baseline genetic material that had been prepared in the profiling exercise. Without an original source, cloning of second-hand strands would increasingly introduce more and more corruption, to the point where the repair material is in an equally bad or even worse state than the damaged strands being targeted for repair.

The second item on the list for confidential discussion was to inform the Guardians that they were facing their own doomsday scenario inside the bunker.

Essentially, unless they could come up with an alternative strategy that would magically make some of these problems go away, they were all going to perish.

CHAPTER 8

Day 71 - Time Travel is the Only Solution

Date 9th June 2612 AD. Time O6h00 GMT.

They all gathered in the large conference room to be briefed and contemplate their next move.

Orb delivered the results of their previous investigations and then put up a slide that reported the second item of the Guardians' previous day's confidential discussion. He started by saying flatly, "The debris cannot be moved without risking the lives of everyone in the bunker."

Marc Gibberson, who liked to be called Gibbs, was considered the nuclear boffin on the team, added, "We are at risk of contaminating the whole bunker if we breach the buffer zone. If there is a breach and the nuclear radiation finds its way into the living quarters or into the stasis chambers, we will all perish as a result of radiation poisoning or freeze to death outside if we try evacuating."

Gibbs carried on to say, "The ice melt without a "Snowball Earth" scenario is projected to take at least 15,000 years and our fuel storage was only ever designed to keep the bunker powered for 5,000 years. If we were able to reprogram the decrement cycle protocol, it would mean that everyone would come out of stasis in 3,250 years' time, which was 1,250 years short of the original target. And," he added, "if a full blown "Snowball Earth" did actually occur, there would be no point in discussing fuel rationing, as there would not be sufficient volcanic activity to enable Earth to ever recover."

Joe then stood up and said, "essentially, we have to come up with an alternative strategy that would magically make some of these problems go away."

There was a long contemplative silence, eventually broken by Lana.

She said, "If it is agreed that we are absolutely unable to resolve the issues in our present state, we have to go back to a previous time-line and alter the steps leading up to the series of dreadful events which led us to where we are today. We have to understand what led up to the nuclear holocaust of December 2111 and do what we can to change things so that it won't happen."

In the silence that greeted her remarks, you could have heard a pin drop. Nobody dared to comment, as it sounded too ridiculous to even contemplate. They all thought she had lost the plot and was living in a fantasy world. It was like an old Star Trek episode where Seven of Nine was recruited by a Federation Star ship from the twenty-ninth century to save Voyager from being destroyed in their past.

Lana stood up, looked at everyone with a quizzical expression on her face, walked over to Orb and Joe and whispered something into their ears. Orb looked surprised, frowned, and asked Joe if he could be excused. He and Lana left the conference room in haste.

As the door closed behind them, the room burst into noisy debate.

Joe took the lead and asked them to calm down, saying that maybe it wasn't as far-fetched as it sounded, and perhaps they should give some time to considering what they thought had gone wrong which led to the destruction of mankind.

"OK," he said, preparing to start writing bullet points on the whiteboard. "Who wants to go first?"

Suddenly, there was an air of expectation in the room: the debates were going to be fierce and contentious.

CHAPTER 9

Day 72 – What caused Mankind's demise?

The first point to hit the whiteboard was "Values and Moral Decay."

One of the work-group members, Mikhail Onderhoudt, who had a Doctorate in Social Sciences, was asked to put his views forward.

"During the last twenty-five years of the second millennium, humanity witnessed the degradation of good, clean, honest living values and a moral decay that took human behaviour such as greed and selfishness, self-importance, and self-righteousness to heights that humanity had never experienced before. The people of the time saw an increase in serious and violent crime, devaluation of human life, terrorism, mass murder and pervasive political corruption. Mankind was on a downward spiral and there was no braking mechanism to pull it back from the brink."

Dr. Karyn Hodges, a Scientist specialising in Global Politics and the sixth Guardian, added, "This wayward behaviour started to get a foothold in the mid-1960s, when the "hippies" or "flower power" movement started advocating that children had minds of their own and that discipline was unnecessary because things could be rationalised with them and they would know instinctively what to do. This generation became known as the Dr. Spock generation. These children grew up not knowing where the boundaries were, not respecting other people's property, or being able to follow rules that society has in the real world to maintain order and not realising that the world was not all about them. This was the first generation that lost many of the basic building blocks that would have helped them formulate the very fabric of the basic human decency and good morals they needed."

Mikhail smiled at her accurate description and added, "Dr. Spock came under fire for this political activism. Critics branded him the "father of permissiveness" and said he was responsible for a "Spock-marked generation of hippies.""

"Good pun," said Karyn with a smile.

Mikhail said, "I wanted to say that in the 1960s, a number of high-profile people such as the USA's Vice President Agnew, Chicago Mayor Richard Daley, and New York Methodist Episcopal minister Norman Vincent Peale publicly attacked Spock, arguing that his methods of bringing up children had caused a "breakdown in discipline and a collapse of conventional morality." From his pulpit, Peale preached, "And now Spock is out mingling with the mobs, leading the permissive babies raised on his undisciplined teaching." Mikhail concluded, "This generation were the first to suffer a self-inflicted man-made disease that was not a physical sickness; it was decades of a lack of discipline which led to inbred disrespect for others, insubordination and laziness, exacerbated by a total disregard for personal achievement and lack of self-pride and personal integrity."

Karyn said, "Yes, that was how it must have looked to those who were still in touch with the religious moral values people held in earlier days, the values taught and handed down to generations by their parents and grandparents. They must have witnessed the slow demise of the good in people. The difference between those who had these values and those who did not was more about upbringing and the environment in which that occurred rather than age or generation differences."

"How could that be?" someone asked.

"Very simply, because by the turn of the second millennium they had third and fourth generation children who had been brought up by parents who did not have those values instilled in them as children. There was a vacuum of moral values, the very knowledge and experience that was handed down century after century to each new generation. Those values were the building blocks that helped humanity to evolve into responsible, intelligent, adventurous human beings, capable of living with integrity, love, mercy and empathy, in short, the ingredients the latest generations appeared to be lacking. For humanity to not only survive, but continue to evolve to a higher state, they needed to assimilate basic values like good manners, respect for people, their property, and living with integrity, and to re-adopt good healthy moral values back into society." She paused and looked sadly around the room. "Without those essential building blocks to guide human behaviour, mankind was set on a path to the very depths of hell and oblivion, as we have all witnessed."

Joe looked at this slightly built, attractive woman with interest. She was softly-spoken, yet carried an air of conviction when she aired her views – views that were very similar to his own. Bringing himself back to the discussion, he said, "So, assuming that we could go back to try to fix this, the question we need to explore is how humanity could be reprogrammed to adopt these basic good moral values as the foundation of good character. We know what failure means for humanity."

The second point to hit the whiteboard was "A flawed political system."

Karyn opened up the discussion with an immediate segue into the evils of politics.

She said, "Unbeknown to most people, mankind was unfortunately sent down the pan by a poor implementation of democracy which evolved over centuries and was overwhelmingly infiltrated and corrupted by something more evil and objectionable …. Progressivism.

"This vile blight on mankind created strategies to control the populace by making society weak, and by creating a society of feeble-minded "sheeple", a flock that may not have contributed much to society or worked and paid taxes. These people were programmed to think the government would look after them and they had rights and were entitled to handouts. There was a growing apathy amongst the masses because they felt they could not change a corrupt system, which they misguidedly believed were being controlled by the evil rich elite, so it was easier to let the government take care of them regardless."

"The wealthy people in positions of influence were, naively, directly and/or indirectly responsible for the ultimate destruction of a society that had previously believed in productivity and a good work ethic."

"Some of the apathy mankind had developed, referred to voting in political elections, which was because of the distrust the public had for the corrupt political and media systems. A distrust caused primarily because of corruption, which could also be partly put down to the entertainment industry, including Television and Movie industries, who had systematically *"dumbed"* down their programs with celebrity and sensational material, so that entertainment had become the opiate of the people as Karl Marx once stated about "Religion." We know from history that he said that religion was a way of controlling the masses."

"It was plain for the world to see that the US government and other political "actors" such as the Progressive actors had exploited Hollywood to "program" the masses and the rest of the world for that matter."

"Even though many of the masses realised that the integrity within the Entertainment industry as well as the News Media industry were somewhat suspect, because the Media consistently; blatantly manipulated the truth for sensationalism or for political point scoring against anyone who did not agree with their political point of view, which became known as "Fake-News.""

"People who were objective and rational thinkers referred to all dishonest Media businesses, which reported untruthful, blatantly biased material and were patently unable to remain objective and fair when questioning, reasoning or listening to those they are engaging with. This applied to all media, irrespective whether the Media business was a Conservative or Liberal media business, if they behaved in the way described, then they were labelled as the "Lamestream *Media"* in over 990,000 Internet articles in 2012 alone*!"*

"According to the bloggers on the Internet, the term *"Lamestream Media"* was said to be a play on the phrase "Main Stream Media (~MSM)." It was intended to promote the idea that.... *most of what passes for news in the world in the twenty first century is controlled by liberal personnel who no longer are interested in reporting objective facts. They want to ensure that the information is slanted to promote liberalism and denigrate Conservatism, which suits their propaganda strategies. They go on to claim that this is the case because most of the Journalists are educated at highly liberal colleges like Columbia."*

"Frankly, many people, who were not taken in by by the propaganda put out by Hollywood and the News Channels, believed that if a journalist was unable to be honest and objective when they were reporting or interviewing people from political parties, then they were considered to be corrupt... full-stop!"

"A corrupt media and their spreading of fake news on behalf of the New World Order (NWO), was the biggest threat to harmony during that era........" she said.

Karyn described Progressivism: "Firstly, being a progressive thinker is different from being a Progressive...... with a capital "P."" It was the specifically American development of liberalism and populism that sought social justice above all else, and especially with reference to the obstacles posed to social justice by large corporations or those who attained wealth. Though the Progressive movement strongly supported civil liberties, the word "progress" in Progressivism was thought to stem most fundamentally from a belief in ensuring "justice for all" and "equality for all." This was a smoke screen and hidden agenda for wealth re-distribution and big government," she said.

"Essentially, the primary objective of the Progressive movement was to create a global *new world order* that redistributed the wealth of the middle classes and the wealthy to the poor and needy on a global basis. Progressivism condoned people's lack of personal culpability and personal responsibility for their own actions and behaviour, such as blaming the actions of the "white racist colonials" of the past for their misfortune and poverty or "the previous governments" for the ills and woes they now experienced."

Mikhail Onderhoudt asked, "How does this relate to fixing what is purportedly a broken political system?"

Joe interrupted and said, "Let me see if I can help.

"The "Progressives" lacked the common sense and ability to understand the damage they caused through their inability to impose stricter laws and disciplines in society to prevent or eradicate the bad behaviour and deadly traits afflicting mankind. Sadly, this helped to accelerate the downward spiral to society's self-destruction. Aside from some of the beautiful and positive aspects of humanity, such as generosity, love and kindness, mankind's evolution was a journey fraught with corruption, mistakes, violent crime, murders, mayhem, starvation, religious wars, water wars and widespread disease, culminating in the eventual mass extinction of humankind. Unfortunately, that extinction was brought about, at least in part, by the very do-gooders who thought their philanthropic ideas were the right way to improve quality of human life and prolong life for all those unfortunate people that became addicted to and reliant on their handouts, charity and social welfare."

He could see Karyn nodding enthusiastically, and smiled at her.

Mikhail replied, "You seem to be saying that a percentage of mankind was in a sorry state, the masses were being treated like sheep, slowly sleep-walking in a state of hopelessness into dependency pens created by the wealthy and those in government so that they could control them."

Karyn interjected, "Yes, their altruistic and philanthropic ways, which appeared so magnanimous actually engineered a mental state which became known as the "Poor me malaise" a contagion easily spread by mankind's new-found laziness and sense of individual entitlement being passed down to subsequent generations."

She went on, stating, "Those "entitlement" generations were the generations and sections of society that believed the world owed them a living, or those that deemed they were owed compensation for what happened to their forefathers. There were also those in society who took to crime because they felt it was the only way to get what they wanted. They felt that they were owed this because of injustices that may have happened in the way distant past like elitism, class prejudices, colonialism or slavery."

"Interestingly, as was stated by Robert T. Kiyosaki in his best seller book entitled; *"Rich Dad Poor Dad"* first published in 1997, a lot of the issues that arose during that period were very much down to the lack of education or simply poor education. For example, who recalls the stories of Robin Hood Karyn asked?" Watching them all nod their heads in recognition of the British tale about a woodsman in

Nottingham Forest who took on the system, robbing the rich to give to the poor.

She rambled on "that Robin Hood story was promoted and told by the rich as a cover for the real heist that happened in 1874, when permanent taxation was voted into law by the masses, because they were told it would punish the rich like Robin Hood was doing. The masses were deceived into getting behind this new law. However, very soon the government was addicted to having this revenue and wanted more. So very soon the tax laws were expanded and became a punishment for the poor and middle classes. However, as soon as that happened the rich outsmarted the taxman by putting their earnings in different vehicles / companies that limited their tax liabilities and enabled them to spend pre-taxed money on expenses. So as the tax from the rich dried up the government was forced to push more tax levies further down the hierarchy in order for them to maintain the benefits of income for the treasury."

"The rich simply used intellect and outsmarted the taxman because they understood balance-sheets and that assets needed to generate revenue instead of just being '*stuff*' they bought on a whim, which added to their liabilities, hence they accumulated wealth, and were known as the "*Have's*", whereas the poor never showed signs of grasping the meaning of assets working for them, thus they always spent their wages on '*stuff*' and because they were never able to accumulate wealth, they became known as the "*Have-Not's.*'"

This battle between the "*Have's*" and the "*Have-Not's*" carried on for centuries."

Mikhail added, "The "*Have-Not's*" seemed to get the rough-end of the stick everywhere, for example, there were those countries that had for decades been receiving monetary Aid, who had governments that were so corrupt they chose to line their own pockets with the Aid money and not to invest in their own countries' infrastructure or to really help their people and businesses to grow so that their people could become productive, wealth creating members of society instead of net consumers or takers."

Warming to his theme, he continued, "This "victim mentality" that

Karyn mentioned became one of the biggest problems that humanity had to face in its twilight years. Hundreds of millions of people became unwitting actors in the disaster that unfolded. The decades of aid that was sent out to African and Asian countries took a devastating toll on their people's ability to help themselves and become productive contributing members of society, instead the system ensured they remained as "*Have-Not's*", which ultimately was a means of controlling the masses by making them dependant on the State, or Aid handouts. The political party running the country would then make all sorts of promises to address the wealth gap, which was how political parties herded their loyal misguide, "poor-me-malaise" sheep into their corrals when it came time to vote once again."

"It wasn't only third world countries that were affected," he went on. "In the United Kingdom there were many tens of thousands of people who lived in households where nobody in the family unit had worked for a living in over three or more generations. These people had indeed lost the basic instincts to survive autonomously or operate in a working environment; their parents had collected the "Social" or the "Dole" as their own parents and grandparents had done. So, new generations came into the world with little opportunity of ever becoming a contributor, they only knew how to be dependent on the State."

Joe then said, "So those in society who worked hard for their money were growing tired of giving to those who had an expectation of entitlement. Essentially, the contributors saw the receivers as '*spongers*'. Perversely, this was essentially a modern form of enslavement."

Karyn chipped in again. "Yes, in response to what was being portrayed by the media as the greed of the wealthy, the non-contributors and the trade unions created mischief and unrest through protests and rioting over a sustained period, which merely exacerbated and perpetuated the economic challenges of the time. For some reason, certain elements of the populace just could not see that their country was bankrupt and that brutal cuts in government spending had to be made if the country was to survive. These same elements wanted the

Progressives to redistribute the assets of the middle-class and wealthy to them."

She went on to explain just how Greece was bankrupt in the early part of the twenty-first century, and how bad the riots and protests were during 2011 and 2012. After already having received an initial 110 billion Euros issued in 2010, under a second bailout the EU plan for Athens, Greece would receive an additional 130 billion Euros in direct loans by 2014, in return for tough new austerity measures and granting tighter oversight access of the Greek economy to the European Union and International Monetary Fund overseeing of its economy. The conditions attached to these bailout loans were, as far as the Greek people were concerned, an insidious and surreptitious colonisation of Greece by Germany.

The emotions and sentiments of the citizens of both countries were diametrically opposed, as the Greeks believed Germany still owed them billions in reparation for all the looting the Nazis had carried out in Greece during the Second World War, whereas the Germans felt the Greeks had not managed their pension funds properly and had run the country into the ground because of a broken work ethic.

She went on, "The political landscape in the first quarter of the third millennium was not helped by the resounding re-establishment of the Progressive movement, an initiative touted by many of the politicians in the west. In 2008 the Progressive movement was given a boost when President Barack Obama was thrust on to the world stage, becoming the first non-Caucasian President of the United States of America.

"Remember," she continued, "the "Progressive movement" was all about equality and wealth redistribution, under the guise of social justice and social welfare. This created a dependency on government and thus enslavement to their cause and ideals – which essentially amounted to them staying in power!"

"Taking from the rich and giving to the poor, but notably leaving the Uber-rich free to do as they please," added Joe.

"Yes, like Robin Hood." Karyn smiled at Joe. "In May 2010 the new Prime Minister of Great Britain, a man called David Cameron, used the words "a more-fair society" and "Big Society", which many thought was another way to soften the blow of wealth redistribution, which some felt would antagonise the British voting public. Don't forget, "fairness" and "equality" were just liberal code words for wealth redistribution, which, if looked at in another way, was just further propagation of the aid or charity blight that affected the African and Asian continents."

She continued, "As you may recall, some countries proved to be incapable time and again of helping themselves because of corruption at high levels within government and the corridors of power. These countries unfortunately became utterly dependent on aid and charity. Sadly, lessons were never learnt and when influential people like US President's and Chancellor's or Prime Ministers of the UK either knowingly or unwittingly perpetuated the "victim mentality" it would prove to be one of the six undoing's of humanity and would eventually contribute to the destruction of mankind."

Joe said, "Thank you Karyn, for such a comprehensive overview of some of the problems mankind faced." He looked around the room to see if anyone else had anything to add, and then wrapped up the discussion by saying that in his opinion, politics was a game played by the rich and powerful to control the poor or the masses. There were murmurs of agreement.

CHAPTER 10

Progressivism – the end of integrity in Politics.

Beverley Cuzen-Baker, a rather outspoken activist in her earlier days at university and was a direct descendent of "Chuck" Wendell Cuzen who was a Special Counsel to President Richard Nixon from 1969 to 1973.

Unlike her great, great, great grandfather, Chuck Cuzen's political and legal career, Beverley was the climate change expert on the team, and she proposed the next topic for discussion, "Climate Change and Aid", and explained her reasons by saying, "To give you all some background, climate change was presented as a serious cause for concern at the same time as the economic downturn, which blew up in 2008. The weather patterns had been changing for some time, and the temperature records showed that both polar ice caps started to melt at a faster rate than expected. The right-wing press appeared to take the line that it was one of the biggest hoaxes ever performed in a modern age, and called it "Climate-Gate", whereas the left-wing press like doe-eyed puppies took the Progressive elite's or their government of the day's stance, that it was dire and remedial action was needed immediately. Governments all jumped on the bandwagon, egregiously, seeing it as yet another instrument by which they could affect taxation by stealth as well as wealth redistribution from those wealthier countries to the less wealthy countries. This ploy turned out to be the nemesis of their strategy to ameliorate climate change, because activists illustrated that the governments had used doctored data to substantiate and support their case. What was in hindsight, a genuine problem for the world as a whole, was sadly undermined and never received the real attention it needed because of corrupt politics and liberal scientists."

"So," she reminded them, "the seas continued to rise, the weight of the sea on the earth's crust was slowly being redistributed from the polar areas, causing the tectonic-plates to start shifting to compensate. As a result, there was more volcanic activity, more frequent and more violent hurricanes, an increase in the size and severity of typhoons, more floods, both lower and higher temperatures and more natural disasters. All of these intertwined with the "Charity-Age" we were just hearing about, because as these disasters increased over the decades so did the demand for Aid, with the result that the poor people in the country's most affected actually began to become overly dependent on those richer western countries."

Mikhail asked, "So you're saying that people in countries worst affected by natural disasters grew up with the belief that their dependency on aid was their means of living?"

Beverley nodded. "Yes, in some cases. As each natural disaster hit these regions, it was in most cases the same countries putting out their hand for more aid, although in some nations, where national pride and personal accountability was still intact, they simply looked inward, rallied together, gritted their teeth and sorted out their own woes. The problem was that there were many nations who lost the ability to help themselves and became content to rely on aid from the rest of the world. And nobody in the governments of the western world had the courage to re-evaluate what was happening for fear of being branded a fascist or a racist."

"Thanks, Beverley," said Joe. "We will certainly discuss that issue."

Karyn said, "The erosion of moral values should be examined, too. This was starkly illustrated during the 2008–2009 MPs' expenses scandal that hit the media in England. The scandal was very quickly buried, hidden from public sight, and only a small handful of the 80 MPs implicated were prosecuted. In fact, many of those MPs who had allegedly "fiddled" their expenses were again put up by the political parties for re-election and incredulously they were voted back into office." She raised her hands and looked around. "How amazing was that? And it simply reinforced the general public's impression that crime or deceit at every level was an acceptable norm in society during that era."

The debate then turned to "Politics and the Corruption of Democracy."

Karyn presented a simplified definition of democracy; "Democracy is a political system wherein the supreme power of the government purportedly rests with the people; the citizens who elect officials to lead and represent them. Democracy is the procurement of a government supposedly ruled by the people for the people, which was essentially based on a popularity contest."

She carried on to say, "In fact, democracy was a big deception orchestrated by the aristocracy. For example, for a period of eighty-six years after 1832, the aristocracy and landed gentry in Britain slowly gave way to discontentment and unrest and were forced to allow more and more segments of the populace to vote. This compromise served as a means to "placate the sheep", as Joe described earlier, who continued to be duped and manipulated by the relatively rich, primarily rural land rich aristocracy, the very wealthy, and those already in seats of power.

"As an example, following the Great War of 1914–1918, in Britain the Representation of the People's Act was passed in 1918, which enabled all males over twenty-one plus women over thirty who were ratepayers or married to ratepayers to vote. Finally, in 1928 after the suffragette movement, all women received the vote on the same terms as men," Karyn said.

Karyn went on to explain that there was criticism of democracy throughout its life span.

"Economists had strongly criticised the efficiency of democracy. They based their belief on their premise of the irrational voter. Their argument was that voters were highly uninformed about many political issues, especially relating to economics, and had a strong bias about the few issues on which they were fairly knowledgeable and which were dear to their own heart."

Mikhail commented that moral decay, as discussed earlier by the Noah 5000 project members, served as another example of how pervasive this decay was in everyday politics in the second and third millenniums.

He pointed out, "In traditional Asian cultures, in particular those based on Confucian and Islamic thinking, they believed that democracy resulted in the people's distrust and disrespect of governments and religious sanctity. The distrust and disrespect became pervasive throughout all parts of society whenever and wherever there was a relationship of seniority."

"What do you mean by "a relationship of seniority"?" someone asked.

"Well, between a parent and a child, for example, or a teacher and a student, or even a government and the populace," explained Mikhail.

Karyn continued, "By 2020, democracy had been criticised widely for being prone to corruption and not offering enough political stability. As governments were frequently elected every four to five years, there tended to be frequent changes between left and right leaning policies of these democratic countries, both domestically and internationally. Even if a political party, maintained power, vociferous, headline-grabbing protests and harsh criticism from the mass media were often enough to force sudden and unexpected political change. Frequent policy changes with regard to issues such as business and immigration were perceived to deter investment and so hinder economic growth. For this reason, many people put forward the idea that democracy was undesirable for a developing country in which economic growth and the reduction of poverty were a top priority."

Joe pointed out that the media had on numerous occasions surreptitiously dictated the outcome of elections, as the journalists who went to left leaning universities, came out indoctrinated with an inherent bias towards liberalism or progressivism propaganda and tended to be anti-conservative.

"The gross ineptitude and ignorance the press demonstrated was unforgivable," he said. "They were so arrogant and blinded by their hatred of conservatism that they could not see that they were mere stooges for the insidious and poisonous Progressivism movement and the New World Order that drove and controlled global affairs and perpetuated the lie. There were Progressives embedded in political parties on both the left and the right side of the political divide. In fact, over a hundred years, the Progressives managed to infiltrate all walks of life, having people in positions of influence through government and industry."

"Yes, you're right there," agreed Mikhail. "The journalists in both the printed medium and in digital media were just too blinded by the hatred of conservatism they were indoctrinated with, to recognise who the real enemy was. This became apparent when the UK's premier British Broadcasting Corporation known as the BBC was losing about a million subscribers in 2018, because the people woke-up to the bias and corrupted media they were broadcasting."

Mikhail also pointed out that democracy was also criticised for frequent elections due either to the instability of coalition governments or adverse press attention. Coalitions were frequently formed after the elections in many countries, India being one example, and the basis of alliances was predominantly to enable a viable majority, not an ideological concurrence.

He said, "It was thought that these opportunist alliances not only had the handicap of having to cater to too many ideologically opposing factions, but they were usually short-lived, since imbalance in the treatment of coalition partners, whether perceived or real, or changes to leadership in the coalition partners themselves, usually resulted in the coalition partner withdrawing their support from the government."

Karyn took up the discussion again, saying, "Democratic institutions worked on consensus to decide an issue, which usually took longer than a unilateral decision or a diktat from a central authorised body as was experienced in China."

"Are you advocating dictatorship?" someone asked.

"Not as such," said Karyn. "But it could be argued that the people in government were possibly the least qualified to deliberate the challenges they faced and make decisions about them . . ."

"Why?" interrupted the same questioner.

"Well, because some of those in politics had considerable wealth and were well marketed in high profile media campaigns, creating a manufactured popularity, which resulted in them securing a seat in the Parliament or Senate, or whatever "House" they aimed for, irrespective of whether they had any skills related to the job they would be doing."

"Yeah, and there was vote-buying, too," remarked Mikhail.

"Yes, there was," agreed Karyn. "That was a simple form of appealing to the short-term interests of the voters. It was a tactic known to be heavily used in the north and north-east region of Thailand in 2009 and 2010. The same tactic was widespread in the southern part of Italy, where the local Mafias took an active part in the process. In the USA, there was another form of it, commonly called "pork barrelling" where local areas or political sectors were given special benefits, where the real costs were obfuscated and spread among all taxpayers, who did not vote for that policy."

Karyn paused to take a drink of water, laughed, and said "I could go on forever! I will just make a couple more points, if you don't mind."

"Go ahead," said Joe, who was thinking that he could listen to her for aeons and still be fascinated.

"OK, just remember you said that!" she tossed back at him, her face alive with enthusiasm for her specialist subject. She then went on to explain that the establishment of new democratic institutions in countries where the associated practices had previously been uncommon or deemed culturally unacceptable resulted in institutions not being sustainable in the long term. One of factors that caused such outcomes was when it was the common perception among the populace that such institutions had been established as a direct result of foreign pressure, such as in Iraq and Afghanistan.

Karyn said, "An example of where the democratic system was subject to volatility was where all Canadian political parties were cautious about criticising the high level of immigration in the early 1990s, because the popular newspapers slated the old Reform Party, which they branded "racist" for suggesting that immigration levels be lowered from 250,000 to 150,000 per year."

Joe added, "Principles were sometimes forfeited for personal popularity and the preservation of one's good name, even if the principle was indeed 100% correct."

Mikhail pointed out "in the twentieth century Gaetano Mosca and Vilfredo Pareto, two Italian thinkers, independently argued that democracy was a cruel illusion, which served only to mask the reality of the elite ruling class controlling of the masses." He said, "Indeed, they argued that a group of elitists collectively governing a nation or controlling an organisation, often for their own purposes, was an undeniable law of human nature, due largely to the emotional reactions, apathy and division of the masses in comparison to the drive, initiative, unity and collective goals of the elites."

Mikhail clarified, "According to Wikipedia, they were in fact pointing out that democracy under an oligarchy, or rule of the wealthy, and their democratic institutions would do no more than shift the exercise of power from oppression to manipulation and deceit. Basically, the ruling demographic created a system where corruption was the name of the game."

Karyn added, "Democracy proved to be malleable and could be presented in a multitude of ways that suited the environment or agenda of the elite or wealthy. In larger populations, this took the form of representative democracy, where decisions were made by elected individuals on behalf of their constituents. The West had been pushing democracy for centuries and was quietly proud of its achievements in getting countries across the world to change from regimes that were dictatorships or derivations thereof into democratic societies."

Joe, who with his military background saw the inherent cynicism in what Mikhail and Karyn had just said, suggested, "The reason why democracy was perpetuated for so long was that people felt empowered, thinking that they had a say in the affairs of government. When it was election time the populace would have a barrow-load of promises offered to them and then be asked to tick the box for the candidate that best fitted their ideals or political beliefs. Remember, the specially chosen candidate list was foisted upon the populace, the list of candidates was not a choice made by the populace. The extent of the populace's naivety and gullibility would of course, soon be revealed as almost all those election promises made by their candidate would not be fulfilled, just like the previous election, and the one before that, on an on-ad-infinitum. It didn't matter which end of the political spectrum was actually in power, they all turned out in the end, to be just as corrupt as the previous one."

He looked at Karyn, who was nodding resignedly, and continued, "Sadly, every four or so years, people would be herded like sheep into groups by the elite, the media and the political parties of the day, ready for the brainwashing they would undergo for the next election."

Karyn said, "Yes, but the monotony of repeated broken promises and unfulfilled dreams began to engender apathy in the voters, who were so numbed by disillusionment they did not see the gradual implementation of Progressivism by the NWO, which exploited everyone, including all of the political parties, for their own insidious agenda."

Joe remarked, "unfortunately, it looks like certain forms of democracy employed during that era was mankind's joke on itself! Democracy could have been the biggest crime against humanity, perpetuated by the very governments the people entrusted in the seats of power. It was a crime perpetuated in broad daylight, out in the open, right in front of their very eyes. Because of a corrupt and biased or "bought" media system, which had undue influence over each political party in power, until Donald Trump became the 45th President of America in 2017, no political party would dare be derisory of democracy for fear of being called a dictator, a bigot, Fascist, a Nazi, or even a racist.

As President Trump experienced first-hand, the press rounded on anyone who challenged "Liberalism" or supported him; such people were openly castigated, attacked and demonised. Also, anyone who lent towards Conservatism was set upon by the media and those in seats of power, resorting to calling them racists, bigots, Fascists or Nazis whenever the "liberals" were losing an argument or debate or their elected position was under threat. This was demonstrated in both the 2007 and 2016 American elections, where in 2007 anyone voting against Obama was deemed racist and in 2016, whilst anyone voting for Trump was deemed to be a racist or a misogynist."

By now, Joe could barely contain himself, saying emphatically, "With the exception of President Trump to a certain extent in his first year, those in power, who were voted in to serve by those they had successfully duped, soon dropped the "I am your servant" façade and very quickly, once voted into office, allegedly took up a position of power and self-interest or their party. They then simply did what they wanted and to hell with their electorate and the campaign promises. What really happened when people took office in their Parliament, Congress, or Senate was that many suddenly became enriched, or exposed to opportunities where wealth could be easily accrued! There was a good example in the twenty-first century American press, where the Speaker of the House for the US Senate between 2008 and 2010, allegedly amassed a fifteen-million-dollar fortune of personal wealth, whilst in office reportedly on a package of circa $300,000 a year."

"The liberal media at that time, who had fallen in love with the then President Obama, the first non-Caucasian President of America, the one everybody had hoped would break away from the old traditional style of elitist government. The people hoped President Obama would really act in the interests of everyone in the country with integrity, creating a vibrant growing economy, whilst protecting the interests of the masses from being exploited by the wealthy elite and political machines. The liberal media fell *"hook line and sinker"* into that dream of liberal socialist nirvana and anything liberal, thus could not see any reason to investigate these questionable "anomalies" manifested by Democrats because they were so sold on the dream of progressivism, liberal-democracy and the intoxication of liberals being in power. Sadly, President Obama did not fulfil their hopes."

"Interestingly" Joe added, "this was the very same Democrat Party who were the ones that wanted to keep slavery going in America and voted against abolishment amendment on April 8, 1864, whereas it was the Republicans who argued that slavery was uncivilized and that abolition was a necessary step in the right direction. One might have thought that President Obama would have had a distinct dislike for the Democrats and Progressives."

Mikhail sighed, and said, "Yes, we have the advantage of hindsight, which could be used intuitively if only we could travel backwards and forwards in time. We could influence the so-called *"New World Order*

(NWO)", as allegedly touted by the Bilderberg Group that allegedly attracted billionaires like George Soros, a global system of governance for countries based on democracy and not dictatorships, and those in power saw to it that every other country had adopted their form of democracy by 2050.

"We can look back at various attempts by the western world to rid themselves of dictators who were not toeing the NWO line. Remember the 2002 Iraq War, where the then President of the USA, George W. Bush, was so hell-bent on removing Saddam Hussein from power, because of supposed weapons of mass destruction (WMDs), which was a falsehood. Sadly, that episode in history cost the West over a trillion dollars, but to what end as no WMDs were found?"

Joe, looking at his watch, said, "Well, it appears we have kicked the tyres to death on that topic, but if we are to try to formulate a solution, do you think it's best if we fully understand what different forms of democracy there are, as well as look at all other forms of government other than democracy or dictatorships?"

There were murmurs of agreement from everyone in attendance, but several said they needed a short break. One quipped, "Hey, the mind can only absorb what the backside will tolerate."

"OK," said Joe, smiling. "A short break for everyone to stretch their legs, grab a drink or whatever, but we continue in fifteen minutes!"

He intended to use his break to chat with Karyn.

CHAPTER 11

Can Politics exist without Corruption?

After the break, which she had spent talking animatedly to Joe, Karyn started to explain some of the better-known forms of government.

"Firstly, there is Meritocracy, which is defined as a system in which advancement was based on individual ability or achievement. Meritocracy is where a government is composed of a country's people who have earned the right to rule through demonstrating virtue, intelligence, personal capability and skill. Meritocracy is a system that does not accept mediocrity. Meritocracy describes a type of society where wealth, position, and social status are assigned through competition or demonstrable talent and competence, on the premise that positions of trust, responsibility and social standing and prestige should be earned, not inherited or assigned on arbitrary criteria or quotas.

"Then there is also an Oligarchy, which means "to rule and command by a few", a form of power structure in which power effectively rests with a small number of people. These people could be distinguished by royalty, wealth, family ties, corporate, or military control. Such states are often controlled by a few prominent families who pass their influence from one generation to the next. OK so far?"

There were murmurs of assent, so Karyn continued.

"According to the definition in Wikipedia, Parliamentary democracy is another fair and free election system, which is a representative democracy where government is appointed by representatives as opposed to a "presidential rule", unlike where the president is both head of state and government elected by the voters. Under a parliamentary democracy, the government is exercised by delegation to an executive ministry subject to ongoing governance reviews.

These are necessary checks and balances for legislative parliament elected by the people.

"Whereas, in a presidential democracy, the public elects the president through fair elections. A president serves for a specific term not exceeding the amount of time agreed by the legislature. Elections typically have fixed dates. Combining head of state and government, makes the President both the face of the people and the head of policy as well.

Unlike a Parliamentary Democracy, the President has direct control over both the cabinet and the members who are appointed by the President.

The legislature cannot easily remove the President from office and vice versa.

By being elected by the people, the President is the choice of the people and for the people.

"Moving on, constitutional democracy is a representative democracy in which elected representatives exercise decision making power. They are subject to the rule of law, and moderated by a constitution that emphasises the protection of the rights and freedoms of individuals. This places constraints on leaders to the extent to which the will of the majority can be exercised against the rights of minorities, as in the case of civil liberties. In a constitutional democracy, it is possible for some large-scale decisions to emerge from the many individual decisions that citizens are free to make such as a Referendum. This means citizens "can change-sides, which equates to voting with their feet or their pockets" or "they can invest-elsewhere, which equates to voting with their dollars", such as in a Referendum resulting in informal government-by-the-masses." Karyn paused to drink some water, and asked, "Are you all still with me? Right, then let's move on to consider inventing an enhanced form of democratic government, because, sadly, none of the systems from Wikipedia I have described up to now was perfect.

"They all had flaws that would over time, undermine the efficacy and integrity of their democracy. A new, well thought through democracy needed to be established, based on a fair and well-balanced constitution that better protected the people, ensured a productive society, viable capitalism led economy, with a set of protocols implemented that would prevent corruption from destroying the integrity of a working democracy. Mankind really needs a more pragmatic form of democracy that engenders a more positive, honest, accountable and transparent political mechanism.

"Let's call it the "Positics Democracy", which enlightened, compassionate and empathetic hardworking humans of our past, envisaged a system where the public elects the Politicians, the Prime minister or President through free and fair elections. It would borrow the good elements from other democratic systems, such as those in a parliamentary and constitutional democracy and merge them with the principles of the meritocracy democracy. So, what do we think of that?"

"Well," said Mikhail, "it sounds pretty good, but even meritocracy could be open to corruption. It would be down to process and law that would make such a system work, not the philosophy itself, so a fair and balanced Constitution based on integrity and accountability is necessary."

"Yes," agreed Karyn. "But a society functioning within the framework of this new Positics democracy, I would suspect, become the populace's most desired democratic system of government because it would be based on a government filled with people who were voted in because they had demonstrable merit, by which I mean ability, talent, life and work experience and integrity, rather than those foisted upon the people because of their status, which includes wealth, family connections (nepotism), class privilege, cronyism, popularity (as in celebrity) or other historical determinants of social position and political power."

Joe chipped in, saying, "Let me remind you, that there was an insidious movement that was worse than a democracy corrupted by the liberal or conservative media, and that was Progressivism. How would the Positics Constitution combat that disease from corrupting the system?"

Karyn smiled at him. "I wondered when you were going to wake up," she joked. "Give me a break and remind us all what "Progressivism" was."

Joe grinned slightly sheepishly, for the truth was that he had been just enjoying watching Karyn. "Your wish is my command," he joked back. "OK, here goes."

He stood up, stretching to get the stiffness out of his limbs. "Right, Progressivism was the specifically American development of liberalism and populism that sought social justice above all else, and specifically with reference to the obstacles posed to social justice by large corporations. Though Progressives strongly support civil liberties, the "progress" in Progressivism is thought to lie, most fundamentally, in "justice and equality for all.""

"What was wrong with that?" asked someone in the audience.

"I'm getting to that," replied Joe. "Bear with me."

He continued, "In the United States there have been several periods where progressive political parties had developed. The first of these was around the turn of the twentieth century. This period notably included the emergence of the Progressive Party founded in 1912 by President Theodore Roosevelt. This Progressive Party was the most successful third party in modern American history. The Progressive Party founded in 1924 and that founded in 1948 were less successful than the 1912 version. There were also two notable state progressive parties: the Wisconsin Progressive Party and the Vermont Progressive Party. The latter was still in operation when the unfortunate 25 December 2111 incident occurred, and at that time members of it had several high-ranking positions in state government."

Mikhail added, "Some think-tanks had argued that early twentieth century progressive US academics such as Reverend James Augustin Brown Scherer and Rabbi Judah Magnes were contrarian thinkers who foresaw the eventual decline of European colonialism in the Middle-East and Asia. They correlated the rise of America – notably through the development of US institutions of higher learning abroad to indoctrinate young minds with their form of propaganda and the creation of massive wealth through the funding of wars across the globe. War was profitable if you printed FIAT currency, gave away billions in AID with conditions attached to buy armaments and military weapons, then sold them the very weapons then finally helped them recover devastated war zones they helped destroy. This was something America became very proficient at doing. (Note: FIAT currency is printed & digital money backed by nothing).

"At the beginning of the third millennium, most progressive politicians in the United States associated themselves with the Democratic or the Green Party. But not all, many of the Conservative or Republican party members, had also succumbed to the Progressivism propaganda as well. In the US Congress there existed the Congressional Progressive Caucus, which was often in opposition to the more conservative Democrats, who formed the Blue Dogs caucus. Some of the more notable alleged progressive members of Congress between 2000 and 2010 allegedly included Ted Kennedy, Russ Feingold, Dennis Kucinich, Barney Frank, Bernie Sanders, Al Franken, John Conyers, John Lewis, Nancy Pelosi, and Paul Wellstone."

Joe interjected, "If ever there was a scenario that depicted the recipe for mankind's demise, the modern Progressive movement was truly beginning to be apparent during this period."

Karyn claimed that Progressivism was the true enemy of any democracy. The Progressive movement was allegedly funded by billionaires such as George Soros and Rockefeller Jnr, who were reported to be funding all sorts of Progressive initiatives that surreptitiously undermined the people's real power and introduced socialism, globalisation and big government into the very heart of world politics. Big government helped to create a dependency on entitlement and low wages for many millions, who were consequently enslaved to the large corporations and Government taxes.

"The Progressive movement could not abide dictators; it went completely against their philosophy, just as Meritocracy was negatively termed by the Progressives and mainstream-media, as the "elitist" evolution of Democracy." Mikhail said.

Joe added, "One just has to look at the 2002 Gulf war, where the USA declared war on Iraq, on the two false premises' of Saddam

Hussein, Iraq's leader, being a supporter of Al-Qaeda and having weapons of mass destruction, which the then President Bush said Saddam would not hesitate to use. If only President Bush had the same hindsight and knowledge we have now, he would be embarrassed to see that in the annals of history he was seen as the stooge of those who truly held power – the military and the oil industry. The reality was that Saddam Hussein had no connection with Al-Qaeda, and there were no weapons of mass destruction. The whole reason for going to war was on the pretext of ridding the world of yet another tyrant dictator, gain access to their oil, to maintain the money machines that funded the wars – the bankers and military industrialists were all at it with their greedy snouts in the trough."

"Oh yes", said Mikhail. "There was state corruption on a global level, and this was being orchestrated in concert with the large banks."

Everyone in the conference room appeared to be in various states of agreement with sentiments postulated earlier in the debates, that greed and corruption were two of the biggest blights on mankind and the world itself.

Mikhail commented, "When was greed first acknowledged as a human trait? The Bible has many instances where greed was spoken about; the most famous of all was Judas and his betrayal of Jesus for thirty pieces of silver. It is nothing new, so why has it become so main-stream in modern times?"

He cited examples of this. "During the 1980s and 1990s, governments needed the populace to start owning their own homes. The primary reason was to remove the burden of housing costs off the State's balance-sheet and put the onus on the individual. There was also the opportunity of creating new or additional wealth through new taxes that related to home ownership, buying and selling of houses, and inheritance taxes. Margaret Thatcher, the then Prime Minister of Great Britain, was alleged to be the first premier in Europe to embrace and accelerate the private home ownership concept.

"Mrs Thatcher was belatedly credited with the alleged manifestation of a new type of corrupt individualism, creating people whose ideals would infect a generation who became very selfish and mercenary. A whole "self-serving" generation, who looked only after themselves, thought nothing of cheating others, and had absolutely no conscience about swindling innocent people. Over a thirty-year period, the shape of the housing market changed significantly. House prices skyrocketed as people saw trading houses as an asset, or means of creating wealth or to make a living. People from all walks of life were desperate to get onto the housing ladder, so that they too could take advantage of this monthly price rise escalator effect that was accelerating before their very eyes because of the unfettered immigration started by the Tony Blair government."

Karyn pointed out that in the UK this orchestrated boom occurred because the City was awash with money, discounted council houses were bought by the thousands, mortgages emerged as financial products and the new "housing-stock middle class" saw an opportunity to make some real long-term wealth by buying and selling a home rather than just renting.

"Naturally, Tony Blair and Gordon Brown's governments as well as successive governments did little to rein in this phenomenon", she said, "because of the windfall they had in stamp duties, taxes, etc. The higher the price, the more taxes, and the more times a single house sold the more the government earned. As long as the government could guarantee the rising price economics, it looked like a win–win situation for all concerned; buyers and sellers were getting rich, the governments were raking in the taxes, and the banks were earning money hand over fist. There were no losers, everyone was a winner, or so they thought."

"Not true, of course," interposed Joe. "No," agreed Karyn. "In fact, it was a perfect environment for a "bubble"; it was like a pyramid or Ponzi scheme, but a legal one because it suited the governments' aspirations to have more houses owned by the private sector. And, because they were earning so much tax from the housing markets, it was in their interests to get the banks to make it easier and cheaper for consumers to borrow money by taking out mortgages to buy the houses of their dreams. The trouble was greed. It had crept in and had suppressed "the house as my home" concept; houses had become a commodity, which were traded like jumpers at a flea market or like stocks and shares on the Exchange."

The discussion then moved on to the fact that the false boom in house prices meant that some people saw an opportunity to exploit the system and make a lot of money. Driven by greed, they acquired second and third houses, stacking them like skittles in the bowling alley waiting for a hit. The market was on fire, fuelled by easy loans, cheap loans, loans without any deposit or collateral, and towards the end of the bubble there were even reports of loans being given out to people that were six and seven times what they earned annually. This was a recipe for disaster; it was a cauldron of pain and hardship brewing under the surface, which the governments ignored.

Nobody asked how house prices could continue to rise when there was absolutely no additional value being added to the house in the interim to justify this. In fact, wealthy Hedge funds got in on the act, buying up large swathes of middle-class properties, driving up the prices, then selling them off to the gullible and often frantic public who were terrified of not being able to get onto the housing ladder because prices were racing away from affordability.

Mikhail said, "Yes, it was a perfect storm brewing, and nobody was interested in maintaining the upkeep of these houses; they were just interested in how much they appreciated in price each month and were looking to cash in or trade up. The household pride of the old school had disappeared; it was a buyer's market. One would hear on a regular basis, "take it or leave it, there are many people queuing behind you to take a look and snap this up." Maintenance became the responsibility of the new owners, who had to invest in their new home to make it habitable, and so off to the DIY shop they would go, spending their hard-earned cash. And so, the economic carousel turned.

"The governments had created what they believed was an engine of perpetual wealth generation for the masses, an engine that not only generated lots of taxes, but also helped to move an entire layer of society – the poorer "un-landed class" that were historically reliant on the state or local council for housing – into the middle classes, or what became known as the new "home-owner class." Those in power thought they had perfected the economics of government and would be able remain in power forever.

"When the Labour Party took power, the bubble was perpetuated because they heard Gordon Brown, the then UK's Chancellor, say many times over, "Labour has created an economy with no more boom or bust.""

Joe added laughingly, "Yep, but unfortunately, what goes up must come down as history eventually illustrated."

CHAPTER 12

Politics and Banking – a recipe for deception!

Mikhail agreed, saying, "In October 2008, there was a massive market crash that reverberated throughout the global financial sectors and that would also be felt in every household in the world. The housing bubble had burst. Lehman Brothers was a financial institution that was a big player in the American mortgage-backed securities market. Mortgage-backed securities were created by purchasing a parcel of mortgages, mixing them in a pool of other mortgage types and then selling off shares of that toxic pool. They worked fine until a lot of home-owners started to default on their mortgages, which is what happened when interest rates rose globally and house prices started to fall.

People suddenly found they owed more on their mortgage than their house was worth, a term known as being "under-water or negative equity."

"Lehman Brothers, who was viewed as one of the most prolific and astute institutional investment brokers, found themselves in possession of highly structured, highly geared complex derivatives that were created to carry the risk of all of these cheap, highly risky mortgages. For Lehman's it was curtains. They were unable to meet their "mark-to-mark" regulatory requirements and were forced into liquidation. For the rest of the industry, it was also a time of reckoning, as they too were sitting with truck-loads of these toxic instruments, as well as the fortune of debt owed to them by the newly defunct and bankrupt Lehman Brothers."

He went on to explain that in 2008, over one weekend, the whole financial services industry was in total disarray. There was a flurry of government-driven take-over initiatives to bail out some of the large American banks. Merrill Lynch was rescued by Bank of America under the guidance of the US Federal Reserve, while in the United Kingdom the Royal Bank of Scotland was also rescued, as were other UK banks.

"Although Lehman Brothers filed for bankruptcy on Monday, 15 September 2008, it had actually been severely damaged earlier, on 11th September when the biggest one-day drop in its stock value and highest trading volume occurred." (Notably, this was exactly 7 years after the World Trade Centre collapsed in Manhattan on September 11th 2001),

Lehman CEO, Richard Fuld, maintained that the 158-year-old bank was brought down by unsubstantiated rumours and illegal naked short selling. Although short selling (selling shares you don't own) was deemed legal for Brokers or Banks, the short seller was required to have shares lined up that could be borrowed to cover the sale. Failure to buy the shares back in the next three trading days was called a "fail to deliver." Christopher Cox, who was chairman of the Securities and Exchange Commission in 2008, said in a July 2009 article that naked short selling "can allow manipulators to force prices down far lower than would be possible in legitimate short-selling conditions."

The drop in stock price was caused by "naked shorting", which was technically illegal for individuals. However, while "naked shorting" was considered morally reprehensible, the corrupt financial system allowed institutions to do this. This was where institutions sold great amounts of stock that they never had, which caused the price to fall or crash, and when the price was low enough, they would buy stock within a certain time to avoid being caught out, thus making an enormous profit between the high selling price and the new lower buying price.

Mikhail continued his explanation, according to the Huffingpost. "By 11 September 2008, according to the SEC, as many as 32.8 million Lehman shares had been sold and not delivered – a 57-fold increase over the peak of the prior year. For a very large company like Lehman, with plenty of "float" – that's "available shares for trading" – this unprecedented number was highly suspicious and warranted serious investigation. But the SEC, which was criticised for failing to follow up, even after receiving numerous tips that the Bernie Madoff business was a Ponzi scheme, had yet to announce the results of any investigation."

"Hang on, Mikhail," said Joe. "Can you explain what a Ponzi scheme was?"

"Yes, please!" someone in the audience said.

"Sorry," apologised Mikhail. "I do kind of take it for granted that everybody knows this stuff because I do! A Ponzi scheme is where an individual or an organisation sets out to attract investors, usually by offering higher interest rates than the norm, but actually paid them out of their own money, or the money invested by others, rather than as a result of any performance of the organisation in which they had been invested. Generally, what happens in a Ponzi scheme is the success of the investment is hyped up because people talk about how smart they were and how much money they made on their investment, thus other people rush to get in and fail to do their due-diligence. To keep the illusion going, money from the later entrants is used to feed inflated profits to the earlier entrants. The Ponzi scheme takes out a hefty fee for their services and soon the money runs out and all late comers lose everything."

"The issue of corruption takes on more significance in light of the fact that the UK government played a similar role in another collapse the previous year. On 14 September, 2007, frantic customers were lining up outside Northern Rock, the UK's fifth largest mortgage lender, in the first British bank run in 141 years. The bank's shares plunged 31% in a single day. Like the collapse of Lehman Brothers in the US, the bankruptcy of Northern Rock changed the rules of the game. Britain's major banks too had to be saved at any cost, in order to avoid the loss of customer confidence, panic and bank runs that could precipitate a 1929-style market crash.

"With Northern Rock, as with Lehman Brothers, the then UK Chancellor, Alistair Darling, could have saved the day but was forced to back down, because Northern Rock had a willing buyer, who was Lloyds TSB, who unfortunately would have needed a loan from the Bank of England, which the Bank's Governor, Mervyn King, had denied.

"Darling was advised by his staff to overrule the Governor and grant the loan, but this would have cost political capital for the then UK Prime Minister Gordon Brown, who had been widely lauded for giving the Bank of England its independence from Government in 1997."

Joe asked, "Why were other financial institutions saved from bankruptcy, as I recall they were, but Lehman Brothers were thrown to the wolves? You'd think that the decision makers would have realised the dire consequences of letting Lehman go down. Do you think that Lehman was sacrificed Mikhail, and if so, why?"

Mikhail replied, "Some critics point to the consultant appointed by the White House, (a Mr Paulson) allegedly he and his cronies at Goldman Sachs, were Lehman's arch rival. Goldman certainly came out on top after Lehman's demise, but there are other possibilities as well, involving more global players. The month after Lehman collapsed, Gordon Brown and the EU leaders called for using the 2008 financial crisis as an opportunity to radically enhance the regulatory power of global institutions.

"Gordon Brown spoke of "a new global financial order," echoing the "new world order" referred to by globalist banker David Rockefeller when he said in 1994, *We are on the verge of a global transformation. All we need is the right major crisis and the nations will accept the new world order."*

Mikhail went on to explain that Richard Haas, President of the US Council on Foreign Relations, wrote in 2006,

> *"Globalisation . . . implies that sovereignty is not only becoming weaker in reality, but that it needs to become weaker.*
> *Sovereignty is one of these cherished rights that nations will give up only with the right major crisis."*

Gordon Brown had allegedly put it like this:

> *"Sometimes it takes a crisis for people to agree that what is obvious and should have been done years ago, can no longer be postponed. . . . We must create a new international financial architecture for the global age."*

Essentially what Richard Hass said was saying was that all this globalisation experiment led to a diabolical mess.

Karyn added, "As was documented by Ellen Brown, a frequent contributor to Global Research, in April 2009, Gordon Brown and Alistair Darling hosted the G20 summit in London, which focused on the financial crisis. A global currency issuance was approved, and the establishment of a new international organisation, known as the Financial Stability Board (FSB) was agreed to as a global regulator, which was to be based in the controversial Bank for International Settlements in Basel, Switzerland.

"The international bankers who contributed to the financial crisis were indeed capitalising on the crisis by being given interest-free money to stabilise their balance sheets, consolidating their power in "a new global financial order" that furthered their mission for top-down global control."

Mikhail said, "Let's take a closer look at the banks and how they fit into this new global financial order."

He went on to talk about the US Federal Reserve, known colloquially as the FED, which was privately owned by a cartel formed in 1910 by some of the most prominent bankers in the world, who convinced the US Congress that this was done to protect the public. "Hah!" scoffed Mikhail. "It was actually created to protect the members of the banking cartel from competition. By deciding not to use the word "bank" in its name and by creating a series of regional entities, they managed to fool the public into thinking that it was a body created by the government to act in the interests of free enterprise, commerce, the public and the nation."

"I guess from what you are saying that wasn't exactly the case?" said Joe.

"You guessed right," answered Mikhail. "It was a massive deception, which was brazenly executed in broad daylight, serving the interests of the cartel and their friends."

They then discussed the Bank of England. Up until 1946, that was also privately owned, the shares sitting in the government's treasury. However, they were bought through massive loans given to the government by banks, for which the government paid interest. So, although control appeared to rest in sterile shares in the treasury, the benefit of the investment actually went to the bankers who funded the purchase of shares through Government Bonds.

The Central Banks, as in entities similar to the Federal Reserve and the Bank of England were known, created money from nothing by printing more cash when they felt it was prudent to do so, such as when they were stemming a run on the banks, or funding a bail-out. This printing of money, known as "FIAT money", which is currency that a government has declared to be legal tender, but is not backed by a physical commodity. The value of fiat money is derived from the relationship between supply and demand rather than the value of the material from which the money is made. The governments of the time began lending it cheaply to the banks was to become known as quantitative easing (QE).

Since the FED's inception, it had presided over the crashes of 1921, 1929, the great depression of 1929 to 1939 and consequential recessions in 1953, 1957, 1969, 1975 and 1981, and the stock market crash on "Black Monday" in 1987. The FED had successfully managed to manifest 1000% inflation and lost 90% of the US Dollars buying power. This incredible loss of value had been transferred into the FED in the form of a hidden tax on the populace, called "inflation", which was caused by the regular printing of money for which it had no assets on which to base its value.

Inflation became more prevalent because in 1971, the United States Government ended the convertibility of the US dollar for gold, in what became known as the Nixon Shock. Ever since they separated the valuation of currency from Gold and Silver and simply just printed new money, the FED was enabled to make money from thin air under the Fractional-reserve system, where they take your deposits and lend it out ten times over, charging interest each time.

Fractional-reserve banking was and probably still remains a form of banking where banks maintain reserves (of cash and coin or deposits at the central bank) that are only a fraction of the customer's deposits. Funds deposited into a bank are mostly lent out, and a bank keeps only a fraction (called the reserve ratio) of the quantity of deposits as reserves. Some of the funds lent out are subsequently re-deposited with another bank, increasing deposits at that second bank and thus enabling further lending of that same money once again. As most bank deposits are treated as money in their own right, fractional reserve banking increases the money supply, and banks are said to create money from re-lending money they previously borrowed.

When they enabled the fractional system and the printing of fiat money by the Central Banks, the heads of Government literally decimated the buying power of the currency as seen by this chart sent to the British Government in June 2012.

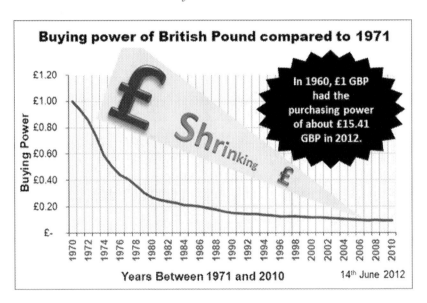

Essentially the US Federal Reserve System and other Central Banks, such as The Bank of England, were a legalised private monopoly for the supply of money that purported to be acting in the interests of free enterprise, free commerce, the public and the nation. Whereas in reality, they operated solely in the interests of the cartel of Banks by using legislation and ignorance of the politicians to move losses incurred by the Banking system to the tax payer or by lowering the value of the dollar's buying power, and thus including their own currencies through inflation."

Ironically, the FED had it fixed so that the banks in the cartel were covered by the government in the event of large corporate or foreign country loans being defaulted on, the banks would be bailed out by the government with tax payer's money, which essentially meant the FED was working for the large banks.

Joe added, "I bet none of you realised that did you? In fact, neither did most of the politicians or the public. The banks and the FED did a fantastic job of obfuscating the truth and making banking and fiscal finance look like a complex business, whereas in reality it was simply a straight-out deception."

"Like giving the QE1 and QE2 money to Banks, which they immorally used to serve-themselves was not morally apprehensible enough?"

Karyn said, "Now that we have a better understanding of what the banks and governments were up to, once the dust had settled after the 2008 fiasco, we can see from the records that the banks were greedy by milking the system through the creation of these structured toxic complex products that obfuscated the real risk by burying the original assets in virtual products. These financial instruments were then spun around and around, creating a whirlpool of money, which was known as securitisation (e.g., the inclusion of mortgage-backed securities into compound and complex financial instruments).

"The faster the whirlpool of money spun around (buying and selling the same products many times over) the more the commissions and interest payments were generated. All the while the real debt was getting more and more toxic as people started to default on their mortgages and housing prices began to fall.

"That said, one of the root causes overlooked by the regulators and investigators was that governments had insisted that banks make those loans to the masses, cheaper and easier to secure, so as to enable easier access to cheap mortgages for the poorer demographic in society. They indicated that the banks should not worry because the rising house prices would more than cover any risk." As history has shown, this only works with rising house prices, which in itself turned out to be devastating for subsequent generations who were unable to get onto the property ladder, which became known as "Gordon Brown and the Labour Party's most egregious policy" as it prejudiced the younger and new generations."

She went on to explain that although many questioned the viability of this "perpetual-money-making-machine", it was a story the "Mainstream-media (MSM)" journalists would not investigate or write about, with the exception of forward thinking journalists like Glenn Beck on GBTV, Bill O'Reilly on Fox News and Max Keiser on RT.com, who were more interested in getting to the truth than seeking fame or ratings. This "perpetual-money-making-machine" deception led to corruption being seen by the populace as widespread, and thus the seeds of distrust of politics and politicians were well and truly sown.

The political system was to suffer years of civil unrest, rioting and the wrath of the people, who were fed up with dynastic rule and corruption. The Unions went on the rampage because they thought the politicians were stealing from their pensions, all the while corporations and the wealthy high-net-worth individuals looked at ways to avoid paying taxes, and the populace became generally disenchanted with each successive government, who arrogantly, but ignorantly continued to sell more of the same old disingenuous, unfulfilled promises just like all the previous governments.

Karyn continued, "The financial crash of 2008 was the beginning of a very slippery road into financial and political oblivion for mankind. The alarm bells began ringing loudly, yet both President Obama and Prime Minister Gordon Brown, appeared unable to grasp the reality of the situation. Instead of just letting the market forces fight this out and that the countries, governments and corporations take their medicine, sadly that did not happen so those ill-equipped Politicians authorised the printing out of more bail out money that went straight to the Banks."

Joe commented, "those politicians in power showed signs that they lacked the fortitude and courage that real leaders would have demonstrated by making the necessary hard decisions and setting things right."

Karyn agreed. "The scene was set for the taxpayers to bail out any organisations the governments saw fit to support for their agenda," she said.

In the USA, the Federal Reserve Bank was printing money hand over fist, perpetuating an ongoing Ponzi scheme under the banner of "quantitative easing", which was in play with the blessing and support of President Obama and his liberal administration, and..... Mikhail took over, saying he would try to explain it.

After the "dotcom" bubble burst in 2000, Alan Greenspan sought to prop up the "irrational exuberance" against which he himself had cautioned, by dropping interest rates from 6.5% down to barely 1% in 2002 – see #2 in the chart "The Years Between 1950 and 2012."

Greenspan's idea was to encourage corporate and private spending by lowering the cost of borrowing money, so that it was much lower than it otherwise would have been in a truly free market, where interest rates are set by the supply of and demand for money.

Interest Rates set by the Federal Reserve Bank of the USA

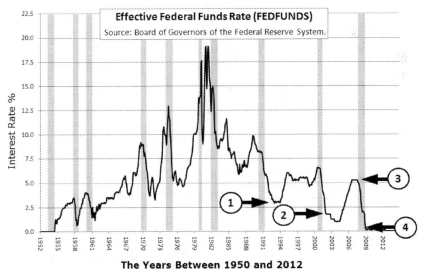

The Years Between 1950 and 2012
Shaded areas indicate US recessions.   2012 research.stlouisfed.org

Post 2000, a free-market interest rate environment was simply a dream or an illusion; it did not exist. The Federal Reserve, rather, simply created as much supply as it wanted in the hope that foolish risk takers would take the bait. Indeed, many millions did.

"Then there was the Federal Reserve's monetary base," continued Mikhail, "which increased from around $800 billion to just over $2.4 trillion."

Supply of Money by the Federal Reserve Bank of the USA

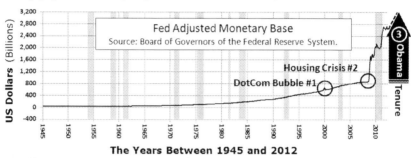

The blip (circled marked #1) was the DotCom bubble that burst in early 2000 and the distance between #2 and #3 was when President Obama took over the reins after the 2008 housing bubble crash.

He carried on to say that the irony of the whole affair was that Banks got bailed out from billions of dollars in bad loans that they claimed they issued at the government's insistence. "Remember," he said, "Governments demanded that banks should not be so rigorous in their testing of customers' ability to repay the loans, reasoning that housing prices would continue to grow and the loans would not become delinquent – the perfect recipe for a housing bubble."

"As part of the "Quantitative Easing" programme – a euphemism for printing money – the banks literally received $1.2 trillion of free money, which they then turned around and invested in their own shares and treasuries, the interest on which history proved to be one of President Obama and Trump's biggest budget expenses during their tenure in office.

"The reason why the banks were not lending money again was quite simple; President Obama and his administration blamed banks entirely for the housing bubble and took no responsibility for their part in the convoluted Fed, Freddie Mac/Fannie Mae Ponzi scheme. The banks were not going to fall for the same trick twice and looked to use the Quantative-Easing money to shore up their balance sheets and to hell with the public, the government or anyone who got in their way."

"By June 2012, the Public were most alarmed and distressed at the lack of accountability and the inappropriate, irresponsible way taxpayer funds were misused by the Banks to prop up their own, as well as their "most favoured" Institutional Client portfolios which ultimately underpinned the companies listed on the FTSE 100, NYSE and NASDAQ and thus propping up the Bank's own balance-sheets, which ultimately served to uphold their own stock market valuations, with little regard for the plight of the struggling Small and Medium Enterprise's."

"To make things worse, the Obama administration continued to spend on government programs, which added to the national debt of the USA – a deficit which by then was growing by approximately $1.4 trillion, annually!"

"What was the real cost of the financial crisis" asked Joe;

"In 2007, the Federal Reserve began pumping liquidity into the banking system via the Term Auction Facility. It wasn't enough. In March 2008, investors went after Bear Stearns, which was rumoured to have way too many of these by-now toxic assets." Mikhail said.

"Bear Stearns approached JP Morgan Chase to bail their Bank out. The FED had to sweeten the deal with a $30 billion guarantee. Wall Street thought the panic was over." he explained.

"How they missed the early clues, God only knows?"

"Instead, the situation deteriorated throughout the summer of 2008. The Treasury Department was authorised to spend up to $150 billion to subsidise and eventually take over Fannie Mae and Freddie Mac. Initially, the Federal Reserve used $85 billion, which rose to $150 billion, to bail out AIG."

"On September 19, 2008, the crisis created a run on ultra-safe money market funds. In just one day, businesses moved a record $140 billion into even safer Treasury bonds. Money market funds are where businesses park the cash to run their day-to-day business. Without these funds, business activities and the economy would grind to a halt. Treasury Secretary Henry Paulson conferred with Federal Reserve Chairman Ben Bernanke and proposed a $700 billion bailout package. It wasn't approved by Congress until two weeks later." Mikhail explained.

At this point Karyn jumped in and said, "However, the taxpayer was never really owed the full $700 billion. Only $350 billion was used in 2008 to buy bank and automotive company stocks, when the prices were depressed. By 2010, banks had paid back $194 billion into the TARP fund."

"The other $350 billion was reserved for President Obama, who never used it. Instead, he launched the $787 billion Economic Stimulus package.

Mikhail retorted, "Yes, he may have done that but that strategy failed with a devastating effect. "In 2010, a Federal Reserve report showed that lending was down 15% from the nation's four biggest banks: Bank of America, JPMorgan Chase, Citigroup, and Wells Fargo. Between April and October 2009, these banks cut their commercial and industrial lending by $100 billion, according to the Treasury Department data. Loans to small businesses fell 4%, or $7 billion, during the same time period."

"Lending from all banks surveyed showed the number of loans made fell 9% between October 2008 and October 2009. But the outstanding balance of all loans made went up 5%. That meant banks made larger loans to fewer recipients."

Mikhail then explained how the deficit in previous administrations had fared. Notably, President Bush was constantly reviled by liberals, including both the media (primarily the "Mainstream-media") and the Democrats during his eight-year presidential tenure because of the $2 trillion national debt that he had accrued and left behind due to the Iraq and Afghanistan wars. While President Bush had actually dragged the debt up to a dizzy $4 trillion halfway through his tenure, there was notably no criticism of the appalling state of the national debt created by the following administration in the first two years of President

Obama's tenure as President of the United States, which was estimated at $13.5 trillion by the end of the first quarter of 2011.

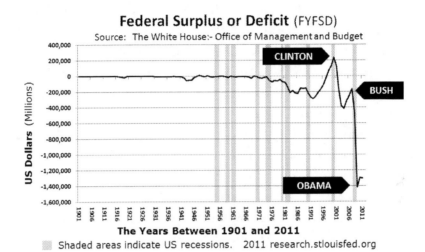

Federal Surplus or Deficit (FYFSD)
Source: The White House:- Office of Management and Budget

Shaded areas indicate US recessions. 2011 research.stlouisfed.org

The "mainstream-media" just did not get it; they were so intoxicated by the dream of a liberalised new world order.... they never challenged President Obama on this issue.

All of this uncontrolled Government spending was being underpinned by the printing presses of the Federal Reserve, the making of yet another gargantuan bubble, as unemployment was being maintained at just below 10% and with interest rates being held at zero per cent, housing prices were being kept high – all artificially.

"If one considers that the action Greenspan took by dropping interest rates to 1% back in 2000 and the monetary base increase when the Federal Reserve printed money to dig them out of a hole sowed the seeds of the boom and ultimate crash of 2008," continued Mikhail, "then you can probably imagine the ultimate cataclysmic outcome of the post-2008 extended course of 0% interest rates and a 300% increase in the Federal Reserve monetary base." One would have thought lessons would have been learnt from the Greenspan FED who had much to answer for in the generation of the tech bubble. Rather than serving as a sobering influence on the market, they encouraged market excess.

Karyn then took up the subject. She said, "There was, however, a glimmer of hope when in 2010 David Cameron took over as Prime Minister in the UK. Cameron stated that the new coalition between the Tory and the Liberal Democrat parties were going to do what was right for the country and be damned with the consequences to their personal political career. The coalition under his tenure made deep cuts in government spending – labelled as austerity cuts – so that the pain would be over within three years, thus avoiding a ten-year "death-by-a-1000-cuts" scenario touted by the Labour Party.

"Essentially, by David Cameron stating that they were prepared to take their share of the lumps over a three-year period, the United Kingdom had begun to climb out of a deep hole of debt left by the previous 13 years of a Labour government."

Joe added, "No matter how much complaining the populace heard from the Unions and Ed Milliband (the then leader of the Labour Party), the majority of the hard-working British citizens could remember the hard times of the past, knew this was the correct thing to do, and so they gritted their teeth and got on with life."

Joe stood up, looked around the room, and said, "I think that's enough for today. Get some rest, and let's reconvene tomorrow, when we should look at the effect of climate change, and what might be done to change that if time travel were possible."

Everyone agreed, and deep in thought, slowly filed out of the room.

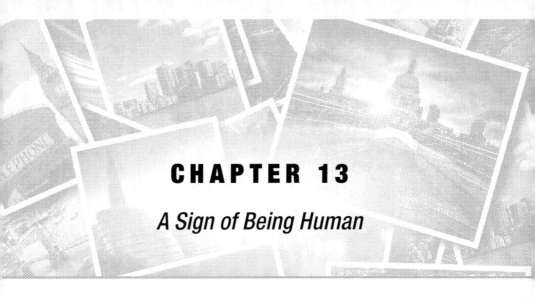

CHAPTER 13

A Sign of Being Human

Joe sank back into his chair, weary to the bone. He wondered whether he was just floating ideas to keep everyone from despairing about their inevitable fate. Maybe he just desperately wanted to believe that time travel was feasible, and that they could change the doomed course of history. His parents would be alive, and his beloved sister would not be lying dead in a malfunctioned stasis pod. Maybe they all wanted to believe it, for similar reasons.

Thoughts of his family caused waves of grief to overwhelm him, and, strong though he was, he felt tears well up, and buried his face in his hands, letting them flow freely. Then he was aware of a gentle touch on his arm, and looked up to see Karyn standing beside him. "I'm sorry," she said softly, seeing his tears. "I didn't mean to intrude, but I thought you might be unwell." She gestured towards her chair. "I left my jacket behind."

Joe struggled to regain control. "No," he said, "I'm not ill, just very tired, and at times like this, I . . . I can't help thinking about . . . all those that I have lost, that we've all lost."

Karyn sat beside him, taking his hand quite naturally. "I know," she said quietly. "It's so hard."

Joe found that he was gripping her hand tightly, and suddenly it all poured out. He told her how his parents had been so proud of his being chosen to lead the Project 5000, and how they had believed this would allow both their children to survive the impending nuclear holocaust, because his sister also had a place. "She was so gifted," Joe said shakily.

"Elizabeth was a wonderful musician, mathematician and just a great person." He stopped suddenly, as the tears threatened again.

"You said "was"," Karyn murmured. "She's in one of the failed pods, isn't she?" Joe nodded, unable to speak. Karyn wrapped her arms around him and held him, making soothing noises. "We have to hope," she said. "We have to beat this."

"Yes," whispered Joe. "We have to, and I have to pull myself together."

"You're human, Joe, falling apart occasionally is part of it."

Joe reluctantly freed himself from her embrace and gazed at her. Then he leant forward and gently kissed her lips, then rested his head on her shoulder. "I've wanted to do that for days," he confessed.

She smiled, holding his gaze with eyes that promised much. "That's part of being human, too."

CHAPTER 14

Day 74 - The Population Growth Dilemma

When they all met again the following day it was now Cassandra's turn to describe her responsibilities to the other Guardians and table a topic that needed to be addressed back in time.

She explained that before she applied for the role on the project, she was involved in several high-profile studies where genetic engineering was being used to advance and enhance plant life to increase yields and resistance to pestilence.

She said, "During the first century of the third millennium, famine was one of the most significant causes of death in third world countries. The world's population had increased to 6.8 billion by 2010, and was expected to reach 9 billion by 2042. Western governments had tried introducing genetically modified crops to help improve yields in drier climates and to produce crops that were resistant to insects and pests like locusts. However, as soon as new strains of the crops germinated, the damn pests showed signs of evolving to the next level and became immune to the resistant effect of the formula. Mankind was fast realising that it could not play God; Mother Nature was equally able to adapt and, because these pests' life cycles were short, so there were many such cycles within a single year, which meant that their evolving state always outstripped the means used to combat them. In the end, the seeds from subsequent harvested crops were found to have lost some of their resistive powers."

Joe asked, "Wasn't there a problem with corruption, as well?" and Cassandra replied that although the intentions of the corporations and governments involved in this activity were to eradicate famine, the execution of the strategy on a global scale was flawed and open to corruption.

However, scientifically significant progress had been made, and Cassandra and her team in Project 5000 had the task of bringing several species of plants and insects back to life after the radiation caused by the catastrophic events of 25 December 2111 had cleared. She continued, "the successful reintroduction of genetically modified plants depends upon seeds being able to germinate without our interference, as we won't have the kind of resources that Monsanto, for example, had at the beginning of the twenty-first century with their large-scale laboratories."

She sighed, and said, "what ought to have been done was to place mandatory curbs on population growth. The drain on earth's resources had already started to show signs of being unsustainable by the year 2030, but nobody had the courage to address the root cause of the problems – too damned many people!"

There were murmurs of dissent from some of the others.

Cassandra folded her arms and looked challengingly at them. "Look," she said, "in just three centuries the human population went from 1 billion to 11 billion. I call that irresponsible, and it led directly to the resource wars at the end of the twenty-first century and the early twenty-second century. It was too bloody late by then!"

Someone muttered something about drought and changing weather patterns, but Cassandra was well and truly fired up now.

"Yes, yes, I know! Those things did have an effect. North Africa was devastated, the deserts crept south each year, and by 2050 over half the land mass of Africa was affected. And then, during the period from 2080 to 2110, there was an increase in terrorists using dirty bombs, which also damaged food production. But essentially there were too many people!"

At the time, she went on, "the popular liberal press, mainstream media had blamed famine on old-fashioned colonialism, financial colonialism, racial inequality, and genetically modified crops (GM crops). They simply ignored the facts and the truth that overpopulation was the primary and root cause.

This sparked heated debate between the six Guardians, with Cassandra arguing that famine was not caused by reckless use of GM crops; there were several outside factors that caused famine to be so prolific.

Joe argued that starvation was a by-product of a much worse disaster, and that by the time of the third millennium mankind's selfishness, greed, and corruption had laid the foundations of a self-made destruction. Man's moral code had evolved down two distinct avenues: there were those who valued the sanctity of all human life and those who saw another's life as worthless as long as it was not their life that was being harmed.

He said, "In certain cultures, another person's life was cheap. To kill someone for a bread crust meant nothing; it was like swatting a fly off a plate. This was noticeable in Latin America, in countries like Mexico and Columbia in the first quarter of the third millennium, with their horrific mass murdering of civilians during their drug wars. It was also seen in Middle Eastern and Western Asian countries like Pakistan, Afghanistan, and Iraq during the period where terrorism against American and British foreign policies was fraught."

"True enough," agreed Cassandra. "And then, of course, We're back with Africa. That unfortunate continent, that did not appear to want to succeed like Asia did. Life was so cheap in many of the African countries, take Somalia for instance, it was because of religious tensions, corruption, crime and lack of compassion - that the governments gave up on even trying to educate their citizens as they were too corrupt themselves and focused on making themselves rich."

"Exactly my point," said Joe.

The lack of compassion and respect for life had a severe effect on the direction of mankind's evolution. Cassandra argued that the split in these two groups became known as the "have" and "have-not's" divide. The press blamed those countries deemed to be part of the western civilisation, for all the failures of the African states, with African governments and activists putting it down to the colonialism they suffered in the past and the purported "asset" pillaging that took place during the colonial period, leaving those countries severely depleted. The truth of the matter was that the infrastructure left behind by the colonial period was in many cases better than that of the colonists' home countries, but sadly the governments of those African states allowed that infrastructure be destroyed because of a number of reasons, such as; their own corruption, lack of investment foresight and/or the gross incompetence of those in power.

The have-nots were often coerced into sleep walking and being led by the state or were too lazy to get the appropriate education, equipping themselves for a life of honest hard work, where they understood the difference between saving for a rainy day or investing every dollar to get their meagre money to grow and eventually work for them or simply spending their salary on "stuff" as soon as they received it.

Instead they found it was easier to blame someone else, like the West for their own shortcomings and lack of integrity, which in many cases manifested in corruption at the highest level. So, for politicians to obfuscate the reality of what they were doing, they fostered an environment where corruption and lack of respect for human life prevailed by outwardly blaming the West for their woes and making excuses for the behaviour of those in their society. An example of this was seen when Robert Mugabe was given the seat of power in the then thriving Southern Rhodesia in 1980. That country, renamed Zimbabwe, was bankrupt by the year 2000 because of Robert Mugabe's poor stewardship and corrupt government. When taken to task about his diabolical failure, he simply blamed it on the West and the previous colonial period. Those countries that were afflicted with governmental corruption and the general malaise or apathy caused by decades of charity and aid found that they were unable to feed their own populations because the entire system and infrastructure had collapsed. What remained was damaged by either terrorism, theft or gross neglect.

"Yes, terrorism," chipped in Gibbs. They all nodded, knowing that this became one of the biggest challenges in the third millennium. The battles between radical religious groups and other disenfranchised factions in society went on for almost a century. Hundreds of thousands of lives were lost due to the bombings and terrorist acts. Billions of dollars were spent by the West to combat threats from the likes of Al-Qaeda or radicalised Islamist groups such as Islamic State of Iraq and Syria (ISIS) the rebranded and significantly more viscous form of Al-Qaeda. Interestingly, although the problems stemmed back to tribalism and religious roots, the primary catalyst that fuelled the Jihad, was the heinous American interventionist foreign policy, spending about $1.5 trillion annually on militarism, imperial wars, and other related policies at a time America had no enemies; so very little investment was made by the Middle Eastern countries themselves to assist the West in their bid to stamp out terrorism. This was witnessed in 2014 when Turkey sat idle on their Syrian border when the city of Kobani was destroyed by ISIS.

All the while, where crops could be grown to feed the populace in countries like Afghanistan, the farmers chose to grow poppies or marijuana because the returns were far larger than what they would get for growing wheat, corn or staple foods. A lot of these funds went into buying arms and ammunition which the war lords used to protect their crops, and as was expected, a lot of these munitions ended up in the hands of terrorists who were allegedly sponsored by states like Iran and Saudi, targeting groups such as the Taliban to create disruption to the American war effort in Afghanistan.

It was a vicious circle, the more the West attempted to stamp out the drug trade and terrorism, the more determined the Taliban became and the more vociferous the Al-Qaeda terrorists became. In the meantime, the government of Afghanistan was asking for western Aid to feed their population.

All of these factors contributed to the massive famine experienced by the world on a global scale in the third millennium.

"Well," concluded Joe, summing up the debate. "At least now you are in a position of advantage, Cassandra. You won't have corrupt governments or terrorists getting in your way."

"Yeah," Cassandra said, with a wry grin. "I knew there had to be some upside to a nuclear holocaust and 500 years of a nuclear winter's ice age."

CHAPTER 15

Day 74 - The Climate Change Fiasco

After lunch it was the turn of Beverley Cuzen-Baker, the climate expert, to hold the floor.

"Yesterday, we talked about the finance, banking and political deceptions during the previous 150 years leading up to the 2111 Armageddon on the eve of Christmas," she began. "All pretty depressing, I think we can agree."

There were nods of assent.

"Yes," she continued, "but if all that was not bad enough, another of the biggest deceptions that was exposed was the narrative of global warming.

"The evidence we have access to and have researched shows that a big debate held during the early part of the third millennium was on the subject of whether mankind contributed towards what was commonly known as climate change, or, indeed, what was the primary cause of this phenomenon. The issue became polarised: there were those who believed it was entirely a human phenomenon who were at one end, while at the other end of the debate there were those who believed it was a natural phenomenon and that governments were using this unfolding disaster as a means of gaining more control over the masses and as a mechanism to aid in the impression that they were re-distributing wealth from the wealthy to the poor. The reality was quite the opposite was true.

"Unfortunately for the "man-made disaster" contingent, the western government's such as the USA, who had made desperate attempts to convince the world of an impending disaster and that people should fall into line with their respective government mandates, legislative controls, and accept the new taxes being imposed to tackle climate change was rather scuppered by the greed and corruption that crept in. For instance, they introduced evidence that had been tampered with to the Copenhagen Climate Change Conference in December 2009. The evidence was not just flawed; it was purposely tampered with to slant the statistics in favour of the arguments being put forward to suit their agenda in Belgium."

"By Belgium, I assume you mean the European Parliament?" asked Mikhail.

"Yes. Naturally, the big question the masses were asking was: "Is climate change real?" There appeared to be clear evidence that the climate was changing, largely due to greenhouse gases, some of which was partly caused by human activities. In the early days, when scientists talked about "climate change", they actually meant warming of the climate system as a whole, which included the atmosphere, the oceans, and the cryosphere – that's ice, snow and frozen ground", she explained. "The observational evidence clearly indicated that the climate system was continuing to warm, including warming oceans and melting snow and ice, both of which contributed to rising sea levels. In other words, there was overwhelming evidence for global warming but very little to substantiate that it was exacerbated by humans."

She continued, "In truth, climate change was not just about Earth warming up, it was about changes to climate at both the cold and warm spectrums. The science indicated that the climate would be altered in many other ways at both ends of the scale. For example, they predicted that there would be changes in rainfall patterns and ocean currents, changes to the intensity and frequency of extreme events such as colder winters, warmer summers, more violent storms, longer drier droughts and more ferocious floods, rising global sea level and ocean acidification."

She glanced around at her audience. "Probably most of you don't know that Earth was, in fact, ice-free for most of its history. For example, the earth was much warmer and had no significant polar ice between about sixty-five million and thirty-four million years ago. Fifty-five million years ago, rapid and massive releases of carbon acidified the oceans and warmed Earth's surface to about 5°C above what had been the temperature of an already warm planet. At peak warming, about 50 million years ago, crocodiles roamed the Arctic amongst subtropical flora and fauna; even though the Sun's intensity was lower than it was in 2111. Much higher carbon dioxide during this time was revealed by various paleoclimate reconstructions, and subsequent global cooling was shown to have followed carbon dioxide decline," she explained.

Beverley carried on to say, "Earth's history shows us that the leading driver of climate change was the concentration of atmospheric carbon dioxide. Not the only driver, but the leading one. It also reveals that climate sensitivity to carbon dioxide was possibly much higher than discussed in policy-making circles. About five million years ago, carbon dioxide was as high as, or slightly higher than, 2009 values, and Earth reached temperatures that were 4°C warmer than in 2111, with sea levels tens of metres higher. The then location of Yale University in the USA was under water.

"Many lines of evidence and study tell us about the effects of carbon dioxide release. In the distant past, large increases in carbon dioxide corresponded to major warming events. It was unwise to think that the increase in carbon dioxide experienced from the late twentieth century onwards would, for some reason, produce a different outcome."

Someone interrupted to ask, "So are you saying people didn't believe that an increase in carbon dioxide in the atmosphere was contributing to climate change? Given the scientific evidence you've just cited, that seems incredible."

"Certainly, very many people were concerned about carbon dioxide levels," Beverley answered, "but most were either apathetic about it, or believed that something or someone, somewhere would find a solution. As history now shows, the scientific predictions were correct and the world changed in ways beyond the recollection of any living human being. Weather patterns changed significantly, storms became significantly stronger and more violent, wetter, hotter, drier and colder seasons were experienced. In addition to this, higher average wind speeds were experienced in storms while winters were also colder with more snow, ice and high-speed winds.

"The Caribbean area was devastated year after year until some of the islands became uninhabitable. The costs in lives, damage to buildings, crops and livelihoods became so extensive that many of the Caribbean inhabitants became climate-change refugees on the world stage."

Mikhail added, "And these changes resulted in a redistribution of the ocean's weight because of water from the melting ice caps in both the north and south poles, which in turn caused the re-seating of the continental plates. That caused a vast increase in earthquakes and volcanic action, some in areas where such things were not expected. The first of the notable earthquakes was the 2010 Haiti earthquake, which totally devastated the main city and left more than a million people homeless."

"Yes, that's right," said Beverley. "Within the first four months of 2010, there were three devastating earthquakes, in Haiti, Chile, and China, that measured magnitude 7.0 or greater. Scientists had stated that 2010 was not showing signs of unusually high earthquake activity, based on the fact that since 1900 an average of sixteen magnitude 7.0 or greater earthquakes – the size that seismologists define as major – had occurred worldwide each year. In 1943, for example, there were thirty-two, whereas in other years, such as 1986 and 1989 there were six." If you take a look at the chart below you can see there is a gradual upward trend since the beginning of the industrial revolution.

Mikhail decided to help out again, saying, "So there was considerable variability from year to year. From 15 April 2009, to 14 April 2010, there were eighteen major earthquakes, a number also well within the expected variation. That said, between 5 January and 26 April 2010, there were twenty-six earthquakes that measured 6.0 or more."

Mikhail consulted his notes and added, "In 2010, a Dr. Michael Blanpied, who was the associate co-ordinator for earthquake hazards for the US Geological Survey, said that while the number of earthquakes was thought to be within the range considered normal, that did not alter the fact that they had caused extreme devastation and loss of life in heavily populated areas."

Mikhail went on to add, "The first twenty-five years of the twenty-first millennium witnessed an increase in the number of catastrophic natural disasters, the ferocity of which mankind had never before witnessed, like the Fukushima disaster. This was the most powerful earthquake ever known to have hit Japan, a magnitude 9.0 undersea mega-thrust earthquake that occurred off the coast on Friday 11 March 2011, which was immediately followed by a devastating tsunami.

This event was one of the five most powerful earthquakes in the world since modern record-keeping began in 1900.

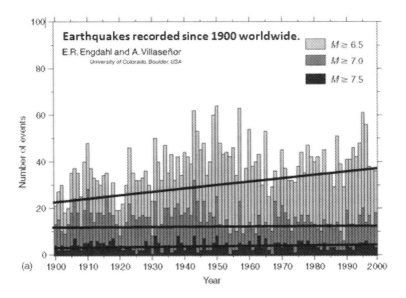

The year of 2018 was a busy year with 17 major quakes, Indonesia was hit particularly hard. More than 500 people died in Lombok in August and a major tsunami struck the Palu region in September, with more than 2,000 casualties. Other deadly events took place in Papua New Guinea, Japan, Haiti, Taiwan and Mexico.

Governments were in a bind. No sooner had they cleaned up one mess, then another disaster would occur and the cycle would repeat itself over and over again. As has been mentioned before in our discussions, the western world became fatigued by the continual requests for aid from the third-world countries. The philanthropic wealthy were fast depleting their resources, while the media were castigating the western countries time and time again for not giving enough aid to those in dire need."

Karyn now brought in the political element. "The global financial economy had never really recovered from the 2007 - 2008 crash. In fact, it was crippled by a new disaster, each time the economy looked like it was starting to gain momentum, such as when the United Kingdom voted to leave the EU in 2016, in what became known as Brexit and Greece, as a result of their own EU driven bankruptcy, dropped out of the EU by 2028. The US political system went through an upheaval in 2012, when the US elections returned President Obama back into office for a second term as President. That event simply furthered the "Progressive Agenda" instead of exposing it for what it was. Unfortunately, not even having a new Republican President was going to save the day - that would come too late to save the American way of life.

While President Obama was in office, in his first term had already ran up the US National debt to $17 trillion plus, which totalled more than what the previous twelve presidents of the USA had accrued in debt collectively. When President Obama took office, total debt stood at only $10.6 trillion, which meant it had increased by over $8 trillion— roughly 70 percent—during his 8-year tenure as President. The fact was, in 2017 the newly inaugurated President Donald Trump had been handed a US debt of $20 trillion and a political poison chalice by the liberal elite and Democrat Party. The very fiscal survival of America had been placed on a precariously slippery slope by the former Obama administration," she said.

"The Republican Party in the USA tried hard to get President Obama to stabilise the economy between 2011 and 2013, which would have been quite promising. However, the environmental damage was already irreversible and catastrophic disasters started to take their toll domestically in the USA with all the tornadoes and hurricanes that followed. This was exacerbated by the world-wide environmental disasters, as the call for human aid was immense. What was asked for in just ten years equated to what was invested in the previous fifty years! The wealthy G20 countries were themselves in a terrible financial state, having to print trillions of dollars to maintain some sort of financial stability within their own countries. The knock-on effect was drastic. Inflation and more unrest because of rising prices, a weaker dollar, and less buying power for each dollar people earned."

She went on to detail the unrest and domestic riots that broke out during 2011 and 2012 in over 60% of western and middle-eastern countries, with their populations becoming increasingly disenchanted with corrupt and unfair financial and political systems. This led to a series of middle-eastern wars, for example in 2016 a coalition led by Saudi Arabia launched military operations by using airstrikes to restore the former Yemeni government and the United States provided intelligence and logistical support for the campaign. According to the UN, from March 2015 to March 2016 over 6,500 people had killed in Yemen, including 3,218 civilians. Further to this, Saudi Arabia's actions in Syria caused a great deal of anxiety within the Middle East region. On February 4, a military spokesman suggested that Saudi Arabia was ready to send ground troops to fight ISIS in Syria. A week later Saudi Arabia announced that it will send combat aircraft and soldiers to Turkey to participate in the U.S.-led coalition against ISIS.

Three days later the Saudis launched "Northern Thunder," described as the "largest military exercise in the history of the Middle East." Participants from 20 countries sent troops to the manoeuvres run over three weeks in Hafar al Batin in northern Saudi Arabia, not far from the Iraqi and Kuwaiti border. According to a Saudi media outlet, some 350,000 troops were expected to participate in the manoeuvres.

It was clear that Saudi Arabia was sending a strong message that it was willing to fight back. The message was aimed not at ISIS, but at Iran and its allies: Syria's Bashar Assad, Hezbollah and above all, Russia.

"In the United Kingdom at that time," she said, "Prime Minister David Cameron, was himself beset with similar challenges. The British public were very much fed up with the never-ending donations to Aid and Charity, and the UK government was still struggling to dig itself out of the deep hole left by the Labour Party's previous fifteen years in office."

"There were two further devastating Banking scandals uncovered in the UK, which showed that before 2008, Barclays Bank and at least twenty other International Banks were allegedly colluding to rig the Libor rate (the exchange rate between Banks she explained) to enable them to improve their investment yields or help clients recover from dangerous money losing precipices they found themselves. In addition to this the Banks had been converting loans to interest swap products to hedge against Foreign Exchange rate fluctuations, which later turned out to be a win / win model for Banks and a lose / lose model for those clients who converted to that product," Karyn said.

Karyn explained "In response to this debt crisis, governments issued bonds in a bid to get the economy growing again – rather than just letting the bad debts fail and allowing the system to reset itself. By quarter 4 of 2016 the biggest threat to Europe was in Germany, right in the heart of it all. In fact, one German bank had a €46 trillion problem that threatened the entire financial system. Huge debt problems lurked in Greece, Italy, Spain and Portugal. Whilst this debt looked benign, much of it was government debt. Deutsche Bank had been in disarray for years. Their share price was currently down at around $13 – a drop of over 50% in the last 12 months alone.

In September 2016, the US Department of Justice (DOJ) proposed that Deutsche Bank should pay a $14 billion fine – to settle claims it mis-sold mortgage-backed securities before the financial crisis. While this figure had not been set in stone, the bank only had $5 billion to cover it.

Notably, this was not simply a German problem..."

"There was France. France's biggest and third largest banks – which made up two of Europe's "big six" – had been found to have vast "capital gaps" – money set aside to protect the banks in the event of a financial crisis...

Italy's €235.6 billion time-bomb could herald the end of the EU.

"As reported in the Financial Times:

"An Italian exit from the single currency would trigger the total collapse of the Eurozone within a very short period. It would probably lead to the most violent economic shock in history, dwarfing the Lehman Brothers bankruptcy in 2008 and the 1929 Wall Street crash. "Why?" Mikhail asked.... rhetorically

Karyn continued, "Because Italian debt was held by banks in the Eurozone's biggest economies.

France was, by a distance the most at risk of contagion, holding in excess of €250 billion" worth, which amounted to 10% of the country's GDP.

Germany was the next highest on the list with €83.2 billion – with €11.76 billion held by Deutsche Bank alone.

These bad debts were fuelling the coming crisis. They were reported to set the next big crash off, when an Italian bank collapsed under the weight of its own bad debts ("Le Sofferenze") – a mass sell-off of Italian bonds followed, leaving banks across Europe in turmoil.

Italy's economy was ten times the size of Greece's. When Italy started to go down, it was a risk to the entire Eurozone. The country had been unofficially declared "too big to save" by the European Bureaucrats Karyn said.

"The burden of debt appeared to increase, because during the decade spanning 2015 through 2025, the United Nations called on all western countries to donate yet more funds to a UN disaster fund to help the third world with their plight. The media were rampant in their derision of the Western world, claiming institutional racism and genocide when they were unable to give as generously as expected because of the precedents set in the past. By 2025, the Western world was itself depleted of funds, the wealthy were terrified of losing their remaining cash reserves, and governments were engaged in internal conflict with Unions, internal protests and rioting. There were years of upheaval, all of which took its toll," Karyn said.

Mikhail chipped in, saying, "Interestingly, throughout this era, the Chinese Government never once asked the outside world for aid, even though China had their fair share of natural disasters. The financial status of China remained sufficiently stable right the way through to 2025. The trillions of dollars of surplus it had accrued throughout the previous forty-five years and the development of its internal economy helped China to become the largest economy in the world by 2018. By 2022, China became one of the largest donors of Aid, through development aid surpassing the USA and the UK, who had been up until then, two of the largest donors ever."

Mikhail said, "you can see how all of these facets we have discussed are intertwined, one exacerbating the other", going on, he added, "There was a notable absence of empathy and contribution from the Middle Eastern states. Saudi Arabia, which was still one of the largest oil producers in the world, was steadfast in its position of not giving aid to countries that were too corrupt, lazy or incompetent to look after themselves or their people. It argued that Saudi was in a fortuitous position at that point in history because of their oil reserves, but pointed out that once the oil dried up, having millions of acres of desert was not going to sustain the country and that it had to prepare itself for the future of its own people in the longer term. Their focus like other middle-eastern countries was to invest in 1,000's of hectares of Solar energy and battery technology."

"Hmmm," said Karyn. "That unfortunately appeared to be the stock answer of many of the Arab states at that time.

"This lack of empathy and disregard for other countries' plight appeared to compound problems where countries suffered water shortages as a result of the changes to the levels of rainfall caused by climate change. These countries had to start shipping in water from other countries that had plentiful supplies, but soon found that the cost of water was high, almost the same as gasoline per litre. The average price of oil had moved beyond $60 per barrel by 2016, which slowly crept all the way to $200 per barrel by 2025," she said.

Beverley suddenly sprang back to life and said, "If that was not enough of a challenge, those countries that were upstream of the mighty rivers, such as the Rhine in Europe, began creating storage dams to hold water to service their domestic needs, much to the peril and anguish of those countries downstream. This caused great concern and stress for the European Union, which was beset with requests to introduce EU laws to outlaw this practice and to arbitrate between countries that had lost diplomatic ties with one another due to the friction caused by water shortages. The first of what became known as the first "Water War" broke out in 2032 between Spain and France, because Spain was diverting water from various sources in the Pyrenees towards Spanish reservoirs. While it only lasted one week, there were over three hundred casualties after the French Government authorised the bombing of the water diverts with air-to-ground missiles.

"Spain retaliated with bombing raids on French military observation and security posts overlooking Spanish territory. The EU was forced into urgent action, calling for calm to be reinstated so that a diplomatic solution could be found. Both the Spanish and French borders were patrolled by the military for nearly ten years after that incident. France and Spain remained fierce enemies for nearly fifty years after the water war."

On a slightly different tack, Beverley offered, "By 2035, there was not one continent in the world that escaped the ravishing or destructive forces of Mother Nature, or staved off overwhelming financial disaster, which affected 90% of all the countries on these continents. The few countries who managed to stay afloat financially were those with massive oil or water reserves such as China. The USA, the UK and all of the European countries had suffered several drops in their credit ratings – they were being considered to be on the same footing as the best of the third world countries. The G20 no longer existed by the year 2030: it was the new G10, which included Britain, the USA, Canada, Brazil, Germany, Saudi Arabia, Iran, China, India and Russia."

She went on, "by 2040, the world map as it was at the beginning of the millennium had changed somewhat, because of what was known as the Milankovitch cycles, which correlated with the planet's shifting in and out of warm periods and ice ages – these cyclical climate changes had proved to be the most powerful catalyst for period based changes in climate and a force too big for mankind to conquer with the climate change behaviour Governments were foisting upon their populations. Government allegiances changed based on where they could get the resources that would keep their people warm, fed and out of mischief, which meant ever new alliances and trade agreements being drawn up."

Joe then wrapped up the session with a big thank you for the informative educational session, suggesting that they continue to explore the cause of man's degradation tomorrow. He signalled to Karyn that she should stay behind, and when everyone else had left, he asked her if she would help him prepare handouts for the next day's presentation. "It should really be Svetlana who presents it, but she's busy with Orb at the moment," he explained.

"Yes, I wonder what they're doing," replied Karyn. "It must be something pretty important."

"It is," said Joe, very seriously. "I can't tell you exactly what for the moment, but it might just provide us with the answer to our predicament."

"That would be good," said Karyn with a smile. "I'd like the chance to get to know you better!"

Joe reached out and touched her cheek lightly. "Me too," he said. "Me too."

CHAPTER 16

No Time for Regrets, only Contemplation.

When Beverley returned to her quarters, she lay on her bunk reflecting on the significance of what they had just been discussing.

She knew that the topic of climate-change was extremely important to being one of the contributing factors that led to this snow ball effect and that the advent and impact of climate-change on the world had been previously mismanaged by politicians for political and financial gain.

As she lay there on her bunk, Beverley recalled the shameful family secret that had been hidden from the public for almost a century.

Her great, great, great grandfather, Charles "Chuck" Wendell Cuzen had once been known as President Nixon's "hatchet man," Cuzen gained notoriety at the height of the Watergate affair for being named as one of the infamous Watergate Seven, and pleaded guilty to obstruction of justice for his attempts to defame Pentagon Papers defendant Daniel Ellsberg. She recalled the stories her mother had told her about her great, great, great grandmother; Beverley-Ann Baker - a foreign-exchange-student from Que-Que in Southern Rhodesia who had proudly announced that the father of her only love-child had become a devout Christian in 1973. She explained "that was God's calling as it would empower him to endure the seven months, he served in the Federal Maxwell Prison in Alabama the following year."

Cuzen was to be the first member of the Nixon administration to be incarcerated for Watergate-related charges, a period of darkness that started because of the top-secret Pentagon Papers about the Vietnam

War, which were photocopied and released to the media in 1971 by Daniel Ellsberg.

Beverley knew that her great, great, great grandmother; Beverley-Ann Baker was a devout Christian and had dearly loved her illegitimate son, Robert Chuck Cuzen-Baker who had been born on January 8th in 1972 from the torrid love-affair Beverley-Ann had with Cuzen whilst working for him as part of the Nixon Administration as one of Chuck Cuzen's researchers.

Beverley recalled that during that era, it was terribly difficult for a single woman to have a child out of wedlock, especially with someone as well connected as Chuck Cuzen. Her boss was responsible for inviting influential people and private special interest groups into the White House policy-making process for the sole purpose of winning their support on specific issues. In his capacity as one of the Consultant's to President Nixon, he served as the President's political communications liaison officer with organised labour, veterans, farmers, conservationists, industrial organisations, citizen groups, and almost any organised lobbying group whose objectives were compatible with the Nixon administration." Cuzen's staff broadened the White House lines of communication with organised constituencies by arranging presidential meetings and sending White House news releases of interest to these and other groups.

In addition to his liaison and political duties, Cuzen's responsibilities included: performing special assignments for the president, such as drafting legal briefs on particular issues, reviewing and assisting with the vetting of presidential appointments, as well as suggesting names for White House guest lists.

Her blood connection with Watergate, "the dark period" is what had terrified Beverley now as she lay on her bunk in the Noah bunker. The hidden skeletons of Cuzen's history were well documented and if someone were to connect her with the infamous Chuck Cuzen, the importance of what she was saying about climate change might be disregarded as were the sage words of so many scientists during the fifty years between 1980 and 2030, when drastic measure should have been taken to deal with the climate-change threat.

Beverley remembered how she had been counselled by her mother to be careful to hide her family ties with someone who was directly connected with the infamous Watergate scandal. "Luckily" she thought, "the birth certificate of the illegitimate son, stated "Father Unknown".

Beverley turned over, pushing her face into her pillow and thanked her lucky stars that her great, great, great grandmother was more embarrassed about having an illegitimate child than getting the father to own up to their affair and to take responsibility for his son.

The activities of her criminal forefathers kept coming back to haunt her. The corrupt behaviour of those people in power like her great, great, great grandfather, who served President Nixon and advised him what to do about the Pentagon Papers, which ultimately resulted in the Watergate scandal; became known as "the dark period." It was like an insidious stain on her DNA that she was unable to wash off, no matter how hard she tried.

Sleep did not come easily that night.

CHAPTER 17

Day 75 - State Welfare and National Health

Various debates had been going on for days. There were lots of frayed tempers and strong opinions, some defensive, some adversarial, yet nobody in the room could deny that mankind had only itself to blame for their present circumstances. Some felt that the discussions were pointless, and some even felt that certain traits were so undesirable that the human race deserved to be extinguished, which led to the next topic: Personal Health and Welfare.

The historical information prepared the previous evening by Joe and Karyn and presented to the gathering dealt with the development of modern medicine, and was based largely on the model of health care that had existed in the UK. It covered the following points.

Maintaining one's personal health should have been the most important primary objective for every single human being. A healthy body, healthy mind and healthy habits naturally lead to a long and sustained quality of life. Or at least you would have thought so. Sadly, the human race had demonstrated throughout history that it had a propensity for self-sabotage and a total disregard for the type of clean healthy living required to live a long life.

Throughout the ages, humans had consumed too much rich food, alcohol, and had smoked tobacco, all of which were large contributors to ill health and premature death in the then modern world. In the latter centuries, humans used drugs and fed themselves on very rich processed foods, ironically named "convenience food." Even though the media made the public aware of the health hazards of smoking and alcohol consumption, a large portion of the human race threw caution to the wind and continued to abuse their bodies. Interestingly enough, the fact that the medical world had made significant breakthroughs in several fields, such as the development of antibiotics, the discovery of DNA, gene therapy and genetics, and the advances in various elements of surgery, was indirectly one of the contributing factors for this behaviour. The populace assumed they could live life in the fast lane and if things started to fall apart, they could take a pill or have an operation.

In these more modern times, before the turn of the second millennium, a significant proportion of the human race in western countries suffered from obesity, which was thought by some to be largely down to the abundance of rich foods, personal gluttony, and lack of self-esteem. This became the new illness after the turn of the millennium. In fact, it had become so acceptable to be fat that companies started using overweight people as fashion models instead of the traditional size 6 to size 8 skeletal models. Society went so far as to invent medical conditions to give overweight people an excuse for their condition, thus allowing them to continue their lifestyle on the pretext of having an illness. The more these people consumed, the more money corporations and governments were making.

The truth was that while some of these people did have proper medical conditions, the majority were simply had no will power who enjoyed their food too much; to the point where they became so overweight, they became ill. There were exceptions, such as those with genetic or medical issues, but they were only a few by comparison.

Remarkably, it was partly down to the medical facilities and weak-minded politicians that obesity came to be labelled "Globesity" and labelled as an illness, so that doctors could offer medical services such as gastric band surgery. This was a procedure in which a silicone band was placed around the top section of the stomach and tightened, leaving a small opening to the lower stomach, thus restricting the amount a person could eat before feeling full. Inserting gastric bands sounds barbaric and was indeed so. So, where did all this start?

In the 1800s medicine was rather barbaric compared to modern times. It was a miracle that anyone survived any illness prior to modern medicine. However, being a doctor was considered a position of prestige in society, and, like other elite groups they, tended to group together. As a result, in the UK, the British Medical Association – the BMA – was born.

The BMA was founded by Sir Charles Hastings (1794–1866) at a meeting in Worcester Infirmary on 19 July 1832. Fifty doctors were present to hear Hastings propose the inauguration of an Association both friendly and scientific.

Called the Provincial Medical and Surgical Association (PMSA) until 1856, their objectives were to promote the medical and allied sciences and to maintain the honour and interests of the medical profession, a set of noble aims, which remained the same ever since its inception.

In the UK this event was soon to be followed by the birth of the National Health Service (NHS), which appeared to be a natural evolution.

By 1930 the BMA itself had produced its own plans for a "general medical service for the nation." In 1938 these were reissued to incorporate recent BMA policy on hospitals and maternity services. In 1940 the Association set up the Medical Planning Commission charged with considering the future of the British medical services. The Commission's report was published in June 1942.

Later in the same year, in December, the Beveridge Report was published, announcing that a comprehensive health service for every citizen would be established. The Report's scheme was to insure the whole nation against unemployment, illness, injury, and retirement, the funding for this to be achieved through contributions from individual citizens, employers, and the Government.

The White Paper "A National Health Service" was proudly published on 17 February 1944.

From all accounts, if an alien had landed and read the annals of history from that era, they might have thought that this was a great move, very philanthropic and quite socialist. It was the first socialist move made by the British Government that was done for the right benevolent reasons. However, as the years passed by, the NHS started to grow into a massive organisation, growing into a powerhouse of employment for the Government. The NHS became the largest commercial employment entity in the United Kingdom and was seen as a key plank in the "big" government strategy for various governments over a fifty-year period.

By the late 1980s, market forces had entered the NHS. The BMA contested the internal market, and, in the following decades, opposed foundation hospitals on the grounds of potential inequality. Contract negotiations had challenged the BMA in recent years. In the first decade of a new century, the BMA faced many more challenges: the impact of European Union directives on the profession; devolution in the UK; new technological sources for medical advice; and a review of the representative structure and governance of the Association itself.

Even with all this evidence of demonstrating empathy for the patient, one would have thought that the BMA would consciously ensure doctors learn about all new medicine and complementary therapies available such as eastern medicine so that they could give their patients world class, quality treatment. You would have expected to see thousands of doctors with numerous complementary medicine qualifications, giving their patients a more holistic approach to their treatment.

This was not the case; in fact, it was very much the opposite.

A pattern was beginning to emerge; the medical fraternity, including the BMA, had allowed the travesty of big medicine, big costs to be perpetuated. The medical fraternity, doctors and pharmaceutical companies, all became very wealthy from all their patients having to take drugs to fend off illness, all the while having their medicines and treatments paid for by the NHS as part of the "free at the point of delivery medicine for all" promise."

The advent of genetic manipulation, gene therapy and bio-genetics had started to make headway once the human genome was understood. The scientists were very soon able to use gene technology to eradicate diseases, filter out debilitating impediments and degenerate genes and, if required, modify human behaviour.

This was the very area that Svetlana Bowker had specialised in. It was noted by all those present in the common room that Svetlana and Orb were still mysteriously absent.

It was not really in the financial interests of the doctors and the pharmaceuticals companies to truly cure people. Actually, they simply wanted to put a sticking plaster over the problem, or give the patient a pill to take away the pain. Why would they want to expend valuable money to do proper investigations into the root cause of what was ailing the patients? It was a self-perpetuating "money-go-round": keep the patients from feeling the pain, let them gorge themselves, let them smoke, let them live poor unhealthy life styles. All this helped to perpetuate the money-making machine for the governments in the form of taxes levied on cigarettes, alcohol and unhealthy foods, for example, and much sought-after revenue for corporations, the pharmaceutical industry and doctors, all of which the government enjoyed tax income from. The pharmaceutical industry spent billions on lobbyists to do their bidding at government level, whilst they developed all kinds of innovative incentive schemes to get doctors to prescribe their brand of medicine, irrespective of whether any of these drugs or procedures were the best available on the market.

Clearly, the health environment was corrupted, and it suited the governments to allow this to continue, because in addition to the taxes on alcohol, cigarettes, food, medicines and the corporation taxes received, the government had a very large institution that allowed them to create quasi government jobs that helped them to keep people employed - out of the social welfare system and out of unemployment queues, which was good for their image at election time. This symbiotic relationship was win–win for all, except for the health of the patient.

It had to be said that the patients were themselves sometimes their own worst enemy. The weak and undisciplined environment fostered by Dr. Spock's exhortations ensured that many modern-day humans were brought up without the concept of personal accountability, personal integrity, moral values or strength of character; prerequisites that people needed to take control and be accountable for their own life, health and wealth successfully. They were brought up through decades of the "nanny state" era, being told that if all went wrong, someone else would bail them out and give them housing support and free medical aid if they fell ill. So many spent everything they earned and did not even consider why they should not live a life of excess, or why they should be responsible for their own health, wealth and state of mind.

Sadly, a certain sector of society repeatedly proved incapable of taking responsibility for their actions. That was just how Progressivism wanted it – people who were dependent on the state, with a sheep-like mentality so that those in the power seats of Progressivism could steer the nation into a state of numb oblivion, addicted to high profile brands promoted by celebrities, trapped them in low paid jobs, swimming in debt whilst being engrossed in the celebrity culture in the media. This kept their flock of constituents what essentially become known as "sheeple" on the treadmill - out of the Elite's political and financial conniving, spending their hard-earned money keeping the economies going. Corporations, with the help of the Banks and Governments were quite successful at enslaving the masses on low wages, thanks to the Blair, Brown and Obama's naïve policies, as it meant they had a consistent on tap cheap labour to do their bidding.

At the end, Joe said, "I'm sorry that Svetlana was unable to be here to lead a full detailed discussion . . ."

"Yes, where is she?" someone called out.

"I hope to be able to give you the answer to that very soon," said Joe. "In the meantime, I would ask you to be patient and trust that the work we have been doing in discussing all these topics will not be wasted."

CHAPTER 18

Day 76 - If Only We Could Go Back in Time

Date 14th June 2612 AD, Time 06h00 GMT.

At the end of the fifth day of brainstorming, Joe stood up and held up a hand to quell the previous day's post-discussion arguments that were going on. Gradually, the room fell quiet, and Joe said, "Your input into all the debates that we have been having is much appreciated. I am aware that some of you think that there is little point in discussing what might have averted the destruction of the human race, and I can't promise that you are wrong. But I have some news that I hope to God will prove that we haven't simply been wasting time."

Just as Joe finished speaking, Svetlana Bowker and Orb entered the conference room accompanied by a third person, nobody had seen before. All three looked excited and animated. Svetlana smiled at the assembly and said, "Let me introduce you all to my elder sister, Venetia. Orb and I brought her out of stasis a few days ago as we felt she could be the key to solving our problems. She is a renowned scientist who was a specialist on the joint American Military and CIA time travel project."

No one moved a muscle, and the tension in the air was almost palpable.

Venetia then spoke. "There is an artefact stashed in hangar 0555, which is a working time machine originally developed by the Germans during the Second World War, in 1944. It was discovered in Berlin in September 1945 and taken away along with thousands of other artefacts by American soldiers, who plundered anything that looked remotely clever."

A buzz of noise swept round the room and amazement could be seen on every face. Joe held up his hand again. "Let her finish," he said, laughing.

Venetia briefed them as to where they had got to in their trials of the time travel technology. "The team in the US built five more machines, which are also stored here, but had only been able to do short time hops due to the trips being one way. To be able to measure any success, they needed line of sight, for example, a few days apart, whereas what is being proposed in this forum is a much longer trip with no line of sight or feedback as to the successful safe delivery and the efficacy of the transportation. In this case, those of us here will not know if the people we transport were delivered successfully, alive, or indeed in an operational state, or whether the expeditions they would be sent to undertake were indeed successful or not."

She pointed out that there were several known side effects that would have to be ironed out before the technology would be authorised for operational use. "One of the major side effects was loss of short-term memory, which means that the person or persons arriving at their destination might never recall what their mission was unless it was committed to long-term memory before departure, so any last minute intelligence or instructions could be lost in transit, there was also the phenomenon of the phantasmagoria, which is a series or group of strange or bizarre images seen as if in a dream stirred up by the brain circuitry struggling to get up and running again" she explained.

Venetia continued, "The first issue we need to deal with is that all of the Hindsight teams would need to be delivered simultaneously to their respective points in the timeline at their various locations. This is because of the shifting timeline, which will occur as the historical events in the old timeline are changed by each of the teams at the different points along the timeline."

Joe then said, "There is a second issue. We have only six-time travel units that could be made functional and fit for purpose. So, in the interests of having a proper disaster recovery plan, after delivering the primary load one unit will be used by myself and a "Beach Head" team to commute back and forth between the various points in the timeline to co-ordinate the setup and bedding in of each element of the overall strategy."

Venetia pointed out that therefore, the other five units would only be given sufficient fuel for a single trip, and would need to be carefully hidden to avoid abuse. "This is the third issue," she said. "The time travel units are powered by very sophisticated nuclear fission devices, a technology which cannot be left back there in that timeline in case they find their way into the hands of the military of a rogue nation. "That means," she continued, "this would be a one-way trip for the teams in those units, since the devices will eventually be relocated to a safe secure location by the "Beach Head" team after the cargo has been successfully delivered."

So, with the known side effects and other issues to deal with, Venetia explained, "you will have to document the missions very clearly and encrypt the data in their journals or on their laptops to circumvent the risk of a person being discovered in a compromised situation on arrival and having the mission taken from them before they had a chance to refresh their memory as to what their mission was."

"There are also other dangers and failure scenarios that we will need to try and factor out of the transmission," she said, "such as location and obstructions in the landing zone. We will need to target the landing co-ordinates to be in an area where there was open space and the arrival times should be at night so as to reduce the risk of being seen, which would compromise integration into the society of the day."

Joe warned everyone that there were other challenges that the teams would need to overcome. For example, initially the time traveller would arrive without the currency of that specific time and place. That meant they would have no cash resources or means to live. They would only have whatever gold sovereigns they could carry, plus their wits and ingenuity. This did not bode well for any of them, as failure simply was not an option if the "Beach Head" team failed to setup base earlier in the timeline.

As a backup for resources in the event that the 'Beach Head' team were unable to pre-set up the environments according to plan, Venetia explained that each person in the teams that would arrive at a target zone would be equipped with a Sports Almanac for that period prepared by Orb's team." She said, "The almanacs will contain useful data about their location, such as information on lotteries, horse racing, or betting opportunities they could participate in to quickly raise sufficient funds to mount an operation. This would need to be done over a few weeks or months so as not to raise suspicions or attract the attention of the law.

"Finally,", she said, "there is one final thing. It will be a one-way trip, so you will have to prepare yourselves properly before you depart, because you won't ever be able to communicate with our present time line again! After all, if the changes the teams would aim to implement actually come about, the Noah 5000 bunker might not exist as it does in our present timeline. Unless you are ported into another future timeline post your natural timeline life's death, you could also cease to exist shortly before your natural conception; your soul could simply vaporise and vanish into thin air if you are still alive at that point of time, which could render your body a lifeless vegetable. We have not been able to test this hypothesis yet, so we have to assume that your soul cannot exist twice at the very same point of conception and that it is a physical impossibility. So, we do not know what happens when two live souls cross over into a shared time space. Do not attempt this; you may not be able to complete your mission!

"I have discussed the logistics with Joe. He knows all of your approximate conception and birth dates and if the plan we have laid out works, you will not be anywhere near those dates, because you would have been able to live out your natural lives in an earlier timeline and die a natural death, such as of old age if you are that way inclined, before the real you is born."

Venetia paused, and said, "I know you will all have many questions when you've had time to absorb this, but I will tell you now that there is a lot of preparatory work to be done before this mission can be launched, and our estimates," pointing to herself and Orb, "are that we could be ready in about a year if we all work hard."

HINDSIGHT

There was an air of excitement in the room as Venetia finished her briefing. Everybody immediately started hypothesising about the challenges the time travellers would face and who those poor, or maybe lucky, devils would be.

Joe, ever the military strategist, immediately took control of the meeting and started organising working groups around this new strategy.

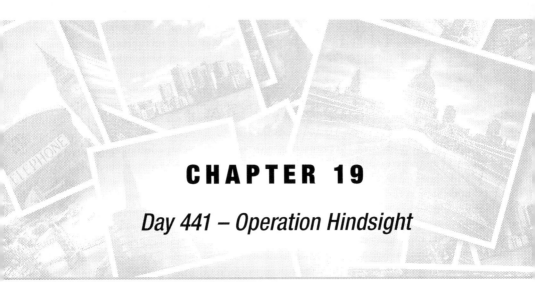

CHAPTER 19

Day 441 – Operation Hindsight

Date 14th June 2612 AD, Time O6h00 GMT.

It was one year to the day since operation Hindsight was initiated. They had all worked like Trojans, and they were now almost ready to put the project into operation and launch the six teams back in time.

The residents of the Noah 5000 bunker were in a precarious situation; if they remained in the same state as they were, they and the rest of humanity would perish. If however, they were to take a big risk and travel back in time on a one-way trip, they could help to nudge mankind down a different path to mitigate the damage caused by corrupt banking, financial and political systems, the degradation of decent moral values and the general breakdown of society. This as well as greed and corruption, climate change, over-population, famine, and the proliferation of arms and weapons.

Joe started the morning with the following statement. "On the basis that a different outcome could be manifested if the previously discussed items were addressed differently, these were the trajectory nudges that we believe would help mankind to take a different course of action, one that we hope would avoid our extinction!"

Joe had listed each "Trajectory Nudge" point in a briefing manifest,

1. Fix the problems with democracy: The first Hindsight team, codenamed "Exceed", will have the most arduous challenge of all; it entails a strategy that will take some decades to

fully implement. Democracy, as it was employed during the nineteenth and twentieth centuries was flawed – it was too prone to corruption! A fundamental change to the voting structure had to be instigated and adopted worldwide. For example, a major influencing of the British Representation of the People Act of 1918, enabled all males over twenty-one plus women over thirty who were ratepayers or married to ratepayers to vote; has to be in place to accommodate the new form of democracy before the implementation of the 1928 Suffragette movement. This means all women would receive the vote on the same terms as men. The media were naïve, which sometimes served unwittingly to corrupt politics and undermine the good intentions of politicians.

History showed that the media were actually more corrupt than the political system itself. In the twenty-first century, the media became polarised, favouring either the left or the right. Because they were so influential and persuasive, this unbalanced the "Ying and Yang" of politics, because 95% of the time it was weighted aggressively with a liberal slant. The Progressive movement leveraged this to their advantage and these journalists thought they were doing the right thing for mankind by shaming and silencing the side opposing side. Governments were sometimes ousted from power by the media, which in most cases was for very wrong reasons. A stable and balanced media needed to be established, where an equilibrium of considered informed debate and political persuasion could be fostered.

This is only going to be made right by influencing the seeds of democracy at the outset in the following ways.

a. Making a sustainable economic environment a mandatory principle of democracy, with a simple fair taxation regime that enables entrepreneurship to flourish in an economic environment that will form the mechanism for wealth creation and distribution based on merit and self-determination, as well as deploying a socialist mechanism only for the needy or disabled.

b. Implementing a more transparent, less corrupt form of democracy.

c. Implementing a more balanced, non-biased, responsible, better disciplined and accountable media with better oversight.

d. Implementing a zero tolerance of corruption within politics and crime in general.

2. Preventing the decay of moral values in society. The second Hindsight team, code-named "Respect", needs to make it very clear to both mankind in general and to governments that the decay of moral and family values in society would be wholly unacceptable and detrimental to society in the longer term. Governments need to ensure that the taxation and legal system favours healthier morals so that good values become pervasive throughout society. The starting point would be be influence Dr. Spock to present a different child-rearing regime to the one he presented to the world in the 1960s. He would need to promote better discipline to ensure that society does not become as delinquent as it did post the 1960s because of his flawed advice. This team will take artefacts from history, such as newsreel, video, newspaper and magazine articles about the problem, to use as tools to convince Dr. Spock.

3. Preventing addiction and dependency on aid and charity: The third Hindsight team, codenamed "Mezzanine", needs to change the basis of giving aid and charity to countries that are in trouble by making their receiving aid or charity conditional on their adopting and implementing the four core principles of a healthy society.

a. Implement a form of democracy that is cleaner, more directed, more accountable, more focused and less corrupt – a democracy based on the principles of the Positics Constitution.

b. Implement zero tolerance on crime and corruption, especially where position of high office or great responsibility are in play.

c. Enable an environment where all religious moral values can be incorporated as part of the fabric of society.

d. Enable a sound economic commercial model in the private sector and a smaller government sector.

4. Climate change – preservation of life and Nature's ecological treasures: The fourth Hindsight team, code-named "Sunshine", needs to make it mandatory for both mankind generally and governments to prevent ecological devastation such as deforestation of jungles, such as those in the Amazon or Indonesia, and the irresponsible killing of thousands of species of animals or plant life. The preservation of life and the ecology should be made mandatory in all government manifestos. Governments should be able to demonstrate that they have implemented initiatives that reduce the emissions of carbon into the atmosphere and should also have a regime where culprits who wantonly flout this requirement are dealt with swiftly and punitively.

5. Implement a global zero tolerance on arms / munitions sales: The fifth Hindsight team, code-named "Concorde", has a dangerous challenge that would take some clever political manoeuvring. After the end of the Second World War and the "Cold War", outlawing the sales of arms to any country is indeed the toughest and deadliest challenge that faces the Noah 5000 Hindsight's six teams.

6. Stabilising the world's population: The sixth "Hindsight team", code-named "Zvakanaka", has to change what has been deemed modern times' biggest mistake, post the Second World War. There were needless deaths of tens of millions of people because of famine, wars and simple neglect, or plainly being unable to support children in the first place. Many people had the notion drummed into them that it was mankind's right to have children. Never once did they ever consider the fate of these tens of millions of babies and young children who died because of famine, neglect, or their parents' inability to afford to have them.

There are five fundamental reasons for human beings to have children:

a. out of love and the desire to nurture;

b. to satisfy one's desire for an heir, or successors to support one in old age;

c. a natural biological urge;

d. out of ignorance or lack of understanding of the consequences of having children when one cannot afford to feed, clothe, or educate them;

e. as a "financial" device to seek benefits and charity, like the single teenage mothers in the United Kingdom during the twentieth and twenty-first century, where simply having a child enabled them to secure a council house and additional benefits for each child.

The question the Noah 5000 residents had to wrestle with was how were they going to make these changes happen and stick fast in a society that was being unintentionally undermined by the "do-gooders", who honestly thought what they were doing was right and good for mankind, especially for those the elite called the unfortunate poor.

The world had to be given a "nudge" towards strategies that would serve to save the world from mankind's own stupidity, ignorance, greed and corruption.

All of these teams would need information on historical data about incidents that happened in the era they were being sent back to. This data would come from Wikipedia, Encyclopaedias or from historical records such as the Almanac that recorded both incidents of history and of betting interest, such as sports results, that happened during that time to be used as convincers in case the likes of Dr. Spock found the idea of time travel too preposterous to believe.

Orb's team of "geeks" had prepared seven state of the art laptop devices, with two terabytes of data, statistics, video evidence and utilities to help each of the teams make their case.

Venetia explained, "Since the technology used in the manufacturing of a time travel device would not have yet been invented during their timeline, it will be impossible to prove that time travel as a concept did indeed work.

"That is why one of the time travel units is being primed with sufficient fuel packs to enable it to go back and forth in time. If it became imperative to convince key targeted people that the concept of time travel was feasible, they might have to take them on a short journey to convince them."

She finished by saying, "Disbelief would be the major risk to the whole Hindsight strategy. We hope this will prove to be a way of mitigating that risk."

Joe then reminded them that the other five units would have to be removed and stored safely or destroyed after delivery was deemed successful, to prevent any possibility of the Time-Travel units falling into the hands of an unscrupulous power. To illustrate this, he pointed out that the so-called "Cold War" was at its height of distrust and volatility during the latter part of the twentieth century, and this technology would create a significant change to the balance of power if it fell into the wrong hands.

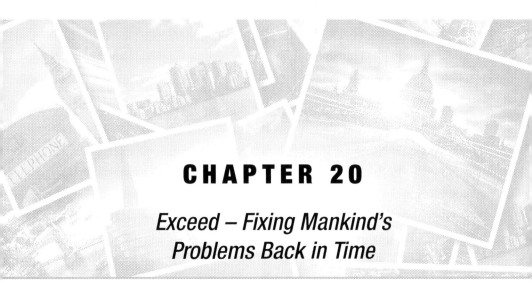

CHAPTER 20

Exceed – Fixing Mankind's Problems Back in Time

Joe, the logistics expert of the group, headed the first team that went back the furthest in time. This team was code-named "Beach Head."

The travel through time had left them all desperately fatigued, but they had reached their scheduled place of arrival, several miles outside of Geneva, at 03h09. The date was 7 April 1920.

Joe immediately looked at his personal briefing note he had held onto tightly in his hands, as they initiated the time-travel sequence. The note helped him overcome the short-term memory loss he had suffered during the trip. Once he had gathered his senses, he immediately set about securing their gear, and ensuring that they were not compromised. He suggested to the team that they immediately get some sleep so that they would have their full wits about them when daylight came.

Joe reminded them, that being compromised and losing control of the time-machine would be devastating and would scupper the Hindsight plan, so security had to be in the forefront of all their minds.

It was a cold yet sunny spring morning in Geneva when they awoke from their slumber to the smell of oatmeal porridge and coffee. Buffa, a burly Australian Special Forces veteran, was making breakfast on a small gas primus stove.

Including Joe, eight people came through the time travel jump. The only female on the Beach Head trip was Karyn, who, with her doctorate in global political sciences would form the nucleus and act as the strategist of the first "nudge" team, code-named "Exceed." The chosen code-name was quite apt, since this initiative had to do better than just excel; it really needed to succeed beyond expectations.

The landing party had all suffered short-term memory loss due to the stresses of time travel, so Joe began the re-briefing from their time travel initiation pack.

He explained the situation to the other six members of his team. "You are all members of the Beach Head team, except for Karyn. We have to make the necessary preparations for the subsequent Hindsight "nudge" team arrivals. We have sufficient information to enable us to secure funds from dormant numbered accounts in Geneva and Zurich which we will be putting into seven trusts, one for each of the other teams coming back in time. These funds will be necessary for us and for the next team if they want to achieve their objectives."

Joe added, "To ensure a successful outcome, each team needs to be aware of the other key elements of the overall strategy so that they can ensure alignment and strategic "nudge" co-ordination where necessary. However, for reasons of security, each team will not know the whereabouts of the other teams until it is safe for them to do so.

"Security is of paramount importance," he said. "This team has to absolutely ensure the safe conduct and execution of all the Hindsight objectives, without exception."

He went on to explain, "We will travel to the target destinations around the globe once the funds have been secured and the Trusts have been established. Once a destination is allocated to you, you will immediately begin setting up your particular mission's base of operation, such as acquiring a property in the appropriate neighbourhood for the team that has been tasked with that specific "nudge" objective."

Joe was confident they would do a good job; he knew that all six members of his team had been handpicked from the Special Forces contingent of "saved souls" in the stasis pool. These members all had field experience and were experts in hand-to-hand combat, small arms combat, and demolition explosives.

The Beach Head team had arrived eight years prior to the scheduled arrival of the first "nudge" team, Exceed, to give them the necessary time to do the leg-work and set up the necessary infrastructure. A key objective would be to secure Swiss identities for every member, not only for the Beach Head team, but for all the subsequent security teams.

Joe reminded them, "The key to our immediate success is to secure and set up our mission base here in Geneva to deal with the logistics in a structured and disciplined fashion, out of sight of the public and officials to ensure Karyn's security while she puts the foundations of the Exceed plan into place."

He glanced at Karyn. In the past year they had both been totally absorbed in the preparation for their mission, like the professional and extraordinary people they were, with almost no time to explore the relationship they both felt was developing between them. He saw that she was completely calm and focused, showing no sign of apprehension or doubt. He gave her a brief smile, which she returned, equally briefly.

Then Joe stood up and barked, "Eat up, and grab your gear. We move out in fifteen minutes."

CHAPTER 21

Influencing Democracy, Starting in 1920

The date was 7 December 1920, the location Sussex Gardens in Paddington, London.

Joe had just safely delivered Karyn's two political science colleagues, Danielle Dunn and Charlie Robson, to her as well as her two security team members. After six months of planning and investigation, Karyn was ready to begin carrying out the actions on her strategy.

Karyn knew that she and the rest of her Exceed team members had to engineer a fundamental change to the voting and political structure of democracy, which needed to be adopted by every country worldwide.

Since they would have arrived too late to influence the British Representation of the Peoples Act of 1918, which enabled all males over twenty-one plus women over thirty who were ratepayers or married to ratepayers to vote. They would therefore have to work on the next legislative changes in British and American politics, which would be the 1928 Suffragette movement, as a result of which all women received the vote on the same terms as men.

The mission of the Exceed team would be to influence key targets in the British Parliament to expand the boundary of the 1928 Suffragette objective and have them convince the then Prime Minister of the United Kingdom, Stanley Baldwin and his Government in power to create a universal constitution that introduced a form of democracy that was based on integrity, fairness, accountability with tighter rules of engagement and implementation.

Karyn warned her team that they had arrived in troubled times.

"The 1920s was sometimes referred to as the Roaring Twenties or the Jazz Age, when speaking about the United States, Canada or the United Kingdom. In Europe the decade was sometimes referred to as the "Golden Twenties" because of the economic boom following the First World War," she explained.

"Since the end of the twentieth century, we have seen that the economic strength during the 1920s could be closely compared with that of the 1950s and 1990s, especially in the US. Those three decades were regarded as periods of economic prosperity, which lasted for nearly each entire decade. Each of the three decades followed a tremendous event that occurred in the previous decade – First World War and Spanish flu in the 1910s, Second World War in the 1940s, and the end of the Cold War in the late 1980s."

Karyn went on to explain, "However, not all countries enjoyed this prosperity. The Weimar Republic, like many other European countries, was about to face a severe economic downturn in the opening years of the 1920s, because of the enormous debt caused by the First World War as well as the Treaty of Versailles. That crisis culminated in a devaluation of the German Mark in 1923, eventually leading to severe economic problems, which in the long term created a fertile environment for the rise of the Nazi Party."

Danielle chipped in, saying, "Yes, and the decade was also characterised by the rise of radical political movements, especially in regions that were once part of empires. Communism began attracting large numbers of followers following the success of the October Revolution and the Bolsheviks' determination to win the subsequent Russian Civil War. The Bolsheviks would eventually adopt a policy of mixed economics, from 1921 to 1928, and also give birth to the Soviet Union, at the end of 1922. The 1920s marked the first time in the United States that the population in the cities surpassed the population of rural areas. This was due to rapid urbanisation starting in the 1920s."

"You're quite right," said Karyn. "The 1920s also saw the rise of fascism in Europe and elsewhere, which was perceived as a solution to prevent the spread of Communism. The diabolical economic problems also favoured the rise of dictators in Eastern Europe and the Balkans, such as Józef Piłsudski in the Second Polish Republic and Peter and Alexander Karađorđević in the Kingdom of Yugoslavia. It was a time of great change. Plus, in October 1929, the devastating Wall Street Crash marked the end of the prosperous 1920s.

"So," she continued, "we know what happened. Our task is to try to change that history in a few subtle ways."

In the eight months since their arrival from the future on 7 April 1920, Joe and the Beach Head team had secured the funding, established identities and accommodations in the respective target locations of the Hindsight plan. Each of the teams had to be well looked after, and financially they had to be seen by their peers of that period as successful and well-connected people of note.

The house in London that had been acquired by the Trust was a magnificent example of Victorian architecture, with high vaulted ceilings finished in artistic coving with wonderful bay windows. Each room had a fireplace in which coal was used to build a fire each day to keep the chill from setting in. The furniture was elegant and suited their needs. While not too extravagant, it left any observer with a feeling that the people who lived there had both money and taste. There were three floors, serviced by a wonderful wooden staircase, with an ornately carved wooden banister, which was sturdy and built to last. Each room had rugs that were imported from the Far East by a local Jewish, merchant, Samuel Rabinowitz, who had an import/export business that was based in the docklands in the east of London.

Karyn had taken an instant liking to Mr Rabinowitz, from the very first time he visited the house when they were shopping for their furnishings. Samuel was extremely helpful and helped Karyn to become acquainted with all her new neighbours within days of her arrival.

Karyn was warned by Samuel to mind her pennies, as there would be tough times ahead. Little did he realise how well she knew that to be true.

However, Karyn was planning a little extravagance to celebrate her twenty-eighth birthday, which would be on 12 December. She had invited Joe, who, having delivered her colleagues would be returning back to the future to monitor things in the Hindsight bunker. So, before he returned to sometime in the future, Karyn ensured they would be together here in 1920 to spend the evening of her birthday with her. "After all," she reasoned. "We cannot work all the time, not even when the work we are doing is so vital." Joe, for his part, had not been too difficult to persuade.

She had planned a dinner for two at home, where they could discuss the progress of the plan, she had put in place for the Exceed team without fear of being overheard, and now she intended to go shopping for a suitably impressive dress.

When Joe arrived on the evening of her birthday and Karyn opened the door to him, he was momentarily stunned. "My God," he eventually managed to say, "you look so beautiful!" Karyn laughed. "It is a bit different from all those sharp suits and hats I usually have to wear!" The dress, which had taken hours to find, was mint green, with a scalloped hem that came to just below the knee, and was richly beaded around the neckline and the hemline. A boa made from ostrich feathers was draped around her shoulders. Her hair had been cut in a bob that framed her small face, and she wore a beaded headband that matched her dress.

Joe could hardly take his eyes off her as she moved around lighting candles and putting the finishing touches to the table. They sat down to eat, and because Karyn had forbidden any mention of their mission until after they had finished eating, they talked about themselves and their backgrounds.

As Joe raised his wineglass to her, wishing her a happy birthday, Karyn said, "It seems weird to be celebrating a birthday when I haven't actually been born yet!"

Joe smiled. "I know," he said. "And somewhere our great-great-great-great-great grandparents are probably about to be born, which is even weirder."

"Tell me about when you were growing up, what you were interested in," Karyn said.

"Well, there was always a lot of music around, so I kind of absorbed that. My father liked classical music, and my mother loved modern folk, too, and my sister," he hesitated slightly, as he always did when speaking about Elizabeth, he continued, "my sister was a pianist."

Karyn reached across the table and put her hand over his. "We *will* succeed, you know, and you will get her back. We will get all of them back."

"No talking about the mission," Joe reminded her, smiling.

"And then," he continued, "I was very keen on sport. I played tennis competitively and loved to ski in winter. I did a bit of diving whenever we were in Greece – we had a little holiday place there – and that was amazing. My career was never in doubt, though. I never wanted to be anything other than a soldier, like my father."

He got up to put more coal on the fire, saying, "But now it's your turn. Tell me about you."

"Oh," said Karyn, "I think I was quite boring. I enjoyed sport, too, especially tennis – maybe I'll be able to thrash you around a court one day!"

"Hah! snorted Joe. "In your dreams birthday girl! But go on."

"I was quite a serious little girl, and as an only child I was probably very influenced by adults. I always wanted to know why things were as they were, and probably drove everyone mad with my constant "but what if . . .." I was actually quite shy, and very studious. I remember –" she stopped suddenly.

"Go on," said Joe. "What were you going to say?"

Karyn blushed slightly. "I was thinking about a boy I knew when I was at school."

"Oh, a boyfriend, was he?"

"No, well, I suppose so, in a way. I went to a pretty strict school with high academic standards, and I did well in exams and things, and I suppose I thought I couldn't go wrong. The school was single-sex, but there was a boys' school on the same site, and some facilities and events were shared. I met this boy, Marcus, at a lecture on political science given by a visiting professor – are you sure this isn't too boring?"

"Not a bit," said Joe, laughing. "I want to hear all about your murky past."

Karyn glared at him in mock anger. "Well, we took an instant liking to each other, and I used to sneak out at night to meet him." Seeing Joe's expression, she added, "I don't know what you're thinking, Mr Gilroy, but it was all quite innocent! Mostly we just talked for hours, putting the world to rights as you do when you are young." She paused. "If only it were that easy," she sighed.

"Anyway," she continued, "losing so much sleep eventually caught up with me, and I flunked my end of term exams."

"You *failed your exams*!" exclaimed Joe, feigning horror.

"No, I didn't *fail* them, but my grades were way down. So that was the end of my friendship with Marcus."

"So, you dumped the poor guy because your grades were down?"

"Yes," said Karen, looking down at her empty plate. "My work and my studies were more important to me." She glanced up at Joe. "See, I told you I was pretty dull."

"Not to me, you're not," asserted Joe. "In fact, if you want to know the truth, I find you endlessly fascinating, not to mention wildly attractive."

Karyn laughed. "How did you manage to get into the armed services with such poor eyesight?" she joked, then looked serious. "Actually," she said, "I think you're not bad yourself. If we weren't so tied up in what we have to do, who knows what might happen?"

"Ah, I see!" said Joe. "I'm going to get the same treatment as poor old Marcus!"

"No," Karyn said softly. "I don't think I could do that to you, even though I am totally committed to our mission, as you are, too."

It was Joe's turn to look away pensively. Then he came to a decision, looked back at Karyn and said, "I don't think I could bear it if you did. I know the mission is all-important, but . . . I also know that I love you."

Karyn was silent for what appeared to Joe to be half a lifetime, then she said, "I think I love you, too, but there isn't much we can do about it for now, is there?"

"Not just now, no, but it's so important for me to know that you might feel the same way about me as I do about you." And Joe got up from the table, crossed to where Karyn was sitting, took her hand and gently pulled her up and into his arms. He sighed deeply, as if he had been lost in a wilderness and had finally found his way home, then bent his head and kissed her mouth. For a few moments they both revelled in the kiss, then reluctantly drew apart.

Joe said shakily, "Look at that for willpower."

"Mmmmm," murmured Karyn. "On both sides."

"I have something for you," Joe said, reaching into his pocket and producing a black box. "It's for your birthday, and I would like you to think of it also as a promise for the future."

Karyn opened the box, and found a beautiful string of perfectly matched natural pearls. Just for a moment she paused, hearing in her head the voice of her grandmother, who used to say, "Pearls mean tears", then she shook off her recollection of what was, after all, simply a superstition. "Oh, they are stunning, Joe!" she gasped. "I was going to say you shouldn't have, but they are too gorgeous!" She draped the pearls around her neck, and asked Joe to fasten them for her. He noticed that she had tears in her eyes, and gently brushed them away. "Thank you so much," Karyn said, as they both looked at her reflection in the large mirror over the fireplace. "I shall always wear them." She turned to Joe and kissed him lingeringly.

"Now," she said, rather tremulously, "I think we should have coffee by the fire and talk about our work."

"Yes," agreed Joe. "Otherwise I am likely to make love to you on the spot."

They hugged briefly, and then resigned themselves to talking over the strategies Karyn and her team were in the process of putting into action.

The first plank in her strategy was to become well entrenched in the realms of high society, where the aristocracy, politicians and people of wealth moved. This would include the Monarchy and the Palace of Westminster, which housed the two chambers of Parliament – the House of Lords and the House of Commons – where one could see much flummery from bygone ages lovingly preserved; a celebration of the much-vaunted continuity of the British constitution and stoicism.

The Exceed team had come well prepared, with reams of historical evidence and research that could illustrate and prove the problems that were going to beset the government when its promises of a better society in which there was supposed to be a higher standard of living and security of employment were not fulfilled. The UK's productivity rate had fallen rapidly behind that of other nations; there was simply too much reliance on the traditional industries of cotton, coal and shipbuilding, all of which were finding it difficult to compete in world markets. Sadly, all of them were managed by those who could not adapt to more modern methods. Britain's economy was being scuppered by their adherence to tradition and old legacy processes and the lack of entrepreneurship. Many countries which had been dependent upon British manufactured goods were now making their own. A great slump in which millions were unemployed was left to work itself out when planned government expenditure would have helped mobilise the unused resources of the economy.

Karyn explained, "This known issue will provide us with a great opportunity to ingratiate ourselves with the current government by showing them alternative ways to resolve this looming problem, such as patenting and licensing their technologies to other manufacturers abroad. I have assigned Charlie to that one."

"Good choice," agreed Joe.

Charles Robson, whose family line came from stoic British Colonial stock, was the brightest economist and political historian ever to have emerged out of Africa. Charlie as he like to be called, had specialised in British history over this period and was well versed with the errors that both the current government and subsequent governments implemented which would have debilitating knock-on effects. During their high school years in Africa, Charlie and his brother James, known as Jim, were avid sports enthusiasts. Charlie loved cricket, squash and rugby while his elder brother Jim loved athletics and rugby. Jim had won medals for the 100-metre sprint, which had elevated his status in his high school days to that of a local icon. While Charlie was no contest for Jim on the track, he did, however, prove himself to be a very savvy and intelligent economist while at University in Natal.

Karyn told Joe that they would have their initial debates with several targeted politicians, in which Charlie could explain that the Liberal

Party, which had done so much to alleviate conditions of poverty and made such significant strides in improving social conditions in general, would begin to lose their standing in the polls after 1922.

It was planned that over a sustained period, the Exceed team would engage with the politicians in power at that time and after having praised them for their foresight and philanthropic ways, they would explain that the political programme of the Labour Party, which advocated increased social security measures, including a national minimum wage, the nationalisation of basic industries such as coal, railways and electricity, and the imposition of higher taxation to pay for social welfare and to reduce the burden of the National Debt, in fact had just one benefit – the "dole." This was a government-funded benefit that allowed workers to survive while unemployed, and it was probably the reason why there was not greater social unrest or even revolution.

In various meetings in the halls of power and exclusive private clubs like the RAC or Carlton Club in the Strand, the Exceed team would go on to explain to the politicians, that what the records from the future demonstrated was that they would need a sustainable capitalist driven economic-model that would run side by side with their socialist policies and provide the necessary balance. This was where the Exceed team would help them focus some of their energies as the second plank within their strategy.

Charlie would need to devise a strategy as to how he could convince the politicians they would have to come up with several feasible initiatives that could be implemented during the first four years of this decade that would help the economy brace itself for the depression that was coming.

In private, Joe had shown the Exceed team a chart of the Prime Ministers during that four-year window and how much turmoil they would have to contend with. This showed that Britain had four Prime Ministers in those four years, the Liberal David Lloyd George, the Conservatives Andrew Bonar Law and Stanley Baldwin, and from 21 January 1924, the first ever Labour Prime Minister, Ramsay MacDonald.

The next stage, Karyn explained, would involve both Charlie and her spending a considerable amount of time talking with dozens of politicians and business people about commercial opportunities that lay within their grasp if they were prepared to stretch their imaginations. They also hoped to advise Members of Parliament on subtle changes the government would need to make to their policies to engage people of all walks of life if Britain was going to be the forerunner and leader of the forthcoming commercial bonanza they had seen from the future.

The key policy change would be to create an equality of pay for services rendered, irrespective of gender, along with a simplified taxation system that would allow for tax incentives to be given as a reward for commercial businesses that implemented philanthropic commercial initiatives along with penalties for those who chose not to participate. Essentially, it would be a way for those who were wealthier than most, which included the aristocracy, the elite and the newly enriched industrialists to become more entrepreneurial and fund people from the working class to create thousands of the smaller businesses that would provide the necessary support for the product manufacturing and services industry that would grow in the next few decades.

This would address the "wealth distribution" issue that the Progressives wanted to see happen, but was abhorred by the elites in society. Basically, by enabling business to thrive and for people to lift themselves out of poverty by taking direct action as to the state of their wealth and being forced by commercial practice to put back into the system when they themselves became successful, this policy would also overcome the "entitlements" issue which plagued Governments in the twentieth and twenty-first centuries.

Karyn said that as part of their strategy to get people off welfare and move them as far away from entitlement as possible, they were going to introduce some of the techniques that were written about by Robert T. Kiyosaki in his best seller book entitled; "*Rich Dad Poor Dad*" first published in 1997.

Karyn explained, "in his book Kiyosaki explains the gulf between the rich who understand the difference between liabilities and assets, thus were prepared to take risks to make money work for them, and the middle-class, who work hard for money all their lives for a corporation or wealthy person but never became rich, and finally there were the "have-not's" who expect the government to take care of them. These are the people who think the world owes them a living, take no responsibility for their own destiny, refuse to be accountable for their decisions or well-being, and always end up with only expenses and overheads because they spend whatever they earn on stuff."

"Kiyosaki shared ten lessons, which if could be taught in schools as part of the education curriculum at every school in the world, the masses would stop blaming the rich for their bad luck, or bad judgement or risk averse strategies they employ to be safely ensconced in a fulltime job, that earns them just enough to pay the rent and barely cover their overheads with very little chance of saving."

"Essentially, it boils down to people being financially illiterate or not and treating every dollar wisely. Knowing how to read a balance sheet, understanding that everything they purchase should be an asset that is capable of appreciation or generating more revenue for them and not adding to their liabilities, like where a struggling person in the middle class borrows money to buy an expensive flashy car to show off and boast about their status in society in the early days of their life, paying off the loan and interest using taxed money. Whereas a rich person would only do that when their assets earn enough to pay all the overheads, mortgage etc, plus stash more into the assets column and if there was any excess, that is what would purchase their expensive car, out of a corporation on pre-taxed money."

"Wow, you have done your homework little miss goody two shoes," Joe said.

Joe and Karyn had talked long into the night, and both of them were exhausted. Joe yawned and said, "I think it's time we said goodnight, birthday girl."

Karyn looked at the carriage clock on the mantelpiece. "My birthday was over more than two hours ago." She smiled. "And, in spite of all the problems we are facing, I think it has been the most perfect birthday of my life." She paused, then said, grinning, "Well, except for when I was eight and was given a rabbit."

"Oh, of course," said Joe. "Being given a rabbit is yards better than having some daft beggar telling you he loves you."

Karyn punched him lightly on the shoulder. "When you're eight it is. When you're twenty-eight, I think being told by someone you love that he loves you probably beats even the rabbit – although it needs thinking about."

"Sorry," said Joe, "but even if I don't quite measure up to a rabbit, I think you're stuck with me."

Karyn gave him a dazzling smile. "Good," she said, and lifted her face for a last kiss.

CHAPTER 22

Influencing Democracy between 1921 and 1928

Over the four years from 1921 to 1924, Karyn and the Exceed team spent their time exerting influence on politicians and MPs, just as she had discussed with Joe that evening on her birthday in 1920.

The first step that would be needed to change democracy for the better was put in place when the Liberal Government under David Lloyd George, the Prime Minister in 1922, had agreed to employ more of a capitalist policy that would help to create a sustainable economy. Thus, the second plank in the Exceed strategy would be embedded by the very government that had already demonstrated their progressive and socialist tendencies for some time. This amendment to their policies would ensure that making a sustainable economic environment would be a mandatory principle of democracy, with a simple fair taxation regime that would have enabled entrepreneurship to foster in a product-based economic environment that could form the mechanism for wealth creation and distribution based on merit and self-determination, as well as deploying a socialist mechanism only for the needy or disabled.

Karyn pointed out that their past history had shown that the Labour Party had proved ineffective in handling the nation's industrial problems, as they wanted to drop anything to do with Capitalism and enforce a stronger Socialist regime with larger government and nationalised businesses which it actually could not afford to fund or even run.

Towards the end of 1924, Britain once more turned to the

Conservatives under Stanley Baldwin as Prime Minister from the 4th November elections.

Charlie pointed out that this would be where the third plank of their strategy needed to be placed. "Further mass unemployment resulted when Chancellor of the Exchequer Winston Churchill returned Britain to the gold standard in 1925. We must prevent that from happening."

The Exceed team lobbied Prime Minister Stanley Baldwin and key members of his cabinet to help them understand the errors that were made during their tenure in office according to history seen from the future.

Charlie urged caution with the Chancellor regarding his intention to return Britain to the gold standard, showing him evidence brought back from the future that was damning in its criticism of that move in the hope that Winston Churchill would seek an alternative benchmark on which to agree the conversion rate and valuation of gold.

Charlie was able to show Winston that because the gold standard conversion rate was fixed at the old pre-war gold and dollar value of the pound, if he went ahead the pound would be devalued; that would create a flight from Sterling and reduce inward investment, which would make imports of raw materials like cotton and textiles, machinery, sugar, ships, cargo rates and other goods and services involved in manufacturing or exporting British goods would become over-priced, and Britain's share of the world export market would decline rapidly. If factories produced less, they would require less coal and steel from the other industrial powerhouses, which would result in unemployment and wage cuts. This would then cause serious repercussions in the industrial areas, where strikes would become common. He presented evidence showing that iron, steel, coal, cotton and shipbuilding suffered the most, the very industries that Britain's free-trade economy relied upon to provide the bulk of the consumer and capital goods exported to provide for the large imports of food and raw materials, and that a devastating general strike would take place in 1926.

Karyn warned that the government's refusal to nationalise would be used against them by the Labour Party and the workers and, if they did not make the necessary corrections, they would see a huge drop in coal exports because of the coal industry's inability to set a national benchmark for minimum wages to be paid by the pit-owners, which would trigger troubling unrest.

In April of that year, the miners' leader, A. J. Cook would coin the phrase "not a penny off the pay, not a minute on the day."

Karyn warned, "the mine owners would refuse to compromise. A showdown would come about when the government indicated that it would not continue negotiations under the threat of a general strike. Although on the 4th of May, 1926 the great strike would go into effect, but lack of support for the unions, the use of volunteers to keep essential services going, the intransigence of the government, and the gradual wearing away of the resistance of the miners by the coal owners would eventually end the stoppage. The grievous damage would be done to the miners earning ability, because they would come out of that affair with longer hours and less pay."

The government was impressed by the accuracy of Karyn and Charlie's predictions and agreed that it would be in the interests of the country to institute a national minimum liveable wage across all facets of business.

This would turn out to be the second piece of the jigsaw that would enable democracy to be restructured in a later timeline, as the Hindsight plan intended.

By this time, Karyn had become a well renowned Professor of Political Sciences at the University of Cambridge, while Charlie had become equally well renown as Professor of Economics and Political Science, a brand-new subject, in which he was leading the charge blazing an exciting trail.

Karyn had spent significant time over the previous four years educating people in a subtle way about the advantages of a meritocracy democracy that would not be so susceptible to the whims of people's mood swings, their pet hates, or their personal prejudices. Once again during a closed debate with Prime Minister Stanley Baldwin and key members of his cabinet, Karyn painted a picture of a democracy that was much more functional and sustainable.

Prime Minister Stanley Baldwin agreed that his cabinet and

members of the shadow cabinet from both Labour and the Liberal Parties would attend a mandatory series of lectures at a secret location, where both Karyn and Charlie could enlighten them about the history of democracy and where it had gone wrong, as seen from the future.

CHAPTER 23

Democracy as you came to know it, will fail

At a secret location, hidden in the Scottish Highlands, there was a gathering of 80 key people, all selected for their influence in industry, or political status or political vocation at the time. The date was January 8th 1925.

When this was being planned, Chancellor Winston Churchill argued that they should invite the Ambassadors from the United States, Canada, France, Belgium, Holland, Switzerland, Denmark, Norway, Spain, Italy, Greece, Egypt, Morocco and Algeria. These eminent people were invited and each attended as emissaries and observers, not as participants.

This forum would be the first of a series of Global Summits, which later became known as the G8 or G20 Summits in the twentieth and twenty-first centuries. This was the very first time that sophisticated technology which had been brought back from the future would be openly and blatantly exposed to an audience of this size.

Karyn began this Global Summit by describing the subject matter.

"Democracy was essentially a mechanism conceived to enable multiple factions of society who had opposing desires to coexist in a co-operative and semi-collegiate environment. The two primary actors in a democracy are the elite and the citizens, of whom the latter were more numerous (the masses); however, this can be further broken down into sub-categories."

She went on to describe the elements that made up the actors in democracy. There was a stunned silence when the projector lit up the screen on the wall and a slide depicting the structure of democracy was seen.

Karyn talked them through what the slide showed. "As I said just now, in a democracy you have the elites, which, as you see, the slide designates as the "uber-rich" or millionaires and in our timeline billionaires, the relatively rich, which includes landed gentry, aristocracy and social elite, and the politicians in power. Then you have the citizens, or the "masses", the working-class comprising the middle-class citizen and the poorer-class citizen."

She continued, "These two primary classes of actors have social choices or desires that are pretty much in conflict with one another. That conflict can be illustrated by the rich individuals – the elite – who oppose redistributive taxation, while the poorer citizens – the masses – prefer a redistributive taxation model, which would direct resources towards them from the rich."

Charlie added, "The wealthy have for centuries used their wealth in numerous ways to attain power and, once attained, to remain in power at all costs. History has shown that they would go as far as bribing other politicians, or the military, or the media to achieve their goal." Charlie also showed them rather unflattering evidence that illustrated how the ruling class in general had colluded and connived to corrupt the political system both systemically and systematically to keep themselves and their friends at the helm and in the halls of power for centuries.

"Also," he said, "the relatively rich can then use their political power to attain more wealth, and history again has an abundance of evidence that illustrates that those in power tend to become wealthy. So, power and wealth go hand in hand."

Karyn continued. "As stated earlier, democracy has been seen as a political system wherein the supreme power of the government purportedly rested with the people, or citizens, who elected officials to represent them. Democracy was a government supposed to be "of the people for the people", which, stunningly, was based on a mere popularity contest or size of someone's wallet."

"Democracy could be deemed to be a system with a methodology that enables political equality, which was designed to placate the masses and to look after their interests, while inversely, non-democracy was a mechanism that was designed to protect the interests of the elite and the privileged, all the while keeping the masses under control, where most of their policies created a distributional conflict. This is how your form of democracy ends up, corrupted."

At this point, there were several guffaws and wheezes coming from the audience.

Charlie interjected and said, "I see some of you are uncomfortable with this description!"

He continued and said, "For democracy to work effectively, a balance needs to be found between the two polarised ends; the poorer masses at one end and the wealthy elite at the other end. The poorer masses desire distributive policies that offer security, fairness and more income choices, whereas the wealthy elite demand wealth protection and non-distributive policies. Therein lays the challenge for any government, finding a solution that makes both sides of that equation happy."

He paused, letting the silence stretch out for several seconds, then said, "Can anyone in the audience who disagrees with this last statement stand up and let us hear your rebuttal?"

There was silence . . . not a murmur came from the crowd, only the shuffling of feet and the rustle of starched collars.

Karyn stepped back up to the podium and thanked the audience for allowing them to continue in a dignified manner and said,

"Unfortunately, history shows us that democracy could easily be corrupted. It was supposed to be one vote per person, but again, as historical evidence we will show you clearly demonstrates, on numerous occasions the voice of some can be heard more loudly because of media bias and, in some cases, those who had resources at their disposal could influence through other types of persuasion, such as bribery and lobbying of other politicians."

"As time marches on, the more political power a group has, the more they benefit from government policies and actions and the more corrupt they become."

Karyn explained, "These power-hungry elites managed to

systematically corrupt and subvert democracy for their own agenda. The *Daily Mail* newspaper reported that over 27,000 charities in the United Kingdom only survived because 75% of their funding came from taxpayers' cash. This information was taken from a report authored by Christopher Snowdon in 2012. The report said government departments should be banned from using public money for advertising campaigns and called for the abolition of unrestricted grants to charities. "Government funding of politically active charities, non-governmental organisations and pressure groups is objectionable", his study said.

"Firstly, it subverts democracy and debases the concept of charity.

"Secondly, it is an unnecessary and wasteful use of taxpayers' money."

"Thirdly, by funding like-minded organisations and ignoring others, genuine civil society is cold-shouldered in the political process."

She then explained "during the 21ˢᵗ century, The Institute of Economic Affairs said that charities such as the School Food Trust – created by the Department of Education following celebrity chef Jamie Oliver's school dinner's campaign – act as "special advisers to the Government and essentially became part of the government machine and bureaucracy.""

Karyn went on, "Between 1997 and 2005, the combined income of Britain's charities nearly doubled, from £19.8 billion to £37.9 billion, with the biggest growth coming in grants and contracts from Whitehall ministries."

The report added: "The political elite had an incentive to transmit their message to the public via third parties because voters regard almost anyone as being *more* trustworthy than politicians."

"In many instances, it becomes difficult to see what services the charity provides beyond policy development, lobbying and enforcement on behalf of the political elite and government, which feels distinctly like a form of dictatorship forcing its terms and conditions on the masses.

"In some respects, a corrupted democracy is much like a dictatorship; certain policies that were designed to protect those in power were put in by brute force instead of persuasion, such as political negotiation and consensus."

At this point, Charlie stepped forward and asked for the lights to be dimmed some more and asked Karyn if she would allow him to show them some material that would illustrate the points made earlier. She nodded.

He clicked on a media icon, which in modern days would have been presented on an iPad or desktop of either a Windows or Apple Mac personal computer, but to this audience it was simply a magic device.

Suddenly, a news bulletin flashed up, showing filmed barbarities imposed on the masses by a dictator who, in their future, did not implement any form of democracy that was acceptable.

The audience's absolute astonishment and initial terror at what they saw was predictable. It was not the content; it was the clarity of full colour video streaming on to their wall. The room erupted with a blast of excited questioning and shouts such as "What kind of witchcraft is this?"

Charlie asked them to settle down and watch the documentary film to understand the point being made by the presenter.

The presenter from their future on what was then a modern-day satellite news channel, Glenn Beck, said, "The primary reason for the democracy collapsing in Zimbabwe was because of failed economics that could not sustain the masses, and the extensive corruption practised by those in power. One can see this by President Robert Mugabe's refusal to step down in 2007, when the then opposition party leader Morgan Tsvangerai won the Zimbabwean elections outright. It was the economic disaster that Mugabe induced by financial distributive policies which caused Zimbabwe's economy to collapse, which ultimately forced the masses to protest. This unrest caused President Mugabe to lose the election, but he simply chose to ignored the result."

This refusal to hand over power to the successor was mirrored in the Ivory Coast in late 2010 and again in Tunisia and Egypt in 2011."

Glenn Beck continued by warning that a succession of rallies and demonstrations would occur in the Middle East, in countries such as Egypt, Jordan, Yemen and Algeria, all of which would be inspired directly by the popular outpouring of anger that toppled Tunisian President Zine al-Abidine Ben Ali. A period of political unrest, which he predicted would lead to a caliphate that would spread disaster right across the middle east in the early 21st century.

The news bulletins showed clips of mass protests that evolved into riots and eventually the overthrowing of dictators or political systems that did not implement a fair and equitable form of democracy.

The map below illustrates just how widespread the unrest was in the Middle-East at that time.

Widespread Unrest Across the Middle-East 2010 - 2012

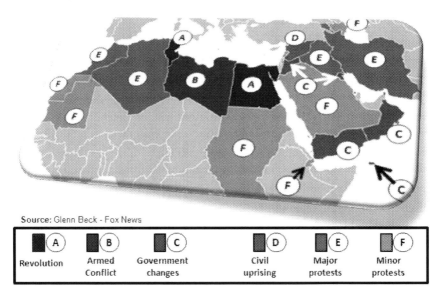

Source: Glenn Beck - Fox News

■ A	■ B	▨ C	▨ D	■ E	▨ F
Revolution	Armed Conflict	Government changes	Civil uprising	Major protests	Minor protests

In Algeria, for instance, riots over rising food prices and chronic unemployment spiralled out from Algeria's capital on January 6th 2011, with youths torching government buildings, shouting "Bring us sugar!" And six days later in the Lebanon, the militant political group Hezbollah and its allies forced the collapse of Lebanon's government, dealing a blow to Washington in the US's battle with Iran and Syria for influence in the Middle-East. Eleven ministers from Hezbollah and their allies pulled out of a thirty-member coalition cabinet after Prime Minister Saad Hariri refused to discredit a United Nations-backed court investigating the 2005 assassination of his father, former Prime Minister Rafik Hariri.

A couple of weeks after that, in Tunisia, the government issued an international arrest warrant for Mr. Ben Ali, the ousted president, and six relatives, accusing him of taking money out of the country illegally, and in the Palestinian territories thousands of Hamas supporters were shown protesting in different locations across the Hamas-ruled Gaza strip. They were protesting against Mr. Abbas and his government in the West Bank, the Western-backed Palestinian Authority, meanwhile in the West Bank city of Ramallah, the seat of the Palestinian Authority, several hundred people were rallying in support of Mr. Abbas.

On January 30, 2011 in Sudan, student protesters calling for the ousting of President Omar al-Bashir clashed with police. The protest coincided with the announcement of preliminary referendum results: south Sudanese voters chose to secede from the north, and ten days later in Jordan leaders of Jordan's Islamic opposition called for a mass demonstration under the slogan "The Solution is by Dissolution" and demanding that the country's monarch dismiss Parliament and call new elections later in the year.

All of that paled almost into insignificance in comparison with the so-called Lotus Revolution in Egypt. On February 11, 2011 Egyptian Vice President Suleiman announced that President Mubarak was stepping down and delegating Egypt's affairs to the army.

The masses in both Tunisia and Egypt had tired of dynastic fiefdoms or having rulers who inherited their power because of birth or class. The mass demonstrations in both countries unseated the then "dictators" and replaced them with a form of democracy. Also, in February 2011, there was damning evidence uncovered that showed that the then Prime Minister Hosni Mubarak had allegedly swindled Egypt out of $70 billion. That was yet another nail in the coffin for corrupt leaders in politics.

Protests in Syria started on 26 January 2011 and were influenced by other protests in the region; on the same day, one case of self-immolation was reported. Protesters were calling for political reforms and the reinstatement of civil rights, as well as an end to the state of emergency which had been in place since 1963.

On 15 April, tens of thousands of protesters turned up, with reportedly 50,000 trying to get into Damascus alone. Al-Assad, Syria's president, responded by saying that emergency law would be lifted, an action that was officially completed on 21 April.

Lifting the emergency law failed to quell the protesters, as on 22 April Syria experienced its biggest and bloodiest uprising, with tens of thousands taking to the streets, and reportedly 100 people killed. On 23 April, funerals for the fallen protesters were held throughout Syria, but snipers were reported killing people at the funeral processions. Later that night, security forces raided homes and arrested activists, with more than 200 people reportedly arrested over the following two days.

These protests and unrest in Syria lasted for years, and eventually culminated in a bloody civil war ignited and orchestrated by the reigning monarch and government as a way of pointing the blame elsewhere.

On 25 April, tanks, soldiers and snipers were deployed to Daraa, reportedly killing twenty-five people. Water, power and phone lines were cut, and the border with Jordan was closed.

In Libya, anti-government protests began on 15 February 2011. By 18 February, the opposition controlled most of Benghazi, the country's second-largest city. The government despatched elite troops and mercenaries in an attempt to recapture it, but they were repelled. It was estimated that at least 6,000 had been killed up to that point.

The UN Security Council resolution 1973 (2011), which referred to the "Libyan No Fly Zone" was agreed on Thursday 17 March 2011. The Security Council referred to the previous resolution 1970 (2011) of 26 February 2011, deploring the failure of the Libyan authorities to comply with resolution 1970 (2011). The UN Security Council expressed grave concern at the deteriorating situation, the escalation of violence, and the heavy civilian casualties, iterating the responsibility of the Libyan authorities to protect the Libyan population and to take all feasible steps to ensure the protection of civilians.

The UN Security Council went as far as condemning the gross and systematic violation of human rights, including arbitrary detentions, enforced disappearances, torture and summary executions.

All of these examples of massive unrest were explained by Glenn Beck of the Fox News channel as a sinister plot being played out by the Communists, Socialists and the Muslim Brotherhood to create chaos and overthrow those governments that were dictatorships or dynasties or governments that were puppets of America.

The documentary went on to show a clip of another program with Glenn Beck during 2010 and 2011, in which he had been talking about the dangers of multiculturalism.

The presenter in the clip shown by Glenn Beck said, "*. . . by then the world leaders were starting to agree with people who had earlier postulated that globalisation and the fostering of multiculturalism in society was a powder keg ready to explode. Instead of having a melting pot, there has been a growing belief that countries and societies should allow segregated groups to flourish with values that run opposite the values and cultures within a single country like America or the United Kingdom.*"

Charlie paused the video and said, "These western countries had slowly come to the same conclusion that their liberal policies of multiculturalism were an utter failure, which was further exacerbating the anger abroad in the Middle East against the West.

"Now listen to what leaders of some of the European countries had to say about the results of a poor implementation of democracy and some of the strategies they employed to guarantee them votes in future elections."

He pressed play on the video, explaining as he did so, "The woman you are about to see is Angela Merkel, the German Chancellor, who, in October 2010 said this: *We are a country which at the beginning of the 1960s actually brought guest workers to Germany. Now they live with us and we lied to ourselves for a while, saying that they won't stay and that they will disappear one day. That is not the reality: this multicultural approach saying that we live side by side and that we are happy about each other – this approach has failed. Multiculturalism is an utter failure.*"

Charlie paused the video again, saying before he restarted it, "And this is David Cameron, Prime Minister of Britain, speaking on February 5th 2011."

The audience was utterly silent, listening to every word, awed by the technology that was allowing them to see these images from the future.

They heard David Cameron say, *"Under the doctrine of state multiculturalism, we've encouraged different cultures to live separate lives apart from each other and apart from the mainstream . . . we failed to provide a vision of society to which they feel they want to belong. We've even tolerated these segregated communities communicating in ways that run completely counter to our values."*

Following that, they watched Nicolas Sarkozy, the French President, speaking on French television on February 10, 2011, when he said, *"We have been too concerned about the identity of the person who was arriving and not enough about the identity of the country that was receiving him. My answer is clearly yes, it is a failure."*

According to Glenn Beck, *"this was only part one of a three-step process these countries would embark on the road to their democracy."* He asked people to be on their guard as stage two was where *"socialism was going to make its play and the insurrection was going to get ugly."*

Charlie turned off the video, and stood looking out into the room, which was blanketed in a stunned silence. Never before had anyone experienced such quietness in a room in which so many important people had gathered.

You could hear a pin drop.

There were looks of utter incredulity, disbelief, exhilaration, sadness and some looks of sheer horror.

Karyn stepped up to the podium once again and gazed in some consternation at a room that was filled with smoke, with sunlight filtering through cracks in the curtains highlighting the grey billows of tobacco smoke and illuminating pictures on the walls.

Coughing a little, she said, "What we have just shown you - is but the tip of the iceberg. We have only just begun to start illustrating the outcome and impact of poorly implemented democracy or totalitarian governments.

"Sadly, history showed that the masses you saw protesting in those news clips had in some cases merely swapped one form of dictatorship for another form of dictatorship, albeit under the guise of a people's democracy. They did not have the gift of hindsight and a fully rounded Positics Constitution."

She and Charlie then described the riots in the United Kingdom during August of 2011. This highlighted deeper troubles to come as a result of the liberalisation and globalisation policies of the previous years.

They showed the audience video footage of how these policies had influenced at least three generations of people, some of whom did not have the benefit of a conventional upbringing because many came from broken or single-parent families. It was postulated by historians this often meant that they lacked structure, discipline, comprehension of boundaries, did not know right from wrong and were of the entitlement culture in society, where they were led to believe the State had an obligation to provide for them and that they had these inherent rights endowed upon them. Many of them wasted their opportunity of free education, instead choosing to adopt gangs as their family, intimidating, bullying, knifing and robbing people. They also had no respect for those around them, or their property and more importantly, they disrespected authority, the police, and were a recipe for an impending disaster.

History would show that this breakdown in society was largely down to the breakdown of conventional family life together with poor and ill-advised lax parenting advised in the book *The Common-Sense Book of Baby and Child Care* written by Dr. Benjamin Spock, a catastrophe he would later apologise to the world for causing.

Some said the UK riots were a free-for-all and those people who participated were plainly and simply criminals, who showed disrespect for the government, the police, their neighbours, their community, their fellow human beings and people's property.

Karyn explained that the riots underwent three phases. The initial spark that kicked this off was a small group of people who genuinely thought they were protesting about the killing of a coloured man, a Mr. Duggan, known by the police as a drug dealer. Unfortunately, this group decided to protest even though they did not have the real facts or any direct personal knowledge of what happened or how those events unfolded. Elements of this riot may have been legitimate for a very short while. That would not last long, as all hell was about to break loose as the criminal element decided to take advantage of the weak UK policies, a police force who were terrified of restraining them due to previous castigation they received from the media after the "Rise in the Cost of Education" riots earlier in 2011.

Then the gangs and independent criminals who had absolutely no respect for people's property or the laws of the country waded in, seeing an opportunity to milk the weak UK liberal system and exploit the ineffective legal system and policies that had been engendered over the past fifty years. In the early stages of this event these people were predominantly people of colour. The footage from the TV channels showed this to be the case for the first eighteen hours at least as the lack of any Police action caused thousands of other opportunistic citizens to jump into the furore and exploit the havoc as they had witnessed in the previous 18 hours.

Finally, the opportunists joined the ranks of rioters. These were the latecomers who saw that the Police were simply standing around for the first day and were not taking any action against the criminal element. So, the "unwashed, poorly brought up, values-challenged" people of all races and walks of life decided to jump on the bandwagon and fill their pockets with goods looted from shops and businesses.

"Sadly," explained Charlie, "as history has shown us, the first two contingents got away with their crimes as the Police stood-by for two days simply observing. It was only when the "Opportunists" jumped in that the police reacted and started arresting people. The irony of the whole sordid affair was that the Politicians, Police and pressure groups were all in denial and politicised the riots to score points and overlooked the root cause of these riots."

He concluded by saying, "I know that the technology that has allowed us to show you these things is pretty amazing to you, some of it will only be available in fifty years' time. We know that your scientists will be working very hard to engineer some of the most marvellous inventions known to mankind. Even in the lifetime of some of you older folks, you will witness both the horror and the blessing of mankind's ingenuity.

"Today, you have the blessing of being given the gift of both hindsight and foresight. How you use it remains to be seen, but the future we have witnessed, which resulted from the current road you are following, will eventually end up in the devastation of the world as you know it and the total destruction of mankind. We know — we were there to witness the full horror."

The audience remained frozen in their stupefied silence for several moments, and then, slowly at first but building quickly, they began to applaud.

Karyn smiled, and then held up her hand. "We'll see you at dinner this evening, where we will continue," she said.

CHAPTER 24

Positics Constitution – Fair and Balanced

At dinner that evening, Karyn opened up proceedings by saying, "Your own history that we have witnessed evidences that the various versions of democracy mankind had deployed had failed in our past for the reasons cited earlier. So now, with our hindsight as your foresight, how are you going to be remembered in the re-writing of your history?

"We can recommend to you that for a democracy to be successful it would need the following elements to be implemented as part of your ongoing policies if you really want to succeed. The question is whether you have the courage to be bold and have the where-with-all to implement this?"

Charlie switched on the projector once more and the slides he showed, detailed various aspects of the Positics Democracy Constitution.

1   Guaranteed personal identification: To ensure the individual's ability to vote and ensure any vote count is not corrupted. Individual identity facilities need to guarantee absolute identification. (ie. Identification documents with Photo and Finger print, in addition they should implement Bio-metric security such as Iris recognition etc.…. when that technology becomes available.)

2   One person, one vote: Democracy should be based on one person, one vote, irrespective of race, religion, creed or gender,

and should be given to anyone older than eighteen years of age who can prove they are a citizen of that country;

a. Voting eligibility: citizens would have to earn and qualify their right to vote by participating in a series of debates or online subject matter induction seminars financed by the government in concert with an independent political media channel, on a neutral basis articulating without bias the policies of the various parties. A citizen's participation should earn them credits, which give them the merits required for their votes to be incorporated in either the lower or middle house or both house elections.

b. There should be a simple but secure dual mechanical and electronic voting system and, when the technology becomes available, which included an internet electronic voting system that can qualify one's ability to vote based on the merits earned for participation – essentially an integrated system to enable voters to qualify for the eligibility to vote. This would necessitate that proper security and identification was implemented to avoid identity fraud and corruption at the polling stations or web servers.

3 Mandatory voting: If the government is unable to institute a law that makes it mandatory to register and mandatory to vote in every election, then they need to consider the following;

a. There should be a modification made to the older / legacy voting mechanisms. They need to introduce a hybrid of both the "first past the post" (FPtP) and the "alternative vote" (AV) systems so that a candidate or party has to secure more than 50% of the qualified votes to declare a victory.

b. While both FPtP and AV systems individually have merits, both will be deemed flawed, unlike the combination of the two FPtP and AV, a hybrid enforces only qualified choices to be selected by the voter and is not a flawed vote collection mechanism. The FPtP–AV Hybrid, called the "Positics voting system", enables a voter to have their vote whilst rating the next four alternative candidates, where a score of 5 is inserted against their first choice, a score of 4 inserted against their second choice, a score of 3 inserted against their third choice and so on. This is a more balanced mechanism that reflects the voters' selection by weighting/ rating their choices, which when toted against the whole electorate the true choices for first and second place with weightings can be taken into account.

c. This hybrid suits both the FPtP and AV mechanisms and does not force anyone to have to choose a third-rate candidate if they do not want to.

4 Sustainable economic system: So that democracy can be fair and equitable to all quarters of society, the government must foster a sustainable and viable economic system in the private sector, independent of the government, which needs to be maintained in that country;

a. The government should reduce red tape / bureaucracy for small businesses, making it easier for them to operate and employ staff;

b. Tax incentives should be given to new start-up businesses for the first three years while they establish themselves;

c. Banks should be incentivised to lend to these start-up businesses, backed by government guarantees so that innovation and entrepreneurial potential can be realised;

d. A 5% portion of the profits from larger corporations should be pooled into a national business and skills education / apprenticeship fund that should be independently managed as a trust on behalf of the government. These funds should also be used for both innovation grants and small business loans.

5   Merit and integrity-based democracy: The political system should be based on a *system of qualification and merit* not birth right, wealth or class status. This would mean that people who were eligible for seats in government had to be properly qualified and able to do the job competently. These roles should be properly paid for, and salaries should be commensurate with the private sector for an equivalent job:

a.   To foster an air of unequivocal trust, there would have to be complete transparency with all payments, expenses, favours, paid assignments, industry directorships or associations and monies given to the politicians.

b.   Corruption in politics should not be tolerated and long jail terms in a hard-labour prison should be the mandatory sentence for politicians or dictators who abuse their positions of power.

c.   The Government should prevent the onerous situation of becoming bloated and overly cumbersome "Big Government" and should be subject to private commercial entities bidding to undertake the same functions of service on a contractual basis to ensure a competitive market rate is paid for the service. This means that;

   i.   No political party in power shall create Government jobs for sake of removing Citizens off the unemployment register to obfuscate their poor handling of the economy.

   ii. No "quasi" Government departments can be setup to employ people for nefarious undertakings as a means of creating employment or unnecessary bureaucracy.

   iii. Governments should always look to small enterprise to fulfil government contracts before looking to large enterprise and should at no point in time have more than 50% of any contracts for government work handed to large corporations.

d. To prevent the globalisation failures experienced in the 21st century, no Government contracts should be given to non-domestic companies or corporations, especially where the majority share in any corporation in held by foreign investors.

6 Balance between the Left, Middle and Right: All political systems in each country should have at least three parties as a minimum. If a new party wants to be recognised, they would need to acquire a minimum of 100,000 supporters in that country to sign up to their party, thus enabling them to become a recognised and funded part of the system. A forum should be made available for the introduction of new parties into the fold; this mechanism should be run every two years, midway between national elections. No election funding should be allocated to a party unless they are certified.

7 Maintaining political and operational continuity: So that both continuity and consistency can be maintained in a balanced and fair way, each political system should have a three-tiered political system with the following structure;

a. The Top House (i.e., House of Lords or Senate) that would own the country's 25 to 100-year plan and deal with matters of strategic and global importance, such as national security, oversight of the law of the land, integrity of the nation, and integrity of the political system. This house would be the custodian of the country's strategy, business plan and mission. These should be voted in positions by way of elections.

b. The Middle House (i.e., Parliament or Congress) would own and have to deliver on the ten-year and twenty-five-year plan, which would cover items of national importance such as the policies on national health, social welfare, Ministry of Defence, national transport, national infrastructure, crime and policing, and defining the law of the land. This house could not in isolation make a radical change on a national basis that would impair the integrity of the nation, which is overseen by the Top House. This is where items that are of national significance would be decided on and delegated to the lower house for implementation. In addition, the middle-house will have specific powers, including the power to establish and maintain an army and navy, to establish post offices, national water, energy and transport services, to create courts, to regulate commerce between counties or states, to declare war, and to raise money. These should be voted in positions by way of elections.

c. The Lower House would own local government in County, District or Town Councils in the areas where people actually lived. This is the house where things would be implemented at a local level on a five-year and ten-year plan. These should be voted in positions by way of elections.

d. The houses described above, (i.e. Parliament, or Congress, or Senate or House of Lords) must have a minimum number of members present in order to meet, they should meet no less than five times per month, and penalties/fines must be levied on members who do not show up more than twice in a row. Also, members may be expelled for persistent non-compliance or dereliction of duties, and that each house must keep a journal to record proceedings and votes, and that neither house can create new holidays and adjourn without the permission of the other houses.

8 To ensure democratic integrity: Integrity must be engineered and qualified throughout the process so that there can be no career politicians, cronyism, political dynasties or any form of political corruption; there should be severe penalties for any politicians found to be corrupt and there should be limits on duration served by any person of any political party or legislative house. So, for each of the following:

a. Heads of State: There should be a maximum of two terms of four/five years for any leader, prime minister, president (eight/ten years in total);

    i. The Head of State should be over the age of 40 years minimum to be electable for office,

    ii. The Head of State must also be a natural-born citizen of the country.

    iii. The Head of State should be paid a salary larger than those paid to elected politicians, which cannot change, up or down, as long as he or she is in office unless authorised by the Middle House.

    iv. The Head of State can make treaties with other nations, and nominate many of the judges and other members of the government (all with the approval of the Top and Middle-Houses);

b. The Top House (ie. House of Lords or Senate): There should be a maximum of three terms of four/five years for Lords or Senators (twelve/fifteen years in total); a Lord or Senator should not be able to enter the Top House unless they have served a minimum of two terms in either of the two lower houses. There should be no hereditary positions, or "gifting" of a seat for favours rendered, or by good fortune of birth into a royal, gentrified or wealthy family. The minimum age to enter this house should be 35 years of age;

c. The Middle House (ie. House of Parliament/Commons or Congress): There should be a maximum of three terms of four/five years for politicians (a total of twelve/fifteen years); The minimum age to enter this house should be 30 years old;

d. The Lower House (ie. County or Town Councils): There should be a maximum of three terms of four/five years for politicians (twelve/fifteen years in total, no more career politicians). The minimum age to enter this house should be 25 years of age;

e. Compensation and Remuneration for members of each of the respective Houses, should be administered independently and their packages should be set by an independent body that has people from the following four sectors in society on the remuneration board;

  i. Government (one person from four sectors);
  ii. Private Commercial sectors (One person from six sectors);
  iii. Politicians (two persons from each house);
  iv. Members of the Public (sixteen persons from various walks of life).

9   Zero tolerance on crime and corruption: The Middle House in each system should implement policies that would dictate the following for all walks of society, including those in the political houses.

a. So that victims of crime are not unduly stressed, there would need to be a policy and law instantiated that forfeits a criminal's human rights if he or she commits a crime that is of any grievous nature against another person. The perpetrator of said crime should be aware that in committing this crime they will forfeit their human rights as soon as they begin to commit the crime.

b. Habitual criminality should be deterred by the implementation of a "three (3) strikes and you are out" policy, where criminals who are convicted three times for serious crimes they have committed, they are sent to prison for a life of hard labour and servitude in a penal system that is geared to manufacture goods that serves the community or populace.

c. Convicted criminals in prison should lose their ability to vote while they are incarcerated.

d. All prisons would have to create a regime of working to pay for their living and for those who resist, there should be hard labour, with no prisoner lazing about watching TV, eating three square meals a day, as it was under the liberalised progressive world of the old.

10 Zero tolerance on arms sales: The Top House of each country would have to work with other countries to ensure that the sales of arms and artefacts of warfare would be outlawed across the globe. Any nation caught selling arms to other nations, especially chemical weapons would be fined billions and be subject to sanctions from the rest of the global community, and ALL Ministers overseeing this industry when the law is transgressed, should be incarcerated for a minimum of ten years hard labour. No exceptions!

11 Funding of political election campaigns: All national elections would be funded out of a central government administered fund, created from the taxpayer's pool; no additional funds should be raised or spent by the political parties or individuals on any campaign. It is essential that elections should not be about the size of campaign funding or celebrity status or popularity. This central funding mechanism would ensure that people at the poorer end of society would have a shot at goal, especially if they qualify by merit:

a. The media should offer balanced and objective material when they make commentary for respective candidates or political parties standing for elections;

b. The media should also offer equal column space / airtime and position for any editorial to each of the parties during the election phase or contest period. Failure to do so should result in heavy fines totally up to ten times their sales for that month.

c. Advertorial or adverts paid for by the fund should be equal in cost per centimetre of copy or number of seconds/ minutes of airtime for all parties or candidates;

d. Breaches of this protocol should be severely dealt with by imprisoning offenders' throughput the chain of command within the media organisation.

e. To avoid cronyism and/or buying favours for votes, any funds submitted / donated by corporations or lobbying groups would be added to the central pool and distributed equally amongst all the participating certified parties.

12 Zero tolerance on media corruption: Each country's media policy should be implemented governing all channels (all internet media & channels, newspapers, magazines, TV/radio channels and any form of advertisement / advertorial media etc.) so that a media organisation can no longer have a single political bias. This should not be a curbing of freedom of speech, but a way to ensure that mankind does not have its politics corrupted by the "Uber-rich" or Progressive "do-gooders" who might happen to own these corporations.

a. The press/media have to be objective and neutral. For example, they should be left-wing or right-wing agnostic. Controls need to be implemented to ensure this is correctly administered; they need to employ an equal number of journalists from the left, middle and right side of the political divide. Funding for editorial initiatives or Programs should be equally spread so that each segment has parity between them.

b. During an election period, the media should print the equivalent wordage/space per party – that is, if they write up a three-page article on a subject dear to the socialist or "left" end of the scale, they have to do likewise for subjects dear to the middle and the conservative "right" end of the spectrum. In other words, the articles should have at least three participants debating the pros and cons of the topic.

c. Neutrality should be measured and monitored, especially during an election period, the media should remain objective and party agnostic: by law, whenever there is a debate or commentary on a political subject, the media should have to field at least three commentators, one each from the left, middle and right side of the political divide as an absolute minimum, or if there were more than three parties, one per party should be represented.

d. The media should not offer their considered opinion, it should report the facts or views of those being interviewed. Failure by media groups to be fair and balanced in their commentary should result in heavy punitive fines and closure of their business after the third transgression, with jail sentences for all the owners and managers of the media organisation.

e. Punitive damages for misbehaviour of the press: large fines should be imposed on any media company that disparages people and destroys their lives in the press for sensationalism, only to find that they were after all innocent. In addition to large fines and punitive damages being paid to the "victim" of their vexatious campaign, in these cases (there were too many annually to cite examples), the exact amount of wordage and exposure that was expended in their disparaging exposé against the individual needs to be used in rehabilitating the victim's reputation by the same media entities and with as high a profile and priority that they used in their sensationalising denigrating reports.

13 The rights of the citizen: All citizens should be equal in the eyes of the government and the laws of the country, irrespective of religion, race, gender or sexual-orientation:

a. All citizens should have the right to express freedom of speech and the right to protest in a peaceful non-violent manner as part of organised protests, without the fear of being intimidated or abused by officials of the state or government.

b. No person shall be deprived of life, liberty, or property, without due process of law, or equal protection of the laws if within the jurisdiction of any country.

c. All citizens should have basic human rights, which can only be forfeited if they commit any grievous crime against another person or sentient being.

d. Due to the over population of the planet and the ravaging / depletion of earth's resources, all citizens should have the right to have children if they can afford to bring them up and care appropriately for those children. No longer should there be children born without thinking about whether, as a parent, one can manage the financial consequences of raising that child in a loving home, without having to rely on State Welfare to support their lifestyle

e. All citizens should have the right to privacy and the government or media should be prohibited from publishing confidential material or personal data that are known to be private.

f. All citizens should have the right to security and should be able to rely on the state / government to implement and run a tough but fair judicial system that would ensure they were not victims of crime both in the physical world and cyber world.

g. No person should be held to answer for a capital, or otherwise infamous crime, unless on a presentment or indictment of a Grand Jury, except in cases arising in the land or naval forces, or in the Militia, when in actual service in time of War or public danger;

      i.   nor should any person be subject for the same offence to be twice put in jeopardy of life or limb (Double jeopardy);

      ii. nor should be compelled in any criminal case to be a witness against himself or the spouse thereof be forced to be a witness against their spouse;

h. All citizens should be protected from all aspects of the Government, (including entities such as Police, Secret Service, Military, Customs and Excise, Inland Revenue and Home Guard) improperly taking property, papers, or people, without a valid warrant based on probable cause (good reason), *unless subject to forfeiture.*

i. The Government guarantees that all citizens;

      i.   should have a speedy trial, an impartial jury, that the accused can confront witnesses against them in court, and that the accused must be allowed to have a lawyer.

      ii. may have other rights aside from those listed that may exist, and just because they are not listed doesn't mean they can be violated, with exception of those which are subject to forfeit because of a grievous crime against another being.

j. All citizens should be protected by the government from slavery, servitude and forced labour, with exception where labour is;

      i.   done as a normal part of legal imprisonment,

      ii. in the form of compulsory military service or work done as an alternative by conscientious objectors,

      iii. required to be done during a state of emergency, and

      iv. considered to be a part of a person's normal "civic obligations."

k. All citizens shall be protected by the government from the retrospective criminalisation of acts and omissions. No person may be retrospectively punished for an act that was not a criminal offence at the time of its commission;

   i. Includes where a criminal offence is one under either national or international law, which would permit a party to prosecute someone for a crime which was not illegal under their domestic law at the time, so long as it was prohibited by international law.

   ii. Also prohibits a heavier penalty being imposed later in time than was applicable at the time when the criminal act was committed.

l. All citizens shall have the right to protect by whatever force or means necessary; their property, both themselves their families and their pets if their house is entered into or invaded by a person or persons illegally without a warrant or not attended by the law who announce and evidence themselves prior to gaining permission to enter. In the event of an illegal invasion, the householder should not be fearful of prosecution as this would be deemed self-defence and the perpetrator would knowingly forfeit all their human rights in committing the crime.

14 Equal respect of all religious practices: All citizens should have the right to practise any religion and the governments of the respective countries should ensure this freedom is respected and citizens are not persecuted because of their beliefs.

a. Separation of religion and government: These two should remain separate, and no country should be governed by a religious body, as this has proven to be a recipe for immediate discrimination;

b. All governments must foster an environment of religious tolerance by having a mandatory minimum of one to two hours a week religious education across all faiths on an equal basis in all of the schools within that country. This includes appropriate lessons for agnostics and atheists.

15 Fair taxation: The governments should implement a fair taxation regime:

a. By taxing those who prospered in such a way that is deemed fair and equitable;
b. By making the initial threshold totally tax free to protect the frail/disabled and poor from taxation, for example the first $12,000 annual earnings per individual should be tax free;
c. To further support the poor, or lower salary earners in society, the governments should seek to introduce a taxation stairway that taxes earnings between thresholds. For example, a possible system could be tiered in a graduated scale structure as follows:

i.   Between $1 and $12,000 at 0% (Zero Tax)
ii.   Between $12,001 and $50,000 at W%
iii. Between $50,001 and $100,000 at X%
iv.   Between $100, 001 and $250,000 at Y%
v.   Any income of $250,001 and above at Z%

d. The governments should seek to introduce incentives for those more fortunate and wealthier in society to receive tax rebates, based on their investment back into society, whereby businesses could create work and entrepreneurial prosperity for all citizens, all of which would result in creating a viable and sustainable economy based on capitalism with corruption mitigation protocols.

16 Education and Health: Both education and health should be primary concerns of all governments and it should be written into law that citizens have access to both services especially if they are too poor (i.e. unemployed or earning less than $50,000 per annum.) to pay for these services.

    a. Also, it should be made into law that a system offering private healthcare should be allowed to run in parallel with any government system, such as the National Health Service (NHS) in the United Kingdom or the equivalent in any other country.

    b. Private healthcare and the government version of healthcare should be in competition with each other to ensure price competitiveness.

    c. For those people or corporations who acquire private healthcare, they should receive a tax rebate of at least 50% percentage of what they contribute towards the government healthcare program in compensation for using a non-government facility.

17 Prevention of corporate or government corruption. It should be put into law that if a Bank, Corporation or any Government department, including the Police or Army or a Charity, commit any crime of fraud that steals or defrauds money from citizens for their own benefit, not only should the culprits who perpetrated the crime be punished, so should the Directors, Chief Executive Officers and Chairman of that organisation be punished to the full extent of the law with penalties that include both incarceration with hard labour along with very hefty fines.

18 Immigration and Migration: In recognition of those people who are prepared to work for a living, are not undertaking criminal activities and do not choose to live off welfare and receive benefits from their hosting country, all countries should look to all implement equal immigration laws that should be

put into law that stipulate the same terms and conditions of how one becomes a legal immigrant if they choose to move to another country, what social services they can or cannot expect in the first four or five years of their arrival, and what contributions over what period need to be made into the system before being able to apply for social services,

a. This includes the introduction of strict border controls for both people and goods including animals of any type;

b. All immigration solutions should employ a points-based system, where merit, qualifications and criminal free records are key considerations of acceptance.

c. In those unfortunate cases where immigrants abuse the laws of the host country and where they are found guilty of crimes committed within the Naturalisation Visa period, those individuals would be repatriated / deported to their home country or last country where they had previous legal status.

Charlie wrapped up the slide show with a simple comment, "In the interests of creating a harmonious, fair and balanced society that should not be too challenging to implement now, should it?"

When the lights came on, Karyn approached the podium and peered enquiringly through the smoke-filled room at Stanley Baldwin, then said, "Mr Prime Minister, you have been given the benefit of our hindsight, which today you are fortunate to be able to use as your foresight. Hopefully, you and the esteemed leaders of all the great countries here today will employ and implement this wisely to prevent mankind making the very same mistakes that destroyed the world in the future we came from."

Charlie added, "The time for petty bickering between political parties, the elite, the aristocracy and the middle and poorer classes is over. Today you have been given the gift of a constitution based on fair principles that will change the way mankind makes and writes history from this day forward. The only thing that should be important from today is that each and every one of you owe it to your families and their children's children and their children's children to find a way to implement this constitution in all countries around the world and be sure to foster religious harmony and a civilised society that does not destroy mother earth as we have witnessed and suffered the consequences of in our era."

The room erupted into a deafening racket of loud questioning voices.

Both Karyn and Charlie were overwhelmed by the massive rush of questions and a common thirst among the guests to hear more of what the future had in store for them.

They were totally exhausted by what had been a very long day indeed, but quietly satisfied by the response they were getting. They were beginning to feel truly hopeful for the success of their mission.

CHAPTER 25

Finally – Integrity based Democracy in Society

Before the Global Summit of January 1925 took place, the history books showed that under the Conservative government of Stanley Baldwin, only a modest program of social reform took place, mainly to appease working class opinion. For example, The Widows, Orphans and Old Age Health Contributory Pension schemes extended the Act of 1911 and insured over twenty million people. In 1928, the Equal Franchise Act gave the parliamentary vote to all women over twenty-one. Under Health Minister Neville Chamberlain, the Local Government Act of 1929 reduced the number of local government authorities and extended the services they provided.

That said, there was still a lack of a coherent policy to deal with the relief of unemployment. Following the election of a Labour government, just as they came to power in 1929, it was the beginning of a world-wide depression triggered by the Wall Street Crash, but like the Conservative government before it, could do little to remedy the situation at home.

However, the Exceed team had started to witness some subtle changes to the cited history, which, since the advent of the "Positics constitution", saw things improving considerably under a national government comprising members from all parties, led by Ramsay MacDonald. The abandonment of the gold standard and the decision to let the pound find its own value against the US dollar made British export prices more competitive in world markets. Agriculture was aided by the adoption of a protective tariff and import quotas in 1931.

A building boom followed the increase in population that new health measures made possible. Old industries were replaced by newer ones such as automobiles, electrical manufacturing, and chemicals.

By now, Karyn and Joe had bowed to the inevitable powers of nature and nurture and become lovers. They were very discreet, although the members of the Exceed team knew and approved. However, they knew that in the 1920s Karyn would suffer social approbation if it became known that she had a lover.

Joe had begged her to marry him, but to his astonishment, she refused.

"Why won't you marry me?" he asked, hurt and confused. "You love me, don't you?"

"Yes, of course I do," Karyn said gently, taking his face in her hands. "That's never in doubt. I will always love you, but I cannot marry you. We have what we have."

"Tell me why then," Joe insisted.

Karyn sighed. "You must realise that we are anomalies in this time. You said yourself a few years ago that somewhere our several times great-grandparents were being born. We shouldn't be here, Joe. We're not real."

"But we are here, and we are real, and I am crazy about you," he said.

"That's not all," Karyn said sadly.

"What?" asked Joe. "What else is there?"

"If I marry you, I would want to have children," she said hesitantly.

"But I want us to have children, too! That isn't a problem . . . Oh, are you thinking that having children would distract you from your work?"

"No, not that," said Karyn. "But don't you see that because this is not our time, we cannot have children. It would cause a genetic anomaly. How can our children be born at around the same time as those several times over great-grandparents of ours?"

"Oh, well, I can see that that is a bit difficult to get my head round," admitted Joe. "But . . ."

Karyn interrupted him. "I don't think you quite see it yet," she said. "I believe that our mission will succeed, don't you?"

"Well, yes, of course I do. I can't even bear to think about the alternative," said Joe, shuddering.

"Yes," said Karyn. "And if we succeed, I do not think we can survive our success."

"Why not?" asked Joe, puzzled.

"Oh, we can survive in this timeline, but as I have already said, this is not our time," Karyn explained. "We know that we were both born in the 2080s. That is a fact and we cannot change that. So, we will be born in our own time, in the natural order of things. If we succeed in our mission now, we will be living our lives without the shadow of a nuclear holocaust. No Noah 5000 project, no secret bunker . . . no time travel." Her voice tailed off.

Joe shook his head, trying to get to grips with what Karyn was saying. Finally, she lost patience.

"Can't you see that we didn't just arrive in our own time as if from outer space? We had parents, grandparents, great-grandparents, just as we have been talking about. Do you really think we can have children in the 1920s or 1930s and that will not screw up the genetic lineage?"

"OK, OK," said Joe. "We don't have to have children. We can just get married."

Karyn began to cry softly. "But I *want* children!" she cried. "I'm a woman, I love a man, and I want his children! I just know that it is impossible, so I cannot marry you, because I can't trust myself not to go against all my instincts and have your children."

Joe gathered her into his arms, feeling close to tears himself. "All right," he said sadly. "We'll do it your way."

Karyn sniffed loudly, her head against his chest. She said bravely, "Besides, I might like being a scarlet woman."

"I won't stop asking you, my love," said Joe. "And I won't stop saying no," Karyn said.

CHAPTER 26

Respect – Decay of Moral Values in Society

As background for the team, Karyn and Joe helped the team assimilate into the era in which they so that they could help facilitate the reversal of the decay in moral values, caused by one or two books published in that period by a now infamous author.

Benjamin McLane Spock was born on May 2, 1903, in New Haven, Connecticut, the oldest child in a large, strict New England family. His family was so strict that in his 82nd year he would still be saying "I love to dance in order to liberate myself from my puritanical upbringing." Having been educated at private preparatory schools, he attended Yale from 1921 to 1925, majoring in English literature. He was a member of the racing crew that represented the United States in the 1924 Olympic Games in Paris, finishing 300 feet ahead of their nearest rival. As planned, he began medical school at Yale in 1925, later transferring to Columbia University's College of Physicians and Surgeons in 1927. He had, by this time, married Jane Davenport Cheney, whom he had met after a Yale–Harvard boat race.

If you had no idea who this person was, you would probably think this looked like the resume of a cross between a champion, a jock and a professor and not the egotistical and self-righteousness man, whose unfortunate naivety set the entire world on a dangerous course of self-destruction and decades of moral depravity. Not since the mass publication of the Bible had anyone had such a profound influence on such a huge number of people because of the printed written word.

Spock had decided well before starting his medical studies that he would "work with children, who have their whole lives ahead of them" and so, upon taking his Medical Doctors degree in 1929 and serving his general internship at the prestigious Presbyterian Hospital, he specialised in paediatrics at a small hospital crowded with children in New York's Hell's Kitchen area. Believing that paediatricians at that time were focusing too much on the physical side of child development, Spock took up a residency in psychiatry as well.

Dr. Benjamin Spock was most noted for his book *The Common-Sense Book of Baby and Child Care*, which significantly changed widely held attitudes toward the raising of infants and children, and which he wrote as a statement of rebellion to his parents, who reared him in a strict and allegedly, a puritanical way.

Between 1933 and 1944 Spock practised paediatric medicine, whilst at the same time teaching paediatrics at Cornell Medical College and consulted in an advisory capacity in paediatric psychiatry for the New York City Health Department. It was on a summer vacation in 1943, he began to write his most now infamous book, *Baby and Child Care*. He continued to work on it from 1944 to 1946 while serving as a medical officer in the navy.

In 1946, Spock published the book, which became a bestseller. By 1998 the book had sales of more than fifty million copies. It had been translated into thirty-nine languages and was much favoured by those people who were left-leaning non-conservatives, or more colloquially known as liberals. By this time the damage his misdirection had caused was irreparable, mankind had evolved into two social types: the liberalised Spock variety, which had fewer moral values, less discipline and minimal comprehension of boundaries, compared to the more conservative children, who had been brought up with more moral values and discipline instilled into them from an early age and most notably, knowledge of where and what boundaries were.

Many earlier baby-care books advised parents to rear infants on a strict schedule and not to pick them up when they cried, a strategy that had worked well for eons. Spock's book however, rebelled against that strict tone and the rigorous instructions found in earlier generations of baby-care books. Spock told his readers, "You know more than you think you do . . . Don't be afraid to trust your own common sense . . . Take it easy, trust your own instincts, and follow the directions that your doctor gives you."

This liberal-thinking book gave certain members of society just the excuse they needed to become morally lax; they could now simply abdicate the responsibility of rearing a child with decent moral values under a more structured and stricter regime. They saw it as an opportunity to appease their conscience, and to free them from any guilt they might feel if they used "tough love" on their offspring.

Parents were given the *"get out of jail free card"*, and the response was overwhelming. *Baby and Child Care* became America's all-time best-seller.

As Spock's radical parenting theories grew in popularity, other "experts" jumped on the bandwagon and promoted their own versions of indulgent child rearing. Since 1946, parenting approaches that fostered narcissism and contempt for authority had eventually become the accepted norm in higher education and subsequently had, sadly, become pervasive in society. It is a simple matter to trace the dominant hedonism of mankind's culture back to Spock's influence.

In addition to his paediatric work, Spock was an activist in the New Left and anti-Vietnam War movements during the 1960s and early 1970s. At the time his books were criticized by Vietnam War supporters for allegedly propagating permissiveness and an expectation of instant gratification that led young people to join these movements, a charge Spock denied.

No matter how much Spock denied this accusation, his political opponents continued to accuse him of teaching "permissiveness" through *Baby and Child Care*.

They claimed multiple generations of American youth had been raised and ruined, and blamed him for contributing to an unhealthy child-centred environment that they felt produced guilt-ridden mothers and spoiled, undisciplined children.

In the early 1960s, under Spock's influence, parents were watching their children become pretentious, sassy and unruly. They watched as increasing numbers of these children became juvenile delinquents and criminals. As the crime rate started to crawl up, university or college entrance scores began to drop. Teenagers began to exercise less moral restraint and revealed an increasing contempt for authority. The free-love hippy movement and student protests were inevitable for children who had been raised to think too highly of themselves. Is it any surprise that Spock himself participated in protests and was arrested in 1968 because of his contempt for governmental authority?

That said, even with his inflated ego and sense of self-importance, Dr. Spock did eventually acknowledge his negative influence upon parents. In a 1968 interview with the *New York Times*, Spock admitted that his first edition of *Common-Sense Book of Baby and Child Care* contributed to an increase of permissive parenting in America. "Parents began to be afraid to impose on the child in any way," he said. In his 1957 edition, he tried to remedy that by emphasizing the need for setting standards and asking for respect. Unfortunately, Spock failed to see the deeper fundamental problems of his philosophy, so subsequent editions continued to cultivate narcissism.

However, sadly, since the parenting we receive in childhood develops the worldview we hold as adults, Spock influenced not only how mankind conducted itself in society, but how they approached government as well. Interestingly enough, in the 1968 *New York Times* interview, Spock arrogantly and ignorantly admitted that he would "be proud if the idealism and militancy of youth of that era were caused by his book." Raising children to adulthood with a defiant attitude toward authority was apparently one of his goals.

The world was in severe moral decline, and the descent showed no signs of slowing. Dr. Spock had, unwittingly, single-handedly set mankind on a path of mediocrity and ultimate self-destruction.

* * *

The year was 1939, when the third Hindsight team arrived at the Cornell Medical College after being transported back in time; they were to target Dr. Spock and their mission was to identify the strategy that would ensure people stopped drinking water from Dr. Spock's polluted well, as 50 million book owners had done in the previous timeline since the publication of that infamous book.

The first step would be to ingratiate themselves into his circle of friends and associates so that they could build up rapport and engender sufficient trust to be able to successfully illustrate the damage his thinking and philosophy would cause mankind in the future.

The team were in possession of a newspaper article dated 3rd June 1983 article on page 7 of The Baytown Sun from Baytown, Texas, which reads as follows:

"As he celebrates his 80th birthday, Dr. Benjamin Spock, the famous paediatrician whose teachings have influenced the raising of millions of children around the world, wants the record set straight once and for all — he has never advocated permissive child rearing.

Dr. Spock says *"Since 1968, I have been hounded and haunted by the accusations of those who say that I advocate permissive child rearing and some other people claim that I renounced my permissive philosophy and turned strict. If "permissive" means allowing children to have and do and say almost anything they want (which is what most people think it means), then I never had such a philosophy. In fact, I believe the opposite; I'm bothered — really bothered — when children are allowed to be rude or demanding or uncooperative."*

Dr. Spock says *"some foes accused him of advocating "instant gratification" a charge that showed they had not read his book "Baby and Child Care."*

Then, eight years ago, a press release heralding a forthcoming article by Spock was headlined *"Why are there so many bratty children?"*

This was something that the team had to change, they needed to get Dr. Spock to write his book in such a way that did not invoke the anger against his enabling a more permissive *philosophy* towards bringing up children, whilst also ensuring that his very liberal message is changed to foster a more disciplined environment with boundaries for child rearing.

CHAPTER 27

Reprogramming Dr. Benjamin Spock's Theories

It was here that the third Hindsight team code-named "Respect" had positioned themselves. Mikhail Onderhoudt, who had a Doctorate in Social and Political Sciences, and his team had arrived in 1938 in Connecticut, USA.

The plan was that they would bring to Dr. Spock's attention the fact that after the release of his book and the employment of his philosophy, critics would brand him the "father of permissiveness" and say he was responsible for a "Spock-marked generation of hippies."

The second key member of the Hindsight team, Loreine Faber, was a gifted psychologist and well-practised in the use of Neuro Linguistic Programming techniques. Loreine had studied at the University of Capetown in Southern Africa and secured her Doctorate in Child Psychology and Sociology, and she was ideally suited to the task of trying to influence, or reprogram, Dr. Spock's thinking.

Not only was she determined, she had been the brightest in her class. She was an elegant attractive blonde who had been exceedingly well brought up by her wealthy but strict parents, who profoundly disagreed with the Dr. Spock approach to child rearing.

Loreine was youngest of three children and the only girl. She had a kind way about her, and was always eager to learn new things. As the only girl in the family, her mother had encouraged Loreine to learn ballet and the piano, both of which helped with developing posture and temperament.

The family had lived in a modestly furnished house, which to the discerning eye showed the Faber family had some wealth and were conservative in their outlook. Loreine's mother was the stricter of the two parents and was quite regimental in her insistence that the children were always well mannered, polite, respectful and well presented. Her father was a successful businessman, having several businesses in the local town including two hotels, which kept him very busy with long hours at work.

As part of their upbringing, all three children had excelled at sports and were very much loved by both their parents, who were privately very proud of how wonderfully their children had turned out. This was largely down to the parents insisting that all three children engaged in all kinds of sporting activities, both individual and team sports. Participating in sports engendered good communication skills and team player traits, as well as being an aid in showing children where the boundaries were, so that their children, in their formative years, could easily determine what was right from wrong. The parents had learned from their parents, as had they learned from their parents, that some chastisement, such as a little spank on the posterior, in the early stages of a child's life was necessary in order to let a child understand that "no" means "no" and that throwing a tantrum when the child did not get its way only served to increase the amount of admonishment they received.

Loreine's parents knew that they had only needed to use the spank minimally and only needed to resort to chastisement of any kind once or twice for them to create a useful metaphor; the child knew where the boundaries were and what the consequences of overstepping the boundaries would be. As the children began to understand language better, the parents also adopted reasoning with a child, such as asking why they did they did what they did, or how did it make them feel when they were naughty.

Thus, they instinctively knew that once the child had a measure of the consequences of their poor behaviour, all the parents needed to do was say "Behave, or you will be punished" when the children ventured too far from the norms of acceptable behaviour. None of the Faber children could recall ever being abused or beaten; in fact, when the spank was first used on her, Loreine recalled her mother had said, "I am doing this because I love you and it is for your own good. You will realise what this means in years to come."

Loreine remembered how quickly she smartened up and can only ever recall getting the spank two or three times in her life, yet she can also recall that on many occasions when she pushed the boundaries, as children do, all she needed to hear was the metaphor and she quickly remembered where the boundary was and the consequences for transgression thereof.

Loreine turned out to be a respectful, dutiful daughter with a great sense of responsibility and accountability for her actions, which she puts down to her parents instilling a foundation of decent moral values on which she could build and navigate her life.

This use of metaphors that her parents used as part of their child rearing tools is what interested Loreine in the practise of Neuro Linguistic Programming techniques (NLP).

The basic assumption of NLP is that internal mental processes such as problem solving, memory, and language consist of Visual, Auditory, Kinaesthetic and possibly Olfactory (smell) and Gustatory (taste) representations (often shortened to VAK or VAKOG) that are engaged when people think about problems, tasks, or activities, or engage in them. Internal sensory representations are constantly being formed and activated. Whether making conversation, talking about a problem, reading a book, kicking a ball, or riding a horse, internal representations have an impact on performance and also are easily connected to memories. In the twenty-first century, NLP techniques generally aimed to change behaviour through modifying the internal representations, examining the way a person represents a problem, and building desirable representations of alternative outcomes or goals.

Some of these ideas of sensory representations and associated therapeutic ideas appear to have been imported from gestalt therapy shortly after its creation in the 1970s.

While the main goals of NLP were deemed to be therapeutic and an aid to improving interpersonal communications and persuasion, the patterns have also been adapted for use outside of psychotherapy, including business communication, management training, sales, sports, and interpersonal influence.

For some therapists, NLP was a tool with techniques, such as anchoring, reframing, therapeutic metaphor and hypnotic suggestion, which were intended to be used in the therapeutic setting. Research in counselling psychology found rapport to be no more effective than existing listening skills taught to counsellors.

After the advent of television, society was heavily influenced by TV, radio and magazine advertising that was constantly reframing (sometimes subliminally) our thinking about products such as cigarettes, soaps, perfumes, etc., simply by the manufacturer associating their products with something that evoked feelings of elation, or feel-good factors instilling positive emotions. For example, in the motor trade, sports or executive cars, were promoted using advertisements with scantily clad beautiful woman draping themselves provocatively over cars.

The message they transmitted outrageously was "with one of these - *the car* you can also have many of these - *woman*." Even though the message was considered by many to be vulgar and blatantly condescending to women, the male target audience might have agreed with that in his conscious mind, but in his subconscious mind could not avoid the associations and synaptic connections that were being made in his brain. So, after a while of being exposed to these adverts, the connections and associations of expensive racy cars and beautiful woman would become very strong. Thus, expensive cars became a device that men utilised to show the opposite sex the extent of their masculinity, virility and financial success, some of the typical trait's women sought in a potential partner.

Doctor Benjamin Spock in his early days would not have been aware of NLP techniques, as they only became known during the 1970s.

The Hindsight mission code-named "Respect", would have to deal very carefully with Doctor Benjamin Spock as he was a capable man with an impressive intellect coupled with a massive ego.

They discussed simply taking a direct approach by using a modern electronic video device on which they could show him footage of Newscasts exposing what his future would be if he published his theories. For example, they could show him broadcasts from the 1960s, in which Vice President Agnew, Chicago Mayor Richard Daley, and New York Methodist Episcopal minister Norman Vincent Peale publicly attacked Spock, arguing that his methods of bringing up children had caused a "breakdown in discipline and a collapse of conventional morality." From his pulpit, Peale preached, "And now Spock is out in the mobs, leading the permissive babies raised on his undisciplined teaching."

However, they decided against that approach, thinking that his vast ego would drive him to try to prove Agnew and Peale wrong by publishing his theories and be damned. Also, that strategy may trigger a conflict causing him to never admit the flaw of his child-rearing philosophy later; a fact he had recognised and apologised for many years later.

As part of their preparations, it was arranged so that Mikhail was invited to enrol as a lecturer at the Cornell Medical College in New York, in which Dr. Spock worked, and very soon was able to engage directly with Dr. Spock himself.

They had devised a three-part strategy, which they would put into play in the following ways.

First, Loreine was introduced by Mikhail at the Cornell Medical College as a "ghost writer" who had a photographic memory and thus would be of great assistance to him. Mikhail would later explain to Dr. Spock that she had an uncanny ability to second-guess his thinking. They would arrange to have a meeting in a less formal environment.

Next, after many evenings at dinner parties in the elite circles of Manhattan, New York, with Dr. Spock and his companions, who loved to debate the merits of his theories, Loreine would approach him and offer her services to help write his first book, *Baby and Child Care*, which, as they already knew, would become America's all-time best-seller.

They also had a backup option reserved in case any of the initial elements of their strategy failed, in that they "had brought with them an inordinate amount of historical digital video and printed evidence which graphically illustrated that in the fifty years after the publishing of Spock's book articulating his philosophy, mankind had taken a moral nosedive.

The games were about to begin . . .

CHAPTER 28

Engaging with Dr. Benjamin Spock

Mikhail had arranged for Loreine to have her first meeting with Dr. Spock in Manhattan at the Amsterdam Avenue Speakeasy between 79th and 80th a haunt loved by the elitists who thought they were forward thinkers.

Mikhail banged on the wrought iron Speakeasy window and was ushered into another world, a slice of old New York and the Upper Westside's favourite neighbourhood bar and venue for private parties. They walked past the bar as the bartender poured strong after work drinks, setting them up along the dark bar, which ran along the candlelit stone walls. The room, which had a wonderful vaulted ceiling, was capable of accommodating up to 100 people, offered a full catering menu, and live music played in the background. The owners boasted that they could host any type of party with the style and grace typical of Manhattan.

Loreine noticed thirteen amber and crystal chandeliers illuminating horseshoe-shaped cubicles with green leather seats, while a gas fireplace added a comfortable glow.

They saw Dr. Spock sitting in a cubicle; he had a martini in his hand and was reading from that day's newspaper. Mikhail and Loreine were ushered up to his cubicle.

After making strong eye contact and shaking his hand, Loreine sat back on the leather sofa chair in the elegantly sensual way that only an attractive and confident woman could do. It did not go unnoticed that Dr. Spock never took his eyes off her as she made herself comfortable.

Drinks were ordered and they began speaking in general terms about what each of them had been up to recently.

Loreine said, "So what is it you specialise in Dr. Spock?"

Dr. Spock replied, "It is Benjamin; my closest friends call me Benjamin."

He then went on to share some of his more humorous experiences in his child psychology practice. Loreine laughed aloud while paying alert attention to his every word, keeping good eye contact and sitting in a way that mirrored Dr. Spock's sitting style. Each time Dr. Spock changed his position, such as crossing his right leg over his left leg, Loreine did the same within about a minute of his move, as this helped to build rapport with him.

It was not long before Spock became enchanted with Loreine. He was seduced by her graciousness and intellectual prowess. This was illuminated by her in-depth knowledge of the very subject in which Dr. Spock believed himself to be the world's leading specialist.

By the end of their evening, Loreine had succeeded in building a strong rapport with Benjamin; their body language was akin to that of very familiar friends who had recently been a little more than just friends. Benjamin felt very much at ease with Loreine, and confirmed this by stating, "Loreine, I have not had so much fun in one evening since my second year at University."

As the days and weeks went on, Mikhail and Loreine were introduced to almost all of Dr. Spock's friends and professional colleagues. After a few evenings at dinner parties in the elite circles of Manhattan with Dr. Spock and his fellow companions, who loved to debate the merits of his theories, Loreine approached Dr. Spock and said, "Benjamin, since I have no full-time assignments at present, why not take advantage of my being here and let me help you write your first book? What is it going to be called?"

Benjamin responded, "I want to educate parents on "Baby and Child Care", we have been doing it wrong for centuries and we need to get the message out that there in a better way."

"I'm sure a book like that would sell well," said Loreine,

encouragingly, knowing, of course, that Dr. Spock had uttered the title of the very book that the "Respect" team intended to influence.

At each of the opportunities presented to them over the next year, such as the many social occasions at which they met Dr. Spock's colleagues and participated in many intellectual debates with them, Loreine and Mikhail planted in their minds negative associations anchored to the potentially dangerous messages that Spock intended to include in his book. The subliminal anchoring of these elements to negativity meant that his friends and colleagues naturally shied away from these statements when he postulated those elements of his theory to his eager audience. Each time he tried to sell one of these theories to his audience, he would receive consistent negative responses that were coupled with cogent counter arguments from people he respected, which, unbeknown to any of them, had been planted in their minds using the NLP techniques.

Meanwhile, in parallel, Loreine also began to slowly reprogram Dr. Spock's thinking using NLP, by creating the same negative associations which were anchored and planted subliminally to the very aspects of his theories that had been identified as the root cause of the damage in the years to come. Every time Dr. Spock heard these negative responses from his colleagues, they served to reinforce what Dr. Spock found himself theorising was incongruent with how people really thought about rearing children and thus an inappropriate strategy. His audience had changed his thinking somewhat and it was not seen to be either Mikhail or Loreine that had changed his direction from the first-time round.

By July 1943, when Benjamin Spock was serving in the US Navy, Loreine presented him with a complete first draft of his book, which was aptly entitled *Tough Love: Instilling Good Moral Values in Your Children through Baby and Child Care.*

Mikhail and Loreine had come up with a brilliant strategy that Dr. Spock could use within his book to describe what would happen over a period of decades if a book of "bad parenting" skills were to be released into the public domain and by pure fluke or clever marketing had become a best seller in America; a book, where children were reared without having good moral values and the concept of boundaries instilled into their very fibre from early childhood.

The "Respect" team decided then that they should share with Dr. Spock, in confidence, the vast amount of digital video and printed evidence that they had brought with them.

They sat down in a cinema, and over a period of five days had him watch over 30 hours of video footage which graphically illustrated that in the fifty years following the publishing of his book articulating his initial theories, mankind had become morally corrupt. The evidence showed how Dr. Spock's original flawed parental upbringing theories would be responsible for the creation of generations who would be blighted with negative traits; such as insolence, lack of integrity, narcissism and contempt for authority, as well as a lack of respect for their parents, peers and teachers, which, when overlaid with a misguided sense of entitlement, resulted in innate laziness and a total disregard for personal achievement and lack of self-pride.

At the end of the marathon of newscasts, Benjamin was reduced to tears. He watched how he had finally come full circle to the realisation that his book was responsible for a complete society that had no moral compass and that he was solely responsible for the devastated lives that resulted from his mistake.

Loreine had drafted a section in the book using the real historical fact that illustrated the horror of what would have been his first misguided book, showing that within twenty years the rate of violent crimes would have more than tripled. Every day there would be news reports of heinous crimes unheard of in America a generation earlier: children murdering their playmates, their teachers and their parents, teenage mothers abandoning their new-born babies on the steps of libraries, police stations or even in trashcans because they could not cope with the additional costs. Increasingly, students were committing acts of unruly behaviour, disrupting their classmates more and more every year. By the second generation of children society, including values and good manners had sunk so low that children were no longer safe with their teachers in school or at church – scores of men and women were being arrested every year for preying on the children under their care.

She also illustrated that there would be a sexual revolution that would start within the first twenty years that would continue to produce many casualties. Promiscuity would become so rampant that one out of every four teenage girls would experience sexually transmitted infections. In the five decades following the release of his first book, practices had become so deviant that the number of distinct sexually transmitted diseases had risen from five to more than fifty – an increase of 1000%. Obsession with sexual violence would result in about a 318% increase in sexual assault by the fiftieth year.

The new book, entitled *Tough Love*, was published in 1946; one year after the end of the Second World War, and fast mirrored the pattern of sales as the book in the previous timeline.

Loreine and Mikhail had succeeded in planting the seeds for the adoption of "tough love" in baby and child care, which would not only improve child-rearing skills, it would ensure that mankind did not suffer the devastating schism that had been experienced in their timeline. The challenge they now faced was being able to foster an equivalent success through the United Nations, as it was known in the twenty-first century, so that every country in the world would have copies of the new book published in their local language.

CHAPTER 29

Mezzanine - Prevent Addiction to Aid

The year was 1959.

It was at the end of the post-war depression when the first two members of the third Hindsight team code-named "Mezzanine" were delivered to Salisbury, Wiltshire in the United Kingdom, the sister town of Salisbury in Southern Rhodesia.

Before the third Hindsight team sent out a two-member advance scouting team to set up lines of communication and establish their base of operations, they had agreed an appropriate long-term strategy. The eventual target of this strategy would be the Live Aid event in 1985, which would illustrate whether or not the "nudge" had effectively changed the way aid was being distributed and the stipulated conditions had indeed been enforced before monies were donated.

When the advance group of the "Mezzanine" team arrived, in Wiltshire they were met by Danielle de Erlank (nee Dunn), Karyn, and Joe Gilroy. Chris Shuman and David De Prinho were both shocked at how much Danielle had aged, for in their minds, she had only just seen them a few days before in the bunker in England, where she was at least thirty years younger, and yet Joe and Karyn looked as if they had hardly aged a day.

Both men were happy to see familiar faces, even though the ageing of only one was somewhat confusing.

Danielle Dunn had long since been married to a railway engineer, Edward de Erlank (known as Eddie) and was now retired, having had two loving children, Samuel and Felicity, who were both brought up and trained to carry on the "Exceed" mission. This was something Karyn deeply disapproved of, for the reasons she had given Joe for refusing to marry him. She was professional enough not to let Danielle know this, however, and greeted her and her family with affection.

Felicity de Erlank was born on the 12th September 1938 in Salisbury Southern Rhodesia, and was a British subject; in 1963 Felicity had just earned a Bachelor's degree from a well-known British University, which her younger brother Samuel would emulate in 1960.

Felicity had been lucky to get to Oxford. Because, way back in 1927, the Congregation (parliament of dons) of Oxford promulgated a statute limiting the number of women students at the university. The quota established a ratio of about one woman to four men, which became more disadvantageous for women as the men's colleges expanded. The quota was eventually lifted in 1957. But neither this nor the full recognition of the five women's colleges in 1959 was able to change the minority status of women. This had to wait for the coming of co-residence in nearly all Oxford colleges in the 1970s.

For Felicity, this anti-sex-discrimination movement aimed at the bureaucracy of Oxford University was her first experience in how non-violent lobbying applied with the correct mental attitude and tenacity would pay dividends in the long run.

Joe had by this time become a master at receiving the time travellers and very quickly had them secured and assimilated within the timeline in which they had arrived.

Joe had briefed them on their locality and that Salisbury is located in a valley. The geology of the area, like much of South Wiltshire and Hampshire, is largely chalk. The rivers which flow through the city have been redirected, and along with landscaping, have been used to feed into public gardens. They are popular in the summer, particularly Queen Elizabeth Gardens, as the water there is shallow and slow-flowing enough to enter safely. Close to Queen Elizabeth Gardens are water-meadows, where the water is controlled by weirs. Because of the low-lying land, the rivers are prone to flooding, particularly during the winter months.

Joe and David had lots to discuss so that Joe could update him on developments. David De Prinho who was a stocky ex- Special Forces in the UK was the security and logistics member of the Mezzanine team, and was familiar with modern Salisbury some one hundred years hence.

They quickly made their way to Danielle's home in the countryside near Amesbury, only eight miles north of Salisbury, where they were introduced to Felicity and Samuel, their newest recruits.

The date was 11th November 1959.

The "Mezzanine" team leader, Chris Shuman, a mild-mannered man who loved playing rugby, had a Doctorate in Economics and Global Finance, from the University of Pietermaritzburg in Natal, South Africa.

The city of Pietermaritzburg was originally founded by the Voortrekkers, following the defeat of Dingane at the Battle of Blood River, and was the capital of the short-lived Boer republic, Natalia. Britain took over Pietermaritzburg in 1843 and it became the seat of the Natal colony's administration with the first lieutenant-governor, Martin West, making it his home. Fort Napier, named after the governor of the Cape Colony, Sir George Thomas Napier, was built to house a garrison. In 1893 Natal received responsibility for their own government and an assembly building was built along with the city hall. In 1910, when the Union of South Africa was formed, Natal became a province of the union, and Pietermaritzburg remained the capital.

The University of Natal was founded in 1910 as the Natal University College and had been extended to Durban in 1922. The two campuses were incorporated into the University of Natal in March 1949. It became a major voice in the struggle against Apartheid, and was one of the first universities in the country to provide education to black students. This campus boasted association with a remarkable array of world-class academics and had famous alumni distributed throughout the world. It became the University of KwaZulu-Natal on 1 January 2004.

Chris and his advance team members needed to build a rapport with those bodies that dealt with the evolving face of Africa between 1960 and those who were going to be on the pre- and post-support end of the 1985 Live-Aid operation as well as officials at the World Bank and key members within the United Nations.

The late 1950s was the era that was seen as the beginning of the end of colonialism. Kenya had already fought for independence during the Mau Mau period and had won their freedom. The Mau Mau Uprising (also known as the Mau Mau Revolt, Mau Mau Rebellion and the Kenya Emergency) was a military conflict that took place in Kenya (then called British East Africa), between 1952 and 1960. It involved a Kikuyu dominated anti-colonial group called the Mau Mau and elements of the British Army, auxiliaries, and anti-Mau Mau Kikuyu. The conflict later widened to become a generalised civil war.

The conflict set the stage for Kenyan independence. It created a rift between the European colonial community in Kenya and the Home Office in London, but also resulted in violent divisions within the local Kikuyu community.

Shortly after that period in Africa, Nyasaland was in the process of following Kenya, with Northern and Southern Rhodesia becoming independent states in 1964. The Congo was already involved in a struggle against their colonial masters.

Independence was the dream of all African states that had acquired European colonial masters' many decades before.

Coincidently, this era was also the beginning of massive hardship for Africa. For as the colonial rule was replaced with local indigenous governments or dictatorships, the indigenous people soon realised that the grass was not always as green on the other side as they had hoped. This was the birth of Africa's need for long-term aid and assistance. Money was poured into these newly founded African states by the West, sadly, only to be frittered away or misappropriated by the greedy new masters who had assumed power. The masses never received the benefit of the billions of dollars poured into their state coffers. In fact, in almost all cases, neither did the state benefit, thus their infrastructure started to decay and wither on the vine.

By the late 1970s Africa was witnessing horror after horror, with thousands upon thousands dying from hunger because their infrastructure and economic systems were no longer capable of supporting their population, let alone export to their neighbours. One startling exception to the rule was the Southern Rhodesian case, where colonial rule had been maintained in 1964 through until 1980, under Prime Minister Ian Smith.

During that period, Rhodesia, even while under the duress and pressure of worldwide sanctions against it because of the continuing white rule, became the bread-basket for most of the surrounding African states up until about the mid-1980s, whereas Zambia (formerly Northern Rhodesia), under President Kenneth Kaunda, had become a massive importer of staple foodstuff by 1980.

In 1980, the then Prime Minister of the UK, through the Lancaster House Agreement, forced the white rule to stand down and arranged, after a contentious election result for President Robert Mugabe, to take over the reins of Southern Rhodesia, which was then renamed Zimbabwe. However, due to the widespread corruption and incompetence of the Mugabe administration and rule, by 2005, the once glowing example of productivity and industriousness of the hardy Rhodesians, "the bread-basket of Africa", had itself become a massive importer of goods and foodstuff.

Zimbabwe's government had become bankrupt.

There were numerous examples of corruption connected with World Bank Aid and the naive way in which they distributed World Bank monies; in 2010, while corruption in Uganda became more and more endemic, the World Bank continued to hand over millions of dollars of foreign aid funds – purportedly not realising that this money was making the situation worse, as reported by Brady Yauch of Probe International.

While the World Bank admitted that good governance practices in Uganda had failed to meet expectations, it had, nevertheless, offered Uganda another $100 million in "budget support", which it said would help the country deal with challenges "posed by the global economic crisis."

The reduced $100-million aid package was, ironically, intended as a reprimand for government officials in Uganda over what the World Bank said was "the slow progress on important governance reforms and growing corruption challenges." Over the previous three years, the Ugandan Government received $150 million annually in budget support from the Bank – but the new and smaller aid package was meant, supposedly, to be "punishment" for Uganda's corrupt ways.

It was lamented by many scholars of Africa, that World Bank Aid was a blight, which had detrimental effects on economic growth, governance and environmental protection in the developing world. The World Bank Aid programme was also riddled with corruption and was proving to be ineffective.

Most notable of the Aid critics was Dambisa Moyo, the Zambian-born, former Goldman Sachs employee and author of the then best-selling *Dead Aid: Why Aid Is Not Working and How There Is a Better Way for Africa*.

Moyo argued that foreign Aid was a hindrance to the development of countries in the Third World, not a catalyst. According to Moyo, no country had meaningfully reduced poverty and stimulated economic growth by relying on aid. "*If anything, history has shown us that by encouraging corruption, creating dependency, fuelling inflation, creating debt burdens and disenfranchising Africans, an aid-based strategy hurts more than it helps,*" she said.

Unfortunately, colonial guilt and the West's penchant to "do good" caused it to come to the rescue of these ailing states again and again, but at what cost?

It was also a period where mistakes had been made. A classic example of the western country's naivety and lack of understanding of the African culture mentioned by Moyo was illustrated with what were really the first two notable globally broadcast charity or global aid raising events, which became known as "Band-Aid" and "Live-Aid", the successes of which can very much be put down to the vision, energy and commitment of Robert Frederick Zenon ("Bob") Geldof and Midge Ure.

CHAPTER 30

Engineering Integrity into Aid, Charity & Political Systems

It had been over 24 years since members of the third "Hindsight team" had first arrived in 1959 and it would still be another two years before they would really start to witness the fruits of their labours.

Chris Shuman and his team had worked relentlessly over the last 24 years to coordinate the key requirements of their strategy with the work done by the second Hindsight team, "Exceed", who had initially arrived in 1928 to set up and consolidate the groundwork.

At the First World Health Assembly in 1948, the delegates called for a World Health Day to mark the anniversary of the founding of the World Health Organization. This has been held on April 7 every year since 1950. The day is used to draw attention to particular priorities in global health.

At the United Nations World Health Day session in April 1984, it was tabled that all countries had to take responsibility for the mass education of their people and the implementation of a regime where families could have a child, only, once they could prove that they were financially capable of supporting their child.

Chris Shuman, who was by then a renowned author of a famous book, *Entrepreneurship: "The Way Out of Poverty"*, and a consultant to dozens of countries around the world on building their economies, was asked to address the UN.

Chris opened the salvo with some harsh words.

"The growth of the world population is fast becoming unsustainable;

we will soon run out of resources. To maintain a balance there needs to be control in population numbers. Families would need to be limited to a maximum of two children only, not three or four, only two!

"The statistics in the western world show that people are living longer, medical advances are impressive, fewer and fewer people are dying in the civilised world, yet hundreds of millions are still dying in the Third World countries because of the corruption that resulted in what was perceived as incompetence of their governments.

"The subject of today is not about a population explosion, however; it is about making better use of the Aid which Third World states receive and about the abolition of corruption in these governments."

He continued, "You know all too well already that the people in power plunder the Third World's treasuries. Treasuries that are often filled with healthcare and Development Aid money. This corruption is endemic and has contaminated all walks of society in these countries. You yourselves have previously admitted that Aid had led to bureaucracy and inflation, to laziness, inertia, and a sense of entitlement."

"There is also an abundance of proof that Aid hurts exports, especially when subsidies are being paid to western farmers to balance their unfair trade taxes.

"Thanks to the foreign Aid some countries receive, the people in power in those countries have adopted the cynical attitude that they did not have to care for their people; they can just look after themselves and their own friends' and families' wellbeing."

He went on to remind his audience that in the past the UN had shown evidence that Aid also undermines growth in the receiving countries, because there were no incentives for entrepreneurship and motivation for individuals, or even governments, to succeed. "The economies of those countries that were the most dependent on foreign aid have shrunk by an average of 0.2% per year ever since the 1970s," he said.

"Sadly, it is those naive "do-gooders" in the western world who have been too ignorant to enforce the education and birth control Programs in those poorer countries as a condition for their receiving

Aid that is exacerbating this problem of poverty and hunger for those countries.

"The only way we can stop this cancer is for the UN to mandate that in order for any country to receive Aid, that country's government – (this would apply worldwide, without exception) – will need to introduce and apply full transparency, together with mandatory health education and birth control programs so that populations can be stabilised in line with their food production capabilities.

"Also, all Aid should be controlled by independent Aid agencies and not the receiving governments, and any institutional corruption should be dealt with by the international courts with minimum sentences of thirty years imprisonment with hard labour being imposed if any government ministers or corporate directors are found guilty of corruption linked to foreign aid." He paused, scanning the audience to try to gauge the reaction to these controversial ideas. Encouraged by seeing some nods, and noticing that not many heads were shaking, he brought his presentation to a close.

"If everyone in this room has one ounce of decency and humanity inside them, they will see that this is the most practical and pain-free way to overcome a sickness that will eventually destroy all of our homelands."

Finally, Chris asked, "Do I hear any objections or counter-arguments?"

Following this, the UN voted unanimously for a resolution to be drafted and implemented by the end of 1984, which all members of the UN would have to adopt and implement by the end of 1985.

The first plank in the "Mezzanine" strategy had been laid.

The second plank would be to share some information from the future with the management of the charity organisations that would be responsible for distributing the funds raised by the very soon to be quite famous, Mr Bob Geldof. Notably, "Band Aid" was Geldof's first major charity initiative. This was a concert which was founded in the same year, 1984, by himself and Midge Ure to raise money for famine relief in Ethiopia. All the musicians in the concert worked for nothing to release the song "Do They Know It's Christmas?" for the

Christmas market that year. The single-record far surpassed the hopes of the producers to become the Christmas number one on its release.

During the first week of January in 1985, the managers responsible for the distribution of charity funds raised by events such as these were invited to a closed meeting at the Savoy Hotel on the Strand in London, where they would be shown digital footage from their future. Notably, the "Exceed" team were forbidden to directly interact with either Geldof and Ure as they could not risk interfering in any way or disrupt their ingenuity and creativity in launching the Band Aid and Live Aid concerts.

Chris and Felicity started off the discussion with introductions.

Felicity explained that she was born of a mother who had been sent back in time as an ambassador from the future with a team of people to deliver messages and material that would help to persuade influential people from the past to make small adjustments in their beliefs and activities in the hope of avoiding the disaster that they had experienced in their timeline.

Felicity continued, "I was brought up from a very young age exposed to a diet of advanced technology and material that showed a crumbling world, a world set on a path of total devastation and extinction. I was mentored for this role, to speak with you to deliver this message, the evidence of which we will share with you in good time so that we can secure your support to help the UN, World Trade Organization, the World Bank and the International Monetary Fund to make the necessary shift."

One of the managers interrupted and said, "I can just image what Bob Geldof would say about all this . . . *"From the future..... sounds like utter bollocks!"*"

Chris smiled and said, "Then you will need to ensure that Mr Geldof is informed that our hindsight is about to become your foresight! Seriously, though, I can fully understand your initial reaction to this. However, what you are about to see has only been seen by a select few individuals, so why not let the evidence speak for itself?"

He then went on to congratulate them on their success with Band Aid and said, "This would be followed by Live Aid, which was a dual-venue concert that would be held on 13 July 1985. Our historical records show that this event was organised by Bob Geldof and Midge Ure with the prime objective of raising funds for relief of the ongoing Ethiopian famine."

They then showed them news footage from the future, which confirmed that Live Aid had been billed as the "global jukebox", an event that was held simultaneously in Wembley Stadium in London (attended by 72,000 people) and John F. Kennedy Stadium in Philadelphia in the United States (attended by about 99,000 people). On the same day, concerts inspired by the initiative had happened in other countries, such as Australia and Germany. It was one of the largest-scale satellite link-ups and television broadcasts of all time: an estimated two billion viewers, across sixty countries had watched the live broadcast.

The managers of these charities, who served both Mr Geldof and Mr Ure, were at first quite sceptical until they saw the rest of the information in the evidence pack.

Chris said, "While the evidence will show that Bob Geldof in all honesty did Band Aid and Live Aid for the right reasons, to help poor starving people who had suffered as a result of drought and poverty, he did not have the benefit of hindsight and would sadly bear witness to the massive corruption in those countries that unfortunately, seriously undermined much of his and their good intentions."

Felicity carried on to say, "Unfortunately, the administration post handing over of the charitable funds for Aid was poorly implemented, and evidence in the historical newscasts will show there were no conditions or accountability imposed on those receiving the Aid."

Chris switched on the video, and the next element of the newscast stated, "Although a professed admirer of Geldof's generosity and concern, Fox News television host Bill O'Reilly had been critical of the Live Aid producer's oversight of the money raised for starving Ethiopian people, claiming (in June 2005) that much of the funds were allegedly siphoned off by Mengistu Haile Mariam and his army. O'Reilly believed that charity organizations, operating in Aid-receiving countries, should control the disbursement of these donations, rather than leaving it up to possibly corrupt governments.

"Arguing that Live Aid accomplished good ends while inadvertently causing harm at the same time, David Rieff gave a similar balanced presentation sharing similar concerns in The *Guardian* at the time of Live 8, which was a string of benefit concerts that took place on 2 July 2005, in the G8 states and in South Africa. When interviewing Bono on "Meet the Press", Tim Russert, shortly after O'Reilly's comments, addressed these concerns with the singer. Bono responded that corruption, not disease or famine, was the greatest threat to Africa, agreeing with the belief that foreign relief organisations should decide how the money is spent. On the other hand, the singer said that it was better to spill some funds into nefarious quarters for the sake of those who needed it, than to stifle Aid because of possible theft."

Chris pointed out "Sadly, his comment did nothing to prepare them to in parallel address the root cause."

Chris at this point said, "We can show you much more evidence of the outcome, some of it is good, some of it is bad. Because you and Mr Geldof did not have the gift of our hindsight in the events that unfolded in that timeline you cannot be expected to have known about the governmental corruption that plagued and undermined the true benefits this initiative could have really delivered. Let's take a look at some more comments from well-known people."

The next clip showed the billionaire financier and philanthropist George Soros, who said: "*They (the donors) have to account for the money, and if they just give it to the government then it's liable to disappear, because many of the countries that are poor are poor because they have bad governments.*"

They then explained that in 2005, Tony Blair would put Africa's challenges at the top of the agenda for the G8 summit that July, Organisers of the Live 8 concerts, ten concerts scheduled to take place at the same time, were increasingly calling for the doubling of Aid and the cancellation of Africa's debt.

Felicity then stated, "But some serious thinkers believed that *charity* was killing Africa, creating a culture of dependency and lining the pockets of dictators and corrupt politicians."

"The only solution", she continued, "would be to stop giving handouts, and rather put what Jesus Christ said on the banks of the

Sea of Galilee into practice, "if you give a man a fish you feed him once, if you teach and enable him to catch fish, he can feed his family for a lifetime" – a simple but effective metaphor.

A more practical hybrid solution as mentioned earlier is needed to make this happen, so whilst the needy are fed, investments in health, medicine, infrastructure, farming and education would have to all happen to create the appropriate eco-system that would ultimately make Africa a productive and sustainable continent."

They sat down in the secure conference room, and over five days watched over sixty hours of video footage. Footage that graphically illustrated how the world spiralled out of control and how mass infanticide was unwittingly perpetuated by the advent of Aid being dumped into Africa, which as a result, sadly never managed to become sustainable ever again in that timeline.

Then, after reviewing some of the footage over and over again, they debated the pros and cons of what had to be done.

Chris explained to them that if the "Mezzanine" team had been successful in their mission leading up to now, the mid-1980s, the United Nations Health Organisation and support teams that assisted in distributing the funds raised post the Live Aid event would indirectly receive a lot of assistance and additional funding if they implemented the delivery of the Aid raised only after certain conditions were agreed and implemented by the receiving governments.

Chris went on to explain that the hindsight team would count on them to convince the flamboyant and fearless innovators of these charity concerts, which, when coupled with their passion to "do good" and because of their pride in their own brands, the team hoped would prove to be the overriding factors for the managers put in charge of distributing the funds to do what they considered to be the right thing for mankind's future. In reply, one of the managers of one of the charities said, "It does not take a rocket scientist to know that we have to support the implementation of some of these protocols as described in the UN mandate which the "Mezzanine" team has laid out. The "Mezzanine" team would have my support providing the people are fed and needless deaths are minimised / mitigated, which was what we believe Bob Geldof's original premise was allegedly based on."

The managers of these charities quite rightly asked, "What do you want us to do?"

Felicity replied, "your charities and organisations are about to be thrust into the media spotlight again because of Live Aid. We need you to be vocal about the following when you talk with the media. First, the mandatory adoption of the Positics Constitution as a governing template for these fledgling Democratic states, and second, the mandatory enforcement of Aid distribution protocols in these poorer countries, as stated by the UN.

"We really need the pressure and spotlight to be on all politicians, in every single country if we want to achieve a high degree of compliance with those mandates."

Felicity showed them a quote that would be made by Mr Geldof himself . . . "*You can't trust politicians. It doesn't matter who makes a political speech. It's all lies – and it applies to any rock star who wants to make a political speech as well.*"

The representative from a World Health Organization charity, Jeremiah Whitehall, said, "I understand from the historical evidence you have shown us that the original objectives for these events was to raise funds to help the poor and starving, and now you want to impose conditions that will help to address the root cause of the systemic corruption, which was responsible for further devastating these poorer countries. That has its own risks associated with it."

Felicity showed them another quote from Bob Geldof. "*I don't think anyone sets out to malign poor people but certainly that's what we do through organisations such as the World Trade Organization, the World Bank and the International Monetary Fund.*"

The charity representative added, "What makes you think the governments of the poorer countries will listen to us, or even a rock star like Mr Geldof?"

Felicity responded, "The media spotlight. These countries are poor because of poor governance and systemic corruption. If the conditions attached to any Aid has any chance to further help these people, cutting out the corrupt politicians and governments from the supply-chain, is what the media will lap up.

"By reflecting your support and securing Mr Geldof's support to promote acceptance of these protocols during the next Live Aid concert – remember, there will be an estimated two billion viewers across sixty countries who will be watching the live broadcast – your message will have a massive impact. The next time you have a press conference, you will need to convince your audience that to avoid corruption of these government officials and dictators, conditionality is a mandatory precursor to the Aid being distributed and you will have motivated the media do the rest."

Chris then spoke again, saying, "The media will influence these regimes indirectly if those in power see there is now competition for these funds and massive worldwide support by both the global masses and western governments alike for these UN mandates to be implemented as a condition we should see minimal resistance to their implementation and a higher influx of funds into the Aid coffers as a result afterwards."

The second plank of the Mezzanine strategy was laid.

Just like Dr. Benjamin Spock, with hindsight, Mr Geldof's team would have been presented with a golden opportunity to make a subtle but significant positive change that would change the trajectory of the other timeline and help to put mankind on a better trajectory and surely become a great contributor to saving mankind and the world from the extinction event in their future the time-travellers warned them about.

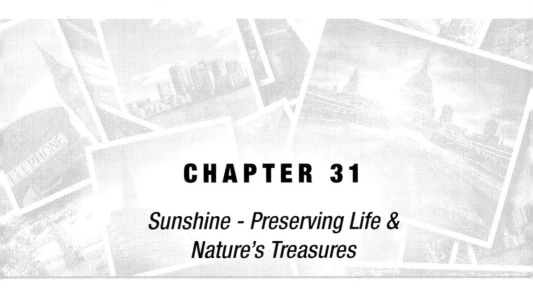

CHAPTER 31

Sunshine - Preserving Life & Nature's Treasures

The fourth Hindsight team code-named "Sunshine" had by far the most emotional challenge of them all: the preservation of rain forests and nature's ecological treasures. The climate change scandal of 2009 and 2010 undermined the position of governments to do anything in a unified and constructive manner or at a United Nations level. The public's trust in science had waned as a result of the establishment fixing the climate change data to suit their political agenda.

Mankind had a lot to thank science for. Since the beginning of the nineteenth century, mankind had evolved in leaps and bounds in medicine, technology, nuclear power, gene therapy, and the mapping of DNA.

Although the success of mankind was largely down to science, there was a chain of distrust about people's intentions and why they pursued the science they did. This distrust was justified in some cases, as was illustrated when "Climategate" was exposed.

When the United Nations Climate Change Conference, called COP 15, began in Copenhagen, Denmark, with thousands of delegates gathered from around the world to discuss the then current state of Earth's climate, they were stumped. In the weeks leading up to the conference, an electronic break-in at the Climate Research Unit of the University of East Anglia and the subsequent posting of emails contained in the servers ignited a contentious debate – dubbed "Climategate" – between those sceptical of the human role in climate change and mainstream climatologists. Some had charged that the emails showed a concerted effort to withhold or manipulate data unsupportive of global warming.

Even though the Climate Change Conference in Copenhagen was also charged with developing an agreement that improved upon and replaced the Kyoto Protocol – the climate treaty ratified by many of the world's countries which was due to expire in 2012 – it was Climategate that commanded the headlines.

The public were left in more of a quandary than was foreseen. While they wanted to support a good cause, how could they trust the scientists or the governments and their so-called evidence? The distrust of science was enhanced.

There was, however, real strong evidence that over the 200 years following the industrial revolution, the CO_2 levels in the atmosphere had indeed increased due to human activity, which led to an overall temperature rise of approximately one degree Celsius.

The key for the fourth Hindsight team would be to enlighten and improve mankind's understanding of the impact, and offer them feasible other options and a solution that would prevent the issue escalating as it had done over that period. The team was armed with a raft of outstanding digital evidence, statistics based on fact and a storyline that was based on history from their timeline.

The challenge would be to get mankind in the twenty-first century to believe them.

CHAPTER 32

Climate Change – Preparing the Environment

Dr. Cassandra Mountain, who specialised in botany and plant life genetic modification, was teamed up with Dr. Beverley Cuzen-Baker, who was a highly qualified meteorologist and was the climate change expert in the fourth Hindsight team, code-named "Sunshine."

Cassandra and Beverley were accompanied by Mark Watson, known as Waddie, who had served several years in the USA Special Forces prior to being drafted to the Noah 5000 project. Waddie, who had a Master's in psychology from Princeton University, was the head of security and the team leader of Sunshine.

These three, with their extensive expertise in their respective fields, made a formidable team.

Before the Sunshine team was despatched, the members had discussed at length what their options were and concluded that the only way for them to succeed was to bathe their audience in empirical evidence that proved beyond doubt that mankind was having an impact on CO_2 build up that when coupled with both seasonal and cyclical epochs, it would accelerate and add to the detrimental effect on the global climate.

The team arrived at their destination near Stanford University; one of the worlds' leading research and teaching institutions, in Palo Alto, California. When the Sunshine team arrived, they were met by Mikhail Onderhoudt and Karyn Hodges, Joe, and the other members of the "Beach Head" team.

The date was 15th June 1972.

The Sunshine team knew that one thing they would have to overcome in presenting the climate change dilemma was a certain amount of confusion caused by the opposing scientific viewpoints as to whether the earth was in the process of global cooling or global warming. However, it was clear that scientists in the 1970s started increasingly favouring the warming viewpoint. A survey of the scientific literature from 1965 to 1979 found seven articles predicting cooling and forty-four predicting warming, with the warming articles also being cited much more often in subsequent scientific literature. In the 1980s, the consensus was that human activity definitely was contributing to the process of warming the climate, leading to the beginning of the modern period of global warming.

The Sunshine team needed to emphasise this viewpoint in the very early stages of the debate so that they could counter objections based on the opposing "global cooling" opinion used by those who were sceptical about climate change, or had vested interests in playing down man's role in it.

They had arrived in Stanford so that they could hook up with Stephen H. Schneider, a Stanford biology professor and a leading researcher in climate change, who would be influential in the public debate on the matter and a lead scientist on the United Nations' Inter-Governmental Panel on Climate Change.

Stephen Schneider had grown up in Long Island, New York. He studied engineering at Columbia University, receiving his bachelor's degree in mechanical engineering in 1966. In 1971, he earned a PhD in mechanical engineering and plasma physics. Schneider studied the role of greenhouse gases and suspended particulate material on climate as a postdoctoral fellow at NASA's Goddard Institute for Space Studies. At the start of his career, he briefly put forward the proposal that the earth could be facing an ice age.

Professor Schneider had claimed, "It is projected that man's potential to pollute both CO_2 and plastics will increase 6 to 8-fold in the next 50 years. If this increased rate of injection . . . should raise the present background opacity by a factor of 4, our calculations suggest a decrease in global temperature by as much as 3.5°C. Such a large decrease in the average temperature of Earth, sustained over a period of few years, is believed to be sufficient to trigger an ice age. However, by that time, nuclear power and other sustainable technologies may have largely replaced fossil fuels as a means of energy production."

Carbon dioxide was predicted to have only a minor role. However, the model was very simple and the calculation of the CO_2 effect was lower than other estimates by a factor of about three, as noted in a footnote to the paper.

The story made headlines in the *New York Times*. Shortly afterwards, Schneider became aware that he had overestimated the cooling effect of aerosols, and underestimated the warming effect of CO_2 by a factor of about three. He had mistakenly assumed that measurements of air particles he had taken near the source of pollution could be extrapolated and applied worldwide. He also found that much of the effect was due to natural aerosols, which would not be affected by human activities, so the cooling effect of changes in industrial pollution would be much less than he had calculated. Having found that recalculation showed that global warming was the more likely outcome, he demonstrated the high level of his integrity and published a retraction of his earlier findings in 1974. The Sunshine team's objective in 1972 was to influence and reinforce that retraction.

Stephen Schneider was an ideal person, being well known and influential in the climate arena, for the Sunshine team to work with to reframe the climate change debate.

Also, the era they had selected was perfect; they had arrived at a point in the genesis phase of the climate change debate that was mature enough to allow for a reframing to take place. At the 1972 United Nations Conference on the Human Environment in Stockholm, it was decided to create the United Nations Environment Programme, as several nations saw enhanced international research co-operation on the greenhouse topic as necessary. Then, in 1979, there was the first World Climate Conference in Geneva, and in 1980 the Brandt report was published, dealing with the greenhouse effect in the energy section.

The Sunshine team would work with Professor Schneider and other leading experts in Washington DC, giving them access to quantitative empirical evidence from the future on which to tune the models that they had previously used to make their projections. The difference between the first time round and this time was that their predictions were going to be accurate up to the year 2611 AD, because the Hindsight team had brought a fancy computer with all the data that Orb, the Noah 5000 computer expert, had prepared for them.

They would target the 1979 World Climate Conference as their launch pad to set the record straight and demystify the science.

Not long after their arrival, Cassandra noticed that Beverley appeared unwell. Her energy levels were way down and she also appeared to be rather depressed and anxious. There were also periods when Beverley insisted on being left alone to think, and did not welcome expressions of concern from Cassandra, who eventually concluded that Beverley was worried or anxious about the subject of their mission. She was wrong.

Within days of their arrival from the Noah bunker, Beverley had realised that she was in the very city in which the woman, Beverley-Anne Baker who would become her great, great, great grandmother was born, who had later worked for someone named Chuck Cuzen, who was her lover. She could not stop thinking about this, knowing the role that Chuck Cuzen would play in Watergate, the great scandal of the 1970s. She was not sleeping well, lying awake at night with a tortured conscience, wondering if things would have been different if Daniel Ellsberg had not stolen the Pentagon Papers, which detailed lies and misrepresentations by successive American governments about the war in Vietnam, from the Rand Corporation and later passed them to *The New York Times*. Then Cuzen would not have tried to discredit Ellsberg on the instructions of President Nixon, for which he was jailed. But at the same time, she knew that lives would have continued to be lost in Vietnam if Ellsberg had been prevented from doing what he did. It was little wonder that she was haunted by what she could do to mitigate both issues.

The stress of the past that haunted her, led Beverley to a difficult and uncomfortable conclusion. She would have to break a firm Hindsight rule and try to meet her great-great-great-grandmother to see whether there was anything that she could do to prevent her lover, Chuck Cuzen, from undertaking the work he did for President Nixon that led to his incarceration and family disgrace. It was a blot on her family history that she might be able to erase. She would have to be careful, though, as she knew what reaction she'd get from her collaborators if they found out.

CHAPTER 33

Unwanted Government Attention

Joe and two of the Beach Head team travelled forward in time to carry out some reconnaissance and intelligence gathering for the targeted 1979 World Climate Conference location, unaware that they were about to face the greatest challenge to their work yet.

As Joe and the others emerged from the time-machine at the landing site, they found themselves staring into the muzzles of guns held by a group of heavily armed men. Still groggy from their time travel journey, and struggling with the problems of short-term memory gaps, the phantasmagoria stirred up by the brain circuitry struggling to get up and running again - they were easy prey. They barely had a chance to recognise the danger before they were pounced on, arrested and bundled into separate military vehicles.

As Joe sat handcuffed in the back of the van with two armed guards, he reflected on the history of that decade between 1972 and 1982, which was about the time when most governments were still paranoid about the infiltration of communism and had become suspicious of everyone or anything that did not fit into their view of the world.

Joe recalled that the security detail in the Noah 5000 project had anticipated that there would be certain government security organisations from several countries that would show interest in the affairs of the Noah 5000 project. In an attempt to avoid being compromised, Joe took measures to ensure his team were very well equipped with the latest covert surveillance and counter-surveillance equipment. Since they arrived at the various execution points, Joe had been informed by those security details that they had become aware of several organisations such as the CIA, KGB, MI5 and FBI that had been tracking down and monitoring the movements of their various Noah 5000 team members and undertaking covert operations to try to steal the Hindsight team's futuristic time travel technology.

Joe looked at the higher-ranking officer who was guarding him and asked, "What's happening here? Why have we been arrested?"

The officer did not even acknowledge that Joe had spoken, merely staring at him with a hostile expression.

Joe said, "I asked you a question. I'd like an answer. You can't just arrest people without . . ."

He got no further. The guard sitting opposite him smashed the butt of his rifle into the side of Joe's head, and everything went dark.

Joe woke up lying on a cold concrete floor with a splitting headache in a small six by four-foot cell, with a gun-metal grey coloured door and an acrid stench of stale urine. He explored his head gingerly with his hand, feeling dried caked blood between his right temple and ear and a large swelling. He also had an incessant loud ringing in his ears.

Joe called out Buffa and David's names, hoping to establish if they were at least OK and somewhere nearby. His calls were met with a resounding silence.

Trying to ignore the headache, Joe began to think about what had happened. The men who had captured them, who he had figured out were government security agents, were waiting at the landing point, which meant they knew exactly when and where the team would be arriving. That meant they had to have been compromised by someone who knew their schedule and what the logistics were for this trip. Because of the sensitivity of this particular initiative, unlike the previous reconnoitring trips that the Beach Head team had carried out, this trip had been widely debated among many of the Hindsight team members during their strategy briefings.

Joe reflected sadly that while they had anticipated potential compromise and had factored that into their security drills, what they had never prepared for was someone from within the Noah teams betraying them.

CHAPTER 34

The Pentagon Papers and Wikileaks

In the short while that they had been at Stanford, Cassandra Mountain had been following with some fascination the Pentagon Papers case, while Beverley had showed signs of being disinterested in it. Suddenly, on July 29th, 1972, the trial of Ellsberg and Russo, charged with stealing the papers and arranging for them to be published, was halted after it was disclosed that the government had wire-taped conversations between one of the defendants and his lawyer or consultants. As a result of that intelligence, it was decided that a stay of the proceedings was necessary until the Supreme Court had a chance to consider the matter. Cassandra was fed up with it.

"What the hell sort of people are in this government?" she fumed. "First, they try to hush up all the cloak-and-dagger stuff about this Vietnam War, then they slap an injunction on *The New York Times* to stop them publishing the papers, and now they're trying to get Ellsberg and Russo. They sound like a bunch of crooks, and these guys should be praised, not thrown into jail for what they've brought to light."

Beverley answered her offhandedly. "They'll get off. There's no need to get so excited. It's not the end of the show."

Cassandra looked at her curiously. "Hey," she said, "we've only just arrived in this timeline. How come you know so much about it?"

Beverley realised that she might have said more than she should, and tried to rescue the situation. "Oh," she said, contriving to look rather bored, "I researched the period's history in detail before we left and, in any case, you should remember that Dr. Schneider, who we're talking with, actually consulted to President Nixon while he was in office."

"Yeah, so what's this court case got to do with President Nixon? I seem to remember he was impeached or was forced to resign because of the Watergate scandal."

"Holy crap girl!" exclaimed Beverley in exasperation. "You're following this case, but you don't know anything about the context! What planet have you been on all this time?" Calming down a bit, she went on, "It was the Nixon lot that set up the "Plumbers' unit" – so named because their orders were to plug leaks in the administration. It was that team that burgled Daniel Ellsberg's psychiatrist's office to find evidence that they hoped would expose whether he leaked the Pentagon Papers. He was a defence analyst, after all."

"Well, who's a clever girl, then," said Cassandra, sarcastically, but Beverley appeared distracted and barely noticed.

"It was in September last year–1971–that a White House aide instructed the ex-agents to see whether they could extract the files and wiretap the offices of the Democrat Party so that President Nixon could keep track of his enemies."

Cassandra abandoned the attempt to take Beverley down a peg or two, saying, "Yes, I remember now, when the Nixon administration decided to pursue Ellsberg and Russo for leaking the Pentagon Papers, it was someone called Krogh who approved the burglary of the psychiatrist seeing Daniel Ellsberg at the time. Wasn't he the head of the "plumbers", running secret investigations?"

Beverley breathed a sigh of relief; she thought for a moment Cassandra was going to say that it was Chuck Cuzen who had authorised the agents to commit those break-ins.

Cassandra mused, "You know, this entire whistle blowing about the Vietnam War was very similar to that Wikileaks fiasco with Julian Assange during the early 2000s."

Beverley, pleased that Cassandra had strayed off the subject of the Pentagon Papers, said, "Yes, and it was actually Daniel Ellsberg who remarked at that time that the Wikileaks case had teased the genie of transparency out of the bottle and that forces in America which operate in the shadows were trying to stuff the genie back into the bottle."

Cassandra laughed and said, "You would have thought that governments and politicians would have learnt their lessons after forty years. They probably wished they had time-travel capabilities so they could go back in time to stem the leaks." She stopped suddenly, aware that Beverley had turned white. "What's the matter, Bev?" she asked her voice full of concern.

"I—nothing," stammered Beverley. "I just don't feel too well all of a sudden."

"Oh, you poor thing. You do look washed out. Why don't you go and lie down for a while?"

"Ye-es, I think I will," agreed Beverley, shakily, and disappeared to her bedroom.

What Cassandra was not aware of was that Beverley had been secretly meeting with her great-great-great-grandmother during her trips to Washington DC; Beverley-Ann Baker, in an attempt to give her pointers to steer her lover, Chuck Cuzen in another direction in the hopes of avoiding the illegal activities he undertook in the previous timeline, which Beverley had listed for her.

Beverley, unable to withstand the temptation to try to change the course of events that, as she saw it, had left a blot on her family's history, had finally plucked up the courage to call on her several times great-grandmother, having first made sure she was at home in Washington DC.

Beverley-Ann answered the door, looking curiously at the nervous-seeming stranger outside. Beverley swallowed hard, forgot all the carefully reasoned introductions she had rehearsed, and blurted out, "Hello, I'm your great-great-great-grand-daughter."

Understandably, her relative looked bemused, then a little frightened. She spoke gently but firmly, "My dear, you must know that is not possible." Clearly thinking that Beverley must have wandered off from some mental health hospital, she asked, "Where have you come from?"

"From the future," replied Beverley, adding quickly, "I know I sound mad, but really I am your descendent, and I and others have returned to earlier times to try to prevent the self-destruction of mankind. Oh, God, that sounds even more insane, but I swear it's true. Please, can I come in and talk to you?"

"No, I'm afraid not," said Beverley-Ann. Still speaking gently and calmly, she continued, "I will have to ask you to leave. You need to see a doctor, as you are clearly not . . ."

"*Please*, you must believe me!"

Now looking quite upset, Beverley-Ann said, "My dear girl, how can I?" and began to close the door.

Desperately Beverley searched her mind for something that might convince her. "Wait!" she cried. "When I was a child, I had a dolls-house that had been in the family for generations. It was my favourite thing. I don't remember who had it first, but if you know of it, I can describe it to you."

Beverley-Ann paused, with the door almost closed. "Very well," she said, obviously trying to humour the mad woman on her doorstep, "tell me what it was like."

Beverley spoke in a rush, her words tumbling over each other in her haste to convince the other woman. "It was painted cream – although that might not have been the original colour, I guess – and it was really big, and it had a red door, and windows with lots of little panes. And . . . and . . . it had real electric chandeliers, with crystal drops, and the furniture was all in antique style . . . I loved the red velvet chaise longue, and used to promise myself I'd have one when I grew up – I never did, but . . . Oh, and it had a garden inside a little picket fence, with rose bushes, and an apple tree . . ." She tailed off, noticing that Beverley-Ann had gone rather pale. "Are you . . . are you, all right?" she faltered.

"I don't know if this is wise," replied Beverley-Ann, "but I think you had better come in after all."

Once Beverley was inside the house, her great-great-great grandmother led her upstairs to a room in which was displayed a splendid dolls-house, just like the one Beverley had described. "It was my mother's," said Beverley-Ann.

Beverley broke down in tears when she saw it. "I loved it so," she sobbed. "I kept it to pass on to my children . . . but . . ."

"So, did I, my dear, so did I. Now I think you had better explain things to me, because Lord knows I'm pretty confused here." And she led Beverley to the more comfortable lounge, made tea, and listened to an incredible story.

Beverley showed her things she had brought to back up her story, such as lists of future Nobel prize-winners, reviews of films and television programs yet to be made, and obituaries of famous people who were still alive in 1972.

Her great-great-great grandmother was an intelligent woman, and realised that Beverley was doing something she should not. Looking searchingly at her, she said, "I'm sure you are not supposed to contact your forebears, are you?"

"No," admitted Beverley.

"So why have you broken the rules in order to see me? It can't be because you wanted to discuss the doll house."

"No," said Beverley again. "I need to talk to you about your lover, Chuck Cuzen."

Beverley-Ann's eyebrows lifted. "Why?" she asked.

Beverley drew a deep breath, and said, "Because I want to try to keep him out of jail, and save later generations the embarrassment of being connected with someone who did the things he did. Your child by him is my great-great-grandfather, and my family is a proud one. I'm trying to clean up their history."

She went on, "You will already know that Chuck Cuzen was appointed as Special Counsel to President Nixon in 1969. What you might not yet know is that in 1971 he authored a memo which became famous, in which he listed Nixon's major political enemies. He also proposed firebombing the Brookings Institution and stealing politically damaging documents in the ensuing confusion."

"Oh, God!" exclaimed Beverley-Ann.

"Obviously we can't change any of that," said Beverley, "because it's already happened. But what will send him to jail is his connection the burglary of the Democratic National Committee offices that sets off what will become known as the Watergate scandal, which will bring down President Nixon in 1974."

She also explained that although the incriminating tapes had not yet been discovered, transcripts would be released of a taped White House conversation between Nixon and Cuzen on June 20th, 1972, clearly showing both men's early involvement in obstructing justice in the Watergate investigation.

"On March 10th, 1973, seventeen months before Nixon is forced to resign, Chuck Cuzen will resign from the White House to return to the private practice of law as senior partner of the law firm of Cuzen and Shapiro, in Washington. On March 1st, 1974, my great-great-great grandfather, Chuck Cuzen, will be indicted for conspiring to cover up the Watergate burglary."

Tearfully, Beverley continued, "Richard Nixon will become the first U.S. president to resign. Vice President Gerald Ford will assume the country's highest office. President Ford will later pardon Nixon of all charges related to the Watergate case, but that pardon will not apply to those following the orders of the President."

The two women hugged one another, sobbing, and agreed that Beverley-Ann would attempt to prevent the love of her life from being incarcerated by telling him what she knew in the hope that he would somehow be able to utilise the information to avoid the charges against him.

Beverley impressed on her that she would have to make him swear to secrecy, and she promised to do so.

CHAPTER 35

Climate Change – Presenting the Case

Both Beverley Cuzen-Baker and Cassandra Mountain had been invited to enrol at the University of Stanford as lecturers and by 1974 were gainfully employed in their respective fields of expertise. Whereas Waddie spent a lot of his time doing research and meeting with other well renowned people in the climate change arena, both Cassandra and Beverley had started to build reputations in their field so as to gain the necessary respectability through peer reviews.

It was two full years before they were ready to arrange a private meeting with Dr. Schneider after having met him on several occasions already during various workshops with the National Centre for Atmospheric Research (NCAR) in 1972. Dr. Schneider was a member of the scientific staff of NCAR from 1973 through 1996, where he co-founded the Climate Project. At their first "Hindsight" get-together, they reminded each other who they were, where they currently worked, and reaffirmed the objectives of their putting their heads together.

After dispensing with the non-disclosure agreements with the lawyers, who were summarily dispatched, Beverley had reinforced the reason why they felt he was important to the "Sunshine" initiative, because, she said, "you are internationally recognized for research, policy analysis and outreach in climate change, Dr. Schneider, focusing on climate change science, integrated assessment of ecological and economic impacts of human-induced climate change, and your involvement in identifying feasible climate policies and technological solutions."

Dr. Schneider also reminded them that he had consulted with federal agencies and/or White House staff in the Nixon administration, which they all agreed was very important. However, both Cassandra and Bev knew that Dr. Schneider would go on to consult and advise the Carter, Reagan, G. H. W. Bush, Clinton, and G. W. Bush administrations as well.

They shared some data with Dr. Schneider that Michael Raider – "Orb" – had prepared for them back at the Noah 5000 bunker. Dr. Schneider was immediately taken aback by the sophistication of the technology they used in their presentation and the enormity of the data-set they seemed to manipulate on a "mainframe" computer that was no larger than a small encyclopaedia book.

They spent hours analysing the meteorology and climate data from all over the globe, watching the patterns of weather changing as each year passed across the screen. What struck Dr. Schneider more than anything else was the verification of what Beverley had mentioned before they began looking at the evidence.

Beverley had opened up by explaining, "The data we have on this computer is real data from the future; the technology is far more sophisticated than anything that will be invented for another 100 years

"You will see that it was the extreme fringes of the weather patterns that change gradually over the next 100 years."

Beverley displayed information about weather changes between 2000 and 2100, showing that summers became hotter, drier and with extended droughts, while winters became colder, with temperatures reaching highs and lows never experienced in some locations since records began. Storms became more violent, with winds reaching speeds never before recorded in those locations, and flooding became the norm in areas which had not flooded in centuries. Hurricanes and monsoons became bigger, more violent, and more frequent.

"Here's some more for you to digest," she continued, showing further information. "As you will see, during the same period of time, desertification increased by at least 30% – remember – we are talking about only 100 years – in numerous areas of the world."

She paused briefly, then said, "Pretty bad, huh? But that's not all.

The polar ice caps continued to melt, gradually causing sea levels to rise by at least 1 metre, CO_2 levels continued to rise, yet the overall temperature rose only 1° Celsius, but it was enough for those weather patterns to change in the way they did."

Cassandra went on to explain, "If you consider the actual surface area of planet Earth, approximately 68.8% of the world's surface is covered by seawater."

She then pointed out that the additional weight of the water produced by the ice caps melting put pressure on the tectonic plates, causing them to re-seat, which in turn caused more frequent violent volcanic and earthquake activity over the 100 years they were looking at.

"One example," she said, "was the Japanese earthquake in 2011 that measured nine (9) on the Richter scale and was followed by a violent and devastating tsunami, which killed tens of thousands of people. This event was one of the five most powerful earthquakes in the world since modern record-keeping began in 1900.

"The Pacific Ring-of-Fire was hit severely over that 100-year period by a series of massive disasters, which included earthquakes, volcanic eruptions and tsunamis.

"The America's west coast was the next to be hit in the series of earthquakes that brought devastation to America, Canada, Mexico and Chile by the end of 2032."

Cassandra explained, "Basically, what we are going to show you is a complete vindication of most of the things you have all been saying, although you have all been saying it in a disjointed, uncoordinated and incoherent way."

After several hours of looking at the empirical data and charts, which fascinated Dr. Schneider, Cassandra went on to share the summarised findings of a report which would be drafted in 2010 by Dr. Michael MacCracken. That summary would give six points, each well established and so serious that it was clear action to reduce emissions was imperative if we were to stand any chance of moderating the very significant and possibly irreversible impacts that might lie ahead.

She said, "The first of these six points dealt with emissions from human activity, and highlighted in particular the combustion of fossil fuels, which were changing the composition of the atmosphere, especially by raising the concentrations of climate-warming gases. That led directly to the second point, which was that these higher concentrations would contribute towards the intensification of the natural greenhouse effect, resulting in global warming and changes in climate that would persist for centuries."

She broke off for a moment to sip from her glass of water, then continued, "Point number three emphasised that changes in the climate were already evident and consistent with human behaviour becoming the dominant influence on top of the cyclical changes that were expected in the late twentieth century."

Quickly, she ran through the remaining three points, which were that future climate change was projected to be substantial if emissions continued to increase without restriction. She pointed out that both the environment and society would be impacted in significant ways as a result of both climate change and the rise in the atmospheric carbon dioxide concentration, and that slowing the ongoing changes in atmospheric composition, would be but one tool in the box of strategies. The climate would require substantial reductions in greenhouse gas emissions over the coming decades in order to limit anthropogenic interference with the climate system and avoid the most harmful environmental and societal consequences.

Based on the futuristic data he had seen, Dr. Schneider marvelled at how astute and accurate Dr. Michael MacCracken's predictions in his report were and appeared excited by the fact that a well-renown scientist and a man of Dr. MacCracken's integrity, intellect and analytical calibre had created an artefact that would prove to be so accurate in years to come.

Finally, before they wrapped up the session, Cassandra explained that the evidence also showed that mankind was unable to slow down the CO_2 build up sufficiently, and, when coupled with the natural evolutionary cyclical climate changing phenomenon the world underwent in its natural cycles of evolution, the climate changing process was already well into its natural cycle and by the year 2030 would prove to be unstoppable through mankind's actions alone.

All three of the Sunshine team members could see that Dr. Schneider was very excited by this new turn of events and was chomping at the bit to get his hands on the data.

He quite rightly asked whether he was able to get a copy of the data so that his colleagues and peers back at Stanford and National Centre for Atmospheric Research could build this into their models.

Waddie stood up and said, "All in good time. We absolutely want the world to see this evidence – that's why we've brought it – and as you can imagine, because of the sensitivity of the source, we need to do this in a secure and structured way that allows for the data to be presented using technology currently available to the scientific establishment.

"Ideally, we should look to work with at least 100 scientists across the world, in a way that allows them to share summarised elements of the data to complete and validate their research activities and give the scientific community an opportunity to present a composite, congruent and unified case for climate change at the first World Climate Conference in 1979." He paused, and then stated simply, "That gives us three years."

Dr. Schneider agreed and suggested, "We should start with the list of climatologists and scientists that are part of a universal working group, of which I am a founding member."

"That's great!" said Waddie. "We're really glad to have you on board."

CHAPTER 36

The Nixon Rubber-Bung Conundrum

During one of their romantic evenings, where Chuck would spend time with Beverley-Ann and lavish her with gifts and promises of marriage, Beverley-Ann shared what she had learnt about the time-travel project with Chuck Cuzen.

Armed with this information and under the express orders of President Nixon, Chuck Cuzen setup a surveillance task force to intercept and monitor communications between Cassandra and Beverley and anyone they came into contact with.

Before Cuzen resigned he explained to President Nixon in the Oval Office "that a complete surveillance programme had been setup to covertly monitor the movements of the Noah project members with a view to seizing their Time-Machine. This team has been codenamed "Rubber-Bung." It has been outfitted with different resources from those used in the Plumbers team. The whole operation had been earmarked top secret from the outset and reports directly to you through me."

Nixon said, "I'll just say again, we have got to keep our eye on the ball. Daniel Ellsberg is the ball. We've got to get this son of a bitch."

Cuzen continued "Once we have sufficient intelligence and know the whereabouts of the time-travel device we will make our move."

Nixon said, "They don't know what's going to hit them when we travel back in time and neutralise the son of a bitch before Ellsberg can get his thieving hands on those damned papers."

Cuzen's "Rubber Bung" plan had indeed worked. They had captured the time travel device, but were none the wiser as to how to operate it, so he was not quite ready to inform the President of his progress.

Cuzen thought to himself, "it shouldn't be long now before we can operate the device, he wanted to be sure to plug the Pentagon Papers leak Beverley-Ann had informed him of."

Meantime, elsewhere, after six days without sleep due to the repeated intermittent interrogations undertaken by several teams of battle-hardened mean looking agents, Joe and his team were beginning to show signs of fatigue. During one of the many periods when his interrogators thought Joe was unconscious, Joe learned that a certain Chuck Cuzen was behind the arrest of himself and the Beach Head team when they arrived to carry out early reconnaissance of the 1979 World Climate Conference location.

Joe knew that it was just a matter of time before his body would start to break down because by being forced to remain awake and alert for days at a time it would have a dramatic effect on his cognitive ability, and may cause temporary increases in stress, depression, and hallucinations. Because of his military training in a more modern age, he knew that if done correctly, sleep deprivation as a tool in military interrogation would increase stress levels increasing the chances, they might divulge important information.

As part of his training to combat interrogation techniques, such as sleep deprivation, Joe and the other members of the Beach Head team were taught that sleep is a very active process, affecting many physical and mental pathways in ways that science before the 1980's had not even begun to understand. The brain is composed of thousands of neurons firing off signals and releasing neurotransmitters. These neurotransmitters act as signalling molecules, giving cues for nearly every process in the body, including sleep. Neurons in the brain release neurotransmitters such as serotonin and norepenephrine to keep the brain alert and awake during the day. During sleep, different neurons fire, inhibiting daytime signals and promoting rest.

Joe and the other Beach Head team members knew too well that sleep deprivation could cause impaired memory and cognitive functioning, decreased short term memory, speech impairment, hallucinations, psychosis, lowered immunity, headaches, high blood pressure, cardiovascular disease, along with stress, anxiety and depression.

As part of their training they learnt strategies to combat the effects of sleep deprivation. The Beach Head team knew that they could last approximately three days or 72 hours without sleep, after, which they needed to start using counter measures like bartering with some futile pre-agreed misinformation for a cup of coffee. They knew that approximately, 200 to 300 mg doses of caffeine mitigated many of the adverse effects of sleep deprivation. From their military training they also learnt that caffeine would significantly improve their visual vigilance, reaction time and cognitive brain functions so that they could remain in control of the situation as best they could, under the circumstances.

They also knew that the FBI, CIA and NSA during that era had not yet fully understood the chemical functions of the brain, so all three of them had a distinct advantage over their interrogators.

By the eighth day, Joe had managed to build up some rapport with one of the interrogators – Bernie. Joe knew, that if he focused on one of his interrogators, and fed only him small pieces of valuable information so that it looked like whenever he was interrogating, progress was made. That would impress his superiors. The key was to select the right interrogator, one that had certain traits that could be easily influenced.

After listening to the standard opening salvo of macho intimidation given each time a new FBI officer took over the interrogation shift, Joe asked, "So, Bernie, you have kept me here for over a week, does that mean you have not fathomed out how to operate the machine yet? How can I help you?"

"You really want to help me; how do I know whether you are just playing for time and have some kind of trick up your sleeve?" Bernie responded.

Joe tried as best he could to laugh through his swollen blood encrusted lips and replied, "Yeah right, obviously I am the one sitting butt naked chained to this damned chair and I am the one with something up my sleeve? I can see why they chose you for this job; you must be the sharpest knife in the drawer, I bet your boss knew your colleagues could never figure that one out."

Bernie laughed, "ok wise guy, you know what I mean. Yes, we do want you to help us understand how to operate that machine."

Joe knew that was the clue he was looking for, as the Beach Head team had a pre-arranged extraction plan that would hopefully work and get them out of their present predicament.

Joe leaned forward as far as his restraints would allow and whispered, "the technology is very sophisticated. The mechanism will only take instructions from verified operators if the control panel can detect certain pre-authorised genes in the breath sample of the operator."

Bernie looked as though he was stunned by a cattle prod, his jaw dropped, with mouth wide open. It took a full five seconds before signs of comprehension appeared in his eyes, then he burst out laughing. After he had regained his composure he asked, "you mean all I have to do is wear your Levi jeans and I will be authorised to operate the contraption?"

This time it was Joe who laughed, causing the scab on his lip to tear open again. As the blood started to trickle down his chin again from the split on his lower lip, Joe retorted spelling out the letters "G...E...N...E...S not J...E...A...N...S you dipstick!"

The look on Bernie's face was that of utter incredulity.

Joe knew the fish had taken the baited hook and Bernie would be thinking how he would be considered the smartest Agent amongst his peers, putting him first in line for a promotion. Bernie secured the prisoner and left the detention facility to work out how he could leverage this information to his advantage.

Later that morning, two armed subordinates under Bernie bundled hand-cuffed and leg chained Joe, Buffa and David into a black van with blacked out windows. The van, part of a three-vehicle convoy, left the detention facility, the prisoners were signed out and heading for destinations unknown by the armed guards.

Only Joe and Bernie knew where they were headed. Joe had described at length to Bernie how the time-travel craft had to be primed before invoking the time travel device.

During the numerous interrogation sessions, as part of a confidence building strategy, Bernie was the only Agent that Joe had purposely discussed time travel and the device with.

As Bernie sat in the lead vehicle, he started visualising how he was going to present his findings to Directors of the CIA and FBI once he had a chance to verify what he had learnt from Joe.

CHAPTER 37

Ambition over-rules Common Sense

The location chosen by Joe was remote from any prying eyes, just like their previous trips, rural locations outside of the target city or town were always selected.

When the convoy arrived at the pre-agreed destination, the time travel device was already there, sitting on the back of a long flatbed truck, covered in a tightly stretched tarpaulin to avoid the device being seen by the public whilst in transport.

During one of their numerous interrogation sessions, as part of his plan to deceive Bernie, Joe explained "it takes a minimum of three people to operate the vehicle, but due to radiation poisoning, which myself, David and Buffa have been inoculated against; it would be lethal for anyone of the Agents to stand near the device whilst it was being primed and prepared for this test trip. I suggest, Bernie that you bring along a single radiation protection suit to protect yourself from Gamma radiation, which is the most penetrating and energetic form of nuclear radiation. Also, whilst gamma radiation will go through most suits the alpha and beta radiation can be easily blocked by the suit - but the inhalation or ingestion of an alpha or beta source is the beginning of a nasty chain of cancerous events."

"Also" Joe explained, "Bernie, you need to bring a filming device with you so that the start-up instructions can be filmed, that way you can ensure the test trip will not be wasted. So if there is anything back in time you dearly want to change, we can go back to that point in time, which will allow you to leave yourself a detailed note that articulates what you need to invoke or do during that period to manifest that particular change."

Joe could tell instinctively that he had chosen the right stooge for his escape plan. Bernie's eyes lit up with excitement at the thought of being able to go back in time to make a change that would enhance his future. Bernie was unable to mask his burning ambition and desire to run his department.

"Yes" Bernie thought, "I know exactly when I need to go back to and what I need to do, to ensure I become the head of this department."

Only the handcuffs were removed from all three prisoners, allowing David and Buffa still in their leg-irons to remove the tarpaulin from the device on the back of the truck.

Joe knew for his plan to work, he had to act quickly, because the pre-arranged extraction plan that was designed to get them out of unplanned predicaments such as this, was about to unfold with a recovery team appearing at a location just several hundred yards from this very location.

Like a child with a new toy, Bernie was so keen to use the device to help him control how his career would develop, he lost sight of common sense by overlooking the risks to his own safety and ordered the other Agents to take cover in their vehicles so that they would not be irradiated by the plasma flux that emits when the device launches itself into the void of time.

Once Bernie had fully donned his radiation protection gear, he armed himself with his Sig Sauer P226 9mm side-arm he climbed aboard, followed by Joe, David and Buffa.

Once all were aboard the time-travel device, Joe wrote something on the piece of paper Bernie had given him with all the coordinates and said, "Bernie switch on the 8mm camera and start filming the start-up procedure" as he entered the coordinates of the location along with the date and time of the period Bernie wanted the device to take him back to.

Standing in front of Bernie, who was confidently holding the 8mm camera in one hand and 9mm pistol in the other hand, Joe began the countdown, "five, four, three, two, one......."

HINDSIGHT

When Bernie came to his senses from his dizzy-lightheaded state after the time-travel device came to a standstill he found himself staring into both the 8mm camera and his own 9mm pistol – he had absolutely no idea of where he was, who these people were and what had just happened – his short-term memory was wiped clean.

David, holding the pistol, explained that Bernie was sent by his boss to help them do some reconnaissance for the upcoming conference.

They knew that by the time Bernie fully realised his mistake, they would have accomplished their mission. Bernie would have been dropped off by the recover team at the second location a full minute after the records would have shown that he departed. Again, Bernie would be none the wiser as to what had just happened and his fellow Agents would be similarly puzzled and sworn to secrecy for the sakes of their careers.

Meanwhile, Joe was already communicating with the other members of the Beach Head team who were going to find themselves in the very near future forming a recovery team to go and find Joe, David and Buffa.

CHAPTER 38

Climate Change – A Change in Philosophy

All three of the Sunshine team members worked with Dr. Schneider to ensure that the data was distributed to over 100 scientists across the globe on technology that was available in that era. They worked in concert with the other Hindsight teams who were focusing on political changes and the United Nations to ensure that the right messages were put forward that would not alienate the populace, as had happened in the previous timeline.

They had managed to get the climate change data fully analysed and interpreted by the time of the first World Climate Conference in 1979.

Dr. Schneider and a panel of other esteemed climatologists presented their findings and suggested routes of remediation across the globe. They also pointed out to the media and the public that they would not allow governments to politicise this issue, as it affected every single living creature on planet Earth.

Eight key issues had been tabled and agreed as manageable solutions which would address some of the root causes of energy wastage. These solutions would need a unified global approach and unanimous acceptance of if they were to be successful.

First, tropical countries needed to cease the slashing and burning of the rain forests and institute a mandatory implementation of a three for one tree replanting regime in managed forests. By 2010, because of greed, over thirty-three million acres of forest was being cut down every year. Timber harvesting and waste burning in the tropics alone contributed 1.5 billion metric tons of carbon to the atmosphere. That represented 20% of human-made greenhouse gas emissions and was a source that could be avoided relatively easily.

Next, mankind would have to find and adopt alternative means of renewable energy including energy from wind, solar power, wave, biofuels, and so on, sources other than coal and oil to generate electricity, like nuclear energy, which would have to be rolled out to all countries to ensure that electricity was no longer produced from coal and oil. Massive investment in low-emission energy generation, whether solar-thermal power or nuclear fission, would be required to radically reduce greenhouse gas emissions.

The third initiative to adopt was that industrial nations would have to apply and utilise low carbon technologies in all factory and mass transport facilities. Laws would need to be drafted and implemented that would mandate the use of energy sources that were alternatives to hydrocarbon sources, without exception.

The motor industry would need to work with the governments to implement the necessary infrastructure to support a hydrogen economy, creating hybrid vehicles that would use hydrogen as the primary source of energy to create electricity through the use of Fuel cells, which are devices that convert hydrogen gas directly into low-voltage, direct current electricity. The cell has no moving parts. The process is essentially the reverse of the electrolytic method of splitting water into hydrogen and oxygen and electricity as the secondary source of energy.

Recycling of all products should become mandatory. Laws would need to be drafted and implemented that would make it illegal to burn or put into landfill anything that was capable of being recycled. Targets for recycling would have to be set at high as 98% if every product had to be recycled in some way once it was depleted or discarded.

All food and excrement waste should be fed into collective digestion chambers located in every suburb or conurbation location, so that it could be used to create methane gas, which would in turn be used to generate electricity. This included businesses, farms and household waste. Laws would be needed which would mandate that no sewage could be pumped underground or into rivers, lakes or the sea. All by-products of the digestion chambers would be used for fertiliser, which would in turn help to put nutrients back into the soil and thus increase crop yields.

Another point dealt with building. All new-build dwellings, office buildings and factories would be obliged by law to employ the latest eco-friendly, energy-efficient material and designs. A target date would be set after which no new builds would be permitted to be erected unless they were compliant and used the latest and best technology available for this purpose. This would include double/triple-glazed windows, insulation in cavity walls, roofs, between floors and under the base floor, as well as heat exchangers to recover any excess heat, used in "passive housing" projects, such as those in Germany, which used "passive cooling or heating" techniques. Passive cooling refers to technologies or design features used to cool buildings in summer or warm in winter without power consumption, such as those technologies described in the "Passive Cooling" projects in Wikipedia.

There would be at least 6.6 billion people living on planet earth by the end of 2010, a number that was predicted by the United Nations to grow to at least nine billion by the middle of the century. The UN Environmental Program estimated that it required at least fifty-four acres to sustain an average human being in 2010; which furnishes food, clothing and other resources extracted from the planet. Continuing such population growth proved to be unsustainable; more humans mean more greenhouse gas emissions. Thus, it was proposed that couples should be limited to having two children only.

Falling birth rates in some developed and developing countries (a significant proportion of which would only be due to government-imposed limits on the number of children a couple can have) would begin to reduce or reverse the population explosion. It remains unclear how many people the planet can comfortably sustain, but it is clear that per capita energy consumption must go down if climate change is to be controlled.

Ultimately, two children per couple would prove to be sustainable to maintain a stabilised human population.

During the next two years, the Sunshine Team and Dr. Schneider worked with the 100 scientists to ensure their respective governments were fully supportive of the recommendations and had begun implementing them.

The Sunshine Team already knew that in January 1981, Ronald Reagan had just been sworn in as the US President; he was a man with a mission and had concerns about how the change in climate would adversely affect mankind. President Reagan's administration proved to be supportive of the climate change suggestions and worked hard over the next eight years on the US Senate and Congress to adopt some of these as fundamental elements of the US energy initiative.

The Second World Climate Conference was an important step towards a global climate treaty. Sponsored by the World Meteorological Organization, the United Nations Environment Programme (UNEP), and other international organizations, the conference was held in Geneva from 29 October to 7 November 1990.

What had been perceived as impossible in the previous timeline had indeed been partly achieved in this timeline; over 80% of the countries in the world had readily started to adopt some of these suggestions, with most of them introducing laws that made it difficult for any avoidance.

Based on the previous timeline data, the Sunshine team saw some positive changes in weather data. Another plank had been laid in the Hindsight strategy.

CHAPTER 39

Concorde - Zero-Tolerance on Arms Sales

The date was December 29th 1957.

The fifth Hindsight team, code-named "Concorde", had a challenge that would take some clever political and diplomatic manoeuvring. Dr. Martin van Ashwegan was the Concorde team leader; like his father, who had been the Deputy Headmaster of an excellent co-ed school in Africa, Martin could, read, write and speak twelve languages. Both he and his father were masterful chess players, so strategy and planning came easily to them. While Martin was an adept rugby player, playing for the high school first team, he was also considered extremely bright and a swot at high school, an intelligence which was confirmed when he easily secured two first class distinctions for Doctorates in both Psychology and Geo Politics, simultaneously. Because of the dangerous nature of this mission, the Concorde team had a four-person security detail and two researchers who were well versed in the arms trade of the period covering the eighty years after the Second World War.

David Mofitt, also a keen and popular sportsman, was Martin's head of security; he had spent several years in the military Special Forces fighting in various wars against terrorists. The one thing David knew well was the business of mercenaries and the arms dealing trade, as that was part of the domain his unit had to monitor and police out in the field in his previous life.

The Concorde team were met by Joe and the other members of the Beach Head team as well as Karyn Hodges and Charlie Robson from the Exceed team, all of whom looked much the same as they did at the Noah 5000 bunker, as if it was only yesterday. Joe and his team had done some extensive research on this subject while on the ground and were well positioned to brief the incoming team.

The team had arrived in Hampshire in the United Kingdom. The Concorde team would be dealing with post Second World War and the "Cold War" politics. So, attempting to outlaw the sale of arms to any country was indeed the toughest and deadliest challenge that faced the six Noah 5000 Hindsight teams.

Soon the teams were settled into their accommodation in Shawford House, near Winchester, which was a Grade II listed building set in around twenty-four hectares of parkland and formal gardens. The estate was river bound on two of its three borders by the River Itchen and Itchen Navigation, giving rise to double and single bank fishing. A Grade II listed folly stood in the grounds. In 2008 much restoration of the landscape had been undertaken.

Located in the beautiful parish of Twyford, Shawford House, was built for Sir Henry Mildmay in 1685 on the site of the pre-existing Dares House. Extensive Mildmay Estate accounts dating from 1653 to 1728 detailed planting, garden work and construction of banquet houses. Its gardens and orchards, planted in 1683, were supplemented with paths, archways and ornaments.

Once the team had gathered and settled in the parlour, which was dressed with ornate carved wooden furniture, sumptuous woven carpets from the Middle-East, and warmed by a coal fire, Joe began to brief Martin and his team.

Joe began with a little sage advice and guidance, warning that those who were in the Arms business had extensive reach and were prepared to go to any lengths to get their way. He reminded them of their history, which would be many years in the future in this timeline. "It was thought by many that Diana, Princess of Wales's untimely death in the tragic accident in Paris 1997 was due to her interfering in the murky world of Arms dealing when promoting the "landmine ban" agenda."

He went on to elaborate, "During her tenure as the champion of "The Ottawa Treaty" Princess Diana visited Angola in January

1997, and walked through a minefield twice. In January 1997, Angola's population was approximately ten million and had between ten to twenty million landmines in place from their civil war. In August 1997, she visited Bosnia with the Landmine Survivors Network. Her work with organisations who were pressing for the total worldwide banning of landmines focused mainly on the injuries and deaths inflicted on children.

"Diana's involvement attracted a lot of interest from the media. When the Second Reading of the Landmines Bill was presented in the British House of Commons in 1998, Foreign Secretary Robin Cook praised and paid tribute to Diana's work on landmines, saying, "All Honourable Members will be aware from their postbags of the immense contribution made by Diana, Princess of Wales to bringing home to many of our constituents the human costs of landmines. The best method in which to record our appreciation of her work, and the work of NGOs that have campaigned against landmines, is to pass the Landmines Bill, paving the way towards a global ban on landmines." Joe continued, "Princess Diana embarked on a crusade for the international outlawing of landmines and to make those companies manufacturing them, culpable for the damage and suffering their products caused the inhabitants in the affected areas. In actual fact, similar precedents of this type were being promoted in industries like the cigarette industry, where they were being made by law to compensate people who became ill with cancer as a result of smoking."

He explained, "There was a stark and fundamental difference, cigarette companies were not militant and armed to the teeth, so governments were prepared to take them on in the civil courts, unlike the Arms dealing industry. There was also a distinct lack of courage and motivation from the ineffective United Nations because the Arms dealers had teeth and could bite back."

Sadly, even with that accolade from Robin Cook MP, the mainstream media, the Governments around the world and Royal family did not give enough credit to this gargantuan break through Princess Diana managed to foster in the reducing the sales of small armaments. The task was herculean and yet she managed to get it through.

At this point, David Mofitt added, "Not only were there hundreds of billions of dollars at stake, there were powerful industry lobbies in countries such as the USA, UK, France and Russia, plus there were those corrupt governments and ruthless criminal gangs in corrupt countries, such as the Balkan states. All of these players caused havoc when challenged to enforce limits or prohibit their selling of arms to whoever had the money to pay for them."

David went on, "To make matters worse, each time any country made a technological break-through, like the stealth planes that the Americans launched in the early 1980s, other superpowers did everything they could to create something equivalent that would help them balance the powerbase. In this case, the Chinese launched their version of the F11 stealth jet in January 2011, which kicked off yet another arms race for supersonic "invisible" jets." Again, we witnessed a major step up in capability when the Russians announced the hypersonic missiles that could out run all known missile of jet technology the Americans had or was on their drawing board.

Martin warned that corruption reached the highest levels of government and their so-called domains of national security, and cited the case of Edwin P. Wilson, a former CIA officer who was convicted of illegally selling weapons to Libya. It was later found that the United States Department of Justice and the CIA had covered up evidence in the case. Arms sales had indeed become a murky business!

Martin said, "Edwin Wilson was born to a poor farming family in Idaho. He initially worked as a merchant seaman, and then earned a psychology degree from the University of Portland in 1953. That same year, he joined the Marines and fought in the last days of the Korean War. He was impressive in the Marines and, when he was discharged in 1956, started working for the Central Intelligence Agency. His main role for the CIA was setting up fronting companies, like Consultants International, allegedly used to covertly ship supplies around the world for the CIA."

Martin added, "In the previous timeline, in the 1970s, through his role in the CIA, he allegedly became involved in dealings with Libya. Wilson would claim that a high-ranking CIA official called Theodore

"Blond Ghost" Shackley had asked him to go to Libya to keep an eye on Carlos the Jackal, the notorious infamous terrorist who was living there. By that time, a strict sanctions regime would be in place against Libya and the country would be willing to pay a great deal for weapons and material. With the blessing of the CIA and under cover of the fronting companies he had set up, Wilson would begin conducting elaborate dealings in guns and military uniforms which would be smuggled into the country.

"The CIA would soon become exposed because they were dealing in arms to get around these sanctions and were about to be embarrassed. The CIA would distance itself and allow a lengthy investigation by the Bureau of Alcohol, Tobacco and Firearms (part of the then US Department of the Treasury), and Edwin Wilson would be indicted by the US Justice Department for firearms and explosives violations."

David pointed out, "After serving twenty-seven years in prison, Wilson was exonerated because suppressed evidence was finally released that showed that the corrupted, not to ever be trusted CIA were indeed complicit and these events took place at their request, and with their blessing and assistance."

David said, "Just to illustrate to you how deep this corruption was and how high it extended up the chain of command, an eminent federal judge ruled that the prosecution had acted improperly. In October 2003, Edwin Wilson's conviction for the explosives charges was thrown out. Wilson was finally released from prison on 14 September 2004. He then initiated a civil action, and filed a civil suit against seven former federal prosecutors, two of whom would by then be federal judges, and a past executive director of the CIA. On 29 March 2007, US District Judge Lee Rosenthal dismissed his case on the grounds that all eight had immunity covering their actions."

He concluded, "So make no mistake, this mission is dangerous and we have to be careful who we liaise with. Remember, they are all known to be corrupt, dangerous and have huge vested interests, allegedly."

Martin went on to explain, "This dominance of the global Arms market was not something in which the American or Russian public or policy makers should take pride in. History showed that a corrupt

America routinely sold weapons to undemocratic regimes and gross human rights abusers, and in many cases, it was these very arms they sold to them that killed American and Russian troops."

Joe added, "Talk about scoring an own goal – the American public should have taken issue with this and retrospectively held all the Congressmen or Senators involved in sanctioning these Arms sales to account and prosecuted them for aiding and abetting mass murder."

"This presented a dilemma for the mass populace, who treasured life and wanted to preserve what little human rights they had," David said, "because the governments they legitimately voted into office were the very problem in this instance. Ideally, the only place into which arms could be legitimately sold would be to the United Nations and NATO."

Martin pointed out, "I do not need to remind you again, the Concorde team needs to tread very carefully, for if we make waves that could be felt by any of those unscrupulous operators, we could be in danger of being killed or maimed for our interference. Our deadliest opponents would come from legitimate governmental security operations in the USA, UK, France, Germany and Russia.

"In order to secure a sufficiently wide support base to establish and enforce a unilateral ban on the sale of arms and munitions unless legitimately sold to the United Nations and/or NATO, the Concorde team would need to liaise with all of those countries that were not involved in the manufacturing of arms or the sale of arms activities to gain their support and then address the United Nations," Martin said.

He pulled out a "target list" to be contacted who in the previous timeline, would be in power between 1958 and 1964 in countries where the sale of arms did not take place. They included presidents and prime ministers of countries such as Brazil, Argentina, France, Germany, Italy, Japan, Canada, India, The People's Republic of China, and Australia.

He said, "We will need to contact each on the target list, so that they can be shown the material we have brought with us, in the hope that they will help us to widen the net and be able to approach people through their good offices when they come into power."

"We will need to setup a combined briefing similar to what Karyn

Hodges and the Exceed Team did back on 8 January 1925 in the Scottish Highlands," Martin said.

David agreed, saying, "I suggest we do this as soon as possible so that we can follow up with subsequent induction workshops through their good offices as they start their respective leadership roles."

David added, "I cannot stress the importance of our succeeding with this mission enough, remember, the combined arms sales of the top 100 largest arms-producing companies amounted to an estimated $395 billion in 2012 according to SIPRI. In 2004 over $30 billion was spent in the international arms trade (a figure that excludes domestic sales of arms)."

CHAPTER 40

A World without Arms Dealers

The Concorde Team worked hard over the next eight months getting people into position and building rapport with each of the targeted leaders. A top-secret two-day conference was arranged in Geneva for 12 September 1958.

The scene was set and the target list had grown to include several other important and prominent leaders such as from the United Kingdom and Belgium. Unbeknown to those attending, Belgium would soon become the administrative home of the European Union.

The Beau-Rivage hotel, where this conference was being held, was a beautiful structure built in 1865. It had always played an important role in the lives of the great famous people who had shaped the history of the world. Beau-Rivage's charm and discretion allied with efficient service, modern comforts and subtle personal attention made this unique hotel one of the most distinguished and charming places in Switzerland.

Beau-Rivage boasted superb views of Lake Geneva and the Alps on the shores of the lake, opposite Mont-Blanc. Joe and Karyn had done the research into the venue and thought that its historical importance would be appropriate, considering the importance of the people being invited.

The hotel's Golden book included the names of King Ludwig II of Bavaria, King George I of Greece, King Alphonse XIII of Spain, Grand Duke Peter of Russia, Prince Philip of Edinburgh, Prince Rainier and Princess Caroline of Monaco, Prince Damrong of Siam, the Maharajah of Patiala, Emperor Akihito of Japan, Richard Wagner and Madame Danielle Mitterrand. The Concorde team hoped they would be thought to be just as illustrious at some time in the future.

The audience was assembled, the conference room was full to the brim, and there was an air of expectation and intrigue.

Martin opened up the conference with an introduction to his team and a brief explanation as to what they were about to see, which would be mind boggling because of both the technology they would be exposed to and the damning nature of the material they were about to witness.

"The evidence brought back by the Hindsight team shows that by the year 2,000 alone, the USA controlled half of the developing world's arms market." he explained.

Martin added, "In the previous timeline, by 2020, the world would be spending some $1,000 billion annually on the military, of which approximately $400 billion would be on arms."

There were gasps of disbelief; the numbers quoted were almost beyond comprehension and well above any financial consideration they could have dreamt of.

Before moving on to the next phase of the conference, Martin suggested that they watch some video footage showing the problems experienced over the years when arms were used adversely. The impact this forty-minute segment had on the audience was incredible. There were gasps and utterances of incredulity, as they watched scenes that were deplorable and frightening to say the least.

After a ten-minute smoke break, they resumed their seats and Martin pulled out of his dossier a chart created in 2010 by Richard F. Grimmett, a specialist in International Security, and said, "Look at this chart below which was created in 52 years in the future detailing arms sales, and notice that approximately two-thirds of sales were to developing countries.

Grimmett's report, a copy of which is being circulated to you all as I speak, showed that developing nations were the primary focus of foreign arms sales, and that most of the weapons were supplied by just two or three suppliers. The global economic climate was pretty poor at the time, yet major purchases were being made by these developing nations, principally India and Saudi Arabia. Their high level of expenditure on arms was a reflection of their modernization efforts since the 1990s."

Martin continued, "Grimmett also pointed out that the strength of individual economies of a wide range of nations in the developing world, for example; the spike in the price of oil, while an advantage for major *oil producing* states in funding their arms purchases, simultaneously caused economic difficulties for many *oil consuming* states, contributing to their decisions to curtail or defer new weapons acquisitions. Therefore, a number of less affluent developing nations chose to upgrade while reducing new purchases."

Arms Sales (agreements) by Supplier 2002 – 2009
(in billions of constant 2009 USD).

SUPPLIERS	TOTAL SALES in USD (Billions)	PERCENTAGE of TOTAL SALES
United States	166,278	40%
Russia	73,965	18%
France	35,175	8%
United Kingdom	29,379	7%
China	13,652	3%
Germany	19,742	5%
Italy	12,531	3%
Other European	43,752	10%
Other	22,459	5%

▨ Developing Countries	**Source:** Richard F. Grimmett
■ Industrialised Countries	**CRS Report for Congress:** Conventional Arms Transfers to Developing Nations 2002 - 2009

He went on to explain that, according to Grimmet, arms suppliers, despite the impact of the global economic situation on sales, found that a number of weapons-exporting nations had increased competition for sales, going into areas and regions in which they may not have previously been prominent. Competition between sellers had only intensified due to the limited growth opportunity.

Grimmet had also noted that just ten developing nation recipients of arms sales accounted for 60% of the total developing nation's arms market between 2003 and 2010.

Martin concluded, "In many cases, it was the same countries that were asking for aid and charitable assistance which were buying these arms, as well as those countries that had dictators, such as Libya, which were the least appropriate countries that should be increasing their armaments."

Martin and David then walked them through a series of slides that illustrated the dichotomy that would prove to be the Achilles heel for mankind a century later, as it was the very weapons that these countries sold to undemocratic regimes and gross abusers of human rights that were used to kill and maim American and NATO troops.

They all agreed that it was clear from the historical records that came from the future that a multilateral Arms Trade Treaty was needed that would control the international trade of conventional weapons.

Martin put up a slide with a famous quote to set the tempo: Oscar Arias Sanchez President of Costa Rica, who would be awarded the Nobel Peace Prize in 1987 for his efforts to end civil wars across Central America through the Esquipulas II Accords, stated:

"When a country decides to invest in arms, rather than in education, housing, the environment, and health services for its people, it is depriving a whole generation of its right to prosperity and happiness. We have produced one firearm for every ten inhabitants of this planet, and yet we have not bothered to end hunger when such a feat is well within our reach. Our international regulations allow almost three-quarters of all global arms sales to pour into the developing world with no binding international guidelines whatsoever. Our regulations do not hold countries accountable for what is done with the weapons they sell, even when the probable use of such weapons is obvious."

Martin explained that in the previous timeline, this Arms Trade Treaty proposal was initially put forward in 2003 by a group of Nobel Peace Laureates led by Oscar Arias, it would be first addressed in the UN in December 2006 when the UN General Assembly adopted resolution 61/89 "Towards an Arms Trade Treaty (ATT): establishing common international standards for the import, export and transfer of conventional arms."

When it came to the actual UN vote, only 153 Member States would vote in favour of Resolution 61/89. The then UK Ambassador John Duncan formally introduced the resolution at the First Committee on

October 18, 2006, speaking on behalf of the co-authors (Argentina, Australia, Costa Rica, Finland, Japan, and Kenya).

On behalf of the EU, Finland would highlight the support for the effort when it stated; *"every day, everywhere, people are affected by the side effects of irresponsible arms transfers . . . As there are currently no comprehensive internationally binding instruments available to provide an agreed regulatory framework for this activity, the EU welcomes the growing support, in all parts of the world, for an ATT."*

David then asked the audience to notice which twenty-four countries would be the ones that abstained, which included *Bahrain, Belarus, China, Egypt, India, Iran, Iraq, Israel, Kuwait, Laos, Libya, Marshall Islands, Nepal, Oman, Pakistan, Qatar, Russia, Saudi Arabia, Sudan, Syria, UAE, Venezuela, Yemen, and Zimbabwe,* explaining that some of those countries would end up being cited as trouble makers and would themselves be guilty of using their weapons to commit heinous atrocities against their own citizens.

However, what would be even more disturbing was that the United States of America, under President George W. Bush, would actually vote against the resolution. Interestingly, the following administration of US President Barack Obama would announce in a statement released by Hillary Clinton and the State Department on October the 14th 2009 that they were overturning the position of George W. Bush's administration, which had opposed this treaty on the grounds that national controls were better. If the Obama Administration could be trusted, the shift in position by the USA, the world's biggest arms exporter with a $55 billion-a-year trade in conventional weapons (40% of the global total), would prove to be a major breakthrough in launching formal negotiations at the United Nations in order to begin drafting the Arms Trade Treaty.

Secretary of State Hillary Clinton would say in a statement; *"The US would support the negotiations on condition they are under the rule of consensus decision-making as an imperative to ensure that all countries can be held to standards that will actually improve the global situation."* Clinton would go on to say, *"the consensus, in which every nation has an effective veto on agreements, was needed to avoid loopholes in the treaty that can be directly exploited by those wishing to export arms irresponsibly."*

Joe stood up at that point and addressed the forum, asking them, "What would you do now that you have the advantage of hindsight? Personally, I would say well done President Obama and shame on you President Bush."

Martin said, "Clearly, 2006 would be far too late; something had to be done much earlier, something radical that would prevent crimes against humanity and mass murder in numerous countries around the globe between 1960 and 2006."

He went on to explain, "What the Concorde team needs to do before 1960, when arms sales started taking off exponentially in the last timeline, is to lobby as many of the United Nations members as possible, showing them evidence from the future that illustrates graphically what damage the arms trade did to innocent people every day and have them support an earlier reading and implementation of the Arms Trade Treaty."

He then showed them an exporter table which illustrated the mighty and powerful manufacturing countries that saw to it that they got their share of the spoils, and where international sales started to slow down or there was a slowdown in domestic and traditional markets for military equipment, newer markets needed to be created or sought after, which was vital for the arms corporations and contractors in order to stay afloat.

"Those countries were active in promoting wars and disunity around the world in order to line their own pockets," David explained.

Joe added, "In the previous timeline, a man called J.W. Smith, an independent economist with a PhD in Political Economics, wrote several books on the elimination of poverty and war. He said that arms sellers were often guilty of overlooking respect for human rights as they sold their instruments of death to known human rights violators.

"Undeniably, too many weapons ended up in the wrong hands. Shipments appeared in countries with dismal human rights records or where they could exacerbate conflict or facilitate repression. History shows that these Arms deliveries were irresponsible."

Martin reinforced the message. "The misuse of Arms was exacerbated by the activities of illicit Arms brokers and traders who conducted their deals by exploiting legal loopholes, evading customs and airport controls and falsifying documents. Such illicit activities violated every United Nations arms embargo, with small arms and ammunition being the main items transferred."

Joe spoke again. He said, "I would like to conclude by quoting J. W. Smith once more. He wrote, *"Heavy militarization of a region increases the risk of oppression on local people. Consequently, reactions and uprisings from those oppressed may also be violent. The Middle East was an example between 2000 and 2013, while Latin America was an example from previous decades, where in both cases sham democracies or unpopular regimes (where oppression - often violent, and authoritarianism rule had resulted), had been overthrown with foreign assistance, and replaced with corrupt dictators or monarchs. Sometimes this also itself resulted in terrorist reactions that lashed out indiscriminately at other innocent people in the name of their cause.*

"Where weapons were abundant and readily available, deeper cycles of violence resulted. The Arms trade may not always be a root cause, because there are often various geopolitical interests etc. However, the sale of arms was cited as a significant contributor to problems because of the enormous impact of the weapons involved."

Joe put up a slide with information cited by J.W. Smith, pointing out that some oppressive regimes were only too willing to purchase more arms under the pretext of their own war against terrorism.

To further illustrate the toxicity of the arms dealing world, in 1994 J. W. Smith stated six key points that harshly criticised the practices and impacts of the arms industry. The first of these was that the armament firms had been active in fomenting war scares and in persuading their countries to adopt warlike policies and to increase their armaments. They also attempted to bribe government officials, both at home and abroad. A further point was that armament firms disseminated false reports concerning the military and naval Programs of various countries, in order to stimulate armament expenditure. His fourth point was that armament firms had sought to influence public opinion through the control of newspapers in their own and foreign countries, while the fifth emphasised that armament firms had organized international armament rings through which the armament race was accentuated by playing off one country against another.

"And finally," Joe said, "Smith made the point that armament firms had organized international armament trusts which increased the price of armaments sold to governments. All pretty disgusting, I think you will agree."

Martin then wrapped up the presentation, saying, "You are present here today because we feel you are the equivalent of the 2006 sponsors and originators of the Arms Trade Treaty, and we look to you to be the forerunners and sponsors of this initiative and arrange for this material to be available, with a presentation, at the next sitting of the UN.

"Now," he paused and smiled expectantly at the Assembly, "are there any questions?"

The room burst into life, with the leaders of over forty nations all asking questions at the same time. Both the Concorde and Exceed teams had their hands full. This was going to be a very long night, and the clock was ticking.

Over the next three hours, during a delicious smorgasbord of superb food prepared by the famous Swiss chefs of the Beau-Rivage Hotel, there were countless excited discussions and pledges of help.

As the evening drew to a close, they secured a unanimous agreement that those who attended the UN were about to get a shock of their life when they were shown footage from the future.

The date was set for the first sitting of the UN in 1959, where all of those present at the Beau-Rivage Hotel would support a Yes vote for a multilateral Arms Trade Treaty.

CHAPTER 41

The 1959 United Nations Arms Trade Treaty

The date was Tuesday 30th April 1959.

At an extraordinary special session of the United Nations Security council in New York, a ferocious discussion took place over a three-day sitting.

The Concorde team, led by Martin, showed video evidence brought back from the year 2611 AD, illustrating the future of those sitting in the session, showing the unacceptable horror and devastation weapons caused all over the world between 1960 and 2110.

The full horror that was yet to play out as in the previous timeline, was laid out in detail, showing how these instruments of death such as the Kalashnikov rifles, landmines and other armaments wreaked havoc and devastation throughout whole continents like Africa, killing millions of innocent people.

Martin and David walked them through the series of slides they had shown at their presentation to the leaders of nations seven months previously.

They stressed that it was clear from the historical records that a multilateral Arms Trade Treaty was needed that would control the international trade of conventional weapons. They also highlighted that an excessive build-up of weapons can lead to tension and insecurity among countries, and more arms also meant a higher risk of misuse and corruption.

For all those reasons, a particular responsibility must be expected from all countries involved as buyers or sellers in the Arms trade.

On Thursday 2nd May 1959, UN member states, led by countries who had based their decision on the personal integrity of their leaders, endorsed a resolution to create and negotiate an Arms Trade Treaty "which would be a legally binding instrument on the highest possible common international standards for the total banning of the sale and or transfer of conventional arms." The Treaty was to be negotiated in a series of subsequent sessions leading up to a negotiating conference in 1960.

At the insistence of the United States, the negotiating conference would need to secure agreement on the treaty which itself needed to deal with a total ban on the sale or transfer of small armaments and conventional weapons, including punitive action against those organisations and countries that participated in the illicit trade in small arms and light weapons in all its aspects. That included the implementation of a convention on the prohibition of the use, stockpiling, production and transfer of anti-personnel mines and on their destruction or the mandatory cleaning up of terrain that had been sown or despoiled with landmines.

It was agreed that while states had previously needed to use weapons in conformity with a UN Charter, they would, after this agreement, need also to do this within the spirit and conformance of this proposed 1959 Multilateral Arms Trade Treaty.

Yet another plank in the Hindsight strategy had been laid. This support and acknowledgement that there was indeed a problem with the sale of arms would prove to be useful in the years to come, as a treaty would take decades to carve out and implement because of the veto power of those countries who were themselves the very entities who were guilty of causing the very mess.

Nevertheless, the Concorde team were confident that this would be done.

CHAPTER 42

Zvakanaka - Stabilising the World's Population

The date was June 1959. New York.

The sixth Hindsight team was code-named "Zvakanaka", which is pronounced "zaga-naga", meaning satisfactory, or it is all good or all right in Shona, a Bantu language from Zimbabwe, formerly Southern Rhodesia and before that Southern Nyasaland on the African continent.

The Zvakanaka team was headed up by Masimba Shumba who had three esteemed colleagues from Africa with him, Cassandra Mountain, Michael Van Straaten, and Petra Adlum. All three had extensive experience with the World Health Organization and had secured a variety of first-class degrees after leaving their respective places of education in Africa.

The Zvakanaka team had to change what was deemed to be modern times' largest man-made disaster post the Second World War.

Explosive out of control population growth and corresponding starvation were intrinsically connected. The United Nations reports that over 7.6 million people die annually throughout the world because of hunger or a hunger-related cause. This means about 21,000 people, on average, die every day because of food insecurity. That's one person every 4 seconds. This means there were needless deaths of tens of millions of people every decade because of famine, wars and simple neglect, or plainly people being unable to support children in the first place.

There was obviously a massive emotive issue surrounding this topic, thus having Masimba head up the team would be a great help.

Masimba found himself dropped into the deep end on their second day. Joe and Karyn had arranged the Zvakanaka team's first meeting to explore a plan of action and to establish who should be invited to a series of enlightenment forums where the information about their future could be shared.

The location for these forums was the New York Marriott Marquis, on Broadway in Manhattan, whose renowned service, creative catering and a variety of meeting rooms and ballrooms made it certainly the most suitable choice for a New York event.

The New York Marriott Marquis brought the energy of Manhattan to its visitors, as it was located in the heart of Times Square and the Broadway theatre district. The hotel was perfect for weekend getaways, as well as for family and business travel. Boasting updated rooms and suites, high-speed elevators and three restaurants and lounges, this hotel in Times Square put its guests in the centre of attractions like Fifth Avenue shopping, Radio City Music Hall, Rockefeller Centre, NBC Studios and Central Park.

It was close to Carnegie Hall, Lincoln Centre, the UN, and Madison Square Garden, so it was the perfect choice for meetings, conventions, and social events.

Masimba opened the forum in the lovely setting of one of the conference rooms, explaining to the 200 strong audience that the data and statistics they were about to see was from the future and should not be taken lightly.

He began with an introduction to the topic, saying, "The recent rapid increase in the human population over the past two centuries has raised concerns that humans are beginning to overpopulate the Earth, and that the planet's finite resources may not be able to sustain the present numbers of inhabitants, let alone an increasing number. Although this information comes from your future, we need to start by looking at the past."

Masimba loaded up a series of slides, giving a commentary on each one.

"Population has been growing continuously since the end of the Black Death, around the year 1400, and at the beginning of the nineteenth century, it had reached roughly one billion, now as you will see from the chart the world population has continued to grow in the second millennium." he began.

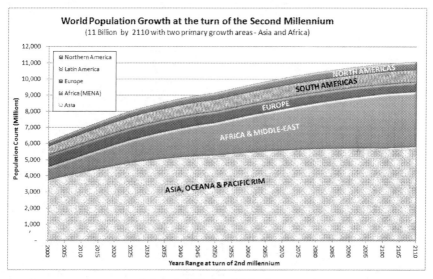

World Population Growth at the turn of the Second Millennium
(11 Billion by 2110 with two primary growth areas - Asia and Africa)

Source: United Nations

"Increases in life expectancy and resource availability during the industrial and green revolutions led to rapid population growth on a worldwide level, and by 1960 – next year – the world population will reach 3 billion. It will then double to 6 billion over the next four decades."

He paused to let that information sink in, and then continued with his commentary as he flicked through the slides. "As of 2009, the estimated annual growth rate was 1.10%, down from a peak of 2.2% in 1963; however, by then the world's actual population stood at roughly 6.7 billion. During the early part of the twenty-first century, projections showed a steady decline in the population growth rate in developed countries, with the population expected to reach between 8 and 10.5 billion between the year 2040 and 2050.

World Population (millions)

Year	World Total	Asia, Pacific Rim & Oceana	Africa (MENA)	Europe	Latin Americas	Northern Americas
2000	6,115	3,729	819	727	521	319
2005	6,513	3,971	921	729	557	335
2010	6,910	4,203	1,033	733	589	352
2015	7,305	4,429	1,153	734	621	368
2020	7,677	4,636	1,276	733	649	383
2025	8,017	4,816	1,400	729	674	398
2030	8,313	4,962	1,524	723	694	410
2035	8,572	5,078	1,647	716	710	421
2040	8,804	5,173	1,770	708	722	431
2045	9,001	5,243	1,887	700	731	440
2050	9,153	5,282	1,998	691	734	448
2055	9,398	5,377	2,134	689	743	456
2060	9,632	5,459	2,271	684	752	466
2065	9,849	5,530	2,408	677	759	476
2070	10,050	5,589	2,544	668	765	484
2075	10,235	5,638	2,680	657	769	492
2080	10,404	5,675	2,815	644	772	498
2085	10,557	5,702	2,949	629	773	504
2090	10,699	5,719	3,080	613	777	509
2095	10,826	5,726	3,209	596	781	514
2100	10,930	5,723	3,336	576	778	517
2105	11,011	5,772	3,364	581	774	521
2110	11,077	5,812	3,388	585	778	514

Source: United Nations

The most noticeable growth, as can be seen in this chart," he put up a new slide, "was in Africa and Asia."

"The frightening aspect of this was that Africa was still the continent with the most rapid population growth and by contrast, suffered the most unnecessary deaths as a result of their inability to regulate themselves. Africa was by far the most unproductive, poor and self-unsustainable continent out of all the continents and was also by far the largest beneficiary of world Aid," Masimba said.

He explained that even during that period, some governments were stimulating population growth for internal economic or religious reasons. Many poor individuals were schooled by governments that they needed large families so that several of their children would survive in order to provide security for their parents' in their old age. This entirely missed the point, which was that, in reality, our societies needed new social systems that would foster less consumption, particularly of non-durable goods, improved resources recycling, a gradually reducing world population, and social models that would take improved care of youngsters and older people.

Masimba continued, "Our records show that you are about to experience a significant change in how society deals with sensitive issues, especially issues that appear to be conservative in nature or seem in any way to interfere with people's human rights. Laws will soon be made around this subject that will only serve to further exacerbate the situation, when solicitors unscrupulously utilise the human rights law inappropriately to manipulate situations for pecuniary advantage and get their clients off the hook on a technicality."

Van Straaten now spoke, as Masimba displayed a slide showing the doubling in the world's population between 1959 and 1999. "Many people had the notion drummed into them that it was mankind's human right to have children as many children as they liked. You can see from the slide that population went from around three billion to six billion in just forty years. It was at 6.8 billion by 2010, and was expected to reach 9 billion by around 2042.

"China was the only country that instigated strenuous controls on population growth in an effort to keep their country's population below 1.1 billion, although it must be said that their policy, structured in the way that it was, did skew the gender balance. If you allow couples to have only one child, as they did, that caused a preference for sons, leading to female foetuses being aborted. This caused a population demographic with two men to every woman in later years."

He went on to add, "That said, in some cultures those couples who did not have children were seen as outcasts, whereas in reality they were actually the enlightened ones. The cultural taboos such as these will need to be addressed."

Cassandra rose from her seat, walked across to the podium and addressed the audience with information on a set of slides she had uploaded.

"According to the World Health Organization in 2007," she began, "more than thirty-six million died of hunger or diseases caused by malnutrition in 2006. Malnutrition was by far the biggest contributor to child mortality, present in half of all cases. Environmental issues with agriculture hampered the finding of acceptable solutions to these problems." She paused, then repeated, "Yes, I did say thirty-six million people." She saw sombre faces as she looked around at the audience.

Van Straaten jumped in to say, "This statistic alone illustrates the diabolical mess that mankind will find itself in. What were they thinking, allowing people to have babies who were then only destined to die painful, horrible deaths because they could not be fed? Dying from starvation is a terrible way to die!"

Joe added, "According to statistics over that period, this was not an isolated incident. This volume of annually recurring deaths had been happening over a sustained period and showed no sign that it was going to improve. Not only was it criminal to allow this to be perpetuated, this had to be one of the cruellest man-made disasters since the Second World War."

The team carried on to say that they believed that no matter what Aid or Charity was being sent to these countries (much of which was being pilfered by politicians or dictators), those governments were guilty of crimes against humanity, starting with the propagation of policies that resulted in mass infanticide and mass murder. The bulk of these deaths could have been prevented if these governments had run education programs and offered free contraception to their populaces, where starvation was prevalent during these periods of distress.

Cassandra then stated, "Sadly, the Western world did not enforce solutions to address the *real-root-cause*; instead they tried several strategies to help overcome these problems which included a "Green Revolution", which involved using genetically modified crops which were deployed in viable land.

"However, the effects of the Green Revolution had been short-lived, resulting in an increasing amount of land becoming unusable for crop production. In fact," she shook her head sadly, "that decade was the only decade on record where less food was produced than was needed to be consumed by humans during that period."

She explained that this had cumulatively resulted in the world's grain stores being almost completely depleted and doubts had been cast over the UN world food programme's ability to feed the increasing number of people being added to the programme. In 2009, a net population gain of seventy-five million people occurred, with the number of people starving increasing from 0.8 billion in 2008 to 1.01 billion in 2010. She added, "By 2020, at least 30% to 40% of the world population had experienced sustained starvation for many years. According to the World Health Organization, each year in excess of fifty million people died as a result of the resource shortages, starvation, and disease-related problems such as HIV/Aids."

Joe spoke up again, saying, "During 2011, the "Save the Children" fund claimed in a series of television adverts in the United Kingdom, when they were yet again soliciting for more funds for Africa, that over eight million children died unnecessarily in Africa every year because of hunger."

He carried on to say, "Never once did these charities or "do-gooders" ever consider addressing the *root-cause* of why these millions of children were perishing because of starvation or neglect. The truth was either too sensitive and they could not bring themselves to offend other people's sensibilities, or they lacked courage to grasp the nettle and do something about addressing the root cause of the problem. The plain fact of the matter was that the parents of these starving children were unable to support themselves, let alone consider having children in the first place."

Masimba said, "Basic common sense says raising a child or children, costs money just to feed, protect and nurture them, let alone educate them."

Van Straaten added, "It may be true that in the early nineteenth century, because of a high infant mortality rate, people felt they had to produce children regularly to ensure some of them survived to look after them in their old age. So why was it, during the hundred years following the Second World War, that the population exploded, with millions of poor families having dozens of children just when medical advances were improving life expectancy, only to let their children die because of neglect or starvation? It might have been a numbers game in the nineteenth century, but in the twentieth, twenty-first and twenty-second centuries it most certainly was not."

Van Straaten showed a slide from Germany's World Population Fund, which showed that one-third of the population growth in the world, was the result of incidental or unwanted pregnancies.

At this point, Petra Adlum, jumped in and stated, "Because of the fear of being castigated, nobody was prepared to say what was necessary to maintain a balanced and stabilised world population." Emphasising her words with repeated stabs of her finger in the air, she said, "If one cannot afford to feed, bring up and look after one's child, then one *should not* have children. One should use contraception to prevent pregnancy."

Joe added, "That was why the Gates Foundation, the world's largest philanthropic organisation, took a unique and bold stance against what the Catholic Church was preaching, they started a charity funded out of the Gates Foundation that made contraception easily available to poorer countries. According to the Blaze News channel, "Unwanted fertility and unmet contraceptive needs were still high in many developing countries, and women were repeatedly exposed to life-threatening pregnancy complications that could have been avoided with access to effective contraception," said Amy Tsui, PhD, senior author and director of the Johns Hopkins Bloomberg School of Public Health, who released a study in 2012 supporting the Gates' perspective.

On Tuesday 10th July that same year, Reuters reported Melinda Gates saying the issue of contraception is "far less controversial than people make it." She pointed to a Gallup poll showing 90 percent of Americans found contraceptives morally acceptable and 82 percent of Catholics are even finding it acceptable. The Gates' Foundation established a much read and followed website "No-Controversy.com" where people were able to pledge their support and share their own stories about birth control. The foundation also released a video that previous week entitled "Where's the Controversy in Saving Lives?"

Joe emphasised, "Remarkably, even with all the media attention and support the Gates Foundation were able to drum up, nobody was prepared to voice the *real-root-cause* of this sustained endemic starvation and *infanticide*, which was caused by people having children when they or their economies were incapable of supporting them. Still it should be noted that indirectly the root cause was being somewhat addressed, whilst not being voiced, because the fantastic efforts made by the Gates Foundation did indeed indirectly prevent millions of unnecessary baby and children deaths from needless starvation over the next few decades."

Joe went on to explain, "If anyone did venture where others feared to tread, there were some people who thought they were doing good by others, together with the media, who would castigate anyone who dared to voice the hard reality or truth of the situation, or questioned the reasoning or rationale for wanton uncontrolled procreation, by calling them bigots, racists or Nazis."

"It was the ignorant and arrogant media that were the real criminals here, they preferred to chase headlines and hound people until they committed suicide, all because they were prepared to state the obvious truth, which was a narrative the media had no stomach for."

Van Straaten asked, "Did anyone ever consider in this equation, the unnecessary suffering of the children who were being born into a certain painful horrific death? No, they simply eased their conscience by throwing money at charities to overcome the resultant negative outcome instead of addressing the root cause!"

Van Straaten added, "according to the Huffington Post, it was for many that the issue was not really about health and free choice for women, but about controlling the world's population which, according to The Olympian, in 2012 world population stood at 7,025,367,636 and was growing by 80 million people annually."

Van Straaten commented, "a very troubling statistic that did not seem to worry journalists or people at that time, because they were either naive or not sufficiently informed to comprehend the magnitude of the mass infanticide problem happening every year and the looming resource challenges."

"If it were not for the courageous and bold moves made by the likes of Bill and Melinda Gates, many millions more children would have died painful needless deaths through starvation. The real shame was on those other so called "do-gooders" who unfortunately lacked courage to step up and publicly, vocally support the Gates Foundation contraception campaign and insist on educating the mass populace and governments on these issues to avoid unnecessary and unsupportable births? Sadly, many millions did indeed die because, unlike Bill and Melinda Gates, those other so-called "*do-gooders*" were too fearful about potentially offending someone's sensitivities and could not bring themselves to do what was right!"

"Instead they threw money and Aid at the problem to ease their consciences, whilst the problem went on and on for over a century, resulting in many tens of millions of unnecessary painful, cruel deaths."

Masimba stood up at this point, took a deep breath, sighed and said, "The unacceptable number of *starvation deaths* demanded that mankind must now face up to the facts and the brutal truth of this perpetual cycle of Aid-funded infanticide. It is time for us to do what is really needed, which is simply; apply conditionality on Aid, with mass education and the global implementation of a mandatory birth control regime where citizens can only have children once they are able to prove that they are financially capable of supporting and educating them into adulthood."

He went on to explain, "The right thing to do would be to propose that to maintain a balance and control on population numbers, families would need to be limited to a maximum of two children only. In countries receiving Aid, this should be a condition of that Aid being distributed, which should underwrite and promote the educational and birth control Programs in those poorer countries."

Van Straaten added, "The truly tragic fact is that in the past, by not addressing the root cause, they added to these millions of unnecessary deaths, because the world's population had outstripped the available resources. Behind closed doors and in the privacy of their own minds, people knew that Governments worldwide, without exception, would eventually be forced to introduce birth control so that populations could be stabilised in line with the worlds' food production capabilities."

"The time for this unwitting charity sponsored mass infanticide needs to be avoided." He retorted.

Petra emphasised, "What the world really needed was international co-operation for sustainable businesses with a high capacity of employment, food farming development and education, which seems to us to be a more constructive and better focused strategy than simply the old-fashioned *Development Aid*. This is because the latter suggests a dependency position of the recipient country."

She went on to add, "Social development Aid, in line with common spiritual values and moral principles should continue and should remain tax deductible for individuals and corporations. However, government financed or subsidised international co-operation will need to be focused on macro issues, such as mass education, that will lead to socially improved and sustainable localised and regional society productivity models."

Masimba pointed out, "History showed time and time again that when the technical, social, legal and monetary advice – reducing population growth – turned out to be inconvenient for politicians, they tended to ignore it and simply take the Aid money for themselves and do whatever they felt they could get away with."

At this point Masimba asked for the lights to be dimmed, and showed the audience forty minutes of news reel material from the forthcoming 100 years in the future of their present timeline.

The Zvakanaka team observed the audience intently and watched their body language; they could see the absolute horror on some of their faces as the newscasts detailed horror after horror, statistic after statistic on diminishing resources, millions dying of starvation and neglect.

They also winced in embarrassment at those who thought they were doing the right thing; those kind-hearted and generous "do-gooders" who appeased their conscience by throwing money blindly at the problem, decade after decade, to make themselves feel good and maintain their sensitivities' and social status quo.

At the end of the short montage of newscasts from their future, Masimba wrapped things up. He said, "We have lived through the timeline that the actions of your current path created; we have all personally witnessed the horror story you have just seen on the video, and there is only one solution, you have to take decisive action and implement solutions to address the root cause of these problems. You now know what those solutions are. Limit couples to having a maximum of two children, and create sustainable economic models where entrepreneurs can thrive to build and grow businesses that employ many people so that people can work and earn a decent, liveable wage and contribute toward a personal pension to keep them safe in retirement!"

He added, "The UN Environmental Program estimated that in 2010, it required at least fifty-four acres of land to sustain an average human being; land which furnishes water, food, clothing and other resources extracted from the planet. Evidence from the future has proved that continuing such population will be unsustainable, and more humans will mean more greenhouse gas emissions. Resources are finite! That is one fact that is not negotiable or dismissible. Wars that will be fought over these finite resources, between 2080 and 2111 by countries so they that can feed their starving populations, which has proven to be devastating for mankind. Your children's children and their children's children will be faced with that horror unless something is done."

Joe said, "Also, what is clear is that per capita, energy consumption must go down if climate change is to be controlled, which flies in the face of unfettered population growth. This is a multi-faceted issue, which will take a lot of different issues to be addressed at the root cause to prevent these millions of painful deaths per annum."

"Ultimately, only the removal of corruption in the halls of power, the creation of sustainable economic models where entrepreneurs can thrive to build and grow businesses that employ many people, the adoption of a fair and balanced constitution on which to base politics with people's participation in elections in these countries, which allow programmes to be introduced such as the introduction of education and free contraception, along with a maximum two children per couple would prove to be adequate to maintain a stabilised human population. A stable population with extensive recycling will help mankind to live within the limits of available resources. Without this, the planet is doomed to suffer the very extinction we witnessed in 2111," Masimba said.

Van Straaten added, "There is no excuse, you have all now been given the gift of foresight. The evidence we have brought back with us should be considered as an early warning that there needs to be an absolute and mandatory world-wide adoption of these principles, with enforcement through the United Nations, otherwise you will end up being the infamous stars in those TV newscasts you have just reviewed."

Masimba had the last word, "Each of the countries that fail to institute stringent punitive anti-fraud measures or population controls should find their ministers and heads of state guilty of aiding and abetting mass infanticide and murder. They should be made to pay the penalty for those crimes against humanity in The Hague."

CHAPTER 43

Project Hindsight 2022 Progress Review

The date was Friday 19th June 2022, Malaysia

Joe and his security teams had gone back to each of the timelines and brought every member of the six Hindsight teams into the same timeline, at the wonderful tropical location, Langkawi in Malaysia.

The beautiful island of Langkawi, which is unofficially known as the Jewel of Kedah, is an archipelago of 104 islands in the Andaman Sea, some 30 km off the mainland coast of north-western Malaysia. The islands are a part of the state of Kedah, which is adjacent to the Thai border.

The team had assembled at the Andaman Hotel, with its 186 spacious rooms, a one-of-a-kind hotel, with its airy, contemporary design which effortlessly blends with touches of indigenous art and culture, surpassed in beauty only by the breath-taking views of the Andaman Sea and the emerald rainforest cradled between Malaysia's Mat Chincang Mountains and the beaches where centuries-old trees, sparkling limestone outcrops, and dense vegetation offer a window into the islands' history and their abundant wildlife.

On arrival in the lobby of the Andaman Hotel, they were faced with a huge altar-like construction with a vast vaulted teak ceiling and featuring soft lighting and fans. This type of structure is locally known as Singgahsana, which is synonymous with Malay royal palaces.

The lobby lounge has a seating arrangement that overlooks the towering altar as well as the outdoor forest canopies and the beach and sea.

As soon as all the team members had arrived, they were ushered into a conference room on the third floor, where they were briefed.

Joe began by explaining, "Langkawi is one of the most beautiful island groups in Malaysia. Apart from having a distinct and unique morphological feature such as Machinchang ridge and karstic morphology in the limestone area, there are a lot of other interesting geological features which can be dated back to 550 million years ago.

"The historical and geological significance of this area is the fundamental reason why we have chosen Langkawi for this historic, we hope world-changing, event.

Karyn added, "Langkawi was dubbed the birthplace or "foetus land" of the South East Asian region. The various natural landscapes of Langkawi reflect the island's geodiversity and its complex geological history. It has the best-exposed and most complete Palaeozoic sedimentary sequence in Malaysia, from the Cambrian to the Permian period.

"Later, during the Mesozoic period, the islands underwent a major tectonic event that resulted in the emplacement of its numerous granitic igneous bodies. This incredible power, generated by nature from the deep mantle beneath the earth, has driven up huge blocks of older rocks and somehow placed them above a very much younger terrain."

Joe took up the story, and said, "The ecosystems of the old limestone rock formation, the caves, the mudflats and the seas that surround Langkawi have three main elements: the mangroves, the vegetation of the limestone hills, and the fauna of the mudflats and beaches."

Karyn explained, "The significance of the mangrove forests' is that they created a unique root system with a physiology of the plant species that is capable of preventing soil erosion and cleaning the water from contamination of metallic pollutants. The mangroves also serve as the breeding ground to many species of fish, prawns and other sea life. The mangrove vegetation in this area is quite diverse and includes many important species, some with medicinal properties."

Joe concluded the introduction, saying, "After much time travel and going backwards and forwards in our timeline, I felt we needed to find a historic place rich with treasures of mother nature to use as the metaphor for mankind's re-invention, somewhere that represented the ages of time, somewhere beautiful, symbolically powerful, both ancient and young, life-giving, regenerative, and last but not least, healing.

"Welcome to Langkawi, where mankind will, we hope, kick-start "*Take-II*" with a new lease of life, based on integrity and respect for mother earth."

Joe reminded them why they had come here to the wonderful Jewel of Kedah to begin the planning of what was going to be the ultimate summit of all world leaders in four years' time.

The planned summit date would be Wednesday 16th December 2026.

The objective of the 2026 World Re-Invention Summit brought together leaders from every country to elevate the role of responsible honest politicians in government and sanction for investment to bring about the final transformation of a more sustainable, honest political system and inclusive governance with corruption-proof electronic online voting systems.

Up until late 2019, there were still shameful excuses being made by arrogant corrupt politicians in government that voting through electronic computer systems; e-voting – could not be trusted and that they needed to stick with the manual voting systems that had been in operation for centuries.

This was an archaic system and just another way for politicians to deceive their citizens, allowing them and big business to manipulate the systems to their advantage.

History had shown that the public had become tired of the lies and repeated deceits that were fed to them year after year, decade after decade. The power of social media and social networking tools such as Facebook, YouTube and Twitter had proved to be major adversaries to the dictators and corrupt governments that were overturned during the 2011 and 2014 Arab Spring. There were tens of millions of easily influenced young people who were using social networking tools to communicate with each other and potentially with tens of thousands of people at a touch of a single button.

While there was some truth in the claim that electronic computer systems were dangerous, it did not actually relate to the voting systems and their liability to be hacked into or tampered with – it related to a more sinister issue that enables a massive corruption of the truth, which would unwittingly be orchestrated openly by the masses themselves, without their even knowing that they were pawns in someone else's propaganda machine.

Joe pointed out that the Americans had proved twice, beyond any doubt, that the masses can be easily manipulated by what they read in the Internet blogs. In 2004, at the height of the second Iraq war, which was one of the most unpopular wars America had been involved in since Vietnam, the Americans voted in President G. W. Bush, the forty-third President of America, for a second term. The entire world, watched in utter disbelief as the American political machine engineered it so that George W. Bush secured a second term.

The unbelievable happened, even though during that second term election campaign George W. Bush had one of the lowest ratings of any President from the previous fifty years for their second election. What makes this even more disconcerting was that in October 2008, President Bush had the third lowest job approval rating during a second term, with a rating of 25, beating President Nixon, who had a rating of 24, by one point and Harry Truman, who had the lowest rating of 22, by three points.

An Associated Press poll found that President Bush began his second term with a public evenly split about his job performance. His job approval rating was in the high 40s in several other recent polls — this was one of the lowest job approval ratings for a re-elected president at the start of the second term in more than fifty years.

Presidents Reagan and Clinton had job approval ratings of around 60% just before their inauguration for a second term, according to Gallup polls.

President Nixon's approval was in the 60% sector right after his 1972 re-election, which slid to about 50% right before his inauguration and then moved back over 60%. President Eisenhower's job approval was in the low 70s just before his second inauguration in 1957.

Then, again in 2012, there was not an outstandingly strong candidate from the Republican Party to choose from, the very same American public were about to vote President Barack Obama in for a second presidential term. The very same President who in just four years had single-handedly added $6 trillion US dollars to the US debt pile, mounting to an unprecedented $18 trillion US dollar American debt by 2014, the largest debt America had ever experienced. This was the very same President who had also failed to keep 90% of his previous election promises, the President that made people's expectation of "entitlement" as a way of life, and destroyed the American entrepreneurial spirit. Even with that devastating track record, yet again, the American masses proved to be gullible and were being easily duped by the misinformation and propaganda that was written about President Obama being America's best President ever on the Internet and published in the much biased and corrupted mainstream media.

What won the vote of the less educated, less entrepreneurial, less motivated to get off social welfare was the one policy that Barack Obama and his Democrat stacked Senate and Congress houses fought so hard for during his first tenure as President; government run "Medicare." This free medical for all policy, which became known as "Obamacare", was similar to the NHS concept in the United Kingdom, which was sanctioned to be "Constitutional" and legal in the Supreme Court in July 2012 because it was deemed to be structured as a tax and thus was considered to be constitutional.

It was projected by millions of people all over the world that Obamacare was to become President Obama's nemesis, causing Barack Obama's tenure as President of the United States of America to be a one trick pony, and a one term President. As fate would have it, even though Obamacare turned out to be too expensive to run, that did not happen.

Joe reminded the Hindsight team that "President Obama had indeed won a second term, which because of the continual printing of approximately $80 billion dollars of new money every month from 2010, laid down the seeds for the most catastrophic failure of the world's largest economy, a dark period indeed that would give witness to one of the most significant changes in mankind's behaviour on a global scale."

After President Obama's second term, "Obamacare", actually turned out to be the catalyst that would spark a revolt against big government and excess taxation, which would rally millions of people towards the Tea Party movement, who voted decisively against anything that President Obama or the Democrats put forward.

Joe jumped in and said, "by 2014 of the Obama Presidency, the American populace who thought they could simply push that Obamacare panic button for help when they hit hard times, brutally discovered that they could push the button all they liked, but nobody came to their rescue…"

Van Straaten continued, "under President Obama's tenure, US debt had doubled, the Government had let the Banking system defraud the masses whilst at the same time bankrupting America because of the toxic products, including sub-prime mortgages they were fraudulently wrapping up as Credit Default Swaps (CDSs) into complex multi-wrapped parcels of toxic products being sold as quality assets. This was one of the core problems that was identified in the 2007 Markets crash, where the US Government took on these toxic products as part of the Bank bail-out. This repeated bail-out continued under the guise of Quantative-Easing (QE) by the FED during the Obama administration. Sadly, the root cause of this corruption was not addressed early enough, because to this day the FED still have absolutely no idea whatsoever what sits inside the $3 trillion worth of toxic CDS parcels they took ownership of from the Banks in the USA."

Joe continued, "the cold, hard facts showed that by 2022 at least 4 in 10 Americans were unable to voluntarily leave the workforce, regardless of how old or infirm they had become, over 63 million Americans could not afford to step away from the daily grind and 47 million Americans who were on food stamps were suddenly left to starve."

Van Straaten continued, "the leaders during the first 16 years of the 21st century, President Obama in America, David Cameron in England and those fiscally naive Commissioners in the Europe Union, failed to recognise the limits of what Central Banks could and should have done.

Their collective naivety allowed three trends that stood out as

Central Banks moved to provide further stimulus for the economy between 2008 and 2014."

He continued, "Firstly, the fiscally ignorant leaders of that time allowed the Central Banks to step up interventions in government bond markets. The Federal Reserve and the Bank of England held sizeable shares of the outstanding stock of their respective government issues. Including the bonds acquired by foreign Central Banks in their currency interventions, Central Banks hold about one third of all US Treasuries outstanding. The Fed, of course, could not just dump $3tn in bonds. It took them six years to accumulate that, and it was going to take them twice as long to dispose of it. So, the FED needed to offer incentives to get that to work. Those incentives mainly included paying high interest rates to banks for their deposits, offering low interest rates for their loans from the Central Banks, to keep them happy and profitable.

Secondly, Central Banks targeted specific parts of the monetary transmission mechanism which they deemed were in need of repair. They used tools that included specific lending programmes, such as the Bank of England's Funding for Lending Scheme; purchases of government bonds of specific countries, such as the ECB's Securities Markets Programme; the Federal Reserve's continued purchases of mortgage-backed securities; and the Bank of Japan's subsidising of lending, entitled Measures to Support Strengthening the Foundations for Economic Growth.

Third, Central Banks made forward commitments. Most were conditional, such as the Federal Reserve's pledge to continue its balance sheet expansion at least until unemployment reached a certain threshold and the ECB's assurance that, through its Outright Monetary Transactions programme, it would buy government bonds of countries that fulfil certain conditions, which was essentially a bribe to keep those countries compliant with the EU's game plan."

Joe added, "half a decade before that, most, if not all, of these measures were unthinkable. Their emergence showed how much responsibility and burden those leaders of those countries let their Central Banks take on.

This overdependence on Central Banks created significant challenges for the economy as a whole. Progress with repairs and reforms were supposed to make it easier for Central Banks to normalise monetary policy. Clearly history shows that it did not."

Joe reminded them of how America had already cheated the rest of the world once before. "According to the Bretton Woods Agreements, between 1944 up until 1971 the fiduciary dollar was accepted as being as good as gold, with a "promise" that Central Banks would redeem the dollar for gold."

Van Straaten continued, "As it turned out, the "fiducia" or "promise" was misplaced, for in 1971 the US reneged on the Bretton Woods Agreements of 1944, "they closed the gold window" and exploited the creditor countries. No final settlement of international commerce debts took place in 1971, nor has any taken place since then; the world was royally swindled by the Americans.

"The rest of the world were deceived into believing that tendering a Fiat currency (printed & digital money backed by nothing) in payment of an international debt constituted settlement of that debt."

Joe added, "once the false idea – that Fiat money could settle a debt - became acceptable as valid, the problem of the enormous "imbalances" in world trade became an insoluble enigma. Ever since then, the best and brightest economists attempted in vain to find a solution to a problem that could not be solved except by the renewed universal use of gold as the international medium of commerce – move back to the gold standard.

"Regarding national commerce, the same reasoning applied. In reality, anyone engaging in commerce in any country in the world during that period was actually paying for their purchases; essentially, there was not any actual settlement of any debt using gold or silver. All individuals, corporations and government entities were merely shuffling debts (payable in nothing) between themselves, in the form of either paper bills or digital banking money, whether in dollars or any other currency in the world.

Joe says, "Take a look at this chart; you can see how the buying power of the US dollar diminished as soon as they started printing Fiat money."

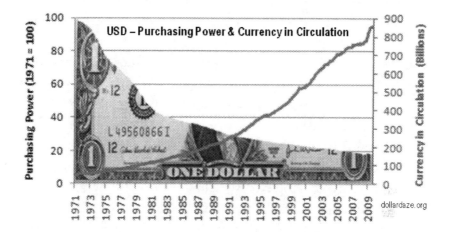

Van Straaten continued, "For smaller value domestic commerce the silver coin was convenient for day-to-day transactions at the popular level and did constitute settlement of debt when tendered in payment, for silver was a merchandise or commodity which, like gold, could participate in commercial exchange as money.

During that period of 2008 and 2015, the European crisis took a turn for the worse, with Greece and Cyprus becoming bankrupt. A deadly precedent was set when the Cypriot government was forced by the European Union's Central Bank (ECB) to confiscate all monies in Bank accounts over 100,000 Euros."

Joe pointed out, "this triggered a world-wide distrust for American dollars, because China and the other great Asian exporters belatedly realised that the dollars they received as "payment" for their mass exports were nothing more than digits in American computers.

"Essentially, if the Chinese did not cooperate with the will of America and Europe, the bankers in New York could simply erase those digits in 20 minutes, and leave China with no reserves. For that reason, the Chinese, Russians and Asians in general started buying gold. That trend continued for an indefinite period - computers could not erase gold reserves."

Van Straaten continued, "the awful truth about China was that the Chinese acquired their formidable industrial and military power in the short span of thirty years at a tremendous cost: essentially, the stark realisation for China was that for thirty years the Chinese people worked for almost nothing. China had built up US$3 Trillion of reserves.

Unless China could find practical uses for those reserves, they had no intrinsic value and China did not know how to exchange these digital dollars for something more tangible of value like gold, oil or investment in infrastructure in Africa countries.

Joe jumped in, "between 2000 and 2014 world-wide, especially in America, England and Europe, 85% of all the well-paid jobs disappeared, leaving people to seek low paid part-time jobs (called 'non-jobs' like dog walking or zero-hour contracts) that did not allow them to create or accumulate any wealth. This incredibly naïve strategy created by those less enlightened people in power at the time was an own goal, because tax receipts dropped by 70%, which only served to further exacerbate the financial dilemma. Their solution was to print more Fiat money, which only served to make the rich - richer and the poor - poorer causing a rapid redistribution of wealth to the benefit of the Elite, leaving generations of younger people without any prospects.

Like many low paid Americans, Britons and Europeans, China worked for thirty years to provide the world with a vast quantity of cheap merchandise, in return for: nothing! Thirty years of slavery, to build an industrial empire!"

President Trump, who already wealthy himself, believed in the American dream and was acutely aware of the feelings of discontent and unfairness amongst the American populace. Because he tapped into these feelings, Trump, always the maverick, saw how the New World Order establishment (Elites and left-wing Progressives) were manoeuvring to protect their wealth no matter what the outcome of the 2020 elections. He was despised by the Elites and left-wing Progressives and they know he had a distinct lack of love for them. Once the DNC had successfully dethroned President Trump, it was not long before the Elite's wealth was being diverted just prior to the start of Biden's inauguration as the 46th President. The alleged financial vandalism of the previous two Presidents prior to President Trump was like a stack of dominoes all lined up ready to be toppled by the new DNC's Communist policies of wealth redistribution.

Van Straaten jumped in, "the biggest financial crash the world had ever witnessed happened, creating the longest, deepest depression ever experienced by mankind, started late 2019/2020and peaked late 2021, the impact of which lasted 20 years." This was exacerbated by the advent of the COVID-19 virus that became mainstream news in Q1 of 2020, where economies world-wide went into shutdown, whilst Governments tackled this flu like pandemic. Within the first 12 months of this outbreak that first appeared in Wuhan in China, over one and half million people died due to the virus, with no vaccination in sight.

"Yes, the American Government had amassed an incredible $19 trillion dollars debt by the end of 2016. According to Washington (CNN) the US national debt stood at $21.974 trillion at the end of 2018, more than $2 trillion higher than when President Donald Trump took office, according to numbers released by the Treasury Department.

"Americans woke up one day to find that their pensions were also bankrupt or underfunded ...- ... Uncle Sam had already begun to drown in its own debt."

"After the disastrous 8 years of Obama, the installation of Trump as the 45th President of America was good for the American people, especially the poor and middle-class. Trump's policies created millions of jobs that were outsourced to China and Mexico during the Bush and Obama years. All Trump wanted to do was run as an ethical President, who delivered on his election promises, which he mostly succeeded in doing. Trump promised to 'Make America Great Again', which started the MAGA movement in America that had some 70 million staunchly patriotic followers during 2020.

Van Straaten continued, "if you think that debt during the Obama tenure, was eye-watering, think again. Under the next Administration, President Trump was forced to raise the US Debt to over $29 trillion due to the COVID virus pandemic. The US Congress authorised over $3 trillion by the end of March 2020, Congress approved, and Trump signed a $2.2 trillion spending bill, the third relief package designed to alleviate economic concerns of small businesses, large corporations, and workers during the COVID-19 pandemic. It allocated $500 billion in loans to large companies, $350 billion in forgivable loans, and provided $1,200 in direct cash payments to most U.S. citizens, among other items.

"America was technically bankrupted by the COVID-19 pandemic, which was made worse when President Biden was parachuted into the Presidency in 2021 due to a corrupt and fraudulent election allegedly engineered by the Democratic National Committee (DNC), who run the Democrat Party.

"Remember who the DNC are, they are the governing body of the United States Democratic Party. The DNC coordinates strategy to support Democratic Party candidates throughout the country for local, state, and national office.

"As a direct result of ousting President Trump, the DNC took America into one its darkest periods in US history. America became a fully-fledged Communist country within 3 months of Biden taking office and by six months, Biden was retired on medical grounds and Senator and Vice President Kamala Harris was appointed the first female non-white President of the USA. President Kamala was seen as a through and through socialist, who immediately appointed Hillary Clinton as her Vice President and Barack Obama's wife, Michelle, as the Attorney General. This all-woman team was a first for America in that it was all female plus it was a non-Caucasian woman who became the President of the United States.

"Sadly, because of the DNC's links to Communism and their hatred for Conservatism and especially older white males, from that point forward, the US was doomed to become a 3rd world country, with a national debt surpassing $35 trillion by 2024.

"America was seen by the rest of the world as non-democratic, corrupt, bankrupt and Communist, just like China. The irony of this period in American history was that the Elites and Celebrities who hated President Trump, were so ravaged by punitive wealth distribution programmes instigated by the newly invigorated and diverse feminist DNC, that they fled to other English-speaking countries like New

Zealand and Australia that had not yet succumbed to their insidious menacing Progressive ways.

Joe said, "Sadly, it was not long before those Progressive Elites poisoned the wells in those last few outlier bastions of Conservatism.

"As you can imagine, the world was sitting on a tinderbox and it was only a matter of time before another American Civil War or World War broke out."

Joe reminded the Hindsight team that they had a lot of work to do and a lot of very important people to get on board.

CHAPTER 44

The 2026 World Re-Invention Summit

This was the busiest the Langkawi airport had ever been. Never before had the airspace been so busy. Thankfully, with the upgrades that were implemented as a result of the June 2022 visit by the Hindsight team, the airport was able to cope with over 160 world leaders and their entourages, the world media and the operational support teams, who were necessary cogs and working parts of the political engine. Aircrafts started landing a week before as preparations for security were being made by the respective countries to protect their leaders.

Every hotel room on the Langkawi Island was booked by a horde of people who attended as participants or were there in a support or security role.

Among the support contingent there were hundreds of people from the media, including the well-known bloggers, newspapers and television.

The Andaman and Datai hotels had made some significant upgrades to their hotel in that short time. The Andaman created a new upper level hidden high up in the rainforest with wonderful sea views and containing secure executive suites that ran the full length of the northern and southern wings. These suites were twice the size of the other hotel rooms and were fully integrated. Similarly, their sister hotel 400 metres to the south, the Datai, which was an exclusive hotel that catered for discerning and well-heeled patrons, had created over 150 stand-alone, self-contained, highly secure bungalows designed to be utilised by Heads of States, Presidents or Prime Minister's and their security teams.

The island had a large military and police presence with thousands of extra resources brought in from the mainland to protect the dignitaries and their entourages; there were over ten thousand people who had made the trip to attend this conference. It was billed as the World Re-Invention Summit, something that the world was indeed very much in need of.

Flights arrived with opportunist holiday makers and back packers, but they were greeted with a big notice on display as they disembarked, informing them that every hotel room or bungalow on the island was fully booked, not a single room remained unoccupied.

As the Heads of States from countries such as Singapore, Japan, America, China, Russia, and Great Britain arrived, they were ushered into private bungalows by their respective security teams to freshen up and be briefed as to the situation on the ground.

CHAPTER 45

Exposing the Horror and Arrogance of Mankind

The date was Wednesday 16th December 2026, location, Langkawi, in Malaysia, the first day of a two-day World Re-Invention Summit.

Each attendee, irrespective of their role, including panel participants, had been fitted with a specialised Perturbed-meter, an emotion sensor which was essentially a very sophisticated lie-detector. This device automatically tracked the biometrics of the individual wearing it, including subconscious emotions as well as the emotions from their conscious mind. The device had a dial that they would turn up or down, depending on how they felt during the video briefings or panel discussions, as well as three voting buttons (Yes/No/Abstain).

Joe explained, "The dial device is simple to operate. The default dial position is in the centre, at neutral (0), which means you feel nothing or are not participating. If you turn the dial anti-clockwise to -1 through -9, it means you feel unhappy, uncomfortable, horrified, disgusted, or fearful about the content of the material you are seeing and hearing, and if you turn the dial to the right, past the zero, or neutral point, to +1 through +9, that means you feel happy, comfortable, delighted, elated or fearless about the contents of the material. The minus (-)9 through plus (+)9 measures the intensity of the emotion one feels consciously, which is then overlaid and correlated with the subconscious biometric readings, which cannot lie. The device will capture both the conscious and the subconscious minds in real time and flag up these aggregate readings from everyone by category on screen during the videos and the panel discussions."

Joe had informed the participants that the Summit needed to be able to maximise the outcome of this exercise, so the names of those who did not participate or had removed the emotion sensors would be put up on the name-and-shame screen, which would reflect the number of minutes that they were abstaining versus the number of minutes recorded. He also explained that the stats would be aggregated in real-time and shown up on the humanity screens. They would keep a static aggregate score and the high–low outliers for each of the segments so that during the course of the day the participants would be able to see just how perturbed or phlegmatic they were as a group. Essential demographics on each attendee had been gathered so that detailed analysis in real-time could be reflected on the screen as to how various segments of the social fabric reacted to the contents of the summit.

Joe emphasised, "The Summit is being translated into thirty-five languages in real-time, and wearing the sensor device is obligatory and necessary for this to work as a collective. Being a President or Prime Minister will not serve as an excuse to not participate."

The conference began with a brief presentation by four members of the Hindsight team, which included the objectives for this conference and the work done to date by the teams. This was followed by a fifty-minute video made up of newscast footage from their future. The video highlighted a future that was corrupt, cruel, horrifying and despicable.

It was a future that no one in this audience would want to have their name associated with, unless you wanted to be seen in a less favourable light, in which case they would have absolutely no right to hold a seat in public office.

The extent of sickened disgust was made apparent by the gasps of disbelief, which were repeated again and again as the human-engineered horror of the future they had previously manifested unfolded on the video. The results of both the subconscious and conscious emotions, which were recorded by the Perturb-Meter sensors, were staggering. It showed a correlation between the two levels of consciousness that tracked in trend with each other, with the exception of the numerous "outlier" spikes that the conscious mind produced when repugnant acts of violence and repellent corrupt behaviour were displayed. It was the sheer size of these spikes that blew the minds of the audience: clearly an underlying hate for corruption, violence and incompetence existed within the psyche of mankind.

When the video stopped, there was absolute silence in the auditorium, not a soul moved, whispered, or ventured to be the first person to talk, in case they were singled out and challenged to comment on what they had just witnessed.

Charlie, from the Hindsight team, was the first to break the silence. He asked the stunned audience if any of them cared to comment on the horror they had created. No one accepted his invitation.

He then informed them, "The video will immediately be followed by a discussion panel made up of highly respected executives from all walks of life, including several religious heads, scientists, doctors, politicians, and military commanders, captains of industry and key members of the Hindsight team."

He reminded them that, "The introduction video was segmented into the following seven categories, which, by the end of the video, had been updated with the aggregated real-time Perturbed-Meter readings, which look like this."

What People Really Felt About These Issues	Yes	No	Abstained
1 Running the State - Should a Religion run any State?	7%	91%	2%
2 Corruption in Politics - Is there enough Integrity in Politics?	1%	98%	1%
3 Arms dealing and the harm that causes - Should it be allowed to continue?	5%	94%	1%
4 Addiction and Dependency on Aid and Charity - Should this addiction be ignored?	14%	83%	3%
5 Decay of Moral Values in Society - Should this be Ignored?	30%	68%	2%
6 Preservation Natures Ecological Treasures - Should we Ingore Climate Change?	8%	90%	2%
7 Worlds Population - Can we afford to let it grow unchecked?	21%	78%	1%
	12%	86%	2%

A slide of the summary and the corresponding chart appeared on the two adjacent screens. The subjects of discussion had been;

1. "Running the State – Should a Religion run any State?";
2. "Corruption in Politics – Is there enough Integrity in Politics?";

3. "Arms Dealing and the Harm It Causes – Should It Be Allowed to Continue?";

4. "Addiction and Dependency on Aid and Charity – Should this Addiction Be Ignored?";

5. "Decay of Moral Values in Society – Should this Be Ignored?";

6. "Preservation of Nature's Ecological Treasures – Should We Ignore Climate Change?";

7. "World Population – Can We Afford to Let It Grow Unchecked?"

Without exception the Perturb-Meters' readings were in the minus range. Charlie went on to explain; "Each one of these subjects would be quite emotive on its own, but when seen in context with all of them and the compounded damage that would be caused as a result of these being poorly thought through or implemented, it was extremely shocking."

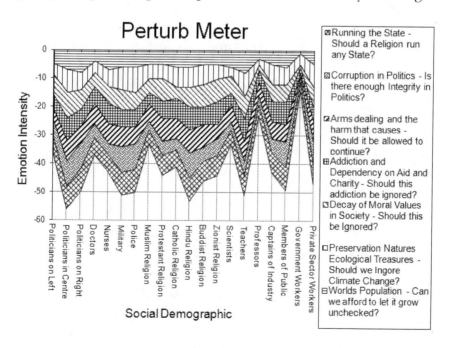

Charlie was the appointed moderator for this Panel, and the fun was just about to start.

CHAPTER 46

The Panel - Emotions Run Hot

For nearly twenty hours the panel members discussed the horror of what they saw on the video.

The debate was not about the authenticity, origin, or integrity of what they saw; it was about the horror and disgust each of them felt as the timeline unfolded.

While they recognised it had to be a faithful reflection of what was to come if they continued on the same path, there was still incredulous disbelief that mankind could be so giving on the one hand, so ingenious and resourceful, yet also cruel, arrogant, debasing and inhuman on the other.

The panel debated the Perturb-Meter results and realised that people had begun to politicise their emotions, which must have happened over several generations because it was no longer a conscious decision, the subconscious or unconscious mind had also adopted this stance as a baseline.

Charlie explained, "What this means is that whenever something happens that goes against your political beliefs, you automatically see it in a negative light and can hardly be swayed to see it in the eyes of anyone else, yet when it supports your political beliefs, you actually cannot see the negative impacts, you see only the positives.

"Let's take the "Unchecked Population Growth" question and look at who was the least perturbed about those implications; government workers, professors, and the Catholic religion all scored the lowest. Why, you ask?

"Government workers generally want to keep the party with the most socialist views in power, because it supports their Unions, a system that will maintain the exorbitant pensions and let them exploit the system to their own advantage. They even accepted strategies where immigrant workers were allowed into the country in droves, then given permanent residency in those countries. All of this helped to keep the socialist or left-wing party in power because those immigrants would initially vote for politicians of that party.

"Professors thought that because they were intellectually superior and had the power to influence generation after generation at their universities, they should have the same as the government workers, plus the added benefit of being able to create their own university curriculum, which they used to inculcate and indoctrinate their left-wing, progressive, liberal socialist thinking and sense of entitlement and dependency on the State into the minds of the younger generations.

"The Catholic religion; Well, this is the organisation that had enough money hoarded in their treasury to settle the world debt three times over in 2011. The same organisation who for decades refused to allow their adherents to use condoms when having sex, all because that would swell the numbers of Catholics in the world. Since Catholics should donate a percentage of their income to the church, the larger the Catholic population, the greater amount of money the church would amass. Unfortunately, as you saw in the video, millions of people died as a result of Aids or Aids-related diseases as a result of that decree."

Charlie wrapped up with, "You can see how easy it is to twist anything to suit your own political or self-serving agenda."

Over the next two hours, the panel pounced on the thread and started debating the merits and impacts of controlling population and exploring whether it was humane and equitable for society and the political machine to do so.

At the end of the first hour of this two-hour debate, Charlie pointed out that they had all totally missed the point: it was not supposed to be a debate on the merits of controlling population or debating whether it was good or bad or morally egregious, it was non-negotiable, it had to be done with immediate effect otherwise they would simply go down the path witnessed in the video they had seen.

The second hour was spent with the Hindsight team being quite controversial in many areas of the debate, pointing them to a solution that would be suitable to be implemented globally and not be morally unacceptable.

It was finally agreed that morally, parents had to be financially able to support their offspring and governments would have to institute birth control programs with free contraception and incentives to ensure a maximum of two children per family. After lunch, Mikhail was appointed as the moderator for the next session of the Panel, which would discuss the question of Arms sales.

CHAPTER 47

The Panel Runs for Cover – Arms Dealing

When Mikhail opened the topic up for discussion after showing some alarming statistics, he saw pain and consternation in the eyes of the panellists. He could see they really did not want to debate this topic: either they were scared or it was too dangerous or challenging.

Mikhail reminded them, "There is no room for half measures, if you do not take decisive action to outlaw Arms sales in its entirety and have the means to police this outrageous business, you will end up starring on those newscasts in the videos from the future you have been so privileged to see. You cannot afford to procrastinate; steps need to be implemented immediately to stamp this out now."

Over the next four hours and forty minutes the panel members discussed the horror of what had unfolded on the previous video and subsequent statistics that Mikhail shared with them. It was very apparent that this was probably the most dangerous topic; the subject matter was ultra-sensitive and steeped in danger, which would inevitably create massive repercussions downstream for the participants and their respective governments. They did everything in their power to avoid talking about cauterising this heinous business.

It was down to the Hindsight team panel members, Joe, Charlie, and Martin to be provocative and to take the hard line. They needed to lead the charge to get a purposeful discussion going that dealt with the real issue and established how arms dealing could be stopped.

Joe said, "Enough time has been wasted in avoiding the hard question. Let's deal with the matter of saving lives, improving the quality of life for millions, and prosecuting those offending countries who sell arms."

There was a lot of fidgeting going on amongst the panel members.

Joe continued firmly, "The current position is untenable, there needs to be a unilateral banning of small arms sales – a total closure of this insidious business needs to happen with immediate effect. There should be no exception, and for those countries who breach this edict, they should be severely punished with global sanctions from the rest of the world."

Martin reminded them of who the largest exporters were and who, by default, were the biggest culprits of exporting evil.

Martin put up a slide used in a previous workshop with world leaders and pointed out that the top five listed countries on this list had so much ground to make up;

Martin explained the chart as follows; "The units in this table are so-called trend indicator values expressed in millions of US dollars at 1990s prices. These values do not represent real financial flows but are a crude instrument to estimate volumes of arms transfers, regardless of the contracted prices, which can be as low as zero in the case of military aid."

World's Largest Arms Exporters

Rank	Supplier	2000	2001	2002	2003	2004	2005	2006	2007	2008	2009	Total
1	United States	7,220	5,694	5,091	5,596	6,750	6,600	7,394	7,658	6,090	6,795	64,888
2	Russia	3,985	6,011	5,773	5,202	6,260	5,321	6,156	5,243	6,026	4,469	54,446
3	Germany	1,603	821	892	1,697	1,067	1,875	2,510	3,002	2,499	2,473	18,439
4	France	1,055	1,270	1,308	1,288	2,194	1,633	1,577	2,342	1,831	1,851	16,349
5	United Kingdom	1,484	1,257	915	617	1,180	915	808	987	1,027	1,024	10,214
6	Spain	46	7	120	156	56	108	757	565	603	925	3,343
7	China	272	496	515	632	282	306	599	412	544	870	4,928
8	Israel	354	360	414	358	612	315	282	379	271	760	4,105
9	Netherlands	280	203	243	342	208	583	1,221	1,322	554	608	5,564
10	Italy	189	217	400	312	214	743	525	706	424	588	4,318
11	Sweden	46	830	185	515	305	537	417	367	457	353	4,012
12	Switzerland	176	193	157	174	250	267	306	324	467	270	2,584
13	Ukraine	288	661	244	430	202	281	557	799	269	214	3,945
14	Canada	110	129	170	255	268	235	231	343	236	177	2,154
15	South Korea	8	165	N/A	104	29	48	94	228	80	163	919

The information was supplied by the Stockholm International Peace Research Institute. (US$M)

The chart showed that the USA was the largest exporter of arms, with a value of almost $65 billion, and Russia was not far behind, with a value of $55 billion.

Joe pointed out, "Russia was by far the most heinous of the top five because of their irresponsible exporting of the Kalashnikov automatic rifle, which was the most prolifically used small arms weapon in modern times. Even the inventor, Kalashnikov himself apologised to the world for inventing and unleashing this instrument of evil."

Joe also noted, "Notice that China, India, South Korea, Greece and UAE were the top importers from those arms exporting countries over that period."

World's Largest Arms Importers

Rank	Importer	2000	2001	2002	2003	2004	2005	2006	2007	2008	2009	Total
1	China	2,015	3,366	2,819	2,207	3,080	3,511	3,831	1,474	1,481	595	24,379
2	India	911	1,242	1,872	2,802	2,227	1,036	1,257	2,179	1,810	2,116	17,452
3	South Korea	1,262	623	461	680	986	686	1,650	1,758	1,821	1,172	11,099
4	Greece	710	725	491	2,241	1,528	389	598	1,796	563	1,269	10,310
5	UAE	243	186	213	695	1,246	2,198	2,026	938	748	604	9,097
6	Turkey	1,170	553	1,009	438	187	1,005	422	585	578	675	6,622
7	Australia	364	1,191	647	798	505	470	682	629	380	757	6,423
8	United States	301	449	453	533	512	501	581	731	808	831	5,700
9	Singapore	622	220	235	88	384	543	52	368	1,123	1,729	5,364
10	Pakistan	158	397	533	592	385	332	262	613	939	1,146	5,357
11	Algeria	418	553	237	197	272	156	308	471	1,518	942	5,072
12	Malaysia	30	26	131	135	48	51	410	546	541	1,494	3,412
13	Saudi Arabia	80	59	555	159	1,161	148	185	64	115	626	3,152
14	Norway	263	148	92	4	6	14	469	494	536	576	2,602
15	Indonesia	171	27	63	398	82	31	58	577	241	452	2,100

The information was supplied by the Stockholm International Peace Research Institute. (US$M)

Martin said, "The evidence speaks for itself; you cannot hide behind excuses or any cloak and dagger arguments of national secrecy. The United Nations must implement a universal law that outlaws the sale of weapons and deals with abusers severely. There should be no option for anyone to veto; this is one event where the might of the United Nations must be felt and feared.

The law should be absolute to deal with those who flout it, by levying immediate penalty fines of ten times what they exported in the previous five years."

CHAPTER 48

A Future with Integrity

The UK, the USA and those countries that employed and implemented elements of the "Positics Constitution" as the basis on which to formulate their democracy had all fared much better, with wealth being created by more people than ever before because of the successful fostering of an innovative and entrepreneurial based fair society.

There were also changes made in the relationship of the UK to her colonies.

Charlie and Karyn had succeeded in planting the seeds for the adoption of mandatory "integrity-based policies" in politics for the more civilised western countries at that stage. The challenge they now faced was being able to foster an equivalent success through the United Nations, so that every country in the world would be based on a similar form of the "Positics constitution."

The United Nations once viewed democracy as one of the five enabling conditions of development and linked democracy to good governance.

In the Positics Constitution, good governance is demanded; integrity at all levels, including the core institutions of the modern state. Positics necessitates the ability of government to carry out policies and functions, including the management of implementation systems.

Finally, Positics necessitates that politicians will be accountable for their actions and that their decision-making is transparent and fully visible for their constituents to review daily.

Only then would, what was needed by a successful United Nations, democracy through good governance, be able to provide a long-term basis for arbitrating, regulating, and managing the many political, economic, cultural, and ethnic strains so that internal tensions that constantly threatened to tear apart societies and destroy states in the previous era would be minimised.

The Positics Constitution balances four concepts: human rights, civil society, fair economics and the integrity of all actors within the field. Prior to this event, the United Nations believed that without a strong emphasis on human rights only, no society could generate either a good government or good governance practices.

They overlooked the economics of fair play in commerce and integrity, which are essential components that would deliver a fair and civil society with sound moral values that excels and prides itself on personal contribution, integrity, and respect for all things.

Therefore, any construct of democracy must focus equally on all four elements with equal tenacity and gusto.

The Positics Constitution necessitates that all four elements be protected by rule of law, as this is essential, if man is not to be compelled to have recourse, as a last resort, to rebellion against tyranny and oppression.

CHAPTER 49

Testing, Testing . . .

Joe and Karyn, like the other members of the Hindsight teams, were exhausted at the end of the second day of the Summit meeting, but they all met in Joe and Karyn's adjoining suite in the Andaman Hotel for a final debriefing session.

Joe began by thanking everyone for their sterling efforts, reporting the results from the other five hindsight missions as being equally as successful, as they had themselves all witnessed subtle changes in how responsive people were throughout this exercise. He then went on and asked them what they thought about the likely outcome.

Charlie said, "I don't see how it could fail. The "Perturb-Meters" readings were exactly what we wanted them to be. It was the equivalent of "not a dry eye in the house.""

"What about the stickiness of the arms dealing question?" asked Karyn.

Martin yawned widely. "Sorry," he grinned. "My misspent youth must be catching up with me. Seriously, I know we had to work hard to get the message across that we must do something about the arms race and the huge amount of dealing in arms that has transpired, but I think they were convinced in the end. It was mainly fear that was the stumbling block, and I believe we frightened them more by what we showed them. Maybe fear and the real power of the people is the key here."

"I hope so," said Joe, fervently.

"Well," said Karyn. "All the teams have now done what they set out to do, so we just have to hope that it was enough. I believe it was."

There was a lull while they all considered what huge efforts they had been making to try to ensure that mankind had a future.

Then Cassandra said slyly, "You could find out, Joe."

"What do you mean?" asked Karyn, looking alarmed.

"Well, he could take the time machine back to the Bunker, programmed for a few days after we all leave."

"No!" exploded Karyn.

"Why not?" said Martin. "What's wrong with it?"

"What's wrong with it is that if we succeeded in our mission there wouldn't be a Noah 5000 project, or a bunker, or a time machine. Joe would simply not exist in that timeline."

"I know," said Cassandra. "That's the point."

Karyn was beside herself. Her eyes filling with tears, she shouted, "So you're happy for Joe to be blotted out of existence, just so that you can know how clever you are?"

"Hey, I didn't say that," began Cassandra. "Forget it. You're right. It's a lousy idea."

Joe had been listening to the argument, watching Karyn closely.

"It would be great to know that, though, wouldn't it?" he mused. "If I disappear in a puff of smoke, at least you guys would know that we succeeded, because I wouldn't be back."

"You can't mean that, Joe," stormed Karyn.

"Oh-oh!" said David. "I sense a lover's dispute. I think we should leave them to it."

Gradually, they all drifted away to their own suites, looking forward to some well-earned rest.

Joe looked at Karyn. "Think about it," he said. "You have made the point so many times that we don't belong in the timelines we've been visiting and living in, and that being here now is a genetic anomaly . . ."

"I know, I *know*!" yelled Karyn, but Joe came to sit beside her and took her hand in both of his. "Hear me out," he said.

Karyn nodded, too choked with tears to speak.

"You know I love you to distraction," Joe said gently, "and I've understood the reasons why you wouldn't marry me. You said you believed in a future for us, but in the right time, in our time, and you wouldn't budge from that view. It's been your steadfast belief that we would succeed that has kept me going so many times. You've kept the hope strong that we would have a normal life, in a world that wasn't going to hell in a hand-basket, that your parents and mine would live and die naturally, and that my sister would not die in a stasis pod, all alone."

"Yes," Karyn managed to say, struggling for control. "Yes, but now I am afraid to lose you. How can we be sure that we would even meet in our own, natural time, sometime near the beginning of the twenty-second century? We only met when we did because we were both in the Noah 5000 project. Otherwise, we could have been anywhere in the world, not even knowing that the other existed. I can't bear the thought!"

"I don't want to lose you, either," murmured Joe, stroking her hair. "Maybe we just have to have faith that we will meet again in our own timeline, just like the faith you have had that we would succeed in our mission in this timeline."

Karyn shook her head. "That's not good enough. If you are even considering doing this, I want to know that there is a failsafe in place to ensure that we do meet in the future."

"How would we do that?" asked Joe.

"Take me back to 1920," said Karyn, suddenly looking brighter. "I have an idea."

"Very well," said Joe, smiling. "So you are thinking of letting me go back to the bunker?"

"Not quite," said Karyn. "If you go, I go with you."

CHAPTER 50

Return to the Bunker

22nd December 2022, Langkawi, Malaysia

Joe and Karyn had completed their trip to 1920, when Karyn had disappeared for a while, telling Joe she did not want him to know what she was going to do, in case it didn't work. He had argued that if it didn't work, he wouldn't know about it, but she was adamant. In fact, she had gone to see Samuel Rabinowitz, and when she returned, she was smiling.

"Right," she said. "Now we had better go back to Malaysia."

"If we're going, we could go from here," Joe pointed out.

"No, we need to leave a note for the rest, in case we don't come back."

"Ah yes," said Joe. "So, we should."

Back in their suite, they composed a letter together, telling their colleagues that they were going to try getting back to the Noah 5000 bunker, and what it would mean if they did not reappear.

They left it at the reception desk, with instructions that if they did not collect it, it should be given to any one of their colleagues the next day.

Then they went to the time machine, which was under guard as usual in a secluded area. They told the guards to stand down, and entered the machine.

"You're sure about this?" asked Joe.

Karyn's chin came up. "I'm absolutely certain. If you're going to fade out of existence, I want to fade out too."

As Joe nodded and began to set the co-ordinates, she said, "Just hold me, Joe."

He said, wrapping his arms tightly around her, "Try and stop me!" They gazed into each other's eyes, smiling lovingly, as the time machine whirred into life, they were both feeling ebullient and like being wrapped in a warm velvet blanket on a chilly evening effused in love.

* * *

In the countryside near the border between Scotland and England, it was a fine spring day. The sun was shining and there had just been a shower, there were sheep grazing in the meadow and birds were singing. The heavens were spanned by a shimmering rainbow with patches of deep blue sky breaking through the remaining clouds, revealing a single vapour trail of a passenger jet that had just flown passed at high altitude.

In the nape of her neck, Joe could smell the wonderful floral and cinnamon fragrance of Karen's Alfred Sung perfume that she loved to wear.

The date on the time machine dashboard showed it was the 14th April 2611, which meant the plan the Noah 5000 Project had executed had worked. They embraced in a hug and soon became overwhelmed with the huge relief and joy that overcame them.

CHAPTER 51

Epilogue

June 2112

Joe Gilroy had just awakened from a peaceful siesta in his family's villa on a Greek island. He had taken some leave and joined his father, also called Joe, his mother Serena, and his sister Elizabeth, who was also taking a break from a tour as a concert pianist.

Joe had decided he needed some peace and quiet after a rather tempestuous break-up with his girl-friend. He was relieved to be out of the relationship, if the truth was told. Melanie had been inclined to jealousy and possessiveness, and Joe had had enough of her tantrums. Besides, he had always had the feeling that she was not the woman he was meant to spend his life with. He regretted having to hurt her, but knew it was the best thing to do for both of them before they did something, they would both regret.

He got up and took a quick shower, then wandered out of his room to see whether anyone else in his family was about.

He had heard Elizabeth playing the piano, and as he passed her on his way to the veranda he said, "Mozart again?" "Who better?" she smiled. "Ma and Pa are still asleep," she said. "Would you like a drink?"

"I'll get them," said Joe. "What will you have - white wine?"

"Mmmmm, please," said Elizabeth, getting up and closing the lid of the piano.

Joe brought two glasses of beautifully chilled white wine out to the veranda, where Elizabeth was already installed in an old, rather battered, but comfy chair, her tanned legs tucked up. He handed her a glass, beaded with cool droplets of condensation, and dropped lazily into an equally old and comfortable chair beside her.

"This is the life, hey?" he said, listening to the susurrations of the crickets in the surrounding fields.

"It certainly is," said his sister. "And I have to say you don't seem too grief-stricken over getting rid of Melanie at last." Elizabeth had made no secret of the fact that she did not like her brother's girlfriend, and thought she was all wrong for him. "Plenty more fish in the sea, so it's time to get your fishing net out!"

Joe laughed. "Yes, you were entirely right about Melanie. She wasn't right, and never would be. It was my fault for not seeing it in the first place."

"Huh!" said Elizabeth. "You probably couldn't see past her chest measurement."

"Oh! Wicked girl! That's not fair! She is quite bright, you know."

"Oh yes, I know," replied Elizabeth, entirely unrepentant. "Bright, but stupid with it."

Joe grinned; enjoying the familiar sibling banter, then frowned, noticing someone approaching the gate to the property. "That's odd," he said.

"What?" asked Elizabeth, who hadn't seen the stranger.

"There's someone coming through the gate. It's not as if We're on a main route to anywhere."

Elizabeth narrowed her eyes to see better against the late afternoon sunlight. "Perhaps she's lost," she said, and stood up, smiling a welcome to the young woman who was now coming down the path towards them. "Hi!" she said. "Can we help you?"

Joe suddenly felt rather odd as he looked at the slim petite woman now standing just below the veranda; a sense of having met her before was nagging at him. She had enormous slightly tilted green eyes, which currently looked rather anxious, and she was nervously fingering a necklace of beautiful natural pearls. Elizabeth noticed that too, and said, "Come and join us. You look a little hot and bothered. Joe, get our guest a drink!"

Joe managed to tear his eyes away from the stranger's face, mumbling something that echoed Elizabeth's invitation.

"No, thank you," the woman said. "You're very kind, but I just came to give you this. I took it to your flat in London, but they told me that you were in Greece." And she handed a slim packet to Joe, smiled at Elizabeth, retraced her steps back to the gate, and disappeared through it.

"How very odd," exclaimed Elizabeth, squinting at the packet Joe held. "It's addressed to you! Do you know her?"

"No . . . that is, I'm not sure. I feel . . ." Joe made a gesture of confusion, and Elizabeth, who had been about to resume joshing him about this mystery woman, looked a little concerned.

"You feel what?" she asked.

"I don't know," Joe admitted. "I had a weird feeling when I saw her, as if . . ." his voiced tailed off again.

"Aha!" cried Elizabeth, her concern gone. "I think you're suffering from coup de foudre!"

"Love at first sight?" said her brother, smiling slightly. "You certainly are keen to get me paired off, aren't you?"

"Well," said Elizabeth, mischievously, "she's certainly a looker. And I liked her instinctively. I wonder where she came from? Open the package, Joe. I'm dying to know what's in it."

Joe looked at the packet in his hands. It felt well-filled. "OK, OK!" he said. "You *are so-ooooo….. nosey*!"

"Just open it, for goodness sake, before the curiosity kills me."

And, sitting there on the veranda, Joe opened the package. In it he found three letters, "Letters!" said Elizabeth. "Who are they from?"

Joe's feeling of weirdness was growing as he looked at the first letter. "This one is from someone called Samuel Rabinowitz, and it's dated 1920!" he said in amazement. He scanned it quickly, seeing that it simply said that the writer had been charged with setting up a legal trust on behalf of one Karyn Hodges, and that Joe should read the rest of the contents carefully and with an open mind.

The second letter was from a firm of solicitors, and explained that they were the current administrators of the trust set up by Samuel

Rabinowitz, and had now discharged their responsibilities by handing the letters to Dr. Karyn Hodges.

Joe ran his hand through his hair, passing those two letters to Elizabeth to read. She looked totally confused. "But if this Samuel what's his name set up a trust in 1920 for Karyn Hodges, and this firm of solicitors have just handed the letters to a Karyn Hodges, then she must be a descendant of the one in 1920. And what's the connection with you?"

Joe, meanwhile, was reading the third and final letter, which was from Karyn Hodges herself. When he had finished, he sat stunned in his chair. "What, what?" cried Elizabeth, consumed with curiosity. "*What is it?*"

Joe looked up at her. "You were right again," he said. "I'll explain later, but I've just met the woman who is going to be my wife. I can't let her go again."

And, leaving his sister mouth agape, he got up from his chair and went haring off to find Karyn, his once and future love.

* * * * * * * * * * * *
* * * **T H E E N D** * * *
* * * * * * * * * * * *

APPENDICES AND REFERENCES

Links to research and quoted texts along with some of the charts and tables referred to in the book, based on research from the Internet.

Chapter 5: Day 5 - Nuclear Devastation and Snowball Earth Effect
Shor's algorithm - https://en.wikipedia.org/wiki/Shor%27s_algorithm
https://www.heritage.org/arms-control/report/what-nuclear-gaming-tells-us-about-new-start
https://quizlet.com/11984144/world-history-chapters-26-30-flash-cards/
Nuclear warfare, https://en.wikipedia.org/wiki/Nuclear_warfare

Chapter 7: Day 41 - Disaster Recovery Not an Option
Wireless Neutrino Network Could Pass Through the Centre of The Earth
https://www.extremetech.com/extreme/122535-wireless-neutrino-network-could-pass-through-the-center-of-the-earth
https://www.bibliotecapleyades.net/Ciencia/ciencia_fisica71.htm

Chapter 9: Day 72 – What caused Mankind's demise?
Greece in "selective default because of austerity measures" on debts - Al Jazeera English
Http://www.aljazeera.com/news/europe/2012/02/2012228156 59488168.html

Chapter 10: Progressivism – the end of integrity in Politics.
Criticism of democracy - http://www.thefullwiki.org/Criticism_of_democracy

Chapter 11: Can Politics exist without Corruption?

Oligarchy Opposition, http://oligarchyopposition.blogspot.com/

The Overcrowding of Prisons, https://educheer.com/the-overcrowding-of-prisons/

Parliamentary or Presidential, https://www.careerride.com/view.aspx?Id=23146

Democracy, http://nyanglish.com/removed-from-office-by

Democracy, https://dal.academic.ru/dic.nsf/enwiki/4576

Democracy, https://www.scribd.com/doc/128911911/Causes-of-Failure-of-Democracy-in-Pakistan

Democracy, https://www.scribd.com/document/109374339/Democracy

Democracy, https://en.wikipedia.org/wiki/Democracy

Progressivism, http://www.liquisearch.com/progressivism/by_country/united_states

Progressive-party, http://nyanglish.com/progressive-party

Progressivism, http://www.thefullwiki.org/progressivism

Democratically, https://en.wikipedia.org/wiki/Democratically

Democracy, http://www.wisegeek.com/what-is-the-difference-between-a-republic-and-a-democracy.htm

Democracy, http://therightplanet.blog.com/2011/09/18/cultural-marxism-and-the-death-of-belief/

Chapter 12: Politics and Banking – a recipe for corruption!

https://www.huffingtonpost.com/ellen-brown/economic-9-11-did-lehman_b_278202.html

https://www.sec.gov/news/press/2008/2008-204.htm

http://thetechnocratictyranny.com/government/brave-new-world/

https://www.counterpunch.org/2009/09/08/did-lehman-brothers-|fall-or-was-it-pushed/

https://www.metabunk.org/debunked-we-will-bury-you-without-firing-a-shot.t942/previous

https://www.huffingtonpost.com/ellen-brown/economic-9-11-did-lehman_b_278202.html

https://www.azquotes.com/quote/1468304

https://www.azquotes.com/author/21902-Gordon_Brown

https://www.globalresearch.ca/china-challenges-us-dollar-hegemony-seeks-new-global-financial-order/5544627

https://www.investopedia.com/terms/f/fiatmoney.asp

https://answers.yahoo.com/question/index?qid=20120610132218AAiWKys

https://www.scribd.com/document/350492408/Financial-Crises

https://www.thebalance.com/2008-financial-crisis-3305679

https://www.scribd.com/document/350492408/Financial-Crises

http://internationalbusinessbest.blogspot.com/2014/04/effect-on-international-business-of.html

https://www.youtube.com/watch?v=c6BdBOprY5E

https://www.thebalance.com/the-great-recession-of-2008-explanation-with-dates-4056832

https://www.thebalance.com/2009-financial-crisis-bailouts-3305539

Chapter 15: Day 74 - The Climate Change Fiasco
https://yaledailynews.com/blog/2009/12/10/bercovici-pagani-park-and-wettlaufer-perspectives-on-climate-change/

Earthquakes, https://en.wikipedia.org/wiki/List_of_earthquakes_in_2018

https://www.dailysignal.com/2014/12/03/since-obama-took-office-federal-debt-increased-almost-70-percent/

https://www.youtube.com/watch?v=tCA9pSlk2WY

https://www.rt.com/news/340912-yemen-oil-terminal-recapture/

https://nationalinterest.org/blog/the-buzz/saudi-arabia-goes-war-15349

https://financialtribune.com/articles/world-economy/62139/eurozone-future-in-serious-doubt

https://www.zerohedge.com/news/2016-10-07/coming-collapse-worlds-biggest-economy

Chapter 17: Day 75 - State Welfare and National Health
British_Medical_Association   https://en.wikipedia.org/wiki/Talk:British_Medical_Association

Chapter 21: Influencing Democracy, Starting in 1920
https://uk.answers.yahoo.com/question/index?qid=20100114083758
AAIDEvO
https://lightgraphite.wordpress.com/art-and-design-in-context/1920-
1925-time-line/
https://answers.yahoo.com/question/index?qid=20090716174805
AA2FO5U

Chapter 22: Influencing Democracy between 1921 and 1928
https://infourok.ru/teoreticheskiy-material-po-teme-istoriya-
anglii-1505862.html

Chapter 23: Democracy as you came to know it will fail
https://www.dailymail.co.uk/news/article-2157373/The-27-000-
charities-survive-taxpayers-cash-lobby-pet-causes-politicians.html
https://www.ndtv.com/world-news/youths-riot-in-algeria-over-high-
food-prices-444359
https://www.wsj.com/articles/SB10001424052748704803604576077
782735649792
https://edition.cnn.com/2017/11/04/middleeast/lebanese-prime-
minister-saad-hariri-resigns/
https://www.fluther.com/115791/massive-protests-in-syria-
demanding-freedom-continue-will-this-end/
http://www.academia.edu/6657182/Arab_spring
https://quizlet.com/11863181/apush-ch-36-39-objective-test-flash-
cards/
https://interactive.aljazeera.com/aje/2017/the-making-and-breaking-
of-europe/2000s.html
https://www.democracynow.org/2010/10/18/slavoj_
https://www.rt.com/news/european-leaders-multiculturalism-f/
https://www.dailymail.co.uk/news/article-1355961/Nicolas-Sarkozy-
joins-David-Cameron-Angela-Merkel-view-multiculturalism-failed.
html
https://vdare.com/articles/will-multiculturalism-end-europe

Chapter 25: Finally – Integrity based Democracy in Society
History of England, The 20th Century Compare text
http://www.britannia.com/history/nar20hist3.html

Chapter 26: Respect – Preventing the Decay of Moral Values in Society
Benjamin Spock Biography - life, family, children, parents, death, wife...
https://www.notablebiographies.com/Sc-St/Spock-Benjamin.html
https://biography.yourdictionary.com/benjamin-spock
https://en.wikiquote.org/wiki/Benjamin_Spock
https://wn.com/Dr_Spock
https://www.wnd.com/2009/01/87179/
Benjamin Spock, https://en.wikipedia.org/wiki/Benjamin_Spock
https://skeptics.stackexchange.com/a/28259
https://skeptics.stackexchange.com/q/28022

Chapter 29: Mezzanine - Prevent Addiction and Dependency on Aid
and Charity
http://nyanglish.com/south-wiltshire
Salisbury UK, https://en.wikipedia.org/wiki/Salisbury
https://wikimapia.org/1900004/Salisbury-City-Centre
Pietermaritzburg RSA, https://en.wikipedia.org/wiki/Pietermaritzburg
http://nyanglish.com/famous-alumnus
https://answers.yahoo.com/question/index?qid=20110523165705
AA3MC1h
http://globalhealth.mit.edu/country-briefing-kenya/
https://QuizzClub.com/trivia/where-was-the-mau-mau-rebellion/
answer/75056
http://www.africa-eu.com/

Chapter 30: Engineering Integrity into Aid, Charity & Political Systems
https://www.timeanddate.com/holidays/un/world-health-day
http://en.wikibedia.ru/wiki/Portal:Philadelphia/Selected_picture_
archive/17
https://thehelplessdancer.wordpress.com/tag/status-quo/
Tim_Russert, https://en.wikipedia.org/wiki/Tim_Russert

https://dal.academic.ru/dic.nsf/enwiki/99362

http://www.abovetopsecret.com/forum/thread413561/pg1

https://www.euronews.com/2010/10/08/on-the-fringes-of-the-un-summit-in-ny

https://www.azquotes.com/quotes/topics/world-trade-organization.html

https://www.telegraph.co.uk/culture/music/.../Bob-Geldof-10-classic-Geldof-quotes.html

Chapter 32: Climate Change – Preparing the Environment
http://maps.thefullwiki.org/History_of_climate_change_science

Stephen_Schneider, https://en.wikipedia.org/wiki/Stephen_Schneider

https://www.turkaramamotoru.com/en/stephen-schneider-593748.html

https://skeptics.stackexchange.com/q/5057

http://nyanglish.com/made-headlines-in

Chapter 38: Climate Change – Implementing the Change in Philosophy
https://unfccc.int/resource/ccsites/senegal/fact/fs221.htm

Chapter 39: Concorde - Implementing Zero-Tolerance on Arms sales
https://wiki2.org/en/Ottawa_Treaty

Chapter 40: A World without Arms Dealers
http://www.globalissues.org/article/74/the-arms-trade-is-big-business

Chapter 42: The 1959 United Nations Arms Trade Treaty Discussions
https://www.tutorvista.com/biology/growth-rate-world-population

https://blog.world-mysteries.com/science/how-can-we-feed-9-billion/

http://legal.un.org/avl/ha/cpusptam/cpusptam.html

Chapter 43: Project Hindsight 2022 Progress Review
http://langkawigeopark1.blogspot.com/2011/05/?m=0

https://www.scribd.com/document/149543001/BIS-Speech

ADDITIONAL SOURCES

- Biraben, Jean-Noel, 1980, An Essay Concerning Mankind's Evolution, Population, Selected Papers, December, table 2.
- Durand, John D., 1974, "Historical Estimates of World Population: An Evaluation," University of Pennsylvania, Population Center, Analytical and Technical Reports, Number 10, table 2.
- Haub, Carl, 1995, "How Many People Have Ever Lived on Earth?" Population Today, February, p. 5.
- McEvedy, Colin and Richard Jones, 1978, "Atlas of World Population History," Facts on File, New York, pp. 342-351.
- Thomlinson, Ralph, 1975, "Demographic Problems, Controversy Over Population Control," Second Edition, Table 1.
- United Nations (UN), 1973, The Determinants and Consequences of Population Trends, Population Studies, No. 50., p.10.
- United Nations, 1999, The World at Six Billion, Table 1, "World Population From" Year 0 to Stabilization, p. 5, http://www.un.org/esa/population/publications/sixbillion/sixbilpart1.pdf
- U.S. Census Bureau (USCB), 2008, "Total Midyear Population for the World: 1950-2050", Data updated 12-15-2008, http://www.census.gov/ipc/www/idb/worldpop.html
- http://www.globalchange.umich.edu/globalchange2/current/lectures/human_pop/human_pop.html

Further reading

- World Population Prospects, the 2010 Revision (United Nations Population Division).
- Symptoms of The Global Demographic Decline

- Central Intelligence Agency (2004). *CIA The World Factbook 2004*. URL accessed on February 13, 2005.
- The World in Balance Transcript of two-part PBS' Nova on World Population
- The Environmental Politics of Population and Overpopulation A University of California, Berkeley summary covering historical and contemporary population dynamics, forecasts, resource scarcity, population control, and environmental concerns

Organizations

- http://www.populationmatters.org/2012/news/urgency-addressing-population-growth-rises/
- The Day of 6 Billion official homepage
- World Population Day United Nations: 11 July
- United Nations (2001). *United Nations Population Information Network*. URL accessed on February 13, 2005.
- Population Reference Bureau *www.prb.org – News and issues related to population*.
- Berlin Institute for Population and Development *"English"*. *Berlin-institut.org. 2010-03-23. http://www.berlin-institut.org/index.php?id=48*.

Statistics and maps

- United States Census Bureau (2004). *Historical Estimates of World Population*. URL accessed on February 13, 2005.
- The AfriPop Project, showing African population statistics
- PopulationData.net (2005). *PopulationData.net – Information and maps about populations around the world*.
- GeoHive *GeoHive.com – World Statistics including population and future predictions*.
- World countries mapped by population size
- World Population from the US Census Bureau in an interactive Excel dashboard

[.................. REFERENCE LINKS GO ABOVE HERE ....]

ABOUT THE AUTHOR

Arden Wedzler lived in the British colonies for the first twenty-five years of his life. After military service, he lived and worked all over the world, including London, Madrid, Munich, Hong Kong, Dallas, New York, and various African countries. He has extensive experience in financial services and investment banking, specialising in e-commerce and IT. He currently lives in Great Britain.

Printed in the United States
By Bookmasters